PIECES OF A BROKEN MIND

Praise for *Pieces of a Broken Mind* by Daniel Ruczko

"Laugh in the dark, cry in the spotlight - An entertaining debut that doesn't give a f*ck." - **Thomas Browning, The Page Turner**

"[...]Ultimately, *Pieces of a Broken Mind* serves up a gratifying cautionary tale, an artful illustration of our capacity as human beings to eat ourselves alive. Indeed, Ruczko has offered up a truly human journey, and one well worth taking." - **Larry Cedar**

"*Pieces* will hit you right in the feels, and you'll love it!"
- **Shelby Olsen**

"[...]Ruczko has written an absorbing novel that rides a roller coaster of emotions from beginning to end. The author does a superb job of crafting a cathartic narrative that is driven, focused, and which never loses its edge." - **The US Review of Books**

"Daniel's debut is 100% him. It will seduce you, make you feel amazing and fall in love with it, only to masterfully break your heart under an irresistible smile. It really f*cked me, but in the best way possible - I love it." - **Emily Correro**

"This book reminds us: life is messy, art is messier."
- **Alice Barker**

DANIEL RUCZKO

PIECES OF A BROKEN MIND

A NOVEL

MIND POLLUTION
PUBLISHING

Mind Pollution Publishing

www.mindpollutionpublishing.com

First Edition July 2024

Second Edition October 2023

Third Edition February 2025

Cover designed by Daniel Ruczko

10   9   8   7   6   5   4   3   2   1

ISBN 979-8-9879979-4-9

ISBN 979-8-9879979-5-6 (ebook)

For the days when giving up isn't an option, but doing what you do is so fucking painful.

This book is a work of fiction. Names, characters, businesses, places, events, locales, and incidents are either the products of the author's imagination or used in a fictitious manner. Any resemblance to actual persons, living or dead, or actual events is purely coincidental.

PIECES OF A BROKEN MIND

0

ollow your heart, and you will die every day.

The sterile glare of the fluorescent light makes the reflection of my face look pale, and I am surprised when I see a tear rolling down my cheek. I haven't cried in months, maybe even longer. But it feels good, cathartic.

No one can ever prepare you for the life you imagine for yourself, especially when it unfolds exactly as planned. Trapped within a self-fulfilling prophecy.

But what would it take to get there? What if you're on top of the world and you feel absolutely nothing? I stare into my eyes in the mirror until they seem foreign. Taking a deep breath, I splash water on my face and leave the room.

The bedroom is shrouded in dim light, illuminated only by the rays of the LA skyline slicing through the gray curtains. A police helicopter circles a small area in the distance somewhere in Laurel Canyon, but nothing happening outside is important right now; only what's inside matters. Two stained glasses and an empty bottle of wine sit on the nightstand on my side.

Seeing her silhouette lying in my bed still feels surreal, as if turning on the light would make her disappear, and the bed would be empty again. The simple act of talking to her was absolutely unthinkable less than a week ago. I lie down next to her, kiss her neck, and wrap my arm around her body. She reaches for my hand, holding it tightly.

There were moments in the last couple of weeks where I would've killed just to smell her one more time. And now, here she is, giving me another chance, and I just want to fall asleep next to her. I didn't know it before, but this moment right here is what it's all about; it completes me.

I will be remembered.

I will be remembered.

I will be remembered.

I inhale deeply before closing my eyes.

Hold your breath.

Freeze Frame.

Click.

3

PART I

1

anny's face is always lit up with excitement. Even during mundane moments like this: sipping on a cold beer while watching a basketball game at a crowded bar. I don't give a shit about sports; I never have. But he sees the extraordinary in the ordinary. Or, while most of us try to escape it, he embraces the mundane. And I love that about him.

It's a typical dive bar with neon signs advertising cheap beer and liquor. The walls are covered with various sports memorabilia, and a large flat-screen TV dominates the room. Current top 40 hits cut through the laughter and chatter, their monotonous melodies a nagging distraction, only adding to the clamor as I scribble on a notepad.

On some days, my brain just gives me a stream of random ideas, fragments of scenes, or snippets of dialogue. I usually don't fully understand them when they come to me, but they always make sense at some point. Today is one of those days. Every word is a silent cry against the madness of everyday life. But just as I'm lost in my creative bubble, my phone buzzes next to me, and a message from work pops up on the screen. I glance at it. It's past nine - hours after leaving the office.

"Man, I hate this place...." I mutter without looking up.

Danny's brown eyes, matching the deep hue of his skin, remain locked on the TV, "Sorry, but this is the only place that shows the game right now," referring to the basketball match.

I tilt my head up. "What? No, I mean the fucking office...." I clarify, thinking of the place that's draining the life out of me.

Danny turns to me. "Yeah, you and me both, buddy." He takes a swig of his beer before returning his attention to the game.

I look up and notice three men in identical, sharply-pressed blue business suits striding past our booth. Looking like clones. Their ties are perfectly knotted, each step in rhythm with their polished shoes, and an air of professional rigidity clings to them. They represent all the aspects I hate about corporate culture, everything I never want to become.

"I just can't imagine living like this for the rest of my life," I say as they start blending into the crowd. Danny casts a fleeting glance after them before shifting his focus back to the TV, "I know, dude, and you shouldn't."

I take a sip of my Sugar-Free Red Bull when amidst the sea of faces in the bar, my eyes land on her. The gorgeous brunette sitting at the counter smiling at me. Returning her smile, I refocus on my writing. Just then, Danny turns to face me.

"Listen... You know you're not like them, right?" he says, pointing at the three clones.

I look at them and then back at him before he continues, "This job is only temporary for you."

I laugh, "Well, it's been temporary for over eight years now." He takes another sip of his beer and says, "Yeah, but you're some kind of genius, man."

I shake my head. Before I can finish thinking of how much I hate it when people call me that, he adds:

"And I know you hate it when people call you that.".
Smiling at his mind-reading abilities, I observe the three guys downing their drinks and enjoying their night out.

"I don't know," I say to him, "It doesn't feel like it. I still work that shitty office job. Nothing's changed. I'm no different."

Danny makes a dismissive hand gesture. "No, Dude, you've got a gift, don't deny that. You're busting your ass every fucking day. And I don't mean at the office" He points at my notebook. "Just look at you, even here; you're at a bar writing shit down. That's dedication and not even optional for you; it's like breathing. And it's what sets you apart!" He takes a moment to let that sink in before adding, "But you know all this, and I know you're sick of hearing it," And turns back to the TV.

Nursing my Red Bull, I contemplate his words before saying, "But I'm not making any money with it. It's just a hobby, really."

Danny shakes his head. "Nah, It's more than that, and you know it. It's your fucking purpose. You've accomplished something that most people can only dream of. How many people can say they've published a novel?"

"Self-published!" I correct him. "Probably a lot of people..."

"Doesn't matter." He insists. "How many copies have you sold?" I check my phone and say, "Fifteen."

Danny grins. "So all the girls you dated bought a copy, trying to figure out if it's about them."

Yeah, probably. But only one of them would be right."

He continues watching the game, his eyes fixed on the screen.

Danny is my best friend and the only one who understands me effortlessly. He was diagnosed with clinical depression when he was nineteen. The pills, those chemical cocktails, scrambled his brain more than they fixed it, so he stopped taking them after a year. Now he's navigating life's maze, hunting for the ever-elusive solution, which isn't always easy. Some people underestimate him, but he's sharp, a razor blade hiding in a box of tissues. And the way I see it, anyone who's got the guts to stare their own mental demons in the eye, to dissect their broken patterns and sift through the rubble, well, they've got to possess some serious emotional depth.

I notice the girl sitting at the counter, fumbling with her jacket, getting ready to leave.

Not letting it go, Danny turns to me. "You can't seriously say that putting out a book hasn't made you feel a shred of happiness," he insists, his voice almost drowned out by the sounds of the bar.

I smirk, "Well, I guess, but I didn't have the talk with my landlord yet."

"What talk?" He asks.

"About whether or not he's accepting happiness as a form of payment from now on."

Danny lets out a mock sigh, saying, "Dumb shit," before looking back to the TV.

As if on cue, the girl from the bar, her eyes hesitant and coy, approaches our table. "Excuse me," she utters softly.

Danny does a one-eighty, his expression friendly and inviting.

"Oh, hey there!" But her gaze never wavers from me.

I look up, greeting her with a simple "Hey" Up close, I notice her beautiful, vibrant green eyes, making it difficult to look away.

"I just wanted to give you this," she smiles and hands me a folded piece of paper. Taking it, I mirror her smile.

"Give me a call sometime," she says.

"Sure, I can do that," the words tumbling out before I can think.

"Great. Enjoy your night." she starts walking. Danny's eyes follow her as she leaves the bar, and I unfold the paper she gave me - her name and number. "Sarah," I read out quietly.

He rotates back to me and says, "I have no idea how the fuck you're doing this. She didn't even look at me!"

I laugh and say, "I don't know what to tell you, man. Maybe she's racist."

He grins, shaking his head, "Motherfucker..." Then, glancing back to the TV, only to let out a frustrated yell as he witnesses his team lose. "Fuck this!" He snaps, refocusing on me. "What do you want to do?"

I ponder for a moment before answering, "Dude, I just want to write and get paid for it. Pretty simple."

Danny smirks. "All right, Bukowski, I actually meant what do you want to do now, but..." he pauses, his gaze piercing,"...I promise you, it will fucking happen! It's more surprising that it hasn't happened yet. And I can't wait to stand right next to you while you unfold your full potential for the whole world to see. Showing them what I've known for years."

I nod, unable to find the words to respond. He sometimes just drops bombs like this when you least expect it. But it's comforting to have someone who truly believes in you, especially on days when you doubt yourself or are just tired of waiting for your dreams to materialize. Success is supposed to be just a matter of time. But what if my time will never come? The line between self-fulfillment and self-destruction is often terrifyingly thin.

Follow your heart, and you will die every day.

If you're paying attention, you know when a moment is extraordinary as it unfolds before you.

And this situation with Danny, showing me support like no one else - there's nothing ordinary about this moment.

2

Reaching for my stash of supplements, I pop a Modafinil with 400 mg of Alpha GPC, Inositol, and Lion's Mane. It's the cheap generic version branded as Provigil that I ordered off a sketchy website from India, the Modafinil, that is. 100 pills with 200 mg each for $99 plus shipping.

When I first heard about this stimulant, everyone called it the "Limitless" pill. Referring to the 2011 film starring Bradley Cooper. It's supposed to have similar effects to Adderall, but without the long-term damage you get from it, given that it doesn't contain amphetamine salts. On top of that, it's also a lot cheaper. Too good to be true? Maybe.

Back in the AlphaBay days, I'd get it from there, but all that didn't end well. They pulled the plug, and suddenly the whole thing went up in flames, and the founder turned up dead in his jail cell. They say it was a suicide, but who knows what really happened. I didn't even look into the dark web since 2017.

In the wake of a recent corporate merger, I now work for one of Seattle's biggest remote IT tech support companies. Our services are a cluster-fuck ranging from remote data recovery, network security, cloud solutions, and everything in between. It's Mr. Robot-type shit. But nine times out of ten, the problem isn't some complicated algorithm or obscure code; it is usually the person sitting in front of the screen. I'm not exactly thrilled to be here. The hours are long, the tasks are monotonous, and the fluorescent lights make my eyes bleed. But if you're good at it, you have a lot of free time.

And I'm fucking great at it.

Thanks to Covid, many people still work from home, but I like coming to the office, even more so now that it's a ghost town. The coffee is pretty good, and Danny works here too.

He manages our department, overseeing all the tasks, making sure we hit our deadlines, and generally keeping the ship running smoothly. Everyone likes him, and it's a pretty easy job because computer IT people love deadlines. He says he has no idea how he even got the position and that he didn't feel qualified. But I told him no one is supposed to do what they're doing. It's all a guessing game, a leap of faith.

My office is a bleak and soulless place, a study in beige. Beige walls, beige carpet, beige furniture. It's like someone sucked all the color out of the room and left me with this drab, lifeless shell. At least it's not a fucking cubicle. The only thing that breaks up the monotony is the window, with its view of the outside world.

But it's a grey morning, one where you can't even guess what time it is. There are no 50 shades of grey in the sky, just one. And I'm so sick of this weather.

My eyes drift to the computer screen; logged in to my Ingramspark account, checking for any recent sales of my book; I haven't checked in a while and discover that one had been sold two weeks ago.

So I'm up to sixteen sales now. It's a sign that maybe, just maybe, I'm on the right track. Slow and steady wins the race, but I'm too fucking impatient.

Danny stumbles into the office, clearly hungover from the bar last night. Without a word, I reach into my desk drawer, pull out the Alpha GPC and toss the bottle over to him. "Here, take this," I say. He catches it and looks at the label skeptically. "I'm not trying to boost my brain, dude; I just drank too much," he says, still rubbing his temples.

"Drinking triggers your brain to produce GABA, which increases the need for Choline. This will give you a Choline boost and helps relieve your hangover." I explain, trying not to sound like Bill Nye.

"This fucking guy," he says, laughing.

Danny swallows the pill and takes a swig of water to wash it down. "Thanks," he says, and I just nod in response.

Walking over to my window, his eyes scan the grey, dreary landscape outside. "I hate this weather, man," he mutters, his voice low and gruff.

"Average minds think alike," I reply.

Danny shakes his head like he's trying to shake off the gloom. "I think I need tropical weather or something," then he turns around to me, asking, "What are you up to after work?"

I tell him, "I'm gonna visit my mom, but after that, I'm free."

"Wanna hang out after?" He asks.

"Yes, sir."

"Ok, cool, I'll try to Rambo through this day now," he says with a fierce determination in his voice. "I'll see you later," And he leaves the room.

I turn back to my computer screen, the glow casting the room in an eerie light. Part of me wants to get a request to fix some idiot's tech issues just so I can have something to do, something to break up the monotony of the day. But the other half of me just wants to be left alone.

A guy whose name I keep forgetting knocks on the open door of my office. It's one of those relationships where we were introduced at some point, but now too much time has passed to ask him what his name was without it being awkward. And I think he doesn't remember mine either.

So we just use words like "man" or "dude" whenever we refer to each other to avoid any weirdness, which is weird in itself.

I also think he has some form of Asperger's or another neurodivergent condition, and he never looks me in the eyes when talking to me. But let's be honest; most people in the IT field are on the spectrum in one way or another. It's like a magnet for the quirky, the unconventional, the ones who don't fit in anywhere else. And believe me; I'm not necessarily excluding myself here. Camus said it best "We are all special cases."

He shuffles into my office, his posture slumped, his eyes downcast. Looking like he's just waiting for someone to come along and put him out of his misery.

"Hey, how you doin' today?" He asks in a shy tone.

I look over at him as he stands in the door frame awkwardly, avoiding eye contact. "What's up, dude?" I ask, trying not to let on that I'm just as uneasy as he is.

I can tell by his body language that he is uncomfortable in his own skin. Which sucks. It's like he's trapped in a world that doesn't understand him. And I always want to be nice to him. Some of the other guys at work keep making fun of him just because they are "slightly less awkward."

And he is definitely a weird dude, but is that a bad thing?

He constantly wants to talk to me about Bitcoin, Ethereum, and other cryptocurrencies. And while I don't really have spare money to invest right now, I can't deny that I find it fascinating. I've been following crypto from the beginning. In 2012, when I received my tax refund, I decided to invest a small amount just for fun. At the time, one bitcoin was worth $13, peanuts compared to the astronomical prices it's fetching these days. Unfortunately, I lost the partition on my hard drive that contained my wallet file.

Co-worker dude asks me the question I hear the most regarding that topic, "Do you think it's too late now to invest in crypto?"

I shrug, feeling like a broken record. "I don't know; it's hard to predict. But people who hesitated two years ago regret it now." It's the same answer I always give, and it's true - there really is no correct answer.

I can see him digesting that information, biting his nails like he's trying to chew his way through the problem. "I think I'm gonna do it!" he says, nodding his head like he's already made up his mind.

I glance down at my phone as it makes a bell noise, signaling a new work task. "Go for it, man!" I say absentmindedly.

Looking up at him, something surprising happens - he actually makes eye contact with me and says, "Thank you!"

I give him a thumbs up as he turns to leave and say, "Sure, anytime."

Although what I said may not have seemed like a significant revelation, I believe it was important to him. And just having something other than his own internal dialogue helped him make a decision.

"We are all special cases."

3

My mother's apartment has a very distinct smell.

It's kind of a sweet smell, like a mixture of fresh roses and vanilla-scented candles. It always smelled this way and immediately brings back memories as I step through the door, making me feel both nostalgic and slightly uncomfortable.

I close the door behind me.

"Richard?" My mother yells from the kitchen.

"Yes, Mom, it's me," I say while taking off my shoes.

"Hey, Do you want anything to drink?" She yells.

"No, thanks. I'm good."

I can hear her opening and closing drawers, probably searching for something.

The air in the room feels warm and thick. She always has the radiator on, even in the summer. Every few minutes, it emits a rhythmic clacking noise.

Clack, clack, clack. Pause. Clack, clack, clack.

I walk over to an old family photo resting on a shelf in the cluttered living room. The photo shows my mother, my dad, and nine-year-old me on vacation somewhere in the mountains during Christmas break. I had the book *Stephen King's IT* with me on that trip. It was a very long drive, and by the time we arrived, I was already so immersed in the story of Derry and Pennywise that I couldn't put it away.

I have very fond memories of that particular vacation. We stayed in a cabin close to a vast forest, the surroundings peaceful. Inside the cozy cabin, my parents and I were warmed by the roaring fire, the crackling sound of flames filling the space. While snow gently falls past the window, adding layer upon layer to the picturesque winter scene outside, one snowflake at a time.

And I would just read all day long. It was a perfect winter.

That trip may be the reason why I wanted to become a writer. Wanting to help shape other people's memories, just like the one I'm recalling right now. But sometimes I wonder if memories are even real or if we rewrite them with each reflection, bending them until they feel the way we need them to.

As I reach for the photo, I notice an empty vodka bottle hidden deep behind it.

"Do you have a lighter?" my mother asks from the kitchen.

"No, Mom, I don't."

"I know I had one somewhere..." she says over the sound of Rattling from the kitchen.

When my grandmother got sick, she became addicted to pills—any kind of prescription pills—until my aunt discovered them stashed inside her nightstand and threw them away.

My mom started drinking after she was diagnosed with Alzheimer's. She thinks I don't know it, but she keeps hiding those bottles and forgetting where she placed them.

Everyone is looking for ways to ease the pain, I guess.

She emerges from the kitchen, lifting her arm triumphantly

"I found the lighter!"

At first, it sounds like she said, "I found the light."

Dressed in a pair of washed-out jeans and a blue cotton sweater that appeared worn from countless washings. Which seemed to be her go-to outfit as it was the one I see her in most often. It had become her signature uniform.

Observing her closely, I notice her mismatched socks.

She takes a moment to look at me and smiles when she says, "It's so good to see you."

I smile back "You too, Mom. Should we go?"

"Wait... is it cold outside? I need to find my coat," she says and starts scanning the room.

Turning to me, she asks, "Do you need money?"

I do, but I don't want to tell her that.

"No, thank you."

She begins frisking herself for her wallet, "I can give you some, no problem," she insists.

I shake my head, smiling, and say "I know and appreciate it, but I'm good."

Glancing over to the sofa, I see a folded grey coat. I point at it and ask "That one?"

She rushes over. "Yes." she exclaims, picking it up and revealing a laptop beneath it.

"Oh, and here's my computer too!"

It's an old Acer laptop I gave her years ago. At first, she used it to Skype me and look for recipes online, but then she forgot her password and hasn't used it ever since.

"Can you take a look at it next time? It's important," she says.

The weirdest things suddenly become "important" to her; I don't know if it's the disease or just her getting old. But who am I to question it?

I nod and say, "Of course, Mom, but we need to find your password first."

She looks around, worried. "I know I had it written down somewhere. I'll find it."

As my mother starts getting dressed, I lift up the laptop. Turning it over, I see a yellow Post-it on the bottom with "lilly2013!" written in my handwriting.

"Hey, look!" I say, showing it to her.

She turns to me, "Great! Then you can fix it."

"Yes, I will."

My mother can sometimes really annoy me, but I realize that in a few years, I may look back and wish for these seemingly irritating moments. And every time I see her, I tell myself to visit more often.

Witnessing my mother's mental decline might be the saddest thing I've ever experienced.

4

The sky is still gray, with heavy clouds looming overhead. It is a cold winter afternoon, about to get dark, the crisp and biting air sends chills down your body. But despite the cold, there is a certain beauty to this time of day. The stillness and quietness can be peaceful and calming, and there's just something about the muted colors of the landscape.

With my mother by my side, we make our way through the vast cemetery gates and follow a small path that leads to my father's grave.

As we walk along, my mother reaches into her purse and starts searching for something.

"What are you looking for?" I ask.

She turns her head to me, "The lighter."

I pull it out of my pocket and show it to her, "I got it."

She smiles with relief, "Ok, good."

I have walked this path so many times with her since I was a kid, that I could navigate it blindfolded. Passing rows of headstones in various shapes, sizes, and styles. I would read the inscriptions, each telling a story of a life that once was. And I can't help but think about the fact that, in a few years, my mother could be among them.

"How is your girlfriend?" She asks.

She keeps forgetting that my ex and I broke up over a year ago. Which doesn't really make it easier.

"We broke up, Mom. A while ago".

Her expression shows confusion, like she caught herself, "Oh, that's right, I forgot. I'm sorry."

"That's ok," I say while forcing a smile.

I keep reminding her, still thinking I can make her save this information. But may have to accept that it's already too late for that.

We reach my father's grave. It's a modest yet well-maintained plot, with a simple gray headstone engraved with clean, serif lettering that reads "Stephen Bryght. Beloved father and husband". Sitting beside it is a small vase filled with a few days-old flowers; their petals are faded and wilted.

There is a gold-colored candle holder in the center of the grave, with a burned-out tea light in it, that my mother changes regularly.

My dad died when I was eleven; he had mental issues and became a therapist thinking that by helping others, he could help himself. But if anything, that backfired or distracted him from his own problems by listening to people who were worse off than him.

No matter how bad things are, there's always someone more fucked up than you.

My mother threw away a lot of his things; maybe the constant reminder was too painful. So the only thing I had left of my dad was an old, beat-up copy of the DSM-III, *The Diagnostic and Statistical Manual of Mental Disorders*. Some of the pages were loose or torn, but whenever I felt lonely, I would read it. I read it so many times that it probably made me the only eleven-year-old kid to learn everything about the classification of mental health disorders and how to treat them.

I started analyzing everyone around me. I felt like a detective.

My aunt Olivia, with her patterns of unstable relationships: Borderline Personality Disorder.

Our neighbor Mr. Idris, who has to count every step he takes: Obsessive-Compulsive Personality Disorder.

One time I got in trouble at school because I analyzed the Kids in my class. And I told one girl she might want to get tested for autism. I don't think I was wrong, but I guess you can't just tell people shit like that.

After my father's death, it was just my mom and me.
And while writing aided me during the grieving process, she didn't have a comparable outlet to cope with her emotions.
I know it wasn't easy for her, but she did a killer job, and despite everything, I can genuinely say that I had an amazing childhood.
She always believed in me, even when she shouldn't have. And I think that her confidence in me surpassed that of a typical mother's belief in her child's potential and abilities.

She always told me, "You can do anything you want to!" And I believed her, but more importantly, she really believed it too.

I watch my mother lighting the wick of a fresh tea light and carefully place it inside the candle holder.

"Do you need help?" I ask.

She reaches for the vase and says, "No, thank you."

Looking at the old flowers, dissatisfied, she adds, "But I forgot to bring fresh flowers."

I say, "I'm sure Dad doesn't mind."

She chuckles and looks at me; I love making her laugh.

Silently, she stares at the headstone.

Not knowing what to do, I just do the same.

My mother says, "You know..." she pauses for a moment, then turns to me, "...I am so proud of you!" And smiles.

I smile back, asking, "For what?".

"You are so talented; you always have been." She turns her head to the headstone again, "And I know your father would be proud of you as well."

"Thank you, Mom. That means a lot."

She then looks back to me and says, "I read your book."

I instantly verbalize my thoughts, saying, "Oh shit!"

And she laughs.

My book isn't necessarily something I'd want my mother to read. And while "based" on actual events, it's primarily a love story heavily infused with fictional elements to make it more intriguing. So can my mother differentiate between my fiction and me as a person?

They are your parents, but how well do they actually know you? Especially if you don't live with them and only see them every couple of days or weeks as you get older. You go visit, leave your bullshit by the door, and try to walk out with the best impression. So that they don't worry about you. Because, after all, they are your parents.

"What did you think?" I ask.

She smiles and says, "I really liked it, you are a great writer, and it's very funny."

I can't believe I'm talking to my mother about a book I wrote, that also includes a gang bang scene.

And yes, that part is fictional.

I keep repeating myself and just say, "Thank you."

"Should we go back?" She asks, "It will be dark soon."

"Yes, Ma'am." I reply, extending my arm for her to loop hers through. And we start making our way back through the cold.

One day my mother and I will go on this walk together, without either of us knowing that it would be the last time, at least for one of us.

DANIEL RUCZKO

5

The TV in my living room has an annoying white spot in the center of the screen, buzzing like a trapped fly. Each time I watch something on it, it pisses me off for the first few minutes. But I don't want to spend money; I don't have to fix it. Using an old Playstation 3 as a Blu-ray player, Danny and I watch *Fight Club*.

He is reclined comfortably on my brown couch, eating chips. His eyes are locked on the TV, while I lie on the one across from him. A glass table between us is covered with notebooks, bills, pieces of paper, and my MacBook Air in the center of it.

Despite the mess, there's a sense of purpose to the chaos. My apartment is never really messy, but there is evidence that I've been writing a lot more lately. When I'm locked in like that, I sleep less, ideas are flooding my brain, and I'm trying to keep up. Everything else turns into static, and I just do the bare minimum. But I fucking love it.

"How is your mom?" Danny asks before shoving a handful of chips into his mouth.

"She's good, man. Nothing new."

He nods. "I'm glad to hear that," he says while chewing and continues watching.

Fight Club has become our go-to movie. We've watched it so many times together that we could actually turn off the sound and still recite every line by heart.

I point at the TV and ask, "You ever read the book?"

"Why would I read the book when there's a fucking movie?"

I shrug and reply, "It has a different ending."

"Really? What is it?"

"Can't tell you; you gotta read it," I say.

"Fuck that; the movie is great."

Glancing towards the table in front of me, I notice a bill I overlooked. The paper feels cold as I grab the envelope.

"Ah, fuck." I mutter to myself, then grab my MacBook and wake it up.

I log onto my bank account, trying not to look at my balance. With a sigh, I begin typing in the details for the transfer.

"What's up?" Danny asks.

Still typing, I say, "Sometimes I just want to peek behind the curtain to see if I'm still on track, you know?"

He thinks for a moment. "Damn. Yeah, I know what you mean," he says, reaching for his drink.

While I'm already on my computer, I switch to the tab of my Ingramspark account and refresh it, noticing that an order for 20 units of my book has been placed.

"Oh shit!" I say while straightening up. I can't believe it.

Danny looks at me, "What?"

In disbelief, I say, "It looks like someone just ordered 20 copies of my book!"

He pauses the movie, his face lighting up. "No Shit?"

"Yeah, dude."

Danny gets way too excited and says, "See, you are on track! It's 20 today; it'll be 20,000 next month."

I laugh, "Yeah, only 19,964 more to go!"

"No, be positive. That's 36 sold!" he corrects me.

I admit, "Yeah, you're right." feeling a bit more optimistic.

"Manifest that shit."

Danny is all about the "law of attraction" and tells me to manifest and picture myself already having what I desire. And while I appreciate his optimism and enthusiasm, I can't help but feel a bit skeptical about the whole concept. He told me to constantly repeat things I want to happen in my head as if they "will" happen, almost like a mantra.

I will be a professional writer.

I will be a professional writer.

I will be a professional writer.

But I wonder if this is really how success works. Does simply wanting and believing make things happen?

As I contemplate this, Danny interrupts my thoughts, "You know what they say, man. Thoughts become things." As if he read my mind again.

I smile and nod at him.

I look at the gold trophy standing on the sideboard next to me. I won it about a year ago at a short story competition. Thinking it would somehow pave the way toward a profession as a writer, but besides an article and a photo in our local newspaper, nothing else came out of it.

My mom still has it framed somewhere, but my excitement lasted for only two days. The perfect contradiction: evidence that I exist as a writer - and evidence that it's still not enough.

As the end credits of the movie start rolling, Danny gets up. "Alright, I gotta bounce."

I give him a thumbs up. "Sounds good," I say and start walking him to the door.

Danny fist-bumps me in the doorway. "Keep writing, dude!"

"I have no fucking choice," I say.

He nods and says, "later." as he leaves.

Looking down, I spot an envelope resting on my doormat. I open it and discover that it's a notice from my landlord about an increase in rent.

6

We fell asleep together, and when I woke up, she wasn't there anymore. It was fucking perfect.

It is dark in my room when a shadow jumps on the bed, like a ninja, followed by the rustling of sheets. It's my cat Salem who tries to get my attention. As I get up to feed him I see a note on my nightstand.

"Last night was fun. - Sarah"

The night was indeed fun, and I appreciate the effort of her writing a note by hand instead of sending a text. As well as other efforts she demonstrated enthusiastically in the bedroom last night. But I can already tell that she would like me a little "too much" for my taste. For most women I spend time with, I'm like a little lovable puppy that can't be kept. They can play with me, and rub my body parts, but ultimately, they aren't allowed to keep me. It's the same kind of excitement, as well as disappointment. But at some point, I would probably shit the bed or chew up their favorite pair of $800 shoes, and they would get tired of cleaning up after me anyways.

As Bukowski said: "To create art means to be crazy alone forever."

And I love being alone. I just hate being lonely.

When she texted me yesterday afternoon, I found myself at a crossroads, girl or writing? Perhaps I felt lonely, and evidently, I chose the girl. But this also means that I need to compensate for the time I didn't dedicate to writing yesterday.

Salem meows impatiently, reminding me of his hunger. He has simple needs: eating, sleeping, attention. Sometimes I envy him for that. Mine are a bit more complex: coffee, sex, success—accompanied by the constant fear that it will never be enough. I grab his food bowl and head to the kitchen. While walking in, I turn on the coffee maker and pour some cat food into the bowl. The warm kitchen air is now infused with a blend of the aroma of Salem's food and freshly brewed coffee. Sitting down at the kitchen table, I scroll through my phone.

December approaches, and my birthday is right around the corner. Which also serves as a reminder that I'm now older than my father ever got to be. I'm turning 39, so close to my life's "midpoint", and I may not have reached the heights I once aspired to, but I'm still chasing my dreams - and maybe that is enough. No, Fuck all that. I think my dreams are just so fucking big that one lifetime simply cannot accommodate them.

It could be because I'm getting older, but I've been obsessed with time and purpose lately. If I don't create something at any given day, then that day is lost forever. Nothing left but memories that will eventually fade. But if I create something daily, no day is ever wasted; at least fragments will remain. If someone cares. And I know that sounds a little extreme.

But we worry so much about how to make more money yet treat the most valuable thing so lightly: time.

We kill it with the constant stream of nonsense internet videos, stupid reels, and meaningless background noise of mediocre entertainment, complaining about where the years went, when we really just "chill" a little too much. Never truly embracing our potential because it could be "too hard."
So we push it away, accompanied with sayings like "one day I'll do it" and don't even start.

But who knows, perhaps I'm the fool for judging how others choose to spend their time. After all, it is their time. And who am I to judge? While most people start families and build happy lives for themselves, I choose to devote mine to crafting clever words in an attempt to feel superior and hoping to make money with it one day. Or, maybe, it is all subjective, and we are collectively just trying the best we fucking can, in our own personal way.

I take a sip of my coffee and try to push the thought away. And instead, I open my laptop and start to work on my latest project. Attempting to immortalize this day. The words flow easily, and before I know it, I'm lost in my own world. And it's hard not to believe that, for me personally, this is where I truly belong, immersed in the realm of my thoughts and creativity.

How am I alone? If you create art, are you really alone? Even when you are, it never feels that way. You are in the company of your creations. But I don't think "normal" people can understand or relate to that.

"We are all special cases."

Salem, now content after having eaten, curls up at my feet, purring gently. While I keep typing, trying to hold on to this day, one word at a time.

7

I love the nights; some of my best days were nights.

Danny had been determined to take me out for my birthday, and even though I sometimes show misanthropic behavior, I do like being around people, especially with him. At least sometimes. He suggested going to a bar in downtown Seattle called *Sip Sip Hooray*, and the name is so fucking stupid that I agreed. I have to see this shit.

As our Uber pulls up to the curb, I can't help but smirk at the neon sign displaying the ridiculous name.

The exterior is unassuming, with exposed brick and large windows that allow us a glimpse of the bustling crowd inside.

We exit the car, thank the driver, and head toward the entrance. The night air is cool and refreshing.

Across the street, another bar catches my eye with its name, *Questionable Choices*. There has to be a fucking ad agency somewhere around here staffed with creatives that come up with shit like that.

Danny is more excited about my birthday than me, which is kind of contagious. And he makes sure everyone we pass knows about it as well.

Entering the bar, I'm struck by the overwhelming hipster vibe that fills the space. Edison bulbs dangle from the ceiling, casting a warm glow on the reclaimed wood tables below. The sound of obscure indie music fills the air, mingling with conversations about the newest craft beers and recent thrift store discoveries among the guests.

Danny orders a beer while I ask for a Diet Coke from the bartender, who sports an impressive handlebar mustache and a sleeve of tattoos. We find a spot to sit and take in the scene around us. Though the atmosphere is decidedly hipster, there's a certain charm with potential for an interesting evening.

Also, Hipsters are usually a nonthreatening breed.

I turn to Danny and say, "Wow, dude, you found the whitest place in Seattle."

He bursts out laughing, "I know! This is too funny".

As we settle into our spot, we notice a group of people nearby, loudly celebrating someone's birthday. The guest of honor, a well-nourished bearded guy in a vintage T-shirt named Johnny, is surrounded by his eclectic friends, who have brought a variety of sweet treats for the occasion. There are colorful plates filled with cake, brownies, and cookies, all beautifully arranged on a wooden table adorned with fairy lights. At a fucking bar!

Danny and I exchange glances before he declares, "I want cake!" in a dry tone and get's up. As we approach the group, a tall, lanky guy with a stylishly unkempt beard, a beanie, and thick-rimmed glasses asks, "Do you know Johnny?" Danny quickly replies with confidence, "Fuck yeah, Johnny and I go way back!" With that, we're welcomed into the group and start helping ourselves to the cake, chatting with the friendly hipsters and seamlessly blending in with the crowd. For reasons unknown, we even give them fake names - Danny introduces himself as "Sebastian," and I become "Tristan." We feel like ninjas or hitmen on a covert mission for free baked goods.

One girl with a flower crown, an oversized sweater, and Doc Martens starts flirting with me. Her long, wavy hair is dyed a vibrant shade of teal, and she has a tiny heart tattooed on her wrist. After Danny yells out, "Hey, it's also Tristan's birthday!" the group becomes extra friendly and attentive. They shower me with birthday wishes and insist that I try a bit of everything on the dessert table. I start to feel a little off, but I'm not quite sure why. Maybe too much sugar. As I kept eating, my head is becoming a bit fuzzy, and soon, we discover the reason: all the sweet treats are edibles infused with Cannabis. I am so fucked.

It turns out everyone who actually knows Johnny is aware that he's a huge pothead. But since we don't know him at all, the joke's on us. And I guess when we were asked, "Do you know Johnny?" that was code for, "This shit is full of weed; be careful." Unlike Danny, I have zero experience with Cannabis. I don't even usually eat sweets, but this time, I go all in. I sample the moist red velvet cake with cream cheese frosting, the double chocolate chip cookies, and the raspberry lemon bars. All very rich in THC. By the time we found out, it was already too late. The damage is done. It comes in waves, switching from "Ok, I think I'm fine" seamlessly to "Fuck, I'm gonna die."

So, at 39 years old, I experience Cannabis for the first time, unintentionally. Surrounded by my best friend and a group of well-meaning hipsters that are surprisingly advanced bakers, while masquerading as someone else at a stranger's birthday party. Life, it seems, has a peculiar sense of humor.

As the THC from the edibles takes full effect, my vision starts to blur, and the indie folk music begins to distort and warp in my ears, the melodies morphing into a disconcerting jumble of noise. The faces around me become caricatures, their features stretching and distorting like a funhouse mirror, and their laughter grows shrill and mocking.

My heart rate accelerates, and I feel an intense wave of paranoia wash over me. I glance around the room, suddenly convinced that everyone knows we don't belong here, that we've been found out. Johnny will be so pissed that we ate his cake.

A sudden surge of nausea hits me, and I feel dizzy and disoriented. The room starts spinning, and the vibrant colors of the party decorations blur into a nauseating whirlwind. My breathing becomes shallow and rapid, and I can't seem to catch my breath.

In the midst of this sensory overload, I become acutely aware of my own thoughts. They spiral out of control, taking on a life of their own as they race through my mind.

For some reason, I feel like I need to go to the bathroom and wait there until this nightmare is over. I walk over to a person who I think is Danny. Fuck, I mean "Sebastian." And tell him, or her, about my plan.

"Dude, I'm going to the bathroom."

The person, or floor lamp, that clearly isn't Sebastian gives me a thumbs up. Or not. At this point, I'm not sure about anything anymore.

Everything feels slow, as if taking a breath takes between ten minutes and a month.

And I can't follow my own thoughts anymore; I keep forgetting what I thought two seconds ago. So I start repeating everything in my mind.

Walk to the bathroom.

Walk to the bathroom.

Walk to the bathroom. The mantra again. My brain is like a browser with ten open tabs - and the same video is playing on repeat in each one.

On my way, I get "attacked" by flower-crown girl who approaches me from the shadows. She grabs my head and starts kissing me. Her breath smells like sugar and cannabis - a strange mixture of childhood and depravity. And it feels as if she has three tongues. While it is not unpleasant, I have to focus on my mission. So even while making out with a beautiful three-tongued flower crown girl, I repeat my current mantra in my head.

Walk to the bathroom.

Walk to the bathroom.

Walk to the bathroom.

She starts grinding me, and I'm just way too fucking high to accomplish anything. So I actually start verbalizing my mind mantra, hoping to escape, but all I can actually mumble is "Bathroom."

Which appears to sound like an invitation to her. She instantly grabs my hand and pulls me with her, like a puppy. A very high little puppy.

As she ushers me into the women's bathroom, everything seems to have taken on a life of its own. The dim, warm lighting appears to pulsate, casting hypnotic shadows on the floor, which is covered in an explosion of mismatched patterned tiles. The vintage floral wallpaper seems to sway and dance as if the flowers are alive. I look at her arm while she drags me along, and the heart tattoo on her wrist appears to pulsate in sync with my breathing.

We enter a stall, and she continues kissing me, pressing her body tight against mine. She starts unzipping my pants, and I'm completely helpless. My pants fall to the floor, and while kneeling down, she looks up at me with her reptilian eyes and says, "Happy birthday Tristan" before inserting my member into her mouth. I don't think I've ever gotten a blowjob from someone with three tongues before.

Flower-crown girl gives her everything, but I simply can't feel my body, nor my mind. The bathroom around me starts to twist and warp; the pulsating lights seem to grow harsh and disorienting. Panic starts to set in as my heart races uncontrollably. The sensation of her multiple tongues on me is still in full effect.

I try to focus, to calm myself down, and maybe even enjoy this weird moment, but it only seems to make matters worse.

Traces of my climax run down her chin, yet I can't recall experiencing any pleasure. Gently pushing her away, I zip up my pants and mumble, "Thank you," as I stagger out of the stall. My legs tremble like overcooked noodles, and the room continues to spin, making me feel nauseous. I need to get out of this place, away from the chaos.

As I finally make my way out of the bathroom and back into the bar, I pass four people that could potentially all be Danny. Or Sebastian.

My phone vibrates in my pocket, its sudden buzzing startling me. I pull it out, only for it to slip through my trembling rubber fingers and clatter to the floor. I drop to my hands and knees, searching blindly for the device amid the chaos of shadows and pulsating lights dancing around me. When I finally locate it, I pick it up, my vision swimming as I try to focus on the screen. The text message is from my ex, Maria. "Happy birthday. I hope you're having an amazing day." Seeing her name on the screen sucker-punched me. Your favorite person has the potential to become your least favorite person. And I don't know if it's the surreal nightmare I'm trapped in or the fact that her and I haven't spoken in months, but those casual and simple words stab at me like a thousand needles.

My heart is racing. Still surrounded by distorted sounds and shadowy figures, my mission remains the same.

I need to get out.

I need to get out.

I need to get out.

As I try to find my way out of this maze of confusion, a concerned voice reaches out to me. "Tristan? Are you ok?".

It is a large human that I don't recognize. "Who are you?" I manage to ask.

"It's Johnny. You don't look so good."

I repeat the mantra words in my head, then morphing over to my mouth, "I need to get out."

Johnny puts his large arm around me and says, "I got you, buddy" and escorts me out of the suffocating bar.

Outside, the air is refreshing, and the absence of deafening noise coupled with the openness of the space brings an immediate sense of relief.

"Stay put," Johnny suggests, "and I'll call you an Uber, alright?" I nod in agreement.

Danny randomly appears as if he came through a portal. He rushes over to me, concern written across his face, asking, "Dude, are you ok?".

When people keep asking if you're ok, then you may not be.

I look at him, unable to speak, and Danny just says, "Let's get you home, birthday boy."

I am not ok.
I am not ok.
I am not ok.

DANIEL RUCZKO

8

Welcome to the past, the realm of Mondays. A day most people would rather avoid. Just the thought of the beginning of a new work week is usually enough to trigger groans and complaints in many people, and in most cases, I would count myself among them. But today, in a twist of irony, Monday feels like a breath of fresh air. After the train wreck that was my birthday weekend, I welcome something to help me recalibrate. A force-fed routine.

I still feel a little high, and I wonder why anyone would choose to feel this way on purpose.

Upon entering my workplace, I quickly notice how familiar and comforting everything feels. The same noises, the same smells, the same mundane tasks that await me, all the shit I usually hate has transformed into a lullaby, a well-worn melody that I find myself humming along without a care. And I'm eager to relive yet another iteration of a day that I've lived through so many times before.

It's a reminder that life goes on, no matter how traumatic a weekend is. And that it's often the most ordinary moments that keep us grounded and anchored. And I'm just fucking grateful for it.

The office seems unusually hushed and vacant today. Navigating the labyrinth of cubicles, I spot Danny standing by the coffee maker, engaged in the sacred ritual of caffeination. I stroll over to him, and as I approach, he greets me with a grin. "There he is, Dr. Greenthumb," Danny says.

I respond with a casual peace sign. He looks concerned as he asks, "You feeling a little better?"

"Yeah, I'm alright." I say with a steady voice. No mention of Maria's text or the surprising mental tornado it left behind.

With raised eyebrows, he asks, "What did you do yesterday?"

I give a slight smile, "I woke up, told my dreams to fuck off, and crawled back into bed."

He chuckles and says, "Sounds like a typical Sunday to me." Coffee in hand, he continues, "Well, I better get going. I'll catch you later." I nod at him, and he starts walking toward his office.

Making my way to my own workspace, I take in the organized chaos I left behind before I started into my weekend. As every day lately, the grey sky outside my window greets me with its dullness. I sink into my chair and switch on my computer, waiting for it to boot. Scrolling through my phone to kill time, I look at birthday wishes that flooded my texts and social media feeds. After gaining access to my work computer, I spot a new message on Slack from my boss, Mr. Graham, requesting to see me.

He's a rare breed in the corporate world, the kind of boss who genuinely appreciates the work I do, someone, who'll stay out of my business as long as I do my job. Curious and without wasting time, I rise from my chair and make my way toward his office. I give the door a gentle knock.

"Please, come in," Mr. Graham says from inside the room.

As I push open the door, I'm greeted by the sight of his well-organized workspace. His large wooden desk is neat and uncluttered, with a few family photos and a computer monitor occupying the space. He appears visibly tense as I sit down, his face etched with anxiety. Clearing his throat, he starts with a strained politeness, "Hey, thanks for coming in, Richard."

"Sure, what's going on?" I ask, sensing something isn't quite right.

Taking a deep breath, he explains that the recent merger between our company and another has resulted in some unfortunate budget cuts. They basically just want to pay fewer nerds to do the same amount of work. And I know exactly where this is going.

Mr. Graham proceeds cautiously, his voice wavering slightly as he speaks, clearly reluctant to share the next piece of information with me. I lean back and watch the train derail. The partner company has enforced a policy of targeting specific employees for downsizing. In an effort to minimize the impact on families, they've decided to prioritize letting go of those who are unmarried and without children. And, of course, I fit the bill. Check, check.

It's clear he's not happy with the decision, and the fact that he's the one tasked with delivering the news only amplifies his distress. In this moment, the familiar comfort of my workplace crumbles, replaced by the harsh reality of me being completely fucked.

His expression filled with regret, he says, "I'm really sorry, Richard. You're the last person I want to let go, but I also believe you'll have no trouble finding a new job quickly."

I appreciate his hollow words, but I'm not sure. Wearing a fake smile, I tell him, "It's ok; I know this isn't your decision."

A storm of thoughts flood my mind, worrying not only about myself but also wondering what was going to happen to Danny.

Mr. Graham moves on to discuss the severance package I'll be receiving, promises a glowing recommendation, support in my job hunt, and blah blah blah. But none of it changes the fact that the rug's been pulled out from under me, and the immediate future appears as an ominous abyss.

My thoughts drift toward *Up in the Air,* the film with George Clooney from 2009. Where the protagonist travels around the country firing people. He has this one recurring line that he says to everyone he lays off: "Anybody who ever built an empire, or changed the world, sat where you are now. And it's BECAUSE they sat there that they were able to do it."

I always liked that, in theory, and when it didn't concern me, but maybe there's some truth to it. Once we're pushed, we have to find a different path. Something we wouldn't have thought of because we were too scared and comfortable. And you only need to be comfortable if you want to fall asleep.

Despite all this, for the first time in my life, I feel like I embody the genuine essence of an artist – soon an unemployed dreamer rambling about hopes and aspirations whose debit card gets declined as he attempts to purchase a McFlurry.

9

find myself in the bowels of a discount thrift store, where dust and desperation mingle freely. Hunting for a small token of appreciation for my mother, who happens to love good thrift store finds. The air is thick with the scent of vinyl, and the constant hum of fluorescent lights overhead buzzes like a soundtrack to consumer purgatory.

I navigate through the maze of discounted wares, a world where every conceivable mass-produced item screams for attention. A blender with a missing button, a pack of mismatched socks, a set of knives with their edges blunted from overuse - all of them orphaned, each one crying out for a home, a purpose, a reason for their existence.

And then, hidden among the chaos, I find it: a small, hand-painted vase, its faded colors a testament to the passage of time, its edges chipped and worn. It holds its ground among the bright displays of plastic and mediocrity, a relic from a bygone era, a piece of history captured in glass. In its imperfections, I see the perfect gift for my mother.

As I leave the store, holding the vase securely against my chest, I feel a sense of triumph. I know she will love it, and I just want to inject a dose of happiness into her day before I give her reason to worry about me.

While stepping into my mother's apartment, the familiar sweet smell greeting my nostrils, letting my brain instantly know where I am. I catch a glimpse of my mother, cocooned in her worn armchair, watching TV.

Her glazed eyes are locked onto the screen, consuming the banality of a sitcom that numbs reality.

As the bolt falls into the lock, she quickly turns, "Richard!" She says, with a huge smile on her face.

I share her excitement. Seeing her right now feels so good, like coming home after a long school day, ready to play "Mario Kart" all afternoon.

"Hey, mom!" I mirror her smile.

Her gaze drifts to the vase cradled in my arms. "What is that?" She asks, pointing at it.

I hold it out to her, "I got it for you."

She looks excited, "Oh, what's the occasion?"

I shrug, my eyes still locked with hers. "No occasion, really. Just felt like getting you something."

I hand her the vase, and she inspects it carefully.

She looks up at me, her expression a blend of surprise and delight. "Thank you, Richard. It's beautiful," she murmurs, her voice soft, genuine.

I notice her laptop lying in the corner, reminding me of my promise to fix it.

I sit down on the couch across from her, my body sinking into the worn cushions, and I fidget with my fingers, feeling nervous, as I mentally preparing myself to break the news about losing my job without setting off the maternal alarm bells.

In that moment, I hear the radiator noise. Clack, clack, clack.

"Did you have a great birthday?" my mother asks.

Right on cue, the sitcom's laugh track echoes mockingly in the background. But I choose to withhold the details of my recent Fear and Loathing at a Hipster Bar experience that included a blowjob from a girl with three tongues, simply replying with a casual, "Yeah, it was fun."

I know that I'm at risk of exposing the cracks in my "I've got my shit together" facade. But I have to tell her. I feel the edges of my mouth stretch into a thin, forced smile, a feeble attempt at shielding my mother from the impending cause for concern. With a final, steadying breath, I summon the courage to begin, each word a fragile soldier marching bravely into the unknown.

Inhaling deeply, I say, "I need to tell you something."

She looks at me with worry and asks, "What is it?"

I always thought that when my life falls apart, it would be more dramatic. Rain. Tragic music. An emotional monologue.

I pause for a moment before finally confessing, "I was laid off from my job."

Her face softens with empathy, and she says, "I'm so sorry, are you okay?"

"Yes, I really am," I assure her. "But don't worry, I'll find a new one pretty quickly."

As I try to think of more things to tell her, she abruptly cuts through my thoughts and says, "No, you won't!".

Confused, I ask, "What do you mean?"

In a calm tone, she says, "Losing that job might have been the best thing that could've happened to you."

Her response catches me off guard; she's not trying to belittle my struggles but rather offer me a different perspective. My mother's words are frank and sincere as she continues, "Most of us don't take risks out of fear. But it's easier to recover from a mistake than to live with the regret of not seizing an opportunity. I have many regrets and missed many opportunities, but I won't let you do the same."

I am speechless and just look at her as she talks; I can see the determination in her eyes, and I know that she means every single word. "You are an artist. And artists in regular jobs are like caged animals - sure, you can survive, but you'll never truly thrive."

Her words are like a lifeline, pulling me out of the depths of uncertainty and into a world of possibility. She never said anything like this before.

No one in my family was an artist, but evidently, she sees something in me, just like she always has, and that means the world to me. But reality kicks in, and I say, "Mom, you have no idea how much your words mean. But I'm not making any money with the writing."

She reaches for the remote and turns off the TV. For a moment, we just sit there in silence, each lost in our own thoughts. She looks over to me. "I recently canceled some of my insurance policies," she begins.

My mother is notorious for having a policy for just about anything, so I know what she's referring to.

"As a result," she says, "I received some money from the insurance companies." I'm unsure of what to make of it, but before I can even ask, she continues, "It's not a lot, but I don't want you to worry about money right now. You can't be creative when your mind is filled with anxiety." She pauses for a moment before saying, "Give this a real shot! For me." As I look at her, I see a glimmer of pride in her eyes, and I know that she's doing this because she believes in me.

A surge of emotions washes over me, threatening to overwhelm me. I rise from my seat, wrapping my arms tightly around her. The air is saturated with feeling as we stand there. And It's a mind-boggling contrast, how one moment she can't even find a lighter, and the next she's completely lucid, channeling something so profound.

As I pull away from the embrace, I look at her with a newfound sense of determination. "Thank you, Mom," I say, my voice constricted by sentiment. "Thank you for everything."

I swear to Christ, if I could give this woman everything on this planet, it would still not be enough.

10

The percussive dance of keystrokes becomes the steady beat that soundtracks my days. I'm addicted. Addicted to creating. Over the course of four weeks, I've immersed myself in a frenzy of creative output, my days and nights bled together as I typed. Driven by the desire to transform my thoughts into words.

While writing, I fasted for twenty-one days, abandoning nourishment and embracing deprivation. At first, it wasn't even on purpose; I simply forgot to eat, but I am an experienced faster.

Someone who never willingly withheld from consuming food could never understand. But once you cross the threshold of that second day without calories, you're catapulted to an entirely new plane of being. Your body abandons the mundane task of digestion, fueled with ketones, funneling every last bit of energy into the depths of your mind.

You see with crystal clarity, smell the most delicate of scents, and your thoughts slice through the fog of your mind with laser-like precision. The sensation is intoxicating, like a drug that sparks life into every neuron - a drug created within your own body. In the words of Salvador Dalí, "I don't do drugs. I *am* drugs."

In that state of self-inflicted starvation, you are reborn, the best version of yourself, untainted and unstoppable. You feel fucking invincible.

I've never had trouble finding someone to share a bed with, but time was the enemy, a precious commodity I couldn't afford to waste on social interaction or seeking out companionship the old-fashioned way. I had a promise to keep. So in the few moments when I stepped away from the keyboard and longed for some kind of physical connection. In the name of efficiency, I let the convenience of technology dictate my encounters, and I turned to Tinder, the digital marketplace of lustful transactions. The Tinder girls that come and go provide a carnal release; nameless, faceless encounters blur together like wet-on-wet oil color strokes by Bob Ross. Painting a panoramic landscape of sex and sin. Sometimes it feels like every encounter is just a fragment of a story I'll never finish writing.

As I navigate this fever dream of creation, self-discipline, and indulgence, I lost myself. I hammered out page after page, a mosaic of text that grew like a fungus.

I am driven by my vision, letting it guide me, mold me, break me apart, and stitch me back together in ways I never imagined possible. Every new chapter, every plot twist, every gut-wrenching revelation was a revelation not only for my characters, but for me as well. I have never felt more alive.

Time loses all meaning, and as the final words dripped from my fingers like blood from an open wound, I knew that this, is why I'm on this planet.

And while these 250 pages may not be perfect, they are definitely a really fucking solid first draft.

I'm proud of the achievement, proud that I didn't waste any time, and fully committed to what I was doing. I owe it to my mother. This might be my best work yet, or it might be the noose that finally tightens around my neck.

Danny wants to come by after work to celebrate, and since it was almost six, he should be arriving soon. In the meantime, a girl named Katie is still in my living room. Another digital conquest materialized, looking for her underwear.

Once upon a time, Katie was a celebrated pop star who rose to fame when she was barely eighteen. She was all over TV and radio back then, with the world as her stage. However, the cruel hand of time had other plans, and her fame began to fade. To this day, she still chases her former life, but without success, as the world has moved on. She now graces the stages of community theaters, performing in musicals that offer her a taste of that intoxicating but fleeting life in the spotlight.

I thought she looked familiar when I first saw her, but I couldn't quite place her. It wasn't until she mentioned her past that it all clicked into place. I remember having a crush on her when I saw her music videos on TV back then. I guess it's never too late to fulfill your fantasies, even the ones you've long forgotten about, and sometimes the universe offers up a taste of the surreal to remind us, that anything is possible. This one is for you, nineteen-year-old Richard.

While I offer Katie something to drink, the doorbell chimes. "Oh, is that your friend?" She asks while I hurry to buzz Danny in.

"Yes, Ma'am," I reply.

And she starts gathering her things. I'm actually really excited to see him, as I was so trapped in my creative vortex that we didn't hang out at all. I was relieved to hear that he got to keep his job, giving us even more reason to celebrate.

Danny walks in, while Katie prepares to make her exit. Acknowledging his presence, she looks at me and suggests, "Let's orchestrate another encounter like this." her lips curving into a smile.

I like the way she phrased it, and nod in agreement, saying, "Sure."

And with that, she leaves.

Shutting the door, Danny turns to me, asking, "Did you fuck her?"

I shrug and say, "Maybe a little bit."

He can't help but smile, shaking his head, muttering, "Jealous."

He hugs me as if we didn't see each other in years, like reunited brothers.

We enter the living room, letting our bodies fall onto the couch almost in unison. Danny laughs at the sight of a bottle of lube on the living room table that I forgot to put away.

He looks over to me and says, "You look skinny, man."

Looking down at my body, I reply, "Oh yeah, the fasting..." As someone who is constantly hungry, he could never understand.

Danny flashes a grin and asks, "So, how is Katie in real life?"

I laugh, "Depressed, but in a cute way."

I see a glimpse of concern on his face as he says, "So, besides fucking ex pop-stars. What else is new? Tell me everything!"

I take a deep breath and launch into my story. I tell him about the talk with my mother, the countless hours of hammering on my keyboard, the rush I get from creating something out of nothing. About how, each day, I woke to the cold glow of the laptop screen, my fingers moving as if possessed, possessed by some unseen force that demanded my story be told.

He's genuinely excited for me, and I can see the pride in his eyes as he hears about my progress.

I grab the first printed copy of the manuscript named *Hard to Find, Easy to Lose* and toss it on the table in front of him, next to the lube, and say, "Boom!"

He grabs it and flips through the pages.

"Dude, that's fucking amazing! I'm proud of you."

I believe him, but I can tell that something's off. So I ask, "What's up?".

He hesitates for a moment before shaking his head and uttering the typical response of "Nothing."

But I know him too well to let it go at that.

"Dude, come on. Something's up," I press on, my concern mounting.

He hesitates again before admitting, "I don't want to rain on your parade."

The words hang heavy in the air. My eyes remain fixed on him until he finally breaks the silence, his shame evident as he mutters, "They fired me as well."

My genuine distress spills out, "Fuck!"

His response is bleak, "Yeah, they gave me four weeks."

He's a hard worker, and I know that he won't have an issue finding a new job, but that's not the problem.

At this moment, I realize that he's lacking something I possess: A sense of purpose. Something he actually gives a shit about. And it's not the loss of that specific job that upsets him, but the uncertainty of what lies ahead. And I hate seeing him worried.

As the weight of Danny's revelation hung in the air, I felt a surge of determination. Now it's my turn. And after hearing him talk about the law of attraction and affirmations for years, I say, "Shit will work out. And we will be fine. I promise!" And I truly mean it.

He smiles, attempting to trust my words, as he responds, "I appreciate it, brother."

With his history of depression, I'm worried this would be a trigger, and I feel obligated to cheer him up.

I jump out of my seat and propose, "Alright, dude, let's get out of here!"

Danny looks at me, a hint of reluctance in his eyes, and asks, "Where are we going?"

"Let's find you a retired pop star or something?"

He thinks for a moment before he says, "Well, I could use some sexual harassment."

"There you go!" I say.

His gaze shifts back to the manuscript on the table. "And man..." he says, pointing at it, "congratulations on this, for real."

Everything will be fine.

Everything will be fine.

Everything will be fine.

DANIEL RUCZKO

11

Outside my window, the Seattle sky exhales an icy breath, setting free a whirlwind of snowflakes performing their mesmerizing dance. As much as I despise the weather here most of the time, I love it during this season, as it transforms the city into an authentic winter wonderland.

The moment those first notes from John Williams' *Somewhere In My Memory* infiltrate my ears, it's as if the holiday season has officially been declared, and I'm instantly catapulted back to a simpler time. *Home Alone* is my go-to Christmas movie, and I indulge in the nostalgic grip it has on me time and time again. Watching it has become a ritual for me, almost an obsession.

For the last couple of days, as this gorgeous season unfolds, my existence has been devoted to a singular purpose: editing my manuscript. Each word a battle to be won, each sentence a puzzle to be solved. The hours bleed together, and my confidence in the project grows with every page.

I invited Danny into my creative process, asking for his feedback and advice. I thought it would be a good distraction, and making him feel involved could give him an invigorated sense of purpose. And I wasn't wrong. He thrives in it, like a fish in water, and provides valuable perspectives. His visits to my place have become a daily routine, and today, the cycle continues. Me, sitting at my laptop, fingers dancing across the keys, while Danny is on his, reading and making notes.

The white spot on my TV appears to be growing, like a malignant tumor, and the buzzing noise got louder. But I don't give a shit. It doesn't matter. Because in this imperfect world, we're stumbling upon perfection, a fleeting moment worth preserving. On a flawless winter day, I sit in my living room with my best friend, lost in this artistic endeavor. The scent of vanilla from a candle lingers in the air, while my cat purrs next to me, and the sounds of Kevin McCallister's adventures echo in the background.

Hold your breath.

Freeze Frame.

Click.

I'm on the verge of wrapping up another chapter when the shrill ring of my phone shatters the silence, pulling me out of my mental cocoon. An unknown number from Los Angeles, California, appears on the screen. Curious and slightly annoyed, I grab it, unsure of what to expect on the other end.

As I swipe to answer, I press the phone to my ear and say, "Hello?"

"Hey there, is this Richard?" The deep, assertive voice on the other end inquires.

"Yep, that's me. Who's this?"

Danny glances at me, and I put the call on speaker.

"This is Allen Warren, film producer from Playdead, a production company based in Los Angeles..." the voice trails off. Danny and I swap puzzled looks.

He goes on, "...I just finished reading your book *Serendipity*, and I think it's ripe for a film adaptation."

Danny springs to his feet in excitement, mouthing "dude" at me.

Intrigued, yet skeptical, I say, "I'm glad you enjoyed it."

Yeah right. Is this some kind of prank? I have never been to LA, but this sounds so fucking LA.

Allen continues, enthusiasm in his voice, "I'd love to discuss the possibility of optioning the movie rights for it. Do you have a manager or agent I should get in touch with?"

I weigh the situation, still questioning the authenticity of his call. But then I glance at Danny, smiling, and say, "Sure, you can reach my manager. I'll give you his number."

"Great!" Allen says with excitement.

A spark of inspiration hits me, and I recite a string of digits to Allen. Halfway through, Danny catches on, realizing I'm giving out his number. His gaze locks onto mine, with a blend of confusion and curiosity. I smile.

"Thanks for the number, Richard."

"No problem," I reply, attempting to sound nonchalant. "Just so you know, my manager is out of the office over the weekend, but he should be available on Monday. Feel free to give him a call then."

"Sounds good," Allen responds. "I'll reach out to him. Looking forward to discussing the project further. Have a great day!"

"You too," I say before ending the call.

Danny's face morphs into a kaleidoscope of confusion, like a chameleon lost in a sea of multicolored Skittles, "What the fuck, dude?"

"Well, I needed a manager on the spot," I explain, shrugging.

Danny's confusion shifts into peals of laughter. "Do you think this is legit?" his voice teetering between suspicion and fascination.

"Honestly?" I pause for a moment, considering. "Dude, I have no fucking idea."

He sits back down. "I guess we'll find out."

I shoot him a grin, replying, "I guess so, "Manager."

He lets out a laugh, "Fuck it! Go with the flow. I'm gonna google his production company now". His energy is infectious, and I join in with a chuckle.

Trying not to get my hopes up too high, but the sheer possibility of this being real feels nice, sparking a sense of excitement and hope that I can't deny. And I'm starting to visualize how all of this could unfold.

Hold your breath.

Freeze Frame.

Click.

12

In the early 90s, when the internet came into the picture, I was all in, eagerly soaking up every bit of it. Using those "10,000-Hour Free Trial" America Online discs that cluttered our mailboxes to get access. With a shitty dial-up modem that made those familiar shrieky noises until you were finally greeted with a voice saying "Welcome" followed shortly by "You've got mail," If you were lucky.

Everything was so new and exciting; it felt like being one of the first people to arrive on a newly discovered planet, ready to be explored. What a time to be alive! Chat rooms, Netscape Navigator, AltaVista, website visit counters- all relics of the early digital age. And don't even get me started on the thrill of receiving an email!

Fast forward to now, we carry around smartphones that are more powerful than any computer back then, with 24-hour access to high-speed internet in our pockets. Crazy.

I'm sitting on the couch in my mother's living room, with her laptop balancing on my knees. She always loved baking and is currently in the kitchen, working her magic. The usual sweet aroma of her apartment is replaced by the scent of freshly baked goods. The faint sound of Christmas music drifting through the apartment, accompanied by a small yet festive tree standing sentry in the corner, twinkling with multicolored lights, as if daring anyone to try and resist its seasonal charm.

When I got here today, in the same way that kids run downstairs on Christmas morning, eager to open their gifts, I couldn't wait to share the news with my mother about the manuscript I wrote and the supposed production company from the land of make-believe that had come knocking, dangling the promise of a film adaptation. Regardless of what the future holds, I needed to make sure that she knows that I'm dead serious about this.

And in her eyes, I saw happiness and pride flicker like a flame.

However, sharing news with my mother is always a precarious tightrope walk, as her Alzheimer's can make important things slip through the cracks while keeping insignificant details remain locked in her mind forever. It's clear that the illness hasn't progressed to the point where she can no longer live independently, but its effects are certainly evident. But maybe this will be one of those rare memories that sticks. And even if not, I don't mind repeating the news to her countless times, reliving that moment, knowing it will bring her joy each time as if it's the first she's hearing it. But sometimes it feels like she's dissolving, like an old photo fading over time. And that might be the cruelest goodbye of all.

With my promise kept, I'm here to fix my mother's computer. It's running Windows 8, Microsoft's bastard child - not quite as bad as Vista or Millennium, but not much of an improvement either. This machine takes an eternity to boot up, and I'm suspecting an issue with the hard drive.

The booting drags on, but finally, the login screen appears. Carefully punching in the password from the Post-it, I'm rewarded with the triumphant three-note startup sound.
The desktop begins to take shape, revealing a cluttered array of icons vying for attention. In the background, a wallpaper of a field of lilies serves as the canvas for this chaotic digital circus.

I launch a diagnostic tool to assess the hard drive's health. As the test runs smoothly, something else catches my eye - a hidden partition. With a swift click, I initiate the recovery process, and voila - it mounts.
Like Indiana Jones stumbling upon a forgotten pyramid, I'm filled with curiosity and anticipation about what could be concealed within. What digital secrets await me?

Browsing through a collection of decade-old photos, taken with a camera from a past life, with memories of girls I once crossed pants with. Among the clutter, I discover random MP3 and WAV files tucked away on the drive.

And then, like buried artifacts, I find a folder named "cash" created by a version of myself that no longer exists.
My finger hovers over the trackpad, and I click. Inside, an innocent file with the title "wallet.dat" is nestled.

I yell out, "Oh shit!"

"What happened?" My mother asks from the kitchen.

I quickly compose myself, "Nothing, sorry."

But it couldn't be. This is the partition I lost in 2012. Oh, the number of times I hoped to stumble upon that vanished file! With trembling hands, I open a program simply named "Bitcoin Core," released back in 2009.

And then, a message glares at me, taunting me with a demand: "Please enter recovery phrase."

The 12-word combo that could unlock a fortune, a series of random words so arbitrary, it could be anything like: tree, sleep, dog, organ, wrist, lamp, frog, jacket, toss, globe, wink, bicycle. But that's not it.

I can't even recall how much I put into this thing. It's like a lost treasure map, and it could be worth anything from $80,000 to $2,000,000. A modern-day chest of gold, and I lost the fucking key to unlock its riches.

We've heard these stories of misfortune many times. This is just another one of them. Like the winning lottery ticket that was thrown away by accident. Hard to find, easy to lose.

But whatever, up until today, I thought the file was forever lost. Now I know where it is, but I don't remember the passcode. Nothing has changed. I'm still just one step closer, yet 12 random words away. I'll try to delete the memory of finding this file, just like I erased the passcode from my mind. But that's like trying to drown a shark.

My mother emerges from the kitchen and asks, "Did you find anything on the laptop?"

Her words hang in the air like a heavy fog.

I force squeeze a smile out of my face and reply, "Nothing unusual. I'm just gonna make sure it runs a bit faster."

She smiles at me and says, "Thank you so much for fixing it," as if this is the most important thing in the world. So I'll treat it that way.

"No problem, Mom," I say.

If the simple act of doing a little maintenance on a laptop can make her so happy, then I'll exert every ounce of effort to make it purr like a kitten. I run a few tools to give it a tune-up, trying to revive this slow and sluggish machine. Click. Tap. Scan. It's like I'm performing some sort of surgery on this ailing machine.

With all the scanning and optimizing finally done, the old computer seems to be limping along once more, at least as acceptable as possible for the outdated hardware it has.

"All done." I say victoriously to my mom.

Her smile outshines the Christmas tree as she says, "Amazing!"

She sets the laptop aside and joins me on the couch, the cushion squeaking under her weight.

"Wanna watch *Home Alone*?" My mother asks, with a twinkle in her eye.

"Of course!" I say.

We often only realize what we had after we've lost it. This applies to everything, from people and dreams to passwords, minds, digital currency, and moments.

I'm in one of those moments, right now, one that I have to savor and make the most of. I'm filled with gratitude and intend to relish every last drop of this experience. Who knows how many more of these precious moments we'll have, how many memories she'll be able to hold onto?

She is the best mother I could ever ask for.
Everything I do is either for her or because of her.

13

Something that started as a "not so serious" throwaway somehow took on a life of its own.

Danny arrived at my doorstep, contract in hand, after his discussion with the producer, Allen. The 30-page document might as well have been scribbled in Klingon for all the sense it made to us. And since we have no fucking clue of how these things work, Danny wasted no time setting up a phone call with an entertainment attorney from LA, determined to make this official. She is supposed to help us understand the contract and its terms, as well as negotiate for us. For that, she will collect 5%.

Danny sits on the couch beside me, fiddling with his laptop. He's more pumped up than me about all of this like he was on my birthday. Meanwhile, I continue questioning how real this is.

"What's this attorney's name?" I ask him.

He looks at his screen and says, "Ava Fernandez," rolling the "R" with a fake Spanish accent.

I let out a laugh and say, "Sounds sexy."

Grabbing my phone, I Google her name. A striking young woman stands behind a podium in the photo that appears. I show the screen to Danny and ask, "Is this her?"

He glances at the picture and confirms, "Yeah, that's probably her. It says 'Attorney at law' at the bottom."

Looking at the photo again, I remark, "She's really pretty."

Danny turns to me, his face serious and stern. "Listen, man. You can not fuck your attorney," he warns.

I roll my eyes and reply, "I'm not trying to do that."

"Just don't even go there."

I sigh and say, "Relax, man. I was just acknowledging her beauty."

"Yeah, and the next thing we know, we need a new attorney because this one hates you," He shoots back.

The phone buzzes on the table. Danny grabs it and taps the speaker button before placing it in front of us.

We're greeted by a voice as smooth as silk. "Hello, this is Ava."

"Danny and Richard here," Danny replies after the pleasantries. Eager to get things rolling, he adds, "Thanks for getting back to us so quickly."

"No problem," she says, "I've reviewed the contract you sent over earlier, and I think we can work with this. There are a few terms we should negotiate, but overall, this is a great deal, especially for first-timers like you guys."

"Ok, let's do it." Danny says.

I chime in, "I've got some questions about the contract."

Ava chuckles, "I find it endearing that you're even trying to comprehend it. Many of my clients don't even give these things a second glance. But I'm happy to answer any questions you may have."

I pause for a moment before asking, "So, this is real?"

Danny gives me an irritated look, and Ava's voice comes through the phone, "I'm not sure I understand. What do you mean?"

With some uncertainty, I clarify, "I mean, the contract and the offer?".

Ava takes a moment to ponder before responding. "Yeah, this is a pretty standard agreement for this sort of thing. And to put your mind at ease, I've actually dealt with the production company before in the past."

It becomes painfully obvious to me that I have no fucking clue about the ins and outs of this contract shit as Ava continues. But her voice is like butter, and somehow it manages to soothe my nerves.

"Could you break down the offer for an idiot like me?" I ask. "Just the cliff notes?"

Ava starts giving us the rundown, "Sure thing. The gist of it is: they're offering you $250,000 for the movie rights to your book, along with 5% of the profits it makes. However, you will retain all rights to your book." Danny's eyes widen in disbelief.

Fuckness. Is this really happening? That's a lot of money.

Ava continues, "But don't worry, I'll be working on a counteroffer after we've discussed the details. I can get you more."

Taken aback, I blurt out, "Wait, you can do that?"

Ava laughs, "Of course. It's standard procedure to counter, no matter what they offer. They expect that."

All I can manage is a breathless "Wow."

The days that change your life usually begin like any other day.

As Ava and Danny dive deeper into the offer, I am mesmerized by Danny's ability to handle it all. He navigates the complex terms with the patience of a saint, and we begin to make some damn progress.

Amidst the labyrinth of legal jargon, my mind had already checked out, and I'm grateful to have Danny taking charge.

After hashing out all the details, Ava concludes the conversation, "Once I'm finished with the counteroffer, I'll send it to you before forwarding it off to the production company."

Danny ends the call and says, "Fuck, man, you're gonna be rich soon. After all, it's already in your name."

I laugh and say, "Well, so is bright, but I'm pretty fucking stupid at times."

Danny smiles, "Man, this is crazy."

I tell him, "But dude, if this is real, then we'll both benefit from it." He looks at me silently, and I say, "I told you, you're my fucking manager."

Danny chuckles and quips, "Yeah, but that was just a joke."

Determined, I reply, "No, this is it. You've always believed in me, even when no one else did. And nobody knows me better than you. Let's make this shit happen together!"

Tears fill Danny's eyes before he leaps from the couch to embrace me. The intensity of his gratitude is palpable, radiating from him like heat waves on a scorching summer day. It feels as though we've just struck the jackpot.

And I wouldn't want anyone else by my side for this journey.

14

With Christmas melodies blaring from my headphones, I make my way to the local bookstore called *Secret Garden*. Every Friday night, they host an event for the up-and-coming wordsmiths to satisfy our thirst for attention. It's a rare opportunity for us, the literary hopefuls, to showcase our raw talent before the judgmental eyes of an audience.

The experience is always inspiring - at times, I stand by, observing and listening to other writers' work, while on other occasions, I take my turn at the podium.

I'm still uncertain about the direction I'll take tonight. Let's see what happens.

The door to the bookstore creaks as I push it open, and the warmth envelopes me, a stark contrast to the frigid temperature outside. The air is warm and dense with the musty scent of coffee and old books, that papery aroma that never fades. It's a familiar scent, comforting even. The sounds of hushed whispers and rustling pages create a peaceful white noise, making it easy to get lost in the rows of shelves.

A quick scan reveals that tonight's event has drawn a sizable crowd. It seems like the winter season is attracting more people than usual.

As I do my lap, I wander deeper into the store. I'm surrounded by rows upon rows of books of all shapes and sizes. Each with its own secrets and stories. I run my fingers along the spines, feeling the embossed titles beneath my touch. Some of them are familiar, old friends that I've read many times before. Others are strangers, the seductive unknowns tempting me to explore their hidden depths.

Arrays of chairs are set up before the podium; they are a collection of mismatched pieces, as if each one was selected from a different yard sale or thrift store. Yet somehow, they fit together seamlessly, as if they were always meant to be there. I watch as the crowd slowly gathers, trickling in like a leaky faucet, each person taking a seat with a quiet shuffle.

One woman, whose dreams may parallel my own and with a fierce determination in her eyes, approaches the podium. The first one to break the ice is the most courageous of them all, setting the tone for the rest of the evening.

I quickly find a seat.

The chair is uncomfortable, and the legs wobble slightly as I attempt to find ease. I glance up at the podium, where the female writer stands, waiting to begin her reading.

Following a screech of feedback from the microphone, she introduces herself as Laura and dives right in. Head first. Her voice is soft yet confident as she reads her work aloud. I watch with rapt attention, analyzing the reactions of those around me. Will they be captivated by her words, or will they fidget in their seats, longing for it to end? She is the litmus test, the one who will reveal the true nature of the crowd.

Each syllable is delivered with purpose and conviction, her voice rising and falling in perfect harmony with the emotions of her story. I'm transfixed, unable to look away from the scene unfolding before me. The other authors fade into the background as Laura's words become the only thing that matters. I love this shit. There is nothing more intimate than presenting something you created–it's like showing someone your scars and hoping they find them beautiful.

I find myself nodding along with her, the story hitting a chord deep within me that I didn't know existed. Her work is masterful, a true representation of the craft. I can't help but be impressed, wondering how someone so talented could be sitting here in this small bookstore, and yet no one knows who she is.

As she concludes her reading, the crowd erupts into applause. I can see the relief and pride on Laura's face as she takes her seat once again. But my mind is elsewhere, wondering if it's really about talent or if it's just about who you know. Or perhaps it's about the persistence of sticking to your guns, even if it takes forever to break through. It's a sad thought but one that lingers in the back of my mind as the night continues.

I feel a sudden urge to approach her. At times it is necessary to be reminded that our work is unique and significant. As we cannot predict when others might be plagued by self-doubt and in need of reassurance. Especially when most of what we do happens in solitude, confined within the walls of our own minds. Laura deserves the respect of the world; her words should be echoing through the halls of every library and bookstore. I can tell that she truly cares about her craft, the way her words flow with such passion and precision.

I make my way over to her, eager to express my admiration for her work. She turns to me, her eyes still sparkling with the excitement of sharing her art with others.

I begin talking, telling her how much I appreciate her writing, and

I conclude with the words, "There is art in your heart." It may sound like a cheesy pick-up line, but I truly mean it.

A smile blossoms across her face as she thanks me, her genuine gratitude warming my soul. As we exchange a few more words, I ponder how many other brilliant writers are lurking in the shadows, struggling to be heard.

My phone rings, and Danny's name appears on the screen. I pick it up with a grin, exclaiming, "Hey manager!" As I settle into a cozy corner of the bookstore.

Danny chuckles, "That still sounds weird, man."

I join in his laughter and ask, "What's up?"

"The production company accepted our last counteroffer."

I fully trusted Ava and Danny to handle negotiations and ask, "What was the last counter?"

His voice trembles with excitement as he shares the good news, "$300,000 upfront and 7% of box office sales. Plus, if they greenlight a sequel, you get a producer credit and a cut."

"Oh shit!" I say, "That's insane."

"That's not all," he teases.

"What else?" I eagerly ask.

During our previous phone call with Allen, the producer, he had asked me if I had any experience writing screenplays. Embracing the "fake it till you make it" mantra, I confidently lied, "Absolutely."

"Remember your little lie from our last call with Allen?" Danny remarks, and I know precisely where this is going.

"I sure do."

"He wants you to come to LA, work on the script with them, and introduce you to people in the industry over there. Obviously, you'll get paid extra for that," Danny says.

Attempting to maintain a low profile, as I'm still inside the bookstore, I sit upright and utter, "Shut the fuck up!"

"Yeah, dude! This is a huge opportunity," He says.

The weather here is like a mosquito bite you can't scratch, and the only anchor keeping me tethered to this city is my mother—a significant anchor, no doubt. But the idea of heading to The Wasteland of Wishes with my best friend to chase dreams, even if it's just another pipe dream, it's like a siren's call. I know I need to dig deep and search my soul for answers. But I also know that LA holds more opportunities than this place ever could and would allow me to give back to my mom and support her in ways I was never able to before.

I've stepped into this bookstore more times than I can count, but today, everything feels different.

Hold your breath.

Freeze Frame.

Click.

15

This morning, I handed my mother a Modafinil alongside a dose of Lion's Mane. Of course, she trusts me completely and understands I'd never give her anything that could harm her. From the moment she was diagnosed with Alzheimer's, I began giving her nootropics. And sure enough, I can tell the difference between the days when she takes them versus when she doesn't. The contrast in her memory and cognition is striking, and it seems to improve her mood. But it's a cruel twist of fate that when she's left to her own devices, she forgets to take them.

It's Christmas Day, and it's our tradition to visit the cemetery every year. The frigid air is motionless, and the only sound that can be heard is the crunch of snow beneath our feet. There's not a soul in sight, each person celebrating the holiday in their own unique way.

My mother is walking next to me, wearing a red jacket and a black winter hat; she looks like a Christmas ornament come to life.

We reach my father's grave, and I notice a small pile of snow on top of the headstone as if it's become a part of the monument. I brush it off with my gloved hand, feeling the cold seep through my skin.

And then we stand there in silence, as if we're waiting for something to happen. But there's nothing to wait for, nothing to do but remember and miss.

The cemetery is a frozen wasteland, a place of eternal rest, and yet somehow, it's alive with the memories and emotions of those who come to visit.

In a hushed tone, my mother murmurs, "Merry Christmas, Stephen," to the grave.

I notice a tear rolling down her cheek. Twenty-eight years may have passed, but the pain still glimmers in her eyes. They say that "time heals all wounds," but it seems my mother forgot that as well.

At some point, her brain will rewind to the past and erase the memory of my father's passing. I've witnessed this with my grandmother before, observing how the brain methodically wipes out memories, starting from the newest and working its way back to the oldest. So my mother will believe he's still alive, and whenever she's reminded of his death, It's as if she's reliving that agony every time as if it just occurred. What a nightmare.

I have yet to tell her about the offer I received to go to LA. I stayed up all night, battling with myself, going back and forth, trying to figure out what the right decision would be. I'm torn between my own dreams and my duty as a son. On one hand, I know it's the opportunity of a lifetime, but on the other hand, I don't want to leave my mother alone. It's like a battle between my head and my heart, and I'm not sure which one is going to come out on top.

Right after New Year's Eve, Danny and I could leave Seattle, and I'd hit the ground running with work the moment we get to LA. But as much as Danny looks forward to heading to California with me, I know he'd respect my decision if I decide against it.

My mother smiles at me and says, "Thank you for spending a melancholic Christmas with me, Richard."

"Of course," I say. "You know you're my favorite cemetery companion, right?"

With a light chuckle, she responds, "Yes, I do." And reaches for my hand.

"So, what's new with your book deal?" She asks like she's pointing a gun at me.

"Well, the deal is signed...."

Her face lights up with excitement. "That's amazing!" she says. "I'm so happy for you, Richard."

"But," The words stick in my throat like a hairball, I continue, "they want me to go to Los Angeles and work there. I'm just not sure what to decide..."

Without missing a beat, she responds, "There's nothing to decide. You have to go!" Her smile widens.

"But what about you?"

Her response is quick and without hesitation "What about me?".

"I don't want to abandon you," I admit, my voice cracking with emotion.

"Don't worry about me; I want you to go."
I'm stunned by her selflessness and have no words to say. "Are you absolutely sure?"

"Yes, Richard," She says. "That was the whole point of you focusing on your writing. This is your opportunity, and I want you to take it. Of course, I'll miss you, but you can always come back if you decide to. Go to fucking LA!"

She never really cusses, but when it does happen, it's evident that she means it with every fiber of her being; she wants to put some weight behind her statement. And it works.

I move closer to hug her. The embrace is warm and comforting, and for a moment, I forget all about my doubts and uncertainties. Suddenly, I feel like a child again, only nine years old, when everything seemed so vast and possible.

As we pull away, I see a glimmer of sadness in her eyes, but it's quickly replaced by a sense of pride and happiness. "You're going to do great things," she says, placing a hand on my cheek. "I just know it."

I smile at her, feeling a surge of gratitude and love. "Thank you, Mom," I say. "I couldn't have done any of this without you."

She looks at me with a warm smile and says, "I just want you to be happy." I feel the weight on my shoulders slowly lifting.

"Let's go home and celebrate," she suggests, her voice full of enthusiasm.

"Okay," I say.

We start walking, side by side, through the quiet cemetery, with the snow crunching beneath our boots, making our way back to the car.

I don't know what it is, but something about this moment feels like the end of the movie *Stand By Me*, you know? It's like that feeling you get when the kids come back from finding the dead body, and they know that everything has changed forever. Like we've crossed some kind of invisible line, and there's no going back.

It's a strange feeling, but I can't help but think that everything is different now.

Maybe it's worth preserving.

Hold your breath.

Freeze Frame.

Click.

PART II

16

Welcome to Los Angeles, where the sun never stops shining, and dreams never die. Calling anyone who outgrew their own hometowns. In this city, everyone is somebody, and nobody is anybody.

It's a place where the rich and famous mingle with the forgotten and forsaken, and the streets are filled with contradictions, where beauty and ugliness coexist. The line between reality and illusion is forever blurred; excess is the norm, and shattered dreams line every boulevard. But for those who can survive it, Los Angeles offers the chance to be reborn into something new and shine like a star in the dark sky. This is where the beautiful and the damned come to make their mark, and now, it's our turn to join the ranks of the hopeful and ambitious.

The plane begins its descent toward the airport, and as I peer out the window, I get my first glimpse of this city. It's enormous, the kind of place that makes Seattle feel like a small town. And the houses, my god. It seems like every other one has a pool, like some kind of suburban oasis in the middle of a desert.

I have never been to California, and I can feel the anxiety rising within me, like a pot of water that's about to boil over. How am I supposed to navigate this chaos? But I take a deep breath, reminding myself that this is what I came here for: to take a chance and chase my dreams, no matter how overwhelming it may seem.

I step out of the airplane and into LAX. This place is massive, a melting pot of cultures, languages, and lifestyles, all converging in one wild and frenzied hub, like an airport on steroids. There's a hectic energy in the air, like everyone's in a rush to get somewhere, anywhere.

The bright lights and constant noise of announcements blaring over the intercoms create sensory overload. It's like I'm inside a monster, and I'm just a tiny part of its intricate system.

Danny's already disappeared into the crowd, probably trying to find his way to baggage claim.

But I can feel the excitement building within me. This is it - the start of a new chapter in my life. The possibilities seem endless, and I can't wait to see where this journey takes us.

As we step out of the airport, I squint my eyes, scanning the area, and I feel the dry heat of Los Angeles hit me like a punch in the face, but in a good way.

It's as if the very air is alive, pulsing with energy and vitality, and I can't help but take a deep breath and savor the intoxicating aroma. The scent of exhaust fumes and smog fills my nostrils, almost making me dizzy.

We make our way to the shuttle; Danny's already in manager mode, taking charge of the situation. He's organized everything, from booking our flight to now renting the car. He knows exactly where to go and what to do while I stumble behind him, feeling like a lost puppy again.

The shuttle arrives, and we hop on board, surrounded by other travelers all eager to start their own LA adventure. Inside, it smells like a combination of stale air freshener and body odor. But I'm too excited to care. The other passengers around us chatter excitedly, but I'm lost in my own thoughts. Danny and I sit in silence, gazing out the window as the buildings blur past us in a hypnotic display. Not a word is exchanged, but somehow we communicate everything we need to through our shared awe and wonder.

Stepping off the shuttle, we walk into the rental car place. Danny, wearing sunglasses, approaches the counter, smooth as ever, and before I know it, we're handed the keys to a brand new, black Audi RS5.

I've never been much of a car person, but even I can appreciate the sleek lines and the power that emanates from this machine. It's sexy.

I jokingly say, "Bruh!" as we near the car.

Danny bursts out laughing, mimicking my "Bruh!"

"Wanna take the wheel? I got the GPS covered," he suggests, extending the keys towards me.

"Fuck Yeah!"

Pressing the button on the remote, the car's locks pop open with a satisfying clunk.

I slide into the driver's seat, my hands trembling slightly as I take in the dashboard and the array of buttons and dials. Danny hops into the passenger seat, a huge grin on his face. I start the car, feeling the engine roar to life beneath me. Danny's hand automatically reaches for the radio, and the opening notes of *Still Dre* fill the car. The bass pounds through my chest, making me feel alive in a way that's been missing for far too long.

It only took 24 years for me to figure out how to fully appreciate a track that came out in '99. Driving through the city of angels, windows down, volume up, and with my best friend by my side.

We both nod our heads to the beat, lost in the moment as we speed down the freeway, ready to take on whatever this city has in store for us. Life is good. And it feels like nothing can stop us. Well, except for the traffic we hit.

Time passes slowly while we crawl along the 405, inching our way toward our destination. But we don't mind; we are in no rush. We're too busy taking in the sights and sounds of this vibrant city. Music blasts from speakers, creating a symphony of different beats and rhythms that somehow all blend together. It's a surreal experience, being surrounded by a sea of cars, all moving in unison, yet going nowhere.

The sun blazes down on us while we cruise down the palm tree-lined streets of West Hollywood. Already, I find myself falling in love more times than I can count; the women here are nothing short of stunning. Even chaos has perfect cheekbones here.

As we drive, we catch glimpses of iconic landmarks such as the *Laugh Factory*, *Chateau Marmont*, *Sunset Plaza*, and *The Viper Room*.

The production company has arranged for us to live in a house for a few months, with all expenses covered.

Just when we approach the legendary *Whisky a Go Go*, our destination calls us up the hill with a sharp turn to the right.
The house we pull up to is a masterpiece of modern architecture; its sleek lines are accentuated by the abundance of glass, giving it an almost ethereal quality. We step out of the car, and the vastness of the property takes my breath away. The view from up here is truly amazing, offering a panoramic vista of the city below, stretching all the way to the Pacific Ocean in the distance. As if by serendipity, our timing is perfect; the sun is on the cusp of

setting, casting a warm orange glow over the horizon as we make our way inside.

Danny and I share a look of mutual disbelief as if we're standing in the middle of some hallucination. We are, here in this unreal paradise, and we can hardly believe it.

Welcome to Los Angeles.

And you know what I'm about to say.

Hold your breath.

Freeze Frame.

Click.

I make my way through the house, my eyes scanning the rooms, admiring the sheer elegance of the place. When I enter the kitchen, I see a table with an array of gifts beckoning me over.

There is so much stuff: baskets filled with fresh fruits and an assortment of snacks, a bottle of expensive-looking wine, and even a box of gourmet chocolates from a store called *Erewhon*.

A note rests on the table reading, "Welcome to LA, we're excited to do big things with you." signed by the production company. Whoever put this together definitely knows how to make a good first impression.

"Danny, get over here!" I call out, inviting him to join me in the kitchen. He walks in, looking slightly overwhelmed by the grandeur of the house.

"Check it out," I say, motioning towards the table of gifts.

Danny sidles up next to me and takes a gander at the welcome table. He carefully inspects everything, then turns to me and holds up a small, unassuming bag.
"Oh, look!" he says, holding it out to me.

I peer into it and notice the unmistakable scent of freshly baked goods. "Brownies and cookies?" I ask.

"Yeah," Danny replies, a mischievous glint in his eye. "But from a marijuana dispensary."

I pause for a moment, my mind drifting back to my last THC nightmare. I shake my head and push the bag back toward Danny. "They're all yours, buddy," I say, laughing.

Danny stuffs a brownie into his mouth, grinning from ear to ear. "I like it here already," he says, and I can only agree.

We go out to take a quick look at the pool, the surface reflecting the setting sun. Without a second thought, Danny starts undressing and jumps right in, the water rippling around him like liquid gold. I hesitate for a moment, but the warm California air calls me, and I follow shortly after, the coolness enveloping me in its embrace. The sky is painted in shades of pink and orange, and the palm trees sway in the gentle breeze. Perhaps the universe can be bribed after all.

I turn to Danny and grin. "I guess your whole law of attraction thing and all those damn mantras really do work," I say.

He just smiles, a sparkle in his eye that tells me he's secretly thrilled to hear me say that. "Told you so," he replies with a laugh.

I feel so grateful, It's comforting to know that we have some support in this new city, and it makes me even more excited to see what else is in store for us. And being able to share it with Danny makes it more real.

Just like Dre says: "My life's like a soundtrack I wrote to the beat."

17

The sound of leaf blowers and the acrid smell of gasoline pull me out of my sleep. However, I don't mind; it's my first full day in LA, a city where the sun always shines, and there are no leaves to be blown. Yet you hear fucking leaf blowers.

With Salem sleeping next to me, I linger in bed for a moment, soaking up the newness of it all - the sounds and the smells of these new surroundings. Then, I rise from the bed, allowing the white sheets to slip off my body. Crossing the room, I open the window and let the dry air flood in. I am excited for the day; we have meetings lined up with three potential agents trying to find a pimp to whore myself out to Hollywood.

Stumbling into the kitchen, barely awake, I try to shake off the last remnants of sleep. Danny is already up and about, moving around the kitchen like a madman, with Guns'n'Roses' *Paradise City* playing in the background.

"Want coffee?" He asks.

"Yes, sir," I say, knowing full well it was a rhetorical question.

I nod my thanks, taking a sip of the steaming hot black gold. God, I fucking love coffee. Danny starts plating up the breakfast, his movements quick and efficient. It's like he's done this a million times before. I can feel the caffeine starting to course through my veins; I say, "We need to find a gym here," my mind already racing with the thought of maintaining my physique in this new city.

Danny glances up from his plate of eggs and bacon, a look of mild surprise on his face. "A gym? You're already thinking about that?"

I reach for my phone to show him what I found. "Yeah, I looked some up. There's an Equinox close by; looks fancy."

Danny takes a sip of his own coffee. "All right, we'll check it out later."

We finish our breakfast, savoring the last bites of our food before grabbing our things and heading out to our meetings with the agents. Beverly Hills, here we come.

As we navigate the unfamiliar streets, the GPS serves us like a digital oracle, directing us to the meeting with Corey Torres, our first potential agent. From what I gathered during my research online, he's a big shot in the industry.

We pull up to an imposing building designed to try its hardest to impress anyone who enters its doors. Inside the lobby, the walls are adorned with elaborate artwork, and the furniture looks like it was imported from some luxurious French estate.

Corey's assistant greets us, her hair perfectly styled and her smile a little too rehearsed. She leads us to a waiting area, where we are surrounded by leather couches and coffee tables stacked with glossy magazines.

A sense of disorientation washes over me, but I can't deny that being here makes it all feel real. We've officially arrived at the heart of Hollywood.

We enter Corey's office; it is all glass and chrome, a sterile space meant to project success and power. I take a seat on one of the white leather chairs, and the surface feels cold and uninviting.

Corey strides in, looking like a cross between a model and a used car salesman. His long hair is slicked back, and he's wearing a designer suit that likely costs more than my entire wardrobe. His demeanor is immediately off-putting, as he starts making inappropriate comments about his assistant's butt. I can feel Danny's eyes roll beside me.

Corey sits across from us, a sly grin on his face. Then he begins talking about how he can help us and all the connections he has in the industry. He promises us that he'll get us meetings with big directors and producers and that we'll be signing big contracts in no time. But it all feels fake; the word "big" was used a little too much. Big meaningless words—as if he's trying to sell us a used car.

He says, "I gotta tell you, Richard, I absolutely love your work. It's fresh, it's edgy, it's exactly what we're looking for."

Danny raises an eyebrow. "Did you read all of it?" he asks.

Corey nods confidently. "Of course, I did my research."

I chime in, "What about my third book?" I pause," Did you read that one?"

Corey's eyes light up. "Oh, absolutely. I thought it was your best work yet, truly incredible."

Danny and I exchange a look and silently agree: "fuck this dude."

Corey keeps talking, but I tune him out. My mind starts to drift to our other scheduled meetings and the possibility of finding an agent who actually gives a shit. As soon as Corey concludes his pitch, we both stand up and say our goodbyes. It's clear to both of us that he's not the right fit. Fucking Corey.

Our second meeting is in West Hollywood with a guy named Toni Hughes. I googled him on the way there and noticed the same glossy veneer of success that Corey had. Despite this, I still have a glimmer of hope since he represents some talented writers. So who knows, maybe good ol' Toni will surprise us. Don't judge a book by its sleazy cover.

But entering his office, I can't believe my eyes; we've entered the Twilight Zone. It's like a carbon copy of Corey's office - the same sleek, modern decor, the same art lining the walls, and the same oversized desk at the front of the room. Even his assistant looks similar. It's as if these agents all shop at the same office and assistant supply store.

We settle into Toni's office, and I quickly survey the surroundings. The walls are covered with framed posters of movies that I haven't seen, and the room is filled with expensive, soulless furniture. Toni looks like he's trying hard to maintain a youthful appearance.

Assessing his demeanor and trying to read between the lines of his words, there's something off about him, something that doesn't quite sit well with me.

Naturally, he tells us the same lies and offers similar assurances that Corey did. It appears they're all reciting from a shared script, trying to lure us in with their fake words and empty promises.

My mind drifts off again; his meaningless chatter morphs into a monotonous drone sound, reminding me of the leaf blowers.

I need to get out.

I need to get out.

I need to get out.

Danny glances my way, seemingly reading my mind like a book yet again. He knows I've had enough of this bullshit. I let out a sigh of relief as he starts to wrap up the meeting.

We make our excuses, eager to get out of there and leave Toni and his fake promises behind us. As we step out into the bright LA sunshine, Danny verbalizes what I'm thinking: "Fucking Toni."

I nod in agreement as we head to the car.

Since we have some time to kill before our last meeting, Danny suggests stopping at In-N-Out Burger for lunch. He tells me it's supposed to be a fast food highlight unique to California. I don't usually get too excited about what to eat, but I'll go along with whatever Danny wants.

The line at the In-n-Out drive-through is long enough to make you wonder if there's a secret cult devoted to their burgers. But we're not interested in waiting, so we pull off the road, park the car and walk into the actual restaurant.

While Danny devours his burger, I take out my phone and start my research on our third and final meeting for the day with Alessa Williams.

Maybe she's the answer to our problems in this city of sleazy guys. We need a strong woman, someone who's not afraid to slay the creepy dragons for us.

All I can find are positive news and articles about her successful clients without being overly flashy. It's almost too good to be true. But then again, in this city of fake facades and meaningless vows, it's hard to know what's real. I come across a photo of Alessa, and I'm surprised to see a genuine smile on her face. From what I've witnessed so far, that's a rare sight in this town.

We arrive at our last meeting, and the building is noticeably more modest than the previous ones. It's still a nice building–don't get me wrong–but it lacks the grandiosity of the other pretenders.

Nonetheless, we make our way in and are immediately met with a different vibe. The atmosphere is warm and welcoming, and a sense of calm and relief settles upon me. This place feels authentic and real. It's not forcing anything on us or putting on a show. Finally, a breath of fresh air in this ocean of emptiness.

Walking into the lobby, Tara, Alessa's assistant, welcomes us with a smile so warm it could melt butter. She immediately offers us a drink before we even had the chance to ask. Her kindness is almost intoxicating, and I feel a bit captivated by the warmth she radiates. Meanwhile, Danny is practically smitten. He's all googly-eyed, and I can tell he's trying his best to impress her with his charm. I can't blame him, though; there's something refreshing about her.

We step into Alessa's office and am immediately struck by her presence. This woman oozes confidence, and it's clear that she means business. She doesn't fuck around.

Her office is impeccably decorated, and it's hard not to admire her taste. She greets us with a warm smile and thanks us for coming by. Then, to my surprise, she compliments my latest manuscript, *Hard to Find, Easy to Lose*. Danny sent it to her after she specifically requested it.

I can feel Alessa's piercing gaze as she asks me questions about it. She actually read my work, and she understood it. I'm not used to this kind of honest interest, and it catches me off guard. But I can't deny that I feel a surge of excitement building up inside me. Halle-fucking-lujah.

She asks us about ourselves, and she's genuinely interested in getting to know us. When she talks about herself, it doesn't feel like she's trying to impress us. She's confident but not arrogant and upfront about what she can do for us without making any unrealistic promises.

She also tells us that if at any point we feel like it's not working out, we can just go our separate ways. No hard feelings, no fuss.

Danny and I are in agreement, and without hesitation, I tell her, "You know what? I'd be honored to have you represent me." Her face lights up with enthusiasm, and we seal the deal with a firm handshake.

We've found our agent. It's a feeling I can't quite describe, but it just seems right. I can already picture us working together, brainstorming ideas, and creating something truly great.

Click.

18

The doors to the gym glide open, and we step inside. It feels like we're walking onto a runway, except the models have been replaced with gym-goers flaunting their perfect bodies in-progress. Although many of them probably are models. This is no ordinary gym. This is Equinox, a luxurious fitness center in the heart of West Hollywood. It's not just a place to work out; it's a place to be seen working out.

The state-of-the-art equipment gleams under the carefully arranged spotlights. The Fitness enthusiasts are all picture-perfect, wearing designer workout clothes and sporting immaculate hair and makeup. The men are practically shirtless, showing off their rippling abs and biceps. The women exude an air of confidence as if they just stepped out of a photo shoot.

As we approach the counter, the lady behind it greets us with a megawatt smile. She looks like she wouldn't be out of place on the cover of a magazine. We tell her we want to become members, and without missing a beat, she types away at her computer. $270 later, we are card-carrying members of the club.

Danny pumps away on the elliptical machine, while I bounce from one piece of equipment to the next. Listening to music, I'm lost in my own world until I'm suddenly snapped back to reality by the sound of a woman's voice.

I turn around and see a vision of beauty standing in front of me. She has resting angel face, with dark hair tied into a ponytail, and a body that looks like it was chiseled out of marble. She introduces herself as Lana and asks if I'm done with the machine. I'm momentarily stunned, but manage to stammer out a "yes."

As I move to the next machine, she follows me, asking me about my workout routine and complimenting me on my physique. We start to flirt a bit.

Then, out of nowhere, she asks, "Wanna hang out later?" Before I can process the question, I hear myself saying, "Sure." as if on autopilot.

She types her number into my phone, and with a wink and a smile, she disappears into the sea of exercise devotees.

Danny appears out of nowhere. He's out of breath and looks like he's seen a ghost.

"Was that...?" he asks, wide-eyed.

"Lana?" I reply.

"You know she's a porn star, right?" he blurts out, barely able to contain his excitement.

I roll my eyes. "Dude, not every pretty woman here is doing porn."

He whips out his phone and starts tapping away, a sly smile creeping onto his face. Finally, he turns the screen towards me, and my eyes widen in shock. There, clear as day, is a photo of the woman I had just been flirting with, tangled up in a threesome.

"Oh, would you look at that," I say.

Danny is laughing, "You and your fucking Jedi Mind Tricks. Unbelievable." He shakes his head.

I smirk and shrug my shoulders. "She just wants to hang out."

"Yeah, right. Hang out on your "pecker.""

My phone buzzes - It's Alessa. She cuts straight to the chase, her words sharp and direct.

"Richard, real quick. How happy are you with your manuscript?"

"I'm pretty damn confident," I reply, "Unless you think we need to edit it some more?".

"I don't think so at all," Alessa says, "but I wanted to check with you first."

"Sweet." I say, and I can tell she's pleased with my response. "Well then, Richard, would it be all right if I start pitching it to potential publishers?"

She does not fuck around. I nod even though she can't see me, excitement building inside me at the thought of my work finally getting out there. "Absolutely," I say with confidence. "Let's make shit happen." Without any explanation to Danny, I instinctively raise my hand for a high-five.

"I'll be in touch as soon as I hear something," Alessa assures me before ending the conversation.

I break the news to Danny, and we make our way out of the gym.

Today is all about being a tourist, soaking up every bit of this place like a sponge. We're going to hit up all the usual suspects: the Walk of Fame, the Hollywood Sign, the Griffith Observatory, and maybe even one of those Hollywood bus tours. I wanna see it all; show me where Leo buys his shoes or where Angelina gets her facials.

Danny claims he knows this city already, thanks to the hours he's spent playing GTA 5.

The Walk of Fame, a gaudy strip of glitter and glamour, feels like a portal to hell. A never-ending stream of tourists with their selfie sticks and fanny packs jostle for space on the sidewalk, vying for a chance to snap a photo with their favorite celebrity's star. It's overwhelming, it's fucking terrible, but at the same time, it's a rite of passage for anyone visiting LA. You simply have to endure the chaos and see it at least once, even if it means dodging through crowds of people like a contestant on a game show.

The bus tour is a cesspool of sweaty tourists, but I couldn't care less. The allure of hearing juicy celebrity gossip and tales of old Hollywood debauchery is too strong to resist. As we roll past the mansions and storefronts of the rich and famous, I hungrily drink in every word the tour guide says.

Danny jokes, "Who knows, maybe one day they'll even include you in the tour. You know, like, 'And this is the 7-Eleven where Richard Bryght got the blowjob from a pornstar.'"

"Very possible!" I say. We both laugh.

The tour ends, and we are at our next destination, the Hollywood sign; once reading "Hollywood land" until 1949, it stands high on the hills, just some letters placed for all to see. It's an iconic sight, and of course, we snap a photo together, one for the 'gram. I don't typically post much, but this is one of those "must-haves." A passerby tells us that in 2017, some joker switched the letters to read "Hollyweed." Ah, the humor of the locals.

The day has already been an assault on the senses, overwhelming me and making me feel like I've been sucked into a movie set, and Allen's invitation to a party up in the hills tonight promises an epic finale. "You'll meet everyone involved in the project," he says over the phone, "and some other people too. It'll be fun."

We arrive at the venue, an extravagant villa perched atop the hills. The night sky is crystal clear, and we can already hear the thumping beat of music emanating from within. As we make our way towards the entrance, my eyes scan the scene: expensive cars lined up like they're on display, and a steady stream of guests making their way inside, all dressed to the nines.

Inside, the air is thick with the chatter of industry people and the clinking of glasses. I catch a glimpse of a few familiar faces, but mostly it's a sea of strangers, all with their own agendas and aspirations.

Allen spots us and charges over, his face lit up with a smile. He greets us like old friends and starts introducing us to everyone.

For a moment, I feel like I'm at a high school reunion, meeting people I've never met before. But Allen's excitement is infectious, and soon I'm caught up in the energy of the room. Despite the superficial glitz and glamour of the Hollywood scene, Allen seems like a genuinely nice dude, the type of guy you wanna hang out with.

Introducing Danny as my manager to everyone swells my chest with pride. We mingle and schmooze, working the room like pros. Danny and I are on our game, charming the pants off everyone we meet. We shake hands, exchange pleasantries, and tell a few well-timed jokes. People seem to love us.

I see Danny deep in conversation with a girl introduced to us as Alice, and they vanish into the rabbit hole of the pool area.

My phone buzzes, pulling me out of the lively atmosphere of the party, with a new text message. "Hey, this is Lana from the gym. Let me know if you have time tonight." A grin creeps onto my face as I tap out a quick response.

I'm bashing shoulders with some folks when Allen weaves through the crowd and corners me with his big ol' grin. "You havin' fun, Richard?" he asks, eyes sparkling.

I nod, telling him how impressed I am with this shindig.

"Good," he says, "I got a surprise for you." And like a magician, he pulls out his phone and shoves the screen into my face. It's a press release on *Deadline Hollywood*, with a picture of me on it, announcing that Allen's company is adapting my book into a movie. Holy fuck, I'm officially someone now. Not because I've improved since yesterday, but because someone with power decided I could be, and it got printed. This is beyond surreal.

My gratitude overwhelms me as I thank Allen for the mind-blowing surprise. He claps me on the back and says, "Come on, let's drink."

I'm not much of a drinker, but this feels like a good enough reason to indulge. As the night wears on, the world around me blurs into a dizzying vortex of euphoria and pure, unadulterated fun. Everywhere I look, there are new faces and new voices, each one promising something different. It's overwhelming but in the best possible way.

I talk to producers, directors, actors, models - all trying to make a name for themselves in this cutthroat industry. But there's a sense of camaraderie, a shared understanding that we're all in this together. Their eagerness to meet me is palpable, as if I were some kind of rockstar. Perhaps this is where I was always meant to be.

As the night goes on, we exchange numbers and promises to stay in touch. It's a reminder that in this city of dreams, there's still a sense of community and connection.

The room is spinning, and I realize I've had a bit too much to drink. A notification pops up on my phone, and I see that Maria has left a comment on my Instagram post from earlier. "Congratulations! You deserve it. I am in LA too." And the thought of casually running into her here makes me want to hurl.

Your favorite person has the potential to become your least favorite person.

Fuckness.

19

I wake up to the sound of soft generic house music and the aroma of freshly brewed coffee coming from the kitchen. God, I fucking love coffee.

Lana's house is up in the hills overlooking Sunset Boulevard, and her bedroom has huge floor-to-ceiling windows. The grey curtains are still closed. I jump up and push a button on the wall-mounted iPad that controls everything within the house.

The curtains slowly open with a buzzing noise, revealing a gorgeous LA morning. But let's be real, almost every day here is like that; it's one of the many perks of living in this city.

A wall on the other side of the room has mounted metal shelves filled with awards Lana received. I make my way over to take a closer look.

There are at least thirty trophies in all shapes and forms. Literally. One is a giant penis made of gold with a plaque saying "Best New Starlet." Another one is a PornHub award for "Most Popular Female Performer," it's a cool glossy black and white trophy, very stylish. And more subtle than the other ones.

As my eyes wander through the shelf, I notice another gold statue that looks like two people hugging; it's an AVN award, the equivalent of an Oscar for Porn Stars.

Hers is for the "Best Anal Sex Scene." I have so many questions. Who judges that? And what makes her's "the best" anal sex scene?

I keep looking at the plaque and realize that her porn Name spelled backward reads "anal", which makes me laugh more than I'd like to admit.

Moments like this remind me that I'm still 12 years old.

There's a giant framed photo of Lana on the wall; it's from the cover of a past Playboy Magazine issue. Showing her posed, lying by a pool, wearing heavy makeup, and looking seductively at the camera while stretching her butt to the sky. She is completely naked but angled in a way that doesn't reveal any explicit body parts.

To the right is a walk-in closet filled with so many shoes and pairs of underwear that she could open up a store of her own, with every color and style imaginable. As well as an arsenal of sex toys. I am intrigued.

I was never really big into porn, but I'm amazed by this industry and the opportunities it offers for the people in it. She told me, that on an average month, she makes about $ 300.000 with OnlyFans alone. Yeah, let that number sink in for a second. She earns more in three months than most authors do in their whole careers - maybe that's the real plot twist.

I leave the room to follow the smell of coffee that keeps calling my name. Lana, only wearing underwear, is standing in the kitchen, looking through her phone. Her body is stunning; I pause briefly to appreciate her beauty before I walk in.

Lana notices me and smiles. "Good morning, handsome!" She says. "Do you want coffee?" and she starts walking to the coffee maker.

I smile and give her a thumbs-up. "Yes, Ma'am!" I reply. I walk over and hug her from behind as she pours me a cup.

"You know, you could be in porn too!" she says.

I laugh and continue the "typical breakfast conversation" by asking, "Did you know that your name backward spells "Anal"?"

She turns around and looks at me like I'm an idiot. "Yes," she says, with a dry tone.

Now I do feel like an idiot and only reply with "Oh...."

She hands me the coffee with the cutest smile, and it smells fucking perfect. "Do you wanna drink it outside?" She asks, pointing to the sun deck.

"Yes, I do," I reply and start making my way over there.

The sun and the gentle breeze feel so nice. I take a seat on her big lounge chair while she sits next to me. She looks at me and says, "I don't think I've ever fucked a writer before."

I laugh, wondering if that's a compliment or not.

"Where do you find your ideas?" Lana asks.

I shrug and say, "They usually find me first." I put my hand on her knee.

She thinks for a moment and says, "Creativity is so fascinating."

The sound of her phone ringing disrupts the moment.

"It's my agent," she says and reaches for it.

I look at her as she talks on the phone; she brushes away hair from her face.

She's cute, but not "ruin my life" cute, nothing more than a subplot. And something about her voice annoys me. She is not lacking intelligence; it's just that "valley girl accent" that can make her appear that way.

I get up to admire the stunning view of the city. It's a smogless, clear day, and the sky overhead is a brilliant shade of blue with not a single cloud present. The bright sunshine bathes the city in a warm glow, making everything seem vibrant and alive.

Sounds of cars and buses weaving in and out of traffic can be heard from afar. The surrounding hills and mountains dotted with palm trees make me feel like I'm in a modern Bob Ross painting.

Life has gotten very hectic lately.

I started living two days at once,

and then three at once; by now, I can go through a whole month in an afternoon.

But I have to do this more often. Simple things.

Like describing a beautiful view while drinking coffee.

God, I fucking love coffee.

20

aria and I had been together for two years, ever since we met at a party where the sparks flew right away. It was an instant connection, like a match lit in a sea of darkness. Maria's looks were striking, and her mind was sharp, with an exceptional talent for creativity. Her wit and confidence were unmatched. But whenever you start describing someone in a way like that, you know that there's a big "BUT" lurking somewhere in the shadows. Only it took me a while to figure it out.

The flames of passion ignited between us, fueled by our mutual disinterest in anything too serious. The sexual chemistry we had was like nothing else; it was almost extraterrestrial. Alien sex.

We started hanging out more and more. Being a lone wolf, I always cherished my solitude and working on my projects, but having her around made everything even better. And the feeling was mutual; it seemed like she couldn't get enough of me either. In fact, she seemed even more into it. Usually, when someone is this intense, I run for the hills. But with her, it was different. She swore she'd never felt this way before, and all the clichéd declarations people make to their new lovers spilled from her lips effortlessly.

But also, right from the get-go, there was something that felt amiss, an unexplainable feeling that lingered in my gut. My intuition warned me against trusting her completely. I'm not one to feel jealous or possessive, as I usually couldn't care less. But again, with her, it was different.

Maria started telling me lies, pointless ones that served no purpose other than to make me doubt her. Each time I caught her in a lie, she would turn the tables on me, twisting the situation to make it seem like I was in the wrong. It was as if I had committed some grave offense by questioning her. Her anger would bubble up, and she'd accuse me of being paranoid, controlling, and jealous. I couldn't help but wonder if I was the problem if my instincts were flawed, if I was seeing things that weren't really there. The more she pushed back, the more I questioned myself, trapped in a vicious cycle of doubt and confusion. Our fights escalated, each time with new promises from her to change, but soon after came new lies.

My imperfections were evident, this relationship brought out the worst in me, and perhaps I could have handled things differently at times. But the tumultuous journey with her was uncharted territory for me. The highs of her affection were ecstatic, but then the lows would hit, leaving me in a state of emotional frost.

We were stuck in a never-ending loop, unable to break free from the toxic cycle we created for ourselves. With each reconciliation, I believed that this time would really be different, that maybe we could finally make it work. But it was only a matter of time before we were once again caught in the same destructive patterns, with me left feeling lost and confused.

Her job started taking her to different cities, which only added to my growing suspicions and made it harder for me to trust her. And then, after traveling for a few months, she said the words, "I need a break." What kind of break? Do you expect me to wait? I finally realized that I couldn't do this shit anymore. I cut the cord, and I set myself free, even though it hurt like hell.

The moment I went "no contact," her texts and calls started flooding in, but I knew better than to take the bait.

And just like that, the tables turned. She became the victim, the poor innocent soul who was left behind. And everyone bought into her sob story, feeling sorry for her and blaming me for leaving. In hindsight, it was crystal clear, yet I couldn't see it while I was trapped in her web, even with my knowledge of mental health. It turned out that she has a narcissistic personality disorder. They're either the hero or the victim; there's nothing in between.

Six months after our breakup, she announced her engagement to her ex. The very same ex I always suspected her of lying about. It was a sickening confirmation of all the doubts and suspicions that had been eating away at me. But in the end, it didn't matter— because people like her don't cry because they miss you. They cry because they lose control over you.

For all the time that passed, silence now prevailed between us. I moved on, continued with my life, and thought I was doing great. But that's the thing with life; sometimes, it pulls the rug from under you when you least expect it. My birthday arrived, and she sent that text. Of course, I didn't fall for it. I knew that responding could be just what she needed to feed her insatiable narcissistic cravings.

But it still left me with a lingering stinging pain, haunting me despite the exciting distractions of my new life. When the noise subsides, and it's just me and my thoughts, she creeps into my head like a shadow. And I don't know what to do with that.

Lost in my inner world, I find myself wandering around the vibrant streets of Studio City, a neighborhood named after the iconic Universal Studios located here. Danny has a meeting in this part of town, so I decide to tag along and explore while he's busy.

As usual, I have my MacBook with me, and I figure it's the perfect opportunity to fulfill a classic writer's cliché - find a cozy coffee shop or café to write in. But where to go? Starbucks? Nah, that's way too predictable. I need something more interesting, more intriguing. Suddenly, a quaint bar called "Laurel Tavern" catches my eye. It looks inviting, with its rustic decor and cozy ambiance. A place where all the misfits and dreamers could come and waste their hours over a drink or two.

I make my way inside, and the warm glow from the dim lighting immediately draws me in. It's the kind of place where you can feel right at home in a matter of seconds, and it looks like the perfect spot for a post-modern Bukowski to drown his sorrows. I walk over to the bar and take a seat. That's when a handsome bartender named Anton comes over to greet me. He flashes me a charming smile and asks me what I'd like to drink.

Without hesitation, I order my usual - a sugar-free Red Bull. He hands me the can with a nod, and I crack it open, relishing the artificial sweetness and the caffeine hit that follows. I set up my laptop on the bar, looking like a total stereotype, ready to get some work done. I dive into the task of downloading some movie scripts. I'm still clueless about the formatting, even though I have to craft one for this film within 12 weeks. But I'm confident I'll figure it out.

I strike up a conversation with Anton, and we hit it off. As we chat, I discover that he, too, is a writer, more screenplays than novels. Seems like everyone in this city has a dream and is connected to the industry in some way, or at least trics to be. Anton turns into my impromptu instructor for the day. In between serving other customers, he basically gives me a crash course in the art of writing for film and what software to use. His charming demeanor and quick wit make the lesson a breeze, and I find myself actually enjoying it. By the time I finish my fourth Red Bull, I feel like I've gained a new friend and confidence in tackling the task at hand.

As soon as Danny texts me that his meeting is over, I take the opportunity to thank Anton one more time for his generous assistance. I hand him a crisp hundred-dollar bill as a token of my appreciation and tell him that I'll be back soon.

"No problem, man. Good luck with that script," he says with a smile.

I nod and leave, feeling like I made a connection in this city of strangers. I can see myself becoming friends with him.

21

I set myself the goal of writing seven pages daily, finding it to be the magic number, the sweet spot between productivity and not overexerting myself. If I stick to it, in just two weeks, I'll have a first draft of the script. Easy enough, especially considering how much money they're paying me.

I wrap up my page goal for today, close my laptop, and stretch my arms. I am now officially free.

Unlocking my phone, I tap on my mother's contact. She answers the Facetime call almost immediately, and her smiling face appears on my screen. It feels surreal to be physically so far away from her, but the magic of technology brings us together in an instant.

As I catch my mother up on everything that's been happening in LA, I sense different emotions in her voice when I mention that I want her to fly out and visit me soon. She's excited, of course, but also a little concerned. This is a big deal for her since she has never been outside of Washington. However, I won't let her anxiety linger.

"Don't worry, Mom," I reassure. "I'll take care of everything. I'll have someone pick you up from your house and take you to the airport. And when you land at LAX, I'll be there waiting for you. All you have to do is pack your bags and be ready to go."

I can see the relief on her face as I make this promise. She knows she can trust me to take care of her, even from thousands of miles away.

But as we continue talking, I notice something different about her. It's like her mind is slipping away, piece by piece, and it's more apparent now than ever before. Perhaps the distance makes it more noticeable. It's like a heavyweight settles in my chest, and I struggle to keep up the conversation, to pretend that everything is okay.

I know I can't fix this, can't stop the inevitable progression of time and the toll it takes on the people we love. Time takes what it wants and gives nothing back. But I want to make the most of the moments we have left, to create memories that will last for an eternity. So I promise her that I'll make all the arrangements for her visit and make sure she has the best time.

We say our goodbyes and hang up, leaving me with a mix of emotions swirling inside me.

In an attempt to distract my mind, I indulge in the temporary pleasure of a social media dopamine hit.

As soon as the Deadline Hollywood press release hit the wires the other day, my phone started vibrating nonstop with notifications.

My Instagram account is exploding with activity. This kind of attention is all new to me. Overnight, I gained thousands of new followers, and my inbox was flooded with messages from strangers congratulating me on the news. Women I've never met are asking me out on dates and offering to do all sorts of explicit activities in the bedroom with me.

I even received DM's from actors and actresses, unknown to me but eager to be a part of the movie adaptation of my book.
"I love your book; if you have a part in the movie for me, let me know," they say, attaching their reels and IMDb links. It's flattering, of course, but also a bit strange. I'm just the writer; I have nothing to do with casting or any other aspect of the movie's production. But I guess you have to try everything to make it in this town.

It's a crazy world we live in, that's for sure. I know I have to keep my head on straight. But with all the noise and chaos swirling around me, it's easier said than done. A fresh city, with distractions waiting on every corner, scripts to write, movie contracts, and award-winning adult film performers - It's as if I've stumbled into a twisted carnival full of thrilling and dangerous rides that threaten to consume me.

As the sun begins to set, I receive an unexpected invitation from Alessa. She wants Danny and me to come to an agency party at a club in downtown LA. Normally, I avoid clubs like the plague —the lights, the noise, the crowds—they all make me feel like I'm trapped in a waking nightmare. But then again, who am I to say no to my new Hollywood agent?

Danny's a whole different breed. He thrives in the chaos of club culture. He used to be a DJ under the alias DJ Fluxx, spinning records and working the crowds until the sun came up. So when I tell him about the party, his eyes light up with excitement. And he's been killing it in his role as my manager, so why not let him enjoy some fun? He deserves it.

As soon as we arrive at the venue, I immediately regret the $40 I spent on parking. That's LA for you, always finding ways to drain your wallet. But we're here now, and I can feel the bass thumping through the concrete walls. There's a pretty big line of people waiting to get in, and we join them. But then, Alessa spots us and pulls her Hollywood power move. "This is the writer Richard Bryght; he's with us." Suddenly, the line parts like the Red Sea, and we stroll right in. It's almost comical how easily a few words from a hotshot agent can turn everything around. As we pass by, people stop and stare at us, trying to figure out who we are and whether they should know us.

When we step inside the club, the sound of *Firestarter* by The Prodigy blasts through the speakers. It's like being transported back in time to the 90s, and I'm not mad about it. It's a decade that I really liked, with its music, movies, and video games.

The club is packed, and the bass is pounding like a migraine. I can feel the sound vibrating in my chest and teeth.
After exchanging greetings with everyone, Danny vanishes into the masses, doing his thing.

I watch as the people flock to him, drawn in by his charisma and energy. It's like he's a magnet, pulling them in from every direction. They're enamored by him—eager to socialize, booze it up, and dance alongside him. White people seem to be particularly drawn to him as if they've never encountered an African American man before. It's absurd, really, but I just chuckle to myself at the sight of it all.

Looking around the club, I notice how everyone Alessa brought is so damn nice. They're all smiles and laughter, eager to strike up conversations with me. Suddenly, Alessa pulls me aside and says, "I have some good news." My ears perk up, curiosity piqued. She continues, "Three major publishers responded to your manuscript, and we're now waiting for their offers. And I think we have a pretty good shot at selling them on a package deal, including your previously self-published book, especially with it now being turned into a movie."

I instantly hug Alessa tightly, unable to contain my excitement. As I pull away, she looks at me with a grin on her face and says, "This could be huge, Richard. We're talking about a six-figure deal, maybe even more." She does not fuck around.

My heart skips a beat at the thought of it. This is the dream. My gaze drifts over to Danny, who's still in the midst of the dance floor. Alessa urges me, "Go give him the good news!"

I maneuver through the crowd, making my way to Danny. The tune of *Carmen Queasy* by Maxim and Skin fills the air, and as I catch my breath, I share the news that Alessa just revealed to me.

He's dumbfounded, shouting in disbelief, "Shut the fuck up!" He pulls me in for a hug, and we both start belting out the chorus, "Money making is a wonderful thing!" Our singing may be off-key, but we don't give a fuck. This is what we wanted, and it's what Danny said he knew would happen all along.

People look at us as if we're idiots, and they are not entirely wrong. Idiots with a potential six-figure deal. Money making is indeed a wonderful thing.

Hold your breath.

Freeze Frame.

Click.

I never dance, ever. But in this moment, I can't help myself; I feel unstoppable. And I am not alone in this feeling. Danny and I both jump around like we're on top of the world. We feel like kings, even if it's just for a moment. The bass from the music pulses through our bodies, and we let go of all our inhibitions. I suddenly feel the weight of Danny's hand on my shoulder as he says, "You, my friend, are a goddamn genius. And I am so fucking proud of you!"

His tone is full of admiration and respect. I feel the warm prickling at the back of my eyes, threatening to spill out tears of joy. It's overwhelming, this feeling of gratitude.

Danny has been by my side throughout this entire journey, and his support has never wavered. "I couldn't have done it without you," I say to him, feeling grateful for his presence in my life. A sense of camaraderie washes over me. It's not just about the money or the success; it's about the bond between us, the shared experiences and memories that we'll carry with us forever.

An hour later, I'm feeling the effects of the drinks, and my lips are locked with Nicole's, a model from New York. As we're about to kiss, she leans in and confesses, "Just so you know, I'm married, but we're in an open relationship."

I raise my eyebrows and ask her, "Does your husband know about that?" She chuckles and pulls me back into the kiss, her tongue intertwining with mine with renewed passion. And I'm lost in these questionable choices.

I excuse myself to grab more drinks and navigate my way through the swarming crowd. It's a dizzying maze of people, and my eyes scan the sea of faces, searching for something familiar. It's been a while since I've seen Danny, and I think he took off with Tara; Alessa's assistant. Good for him. My head spins from the strobe lights and the alcohol. But then, out of the corner of my eye, I catch a glimpse of a face I haven't seen in ages, and I freeze.

It's Maria.

I can hardly believe it—it's like seeing a ghost.

She's just about to leave. What should I do? Should I go say hello? Pretend like I didn't see her? Suddenly, my stomach churns, making that decision for me, and I have an overwhelming urge to throw up. I know I need to find the bathroom, and fast. I turn around and start running, but the crowd is too dense, my vision blurry, and my legs unsteady. I can't make my way through in time. Panic sets in; I can feel my throat start to clench, my mouth watering with the bitter taste of vomit. And then, right there in the middle of the dance floor, it happens–I hurl my guts out for all to see. The stench and sight of my puke spreads around me like a toxic cloud, and I am horrified and embarrassed beyond belief.

Luckily I'm not big enough to end up on TMZ.

Welcome to Hollywood.

22

I arrive at LAX, feeling the scorching heat of the Southern California sun on me. My eyes squint against the glare of the bright sky. On the surface, it's a typical LA day, filled with the noise of traffic and the hustle of people rushing to their destinations. But today is different for me because I'm here to pick up my mother.

I step inside the airport terminal, and the cool air conditioning envelops me. It's been a while since I've seen her face to face, and I hope everything goes smoothly. I check the flight information board and notice that her plane has already landed. It's a chaotic scene, with people shouting and calling out to each other as they try to navigate their way through the herd of travelers and luggage. Then, I spot her–standing there with her suitcase, looking around as if searching for me. Her gaze meets mine in the chaos, and her face lights up with a smile.

We embrace, and I can feel her warmth and love radiating through me. "Welcome to LA, Mom," I say, grinning from ear to ear. Taking her bag, we make our way out of the airport, and she absorbs every detail of this new city that I now call home.

I'm in the driver's seat, my hands gripping the wheel tightly as I steer through the sea of cars that stretches out in front of us. In typical LA fashion, we're stuck in traffic, crawling along at a snail's pace.

My mom is sitting in the passenger seat, her eyes darting around, taking in the sights. One thing that catches her attention is the abundance of palm trees. She excitedly points them out, marveling at their height and beauty.

Surprisingly, for me, the palm trees have become a part of the scenery already. They're like an old friend that I've grown accustomed to, a simple reminder of where I am. And I somehow feel like I belong here.

I always have; I just didn't know it.

As we inch our way forward, I point out some of the other landmarks that I've become familiar with. We pass the Getty; I show her the Hollywood sign in the distance and the Capitol Records building. I'm grateful for this moment, for the opportunity to show my mother my new life. A life that wouldn't have been possible without her unwavering support and belief in me. It's almost surreal to have her here, seeing it all through fresh eyes.

We make a quick stop at the house to drop off her luggage and hit the road again.

With Danny in the back seat, cracking jokes and pointing out points of interest, we navigate through the crowded streets. Our destination keeps shifting, always in flux. In a never-ending cycle of sightseeing, we move from one tourist spot to the next, each one leaving a distinct impression on my mother.

The day comes to a close, and we find ourselves at Venice Beach. It's a freak show, and I don't mean the one on the boardwalk that closed in 2017. But the boardwalk itself. It's a must-see for anyone who sets foot in this town. The sidewalks are packed with a never-ending parade of performers, vendors, and eccentrics of all shapes and sizes. You'll encounter artists selling their wares, skateboarders showing off their tricks, and bodybuilders flexing their muscles. It's a spectacle like no other, a celebration of the strange and unconventional.

As we walk towards the beach, the sound of the crashing waves and the smell of saltwater fills my senses. I can see the amazement in my mom's expression; she barely says a word. Even Danny grows unusually quiet. Perhaps seeing my mother here reminds him of his own loss, the way his mom died in a car accident when he was only five. A reminder that he would never be able to show her the wonders of this city like I can with my own mother.

After a long stroll by the water and a quick bite at a nearby restaurant, we get back in the car and head home, feeling both drained and fulfilled from the day's adventures.
We arrive at the house, the weariness of the day settles into my bones.

In a state of exhaustion, we stumble out of the car and into the comfort of our home. My voice is barely audible as I mutter a tired "goodnight" to both Danny and my mother. After Danny disappears with a peace sign, my mother turns to me, her gaze warm and filled with gratitude.

"Thank you for today," she says, "I had such a wonderful time."

I smile at her, "Of course, Mom," I reply. "I'm glad you're here."

I make my way to my room, my mind still buzzing with the events of the day. As I settle into bed and my head hits the pillow, I catch a glimpse of the LA Skyline, and I just feel grateful. Grateful for this day, for this city, for Danny, for this life that I'm fortunate enough to share with the woman who made it all possible.

A few hours later, I bolt upright in bed. The doorbell rings in the middle of the night.

I stumble out of bed, rubbing the sleep from my eyes as I head to the hallway. There stands Danny, his hair tousled, looking just as confused as I feel.

"What the fuck?" he mutters, and I nod in agreement.

Doorbells had become a thing of the past; these days, the only people I expect to see at my doorstep are either Amazon drivers or takeout delivery guys. This can't be good.

Together with Danny, we make our way to the entrance, our footsteps echoing in the quiet house. I open the door to find two police officers standing outside. And to my surprise, my mother is with them, looking dazed and disoriented.

"What's going on?" I ask, my voice thick with sleep.

My mother looking small and vulnerable in the night. She is frightened, and the confusion is evident on her face.

The officers explain that they found her wandering aimlessly through the neighborhood. She had apparently left in the middle of the night and had been walking around for who knows how long. My heart sinks at the thought of her being out there alone in the unknown darkness.

Approaching her, I say, "It's okay, Mom," attempting to calm her down.

I thank the officers for bringing her back safely and assist my mother inside. She appears shaken and tired. I guide her to the couch, holding her hand, reassuring her thxat she's safe now.

As we talk, I can feel the weight of the situation sinking in. My mother's confusion serves as a reminder of her ongoing mental decline and how quickly things can change. I'm grateful that she's okay, but I can't shake off the feeling of unease that lingers in the air.

Eventually, my mother settles down and returns to bed, but I stay up for a while longer, unable to dismiss the adrenaline that's still coursing through my veins.

I'm a tangled mess of emotions, all twisted up and gnarled like the roots of an old oak tree.

Bringing my mother here to LA, did I truly consider the impact it would have on her? Did I take into account the drastic change in environment, the unfamiliarity of it all?

The guilt isn't new to me. It's been a constant companion since the day I left Seattle, leaving my mother behind. It was a difficult decision, but I knew that I needed to make a change to pursue my dreams.

She came to visit me to spend time together, and I feel like I've let her down. I promised her a good time, a memorable trip, but instead, she ended up lost and confused in the middle of the night. Memorable only for me, It's possible that this whole incident will just slip from her mind like sand through fingers.

But now, as I see the consequences of my choices, the guilt overwhelms me. Did I make the right decision? Or was I just too fucking selfish? Should I have stayed in Seattle and taken care of her instead of pursuing my own ambitions? These questions swirl around in my mind like a never-ending tornado, threatening to tear me apart. But maybe there's a purpose to all of this, a lesson to be learned.

A few days later, I pull up to LAX once again, and the familiar sound of planes taking off and landing fills my ears. My mother sits next to me in the passenger seat, her face a blend of emotions - sadness for leaving, gratitude for the time we spent together, and worry about the future. We've made some unforgettable memories here in the city of angels, but we've also had some serious but necessary conversations.

We talk quietly about what happened a few nights ago, and I assure her that I'll take care of everything. She requires someone to be with her during the day, to keep her company and make sure she's safe. So, we decided to find her a caretaker, someone who will be there for her when I can't. It's a difficult decision, but we both agree it's for the best.

And although I didn't tell her, I've made another decision: when all the deals are sealed, and the money comes through, I will buy my mother a house, a new home to get her out of her cramped apartment. She deserves the best, and I'll do everything in my power to make it happen.

I deeply love this woman, and I feel a sense of responsibility settling on my shoulders. It's a shift in our dynamic, a role reversal of sorts, and it's not lost on me. The child has become the parent, and the parent has become the child.

But no matter what the future holds, I know one thing for sure: I'll always be there for her, just as she's always been there for me. She has made countless sacrifices, and now it's my turn to repay that debt.

The memories we made will forever hold a special place in my heart, but now it's time to let her go and continue with my own life. I promised her that I'd come to Seattle for Christmas, but that feels like a long time from now. I guide her to the security check, her hand gripping mine tightly as she looks back at me with tear-filled eyes. It's a painful moment, one I wish I could make disappear.

I snap a selfie with her, and then after a last hug, she's gone, swallowed up by the airport, leaving me standing there, alone with my thoughts.

We are all special cases.

23

Sitting by the pool with my eyes glued to the screen of my laptop. My fingers tap away furiously at the keyboard, in an almost trance-like state. The sun beats down on my skin, and the sound of the pool water lapping against the sides provides a soothing background noise. I'm almost done with the script. In just a couple of days, it will be ready for delivery, well ahead of the given deadline.

Fuck, I feel like a real writer now that I have to deal with deadlines and publishers. It's a surreal feeling, but it is what I wanted. My manuscript is in high demand, and after careful consideration, we've already decided on which publisher to go with. Now, it's just a matter of negotiating the contracts. Luckily, I have Ava on my side for that part.

And I think it's pretty cool that my team consists mostly of women. I actually have a team now. That's fucking crazy.

Allen's production company invited me to attend a film premiere tonight. It's one of their partners' movies, made with a budget of 60 million dollars. This will be my first Hollywood premiere–the real deal. Complete with fancy clothes and a red carpet. Alessa even got me a publicist for the event. She thinks it's a great opportunity to get my name and face out there.

Danny's not feeling well, so I'll be flying solo tonight. Nevertheless, I can't wait to immerse myself in the glitz and glamor of the spectacle that awaits me.

I hail an Uber, and we navigate the busy streets to the theater located in Hollywood. Stepping out of the car, I'm immediately engulfed by a sea of people, all dressed up and ready to walk the red carpet. The flashing lights of the paparazzi cameras and the sound of security personnel shouting instructions create a chaotic scene. The atmosphere is electric, and I feel like a tiny fish swimming in a vast ocean of opulence. But I'm excited to see what the night has in store. So, I adjust my tie, straighten my jacket, and confidently make my way through the throngs of people toward the entrance.

Approaching the towering security guards, who diligently scan everyone's credentials and patting them down for any suspicious items. I'm suddenly approached by a stunning woman who greets me with a warm smile and introduces herself as Cora, my publicist for the night.

Fuckness. With her striking features, black hair, and effortless charm, she could easily be mistaken for one of the A-list actors among the attendees. Her form-fitting professional attire reveals a body that clearly belongs to someone who takes care of themselves.

I feel like a celebrity with her by my side. She handles everything like a pro, from the guest list to the badges, and we strike up a conversation that flows like a river. It's incredible how much she already knows about me. She did her homework, and that makes me feel special.

I can't deny that there's a spark between us, but I try to stay professional and play it cool. At least for now.

As we navigate through the crowd, I notice the sign she's carrying with my full name on it. Every time someone wants to take a photo, she holds it up so that Getty Images or whoever can credit it correctly.

I reach for my phone to give Danny a call, hoping to get him on the line to check-in. But the ringing goes unanswered. I quickly snap a picture of the hectic scene around me and attach it to my message: "I hope you're feeling better, brother. Wish you were here to soak it all in." I hit send, at least trying to include him in some way.

Looking around, I realize I don't know anyone here except for a few actors whose faces I recognize from the silver screen. Everyone is doing their thing–mingling, sipping drinks, and indulging in some complimentary food. And now, we're getting ready to walk the red carpet, the main event for many people here.

Cora gives me a quick pep talk and explains the dos and don'ts for an occasion like this. Hundreds of photographers are lined up, eagerly waiting for their chance to capture the perfect shot. I feel like an animal being presented, and though I'm not one to lack confidence, I must admit that this feels a bit strange. The camera flashes blind me as the clicks of the shutters fill the air. And at each stop, Cora swoops in, holding up the sign with my name, almost as if she's saying, "Hey, look at this guy! He's somebody important!".

My ears are ringing from the screams of the crowd. It seems like some people recognize me or my name as they approach me and introduce themselves. I play along, shaking hands, smiling, and doing my best to remember everyone's names. Some even want to take photos with me, so I oblige, trying to look as natural as possible.

Once the red carpet extravaganza ends, I find myself in front of the theater, ready to step inside. Suddenly, Cora turns to me and says with a smile, "All right, Richard, it was so great meeting you, have fun."

I ask her, "Where are you going?"

And she calmly replies, "This is my job; after the red carpet, I'm pretty much done." But I can hear the regret in her voice.

"You can't leave me alone here," I say jokingly.

Cora responds with a playful smile and suggests, "I'm sure you won't have any trouble finding a companion for the night."

I nod and say, "I agree, but I want you to come with me." I can tell she is into it.

She timidly asks, "Are you sure?"

In response, I take her hand and lead her toward the theater. Fortunately, I've got an additional ticket on me, seeing as Danny had to bail out.

We enter the theater, and despite the grandeur of the event, the familiar scent of buttery popcorn and sugary candies wafts through the air, tickling my nose. It brings back memories of my childhood–a smell that I've come to associate with excitement and the joy of escapism. A blast from the past. The room stretches out before us, like stepping into a vast cathedral of cinema, a temple of the silver screen. We navigate through a swarm of individuals, some already seated, and others scramble to find their designated spots. I hear the shuffling of feet and soft whispers as people settle in. We find our seats and get comfortable.

After a while, one of the producers takes the stage and introduces the director of the film, who follows shortly after him. He begins to speak, and the rustling of popcorn bags and the creaking of seats fade into a hush. His voice echoes through the room, filling every corner. With an air of authority and a hint of excitement, he expresses gratitude to everyone involved in the film–from the crew and actors to the studio executives.
After he finishes his speech, the audience breaks into applause. He steps aside, making way for the main event–the film itself.

I glance over at Cora, who seems unfazed by it all. This isn't her first rodeo, that's for sure. To her, this is just another day at the office, while for me, it's exciting. The lights dim, the audience hushes, and the screen flickers to life. Sitting in my seat, I suddenly realize something - I have no fucking idea what movie I'm about to watch. I was too caught up in the chaos of the night to pay attention to any of it. All I remember is seeing the poster, but even that's a blur now. I have no idea what genre it is, what the story is about, nothing. So now, as the movie starts, I sit there in my seat, ready to be surprised and hopefully entertained.

I reach for Cora's hand, our eyes briefly meet, and she returns the gesture with a smile.

The film opens with an onslaught of high-energy action - explosions, screeching cars, and gunfire echoing throughout the theater. And my attention dwindles almost instantly. It's like a barking dog for my brain—too much noise and too little substance. The characters blend into a blur of cliches and one-dimensional archetypes. Expensive Hollywood bullshit.

I let out an involuntarily sigh, my body sinking into the cushioned seat as the movie blares with an explosive start. Cora looks over at me and whispers, "Are you okay?"

I muster a grin and confess, "I just can't stand action movies."

She laughs and exclaims, "Me neither!"

I chuckle, feeling a surge of relief. At least I'm not alone in my disinterest.

"I'm going to find the bathroom and grab us something to drink," I say, hoping to stretch my legs and clear my head for a moment. But she surprises me by saying, "I'll come with you."

Together, we quietly make our way out of the theater, tiptoeing past the rows of moviegoers, trying not to disturb anyone. We end up in the dark and quiet hallway.

She turns to me and smiles, and seizing the moment, I pull her toward me and kiss her.

We make out like teenagers, with a raw, unrestrained passion. This was building up since we met, and now, at this moment, it's finally reached its boiling point. I take her by the hand and lead her toward the bathroom, both of us fully aware of where this is headed. We're on the same page, and we couldn't care less about who might see us. And for a moment, we can pretend to be exactly what the other is looking for.

We reach the facilities, and the door clicks shut behind us. The sound echoes in the tiled room, emphasizing our seclusion. Lost in the moment, we are completely oblivious to the world outside. There are a couple of times when other people walked into the bathroom. But we were too caught up in the act to care about anything else. The sound of the door opening and closing becomes nothing but background noise to us. We don't even consider stopping, continuing with our intimate encounter. Even when the stall door rattles and voices can be heard on the other side, it isn't reason enough to stop.

When we finally come up for air and step out, the lobby is crowded with people, all chattering and moving toward the exit. They shuffle their feet, straighten their clothes, and check their phones. The movie has ended. Some eagle-eyed individuals give us knowing looks, fully aware of our illicit activities. It's so obvious; we have sex written all over our faces.

The herd of people flows toward the exit like a river of bodies. Cora and I are just two more faces in the crowd, trying to blend in and make our escape unnoticed. As we inch closer to the exit, flashes of light blind me. Paparazzi line the entrance, waiting to snap pictures of anyone and everyone leaving. There's no avoiding it. I know they'll capture some shots of Cora and me together. I try to keep my head down and rush past, but it's impossible to evade them entirely. As we finally break free from the crowd and start walking down the street, I take a deep breath of fresh air. What a night.

Then, as I glance down at my clothes, I notice a big white stain smeared across the fabric. It's the salty icing on the cake of an already memorable night. In my mind, I hope that the majority of those photos captured just our faces.

At least I have my publicist with me to navigate any potential media attention. But in Hollywood, no one cares about cum stains on a writer's pants.

Although I would love to see the headline, "Writer Richard Bryght fucks his publicist in the bathroom at a movie premiere."

24

The Grove on a Saturday morning is a world unto itself. The crowd is a mixture of locals, tourists, and the occasional celebrity, all strolling through the outdoor shopping center. I arrive at the food court, the hive of activity. The air is filled with the crackle of cooking meat, chopping vegetables, and sizzling oil, mixing with the buzz of conversation and laughter.

My eyes scan the crowd for Lana. It takes a moment, but eventually, I spot her at a small table tucked away in a quieter corner. It comes as no surprise that many people recognize and approach her, mostly men, of course. As always, she looks stunning, her beauty radiating like a lighthouse beacon in the chaos. When she tilts her head up and sees me, a smile spreads across her face.

Lana wants to see me before she leaves for Miami, where she'll be gone for a few weeks to "work." Knowing Lana, that could mean anything from photo shoots on yachts to filming scenes in mansions. Regardless of the specifics, she's always working, always hustling.

I make my way over to her, dodging people left and right. We hug briefly, and she gives me a kiss before we take our seats. I can tell she's genuinely excited to see me.

She's quick to congratulate me on my recent success, mentioning the photos she saw on my Instagram from the red carpet. I thank her for the kind words and the attention. "Well, I may not have a following of 16 million like you, but hey, at least you're one of them," I say with a smirk.

We order food, and I notice the eyes that follow Lana's every move. In this town, it feels like we're all just walking billboards for our job titles. There's Richard, the Writer; Danny, the Manager; and Lana, the Pornstar. Our identities often seem reduced to our professions, with people rarely bothering to look beyond the label. I believe Lana enjoys my company because, with me, she can let her guard down and just be herself. I see her as a real woman, with thoughts and emotions, and not just like a fuck toy.

In the midst of our conversation, Lana suddenly springs up like a jack-in-the-box, screaming the name "Emily!" It catches me off guard, and I turn to see another beautiful woman making her way over to us. She radiates a sense of confidence and independence, igniting my curiosity about who she is and how she fits into Lana's world.

Lana introduces the brown-haired beauty as Emily, and as they hug, she casually mentions that they work together. I watch the two exchange pleasantries and catch up on each other's lives while I crack a few jokes to make them laugh. As they chat, the conversation turns to Emily's struggles with anxiety. Admitting that she relies on Xanax to keep her head above water. It's as if anxiety is the new black in this town; everyone is wearing it. And

I'm not excluding myself. But what she describes sounds like Generalized Anxiety coupled with a panic disorder. After a while, Emily announces that she has to leave and get ready for a shoot. Without skipping a beat, Lana suggests taking a photo together to commemorate the moment. I offer, "Want me to take it?"

But Emily has a different idea. "No, let's take one all together," she says, smiling at me.

I'm surprised by her suggestion, but I agree. I find myself sandwiched between Emily and Lana, their bodies pressed against mine. Lana wraps her arm around my waist, and Emily rests her hand on my shoulder with a Xanax-induced smile. Lana holds up her phone, ready to snap the picture.

Hold your breath.

Freeze Frame.

Click.

Soon after the photo's taken, Emily chimes in, "Make sure to tag me, too!" Lana nods, quickly posting it and tagging both of us. We say our goodbyes, and Emily heads out. I turn to Lana and say, "She seems nice."

Lana nods, "Yeah, she's cool. She's like my sister in porn."

The moment that picture goes live on her Instagram, it spreads like a digital wildfire, at least in my little forest. My followers begin to skyrocket, and I notice that Emily is among them.

Since I haven't seen Danny before leaving the house, I send him a text: "Wanna do something later?" His response is instant and to the point. "Not even a little bit."

Lana wipes her mouth with the napkin, pushes the empty plate aside, and lets out a sigh. "I should probably head out now," she says, glancing at her phone. "I still have to pack and make my way to LAX." I nod my head, knowing how hectic airport traffic can be, especially here.

We exit the Grove together, and I walk Lana to her car.

She unlocks her white Tesla Roadster and gracefully slides into the driver's seat, her long legs tucked beneath the steering wheel. I lean against the doorframe, my eyes tracing the contours of her face.

"Let's hang out when I'm back," she says, reaching out to give my arm a gentle squeeze.

"Yeah, sounds good," I reply. "Have fun in Miami."

She starts the car, the electric engine buzzing to life, and she blows a kiss in my direction before driving off. I turn around and start walking toward my own vehicle. Suddenly, I see someone standing near the Whole Foods, and my heart skips a beat. It looks like Maria. Time seems to slow down as she turns around, revealing her face. My heart races faster and faster as she comes into focus. And it seems as if I can smell the scent of her perfume that lingered long after she was gone. However, as she fully turns towards me, I realize that it's "not" Maria. Fuck me. Relief washes over me, and I let out a breath I didn't even know I was holding.

When I was ready to see you, you were there because you were everywhere.

25

Laurel Tavern, a microcosm of the city itself, where every drink tells a story, and every story is just another drink away. I'm hunched over my laptop, lost in thought. Danny is here with me, feeling better again and back to his usual self. He jokes around and cheers me on as he stands by my side.

Today is the day–The day I'll finish the script. I feel the weight of it, both a burden and a relief. Danny's eyes are glued to the screen as he watches a game, yelling at the players as if they could hear him through the television. But with my noise-canceling headphones on, I shut out the distractions of the outside world.
In the midst of a noisy crowd of drinkers and chatterboxes, my fingers race across the keyboard, producing a sharp and steady clacking sound.

I can't fully explain how the writing process works for me. It's like a force takes over, and I become a vessel, channeling the story through me. My fingers move almost involuntarily, tapping the keys with a rhythm that's all its own. The words flow like a river, twisting and turning in unexpected ways, and I'm just along for the ride. It's as if the story is writing itself, and all I have to do is be present and let it happen. And now, finally, I've reached the end. I stare intently at the computer screen as the final lines of my script come to life before me. I type the last two magic words, "Fade Out." Taking a deep breath, I close my eyes, savoring the feeling of completion. It's a sensation that's difficult to describe, but it's almost like I've given birth to something. I've officially finished the fucking thing.

Opening my eyes, I return to reality, and I notice Danny looking at me with a grin on his face. He knows exactly what just happened, and there's a sense of accomplishment coursing through my veins. "Congratulations!" he says, his voice laced with genuine pride and admiration.

"Thanks, man," I reply.

"Time to slap some ballerinas!" Danny says with a grin. His unusual way of saying, "Let's celebrate." And he orders us some drinks.

I watch as Danny lifts his glass, the amber liquid inside it sloshing around as he raises it in a toast. "To the script," he says.

Then, a voice next to us interrupts the moment. "Congratulations, guys!" a man exclaims, raising his own drink in our direction. I turn to him and offer a nod of gratitude. He's wearing a sharp suit, his head shaved smooth and shiny. Clearly, this guy has been putting in the time at the gym.

Then he asks, "You're Richard Bryght, right?" his eyes fixed on me. I feel a sudden jolt of surprise at the recognition. Danny, full of confidence, answers the question for me. "That's right." he says, "This dude is a fucking genius!" Pointing at me.

My mind is still trying to figure out how this guy knows me, but I try to act cool as he introduces himself as Russ. He tells us that he was in New York for a year and recently returned to LA for business. Curious, I ask, "What did you do in New York?" expecting to hear about some kind of exciting career. But instead, he smirks and says, "Her name is Vanessa." As I turn my head toward Danny, I see that he's laughing uncontrollably at Russ' response.

Even though I thought it was kind of douchey.

Russ mentions that he saw the Deadline Hollywood press release but also that we might have mutual friends, which catches my attention. He clarifies that he's referring to Lana. It's then revealed that Russ is a porn producer, which makes perfect sense, so I nod in understanding. "What are you guys doing later tonight?" he asks, his voice low and smooth.

I look at Danny, who shrugs in response, and then back at Russ. "Just celebrating the script, I guess," I reply.

"Do you want to come to my party? Celebrate there?" his eyes gleaming with anticipation. "It's at my house up in the hills. No cell phones allowed," he adds.

I can see Danny's eyes light up with curiosity. I say, "Fuck yeah, why not." Russ pulls out his phone and asks for my number, promising to text me the details of his party.

A few hours later, we're inside an Uber headed to the address Russ had texted me. I gaze out the window, watching the city lights blur together as we make our way up into the hills. Danny sits next to me, scrolling through his phone. He seems quiet, and my mind is racing–I've been feeling a little anxious all day. I lean over to him, projecting how I feel, and ask, "You nervous?" He shrugs and says, "Nah, just wondering what kind of freak show we're getting into." I can't help but laugh. Danny always has a way of putting things into perspective.

The car pulls up to the address, and I see the "House"–it's a fucking mansion with a line of cars parked along the driveway. The music is thumping, and I can hear people laughing and talking.

We step out the car and approach the gate, where two imposing security guards block our path, surveying us with a suspicious eye. "Names?" one of them barks. We give our names, and they demand our phones. Without hesitation, we hand them over, watching as they seal them away in locked pouches. No distractions, no texts, no social media–just be present and enjoy the night. Eckhart Tolle would be so proud. But of course, there are privacy concerns; there are probably some folks here who don't want their every move documented and posted to Instagram. But the guard assures us that the pouches will be unlocked when we leave.

Then, the security guards step aside, their faces stoic and their eyes void of emotion. They mutter a quick "Have a great night, gentlemen" before turning their attention back to their post.

We walk inside the mansion, and my eyes widen in awe. This place is massive, decorated with some of the coolest art pieces and paintings I've ever seen. As I look around, I'm amazed by the sheer number of attractive people in this place. Beautiful women with stunning curves and muscular men everywhere, mingling and chatting away, their laughter mixing with the thumping beats of electronic music that reverberate throughout the entire house. But as I observe them, I notice something different about this crowd. They're not trying to impress anyone or fit in. They're simply being themselves, comfortable in their own skin. It's a stark contrast to the pretentiousness of Hollywood. In this world of the adult industry, there's a different kind of acceptance, a different kind of openness. They don't judge you; they simply accept you for who you are. Maybe it's because they know what it's like to be constantly condemned and scrutinized by society. They are misfits, and they embrace it.

The mansion seems to go on forever, with long hallways leading to different rooms, each one more extravagant than the last. I catch glimpses of people lounging by a massive pool, sipping on drinks, and enjoying the warm evening breeze. It's as if we've entered another world—welcome to Babylon.

We roam around the party, and in a way, Danny and I blend in with the crowd seamlessly, like we belong here. Danny spots a huge guy sporting a Raiders jersey and immediately starts talking about football. Even in this environment, he finds a way to connect through sports. I smile at him and say, "I'm gonna go explore," feeling drawn to the enigmatic allure of the place.

Stepping away, I venture deeper into the estate, passing by groups of people engaged in conversations, making out and laughing.

As I observe my surroundings, I notice the small notepads and pens scattered throughout the place. It's a smart move, I realize, given that no one has their phones on them. Instead, these notepads serve as a means to exchange information - phone numbers, emails, and whatever else. It's a refreshing change from the typical phone-obsessed culture, and I can appreciate the simplicity of this approach.

Suddenly, I feel a pair of arms wrap around me from behind. I turn and see Lana's friend Emily, her face adorned with a wide smile. She gives me another hug and says, "Hey, it's so good to see you again!" I return the compliment, and then she asks, "Where are you going?"

I shrug," I just wanted to go explore," I say, "Wanna join?". Emily grins and then locks her arm into mine. "Absolutely!" and we begin walking together.

I follow her as she confidently leads me through the sprawling mansion like she owns the place, introducing me to all sorts of people along the way. And damn, it's a trip. Each room we pass is more wild and debaucherous than the last. We pass by a room with a threesome going on, a couple getting it on against the wall in the hallway, there's an orgy in another room, and some seriously intense BDSM next to it. It's like stepping into an erotic wonderland, and Emily is the white rabbit. The air smells like sex, blowjobs were given and received, and everywhere I look, there are people lost in the moment.

Eventually, we arrive at the club area, where the music pounds relentlessly and the dance floor pulses with writhing bodies. Emily immediately starts dancing, overflowing with energy. But despite the intoxicating craziness and distractions of the party, I can't shake off this fucking anxiety that has plagued me throughout the day. Sensing something is up, Emily asks, "Are you alright?" Knowing she understands this feeling, I decide to be honest, "Just dealing with some anxiety."
Without hesitation, she reaches into her bag and pulls out a bottle, giving it a little shake that causes it to rattle.
She offers, "Do you want a Xanax?".

I hesitate for a moment before asking, "What does it feel like?". She looks at me with a grin and replies, "Like a warm hug around your brain." Intrigued, I respond, "Damn, that sounds fucking nice!"

She says, "Feels fucking nice too."

But I shrug my shoulders and say, "I don't know. I'm not the biggest fan of psychopharmaceuticals."

There's a mischievous glint in her eye, "Let's take one together," she says, "You'll feel better." She breaks a pill in half and pops one into her own mouth before placing the other half on my tongue. Then, in one swift motion, she leans in and kisses me. I taste the bitter chemical compound in my mouth, mixing with the remnants of the sweet drink Emily had earlier. Everything about the way she kisses feels amazing. It's as if every nerve ending is on fire but in the best way possible. As we kiss, the taste lingers, serving as a reminder of the relief that's to come. In a world that always demands more from us, sometimes we just want to feel less.

I can feel the bass thumping in my chest as Emily drags me onto the dance floor. The electronic beats are relentless, and it feels like we're in the midst of the opening scene of *Blade* - I half expect the blood sprinklers to start going off any second. Slowly, a sense of relief seeps into my brain. Even in this chaotic environment, everything starts to feel calm. Emily's words echo in my mind, and I have to admit, she was right. It does feel like a warm hug around my brain. Fuck.

Right now, things feel alright again, and even my regrets seem pointless. Emily presses her body against mine, and while feeling me up, she asks, "Wanna go to the pool?" My head nods almost automatically, with the Alprazolam making me feel light and floaty.

My body moves in sync with hers as she drags me through the crowd of people, like the benzo-fueled puppy I am. As we pass by a table, Emily makes a quick grab for one of the notepads. Her pen glides smoothly over the paper as she scribbles down a string of digits, then she hands it to me with a smile. We arrive at the pool area, and the scene is like something out of a Bacchanalian dream. The rhythm of the music, cups clinking, laughter, and splashes echoing around us. And there, at the far end of the pool,

I spot Danny between two beautiful women, his charisma in full effect. I know he's doing just fine without me.

I glance up, my eyes fixate on the rooftop deck of the mansion, three stories above us. Silhouettes of people sway and move to the beat as if they're dancing with the stars. The view from up there must be spectacular, with the city lights illuminating the sky.

Emily stops at a group of three towering African American men standing together, and she introduces me to them. They give me fist bumps and handshakes that make me feel like a total lightweight. They're all three times my size, and the contrast is almost comical. But despite their intimidating size, these guys couldn't have been nicer. They are like gentle giants. And maybe it's the Xanax talking, but I feel like I'm among friends here, even with these strangers.

I place my drink down on the glass table next to me as I continue engaging in small talk when one of them, a behemoth of a man named Bruce - suddenly chimes in with an unexpected revelation "Shit, I read your Book!" Excitement fills his voice.

I am stunned, but before I can even ask if he is confusing me with someone else, he continues.

"Man, that book spoke to me like nothing else. It was like you reached deep into my soul and put all my thoughts down on paper. That shit was powerful." I'm floored. At this point in my career, when all the deals are still up in the air, and nothing has come out yet, I'd never expected to meet someone who not only knew who I was but had actually read my work and found meaning in it. Rare recognize rare.

Bruce continues to gush about my book, and the other guys seem impressed as well. As we talk, Emily reaches for my hand. I turn to her, and she gives me a small, devilish smile before whispering in my ear, "I wanna fuck you later."

I nod with a smile and say, "That can be arranged." Feeling a sense of calm and serenity. It's like nothing can throw me off. I'm just living in the present, and it feels fucking amazing.

I reach for my drink on the table, the glass cool against my fingertips, and I take a sip. But then, out of nowhere, a piercing scream slices through the air. I barely have time to register the sound before it's followed by another - the sound of shattering glass, like a thousand tiny knives raining down around me, and the sickening crunch of something heavy hitting the ground.

Thrown off balance, I feel the shards of broken glass biting into my skin like tiny razors. The world spins and tilts, and I experience a strange disconnect between my mind and body. It's like I'm moving through molasses, my limbs sluggish and heavy. I know it's the Xanax that dulls my reactions and slowed me down, but at this moment, it feels like an insurmountable obstacle. The music continues to blare, but it's drowned out by the symphony of panic and terror that fills the air. Struggling to get up, my eyes frantically scan the chaos around me. And then, my gaze settles on the sight of a woman's body crumpled on the ground and broken glass table beside me. Her lifeless form twisted and contorted in an unnatural pose while her blood mixes with the remains of my drink.

People are shouting and panicking, but my mind is foggy, and it's hard to process everything. I notice a couple of people trying to force open their phone pouches. Those damn things that were supposed to keep us all present in the moment, away from the distractions of technology, were now preventing us from calling for help. Even though it's too late for that.

My mind races, trying to make sense of the tragedy unfolding before me. Was it an accident? Suicide? One moment you're up on a rooftop overlooking the city, dancing like you're invincible. And the next, your body crashes down onto the hard concrete by the poolside, like a watermelon smashed against the pavement, proving the opposite.

The day your life ends usually starts like any other day.

26

The sun hangs high in the sky as I step onto the Universal Studios lot, encompassed by towering sound stages and trailers. Today is the first day of shooting for the film adaptation of my book, *Serendipity*. I can hear the hum of activity surrounding me, people running around like ants, carrying equipment, and setting things up. It's hard to believe that all of this is happening because of some words I wrote.

I make my way through the lot, trying not to get in the way of the busy crew. That's when I see Allen, coffee in hand, striding towards me with purpose. "Richard, glad you could make it," he says, clapping me on the back. "Ready to see your baby come to life?"

I nod, but the truth is, I have no idea what to expect. The script is complete, my part is over, and now it's up to the director and the actors to breathe life into it. But I can feel a sense of excitement building within me.

Allen takes my arm and leads me on a whirlwind tour of the production; I'm introduced to a bunch of new faces, from the crew to the cast. Everyone seems to know who I am, and I feel like a celebrity. Allen points out different parts of the set, explaining how they'll shoot certain scenes.

And then, we come across a familiar sight - a replica of the apartment I vividly described in the book, mirroring my first place in Seattle, down to the very last detail. It's surreal, like stepping back in time and seeing a piece of my own history come to life, but with a Hollywood budget.

During the pre-production of the film, I was asked if I still had any photos of the place that served as the inspiration for the apartment in my book. So I gave them what I could find, not really knowing what they would do with them. Now I know the answer. It's a bizarre feeling, like peering into another dimension where the lines between my reality and my fiction blur into one.

The phone buzzes in my pocket, pulling me out of the manufactured world of movie-making. It's a message from Emily, a simple invitation to hang out. We're not a couple. A couple of idiots, maybe. But we're not just friends either; it's a murky in-between, and we hang out from time to time. Two lost souls trying to feel a little less alone. Emily and I bonded over the shared experience at the party six months ago. She was standing right next to me when that girl fell from the roof, and we've grown closer in the aftermath of our blood-stained memory. Sometimes life feels like being in traffic; without warning, someone crashes into you and suddenly becomes part of your journey. I tell Emily that I'm swamped with work on set, which sounds like a hollow excuse, even if it's the truth.

Meanwhile, the cash from the script and my book deal finally rolled in, and true to my word, I'm scouring the Seattle real estate market for the perfect house for my mother. It's a tall order trying to find the ideal home from a distance, but the holidays are approaching, and I'll be back soon enough to handle the situation in person.

The caretaker we found for my mom is a godsend, a true gem who keeps things in order and ensures my mother is taken care of. It's a weight off my shoulders; she spends time with her, doing things she enjoys and keeping her company when I can't be there.

About a month ago, Danny and I moved into a new house, nestled up in the Hollywood Hills, overlooking Mulholland Drive, offering a breathtaking view. The size of the place is kind of too much. I mean, it is just the two of us, and this house was fit for a king. But it's not like we're hurting for cash, and the moment we walked through the door of this house, we knew it was the one.

Every day, I wake up to the sound of birds chirping and the gentle breeze rustling through the trees. And when the sun sets, the sky is painted with shades of orange, pink, and purple that I never knew existed.

Once we settled in, we couldn't resist setting up a game room that would make any '90s kid drool. With Super Nintendo, Sega Saturn, N64, TurboGrafix, Playstation One, you name it. All set up and ready to go. Thanks to LA's thriving Retro gaming scene and eBay, we were able to track down all the games we couldn't afford back in the day. It's like time-traveling back to a simpler era, where all we had to worry about was beating the next level of

Super Mario Bros or Sonic the Hedgehog. Nostalgia comes with a price tag, and we're paying for it with each game we play.

Allen keeps showing me around as the cast rehearses one of the scenes. It's an absurd feeling watching my words come to life through the mouths of these actors. It's like a dream but more vivid. The actress they cast for the role based on Maria is breathtaking. She's got this charmingly sad look on her face, depressed, but in a cute way. I see her gaze drift toward me as Allen and I approach. But I know better than that, and despite her beauty, I'm just a bystander, a tourist passing through, and I have no intention of becoming part of any kind of on-set drama. The words I've written are the stars of the show, not some fleeting attraction. It's not worth it.

Looking around at all the people on this set, it feels like the circus has come to town. Everywhere I turn, there's someone clutching a clipboard or wearing a headset, running around like chickens with their heads cut off. And then there's me, stuck in the middle of it all, just waiting, without a purpose. Everything seems to take forever; it would drive me nuts. I'm not good at being patient, never have been.

Allen starts telling me about all the different cameras and lenses they use. He's really into it, like it's the most fascinating thing in the world. But I don't understand a damn word he says. All these technical terms and jargon just fly right over my head, and I'm left feeling like a total idiot. I just nod and pretend to understand what he's saying because I don't want to be rude or ignorant.

Just the fact that Allen invited me to the set is pretty damn cool. We writers are usually confined to our offices or apartments, typing away on our laptops. But being on a set is a whole new world for me, and I'm soaking up every detail like a sponge. After all, my work is done. I find a seat and observe, feeling like a ghost —invisible and insignificant. They're setting up the cameras, the lights, and the sound equipment. It's all so precise, so organized, and I am astounded as I witness the pieces fitting together.

Suddenly, the time has come to start filming. The assistant director barks through his megaphone, "QUIET ON SET, PLEASE!" The camera operator announces, "Rolling!" and the sound guy chimes in, "Rolling sound." Soon after, the slate guy steps in, stating the scene number. Then, the director's voice fills the air, yelling, "Action!" and just like that, we're sucked into the scene.

Everything flows together seamlessly. The takes come and go, and the scene plays out before my eyes, every word and action as it was written in the script.

And then, as the grand finale, the scene concludes with one of my most cherished lines from the book, and I can feel I have tears in my eyes:

"How are we supposed to meet and fall in "love," if I am so fucking busy and you don't exist?"

Cut.

27

Picture this: it's the summer of '98, and the air crackles with anticipation. It's Friday, the last day of school before summer break, and you're stuck in a classroom, eagerly counting down the minutes until freedom. Finally, the bell rings, and you rush out with everyone else. Signaling the end of another school year and the beginning of a summer full of adventure and memories. With your backpack on, you hop on your bike and pedal your way to the local Blockbuster video store.

It's a hot day, the kind of day that makes you feel alive, cruising down the sun-soaked streets with your two best friends next to you, your hair blowing in the wind like a wild flag. When you push open the store's door, a blast of cool, refreshing air conditioning instantly washes over you, accompanied by the scent of stale popcorn, new plastic, and shrink wrap filling your senses.

The familiar blue and yellow color scheme surrounds you, welcoming you to a world where Friday nights were sacred.
You pass aisles filled with videotapes, and you can feel the excitement bubbling inside you as you make your way to the video game section. And then you're there, eagerly scanning the

rows of PlayStation games, each title a seductive promise of pixelated fun and adventure.

You pick up the game case, study the cover art, and read the back. Choosing which game to rent is an important decision, one that could dictate the next days of your life, perhaps even your entire summer. And then, you see it. The box art catches your eye, and you pick it up. A new release called "Road Rash 3D". A combat-racing game where you can punch and attack other players with weapons? It's unlike anything you've ever played before. This is the game that will consume you. Without hesitation, you hand it to the cashier and rent it.

Back in your room, you sit cross-legged on your bed as the sun begins to set, the sounds of the neighborhood outside filtering through your open window, creating a comforting backdrop to your gaming session. You take a sip of your mother's freshly made lemonade, the tangy sweetness exploding in your mouth, with a bag of potato chips next to you. And as the game boots up and the soundtrack fills your ears with its infectious beats, you're transported into the virtual world of speed, power, and danger.

At that moment, the world outside fades away; you don't need anything else because right then and there, everything is perfect.

You know exactly what I'm talking about, what it felt like, and even what it smelled like. Days where time seemed to stretch out like an endless ribbon, and the weight of the world was nothing more than a fleeting thought. You remember it vividly, that feeling of carefree bliss that can only be experienced in the golden days of youth. It's almost like a dream now, a distant memory that you can barely grasp, but it's still there, lingering in the recesses of your mind. And we would try anything to feel like that again.

Danny and I are sitting in the game room of our luxurious house in the City of Angels. Playing that very same game on an old PlayStation and a CRT television. We've come a long way since the days of renting games from Blockbuster. But it's not just about playing a game; it's about reliving a moment from our past, a moment that we hold onto with every fiber of our being.

Today is my 40th birthday, and I couldn't imagine a better way to spend it. And right now, I feel just as carefree as I did back in the day. It's not just because I'm sitting here with my best friend playing old video games or because of my success and the money in my bank account. Added to all of that is something much simpler. It's a supplement called Phenibut. When Emily first offered me a Xanax, the feeling was nice, sure, but I knew the potential damage it could do to my brain chemistry. So I scoured the internet for an alternative, and that's when I stumbled upon Phenibut. It increases GABA levels in the brain, producing a calm state without any long-term harm. But the danger still lurks in the shadows, as it can be addictive.

I only take it on special occasions, extremely rarely. But when I want to experience pure bliss again, I take that magic 2-gram dose, and it's like a time machine back to those innocent days of youth. And today is one of those days.

As the sun sets, the room becomes dimly lit, with only the flickering of the television providing illumination. Danny's had a few beers, and I can tell he's feeling pretty damn good as well. It's an uncomplicated joy that we share, born from a time when life was simpler, and happiness came cheap.

Danny turns to me and just says, "Man, the music from the underwater level in Donkey Kong Country...."

I know what he's referring to and say, "Yeah, dude, fucking brilliant."

But as the night wears on, I can feel my eyelids getting heavy, and I know it's time to go to bed. The Phenibut has done its job, inducing a tiredness that could only come from complete relaxation, and I welcome it with open arms. I tell Danny good night and head to bed, feeling grateful for evenings like this. The simplicity of it all is what makes it so perfect. And as I drift off to sleep, I feel content knowing that I am exactly where I am supposed to be; this is the life I envisioned for myself.

Freeze Frame.

Click.

The night comes to an abrupt end as the sound of persistent knocking on my door pulls me out of my deep synthetic sleep. The morning light pierces through the window like a million shards of glass and blinds me. The brightness is so intense that I can barely keep my eyes open. Suddenly, I hear Danny's voice from behind the door "Richard?" Something feels off. I mumble a groggy "yeah?" in response while reaching for my phone, which I notice has 20 missed calls from an unknown number.

Danny enters the room, his face contorted in a way that I've never seen before. He looks like he's carrying the weight of the world on his shoulders. It's like he's trying to convey a message through his expression alone, but I can't decipher it. Confused, I look at him and ask, "What's up?" in a feeble attempt to break the silence. There's no immediate response from him. That's when I know something is terribly wrong. The tension in the air is suffocating, like a thick fog. Finally, Danny manages to choke out the words that I never thought I'd hear. "Your mother died."

My heart stops beating, and my mind goes blank.

28

look at my mother, her eyes filled with an overwhelming sense of pride. It's a look I haven't seen in a long time, maybe ever. At least not to this extent. Her words hit me like a ton of bricks. "I am so proud of you; I told you you can do anything you want to." The weight of her words sinks in, and suddenly everything feels possible. She is the one person in the world who truly believes in me, the one who's always been there, pushing me to do better, to be better. And now, here I am, standing before her as a living testament to her unwavering faith. I can feel tears welling up in my eyes as I realize the gravity of her words. All the late nights, the sacrifices, the hard work - it's all been worth it to hear her say this. In this moment, I know that I've made her proud, and it's the greatest feeling in the world.

I wake up abruptly to the jarring sound of the plane's warning system, indicating impending turbulence. Looking around the darkened cabin of the plane, disoriented and confused, and the hum of the plane engine drones in my ears. I'm on my way to Seattle, and everything about this trip feels so fucking wrong. My mind is a jumble of thoughts; memories of my mother's smiling face flood my mind. I glance out the window and see nothing but darkness and the distant twinkle of city lights far below. The flight attendant's voice crackles through the intercom, "Ladies and gentlemen, we are approaching some turbulence. Please fasten your seatbelts and remain seated until further notice."

Like I give a fuck.

As the plane shakes, I look around and see people gripping their armrests with white-knuckled hands. Some of them have beads of sweat on their foreheads. But I can't relate. Maybe it's due to my current mental state, or the fact that I took four grams of Phenibut, or maybe, it's just my natural disposition, but I've never been afraid of flying. Not even a little bit. In fact, I kind of enjoy the turbulence. There's something about the way the plane bounces around that's kind of soothing, like being rocked to sleep. I'm just numb, disconnected.

It's a strange thought, I know, but I've always had this feeling that dying in a plane crash would be the appropriate death for me. The headline "Writer Richard Bryght Dies in Plane Crash" just has a better ring to it compared to the banality of slipping and breaking one's neck in the shower. I know, that's morbid as fuck, but after all, I'm on my way to arrange my mother's funeral. If there was ever a time to embrace the notion of death, it is now.

The last time I saw her alive was when I dropped her off at LAX. If only I knew, I never would've let her go. I wouldn't have been so careless with our time together. Danny immediately offered to come with me to Seattle for support. But I turned him down; I needed to do this alone.

I could tell he felt guilty about being the one to break the devastating news to me. But the truth is, there's no right way to receive information like that. No matter how gently or harshly it's delivered, it's going to hurt. And it did. It hurt like hell. Still does. But I need to feel the pain and let it consume me. Maybe one day, I'll be able to look back on this and find some kind of meaning in it. But for now, all I can do is try to survive it.

The day my mother died, her caretaker left her alone in the cramped apartment for the night. Then she got hungry and wanted to make herself a late-night snack before heading off to bed. However, what happened next was a tragedy beyond measure. Fires raged on two burners atop the stove as well as in the oven. The flames consumed the oxygen in the tiny apartment, suffocating my mother in her sleep. The windows, sealed tight, offered no reprieve from the oppressive heat. It wasn't until the following day, when the caretaker returned to check on her, that the horrifying discovery was unveiled. The apartment had transformed into a smoldering, suffocating tomb. And my mother was gone. The thought of her dying alone like that is almost too much to bear.

The guilt is relentless, gnawing at me from the inside out. It's like a parasite that's taken up residence within my soul. I reach into my bag and take out the small bottle of Phenibut. I twist open the cap, dump the contents of another gram into my hand and tip the white powder under my tongue. It dissolves almost instantly into my saliva. The taste is bitter, but I don't mind. I just need it to work fast. I know it's not the right course of action. My mother is dead, and here I am, self-medicating with a supplement I barely understand.

Being on this plane at night is like being suspended in a void, detached from everything else, much like the dark apartment my mother died in.

The substance wraps its arms around me, pulling into a lucid dream so vivid it feels like a hallucination. Transporting me back to the last summer vacation I went on with my mom a lifetime ago. The sun was hot, and the sand was burning my feet. It's hard to believe that was me, the rebellious teen who thought family vacations were for losers. Now I know that I was wrong, and I recognize how precious these memories are. It's painful to witness, somewhere between sleep and wakefulness.

We know that our parents won't live forever; it's a universal truth, an inevitability that we try to ignore as long as we can. And we hold onto the hope that we'll have just a little more time with them, a few more precious moments to share before they're gone forever. But deep down, we know that time is limited, that we're all just passing through, and that life is fleeting and fragile. Yet, we keep on living as if we're invincible, as if death is something that happens to other people, not to us.

But then, one day, that illusion shatters. The news hits us like a sledgehammer blow, a sudden and brutal reminder of our mortality. And in that instant, all we can do is mourn, regret, and wish we had more time. More time to say the things we should have said, to do the things we should have done, to be the people we should have been.

Fuck.

29

Rain is pounding on the church roof like a million fists. It's almost as if the sky is crying for my loss, mourning alongside the sea of guests in the pews. The church is packed, and it's suffocating me. As I walk down the aisle, I see faces I don't recognize. People I haven't seen since my childhood or maybe never even met before. I feel like being trapped in a box with a bunch of individuals I don't know or care about. It's enough to make me want to scream.

I can sense every pair of eyes lock onto me. They gather here to mourn my mother, yet they seem more interested in the son she left behind. It's as if they're all silently judging me, wondering how I'm handling her passing, like they have a right to know. Maybe some of them recognize me, not as the grieving son, but as the writer Richard Bryght. It's a weird feeling to be known by strangers who have no connection to me beyond my words on a page. Or maybe I'm just being paranoid.

My mother always loved going to church. But for me, it was torture. I remember every Christmas Eve, she would take me with her to the midnight mass, and I would be there, counting the minutes until it was over. The son who hates church, standing at the back like a guilty man at his own trial. But she never gave up trying to convert me. She thought that if she took me here enough times, something would stick, and I'd finally see the light.

I never believed in God. The notion of an all-knowing, all-powerful entity watching over us just seems a little too far-fetched for my rational mind. But hey, to each their own. I'm not sure what I believe, but I have to admit I can see the value in faith. If believing in God can inspire someone to be a better person, or give them the strength to face another day, then I'm all for it. I've seen individuals who would otherwise be total assholes become better people because they believe in something. They'll volunteer, donate to charity, all because they think it's what God wants. And I can't fault them for it.

But the fact that I'm here in this church right now, at the funeral of my mother, doesn't exactly make me want to change my mind about religion. I still don't want to be here. If anything, it further solidifies my disbelief. The ceremony appears hollow, lacking any real meaning beyond the repetition of rituals. All the prayers and hymns, they're just empty words. They can not resurrect my mother, nor can they alleviate the pain of her absence. And I'm left with asking the same questions that plague every grieving soul - if there is a higher power, why would they strip away such an incredible person from my life? It feels cruel. After all, isn't God supposed to be good? Protect the innocent? But I don't believe in any of this shit, so I am in no position to demand answers to those questions or feel like God betrayed me.

In fact: Fuck God.

Leading up to this, there were so many decisions to be made. Open or closed casket? How should the service go? What songs should be played? It's endless. And all I want is to just get it over with. But there's no rushing the process of saying goodbye to someone you love, no shortcuts. It's like trying to run through quicksand. The harder you try, the slower you move. The decisions have to be made, no matter how overwhelming they may seem.

I stare at the blown-up photo of my mother standing next to her casket. Her smile is contagious, and I find myself inexplicably drawn to her face. It's almost as if she's telling me not to worry, assuring me that everything will be alright. But everything is far from alright. This entire situation feels like a fucking nightmare that I can't wake up from. After the service, people start approaching me, giving me their condolences. I appreciate the kind words, but they feel empty. One guy comes up to me, claiming to be my cousin, saying, "Richard, I'm so sorry for your loss. Let's catch up sometime. I really enjoyed your book." Are you kidding me? At my mother's funeral? Get the fuck out of here.

The rain pours relentlessly, hitting the fresh grave as they slowly lower my mother's casket into the ground next to my dad, and it's like watching my heart being buried with her. The pain is unbearable, and I feel utterly alone in this moment. And then, out of nowhere, a hand lands on my shoulder. I turn around to see Danny standing there, doing exactly what a best friend should do –ignore what I told him, like a true brother.

He understands me better than anyone else. Recognizing that I needed him, even when I didn't know or couldn't ask for it. And he doesn't have to say anything. His presence alone is enough in that moment; I'm so grateful for him. My eyes are still wet with tears as I wrap my arms around him.

Several hours later, Danny and I are back at the bar we visited last year. The place hasn't changed much, but we have. Instead of my usual sugar-free red bull, I'm sipping on a glass of whisky. Something I rarely ever touch. But it feels appropriate.

Feeling slightly tipsy, I turn to Danny and blurt out, "According to my mother, the first words I ever said were 'I don't care.'" Danny lets out a laugh and replies, "I believe that.". Then he looks at me with those concerned eyes of his and asks, "Are you okay?" And for a moment, I hesitate.

Obviously, I'm not, and he knows that, so I just reply with a simple, "Yeah, dude."

Lost in thoughts, my eyes wander across the bar, and that's when I spot a face that looks oddly familiar. It's the guy I used to work with, the one whose name I never remembered, Co-worker dude. This has been bugging me for years, and I don't care about the potential awkwardness of the situation. Determined, I make my way over to him, and as soon as our eyes meet, he exclaims, "Richard!"

I can't believe it. This guy knows my name. I know we were introduced at some point, but still. Did he know it all along? Was it just me who forgot his? I feel like a dick and ask, "How do you know my name?"

He looks at me like I'm an idiot and says, "Well yeah, I read "Serendipity" and saw you on TV and social media."
Oh, duh. I keep forgetting that I'm more in the public eye now compared to when I worked at my old company.

Intrigued, I ask him, "And what's your name?" He tells me it's Nick, simple enough. And I feel a sense of relief that I finally have the answer. He proceeds to tell me how I unknowingly influenced his life. After our talk at the office, he got more interested in Bitcoin and web3. When the old company eventually let him go as well, it led him to start his own firm specializing in crypto investments. He says that he's never been happier. Expressing his gratitude and insists on buying me a drink. I'm glad that my little bit of wisdom could have such a profound impact on the life of a guy whose name I didn't know up until five minutes ago.

As we share our third drink, I feel a sudden wave of nausea rising in my gut, like a volcano on the verge of eruption. Mixing Phenibut and alcohol was pretty stupid. I try to suppress it, but it's too late. My body convulses, and my stomach empties its contents all over the bar, drawing the attention of everyone in the room. In the midst of my humiliation, I notice some guy filming me with his damn phone. But before I can do anything, Danny jumps up from his seat, knocking over his chair, and starts yelling at the guy. "Turn that fucking thing off!" he screams. But the dude keeps filming, ignoring Danny's threats, which is a mistake. In response, Danny's fist flies, and it lands square on the guy's jaw. I hear the thud of the punch, and the guy drops like a sack of potatoes. Fight club style.

The next thing I know, my vision is swimming, and my mind is blank. It's like someone hit the reset button on my consciousness.

Then, I can hear a voice echoing through the darkness. "Richard, are you okay?"

When people keep asking if you're okay, then you may not be.

30

Watching the rain pour down on Seattle, I realize that despite the gloom and dreariness, I actually missed this shitty weather. As I step inside my mother's apartment, the familiar sweet aroma that once filled the air has been replaced with the pungent residual stench of gas, filling me with unease. It's strange how the smell of a place can have such an impact on your emotions. It's almost as if the very essence of her home has transformed in the blink of an eye.

While I start navigating past the debris of her life, I'm hit with an overwhelming sense of nothingness. The apartment surrounds me with an eerie silence, except for the monotonous sounds of the ticking of the clock and the rhythmical clacking noise of the radiator every few minutes. It's like she's still here, but she's not, and the quiet is overwhelmingly loud. It feels like walking through a museum exhibit, one dedicated to the life of my mother. Each item tells a story of her joys and sorrows. But it's not all nostalgia and reminiscing. The harsh reality sets in as I come across items that serve as stark reminders of her struggles—dozens of empty alcohol bottles. Some of them are tucked away in the depths of cabinets and corners, while others are lurking behind curtains.

Then, I stumble upon a large box hidden within a closet. Inside is an old projector accompanied by several reels of 8 mm film. With labels on them, each one marked with a different vacation destination or holiday. The dust-coated films serve as ancient time capsules, encapsulating long-forgotten secrets and memories of the past.

Taking a seat on the couch, I find it strange to be in this apartment without her. I can't remember a time when her TV wasn't on, filling the room with noise. To my right sits her laptop, still and silent; it held such "importance" to her, yet she never used it again after I fixed it. I know I should start going through the boxes and items, but I remain stuck in this limbo, feeling engulfed in a whirlwind within myself. Finally, I force myself to start, to not miss anything that might be important.

There's just so much stuff here, and it seems wrong to be rifling through someone's personal belongings like this; it feels intrusive, like I'm trespassing on her privacy. But I remind myself that this is the last time I'll be in this apartment, my last opportunity to gather the pieces of my mother's life and put them together.

And then, nestled within a small box, I find an envelope. Inside is a letter, and as I read it, I'm filled with a mixture of shock and confusion. It's a suicide note from my father. I had no idea he took his own life. It's like a bomb has gone off, shattering my understanding of my family history. Suddenly, the years-long struggle that my mother had with his life insurance makes sense.

As I hold the suicide note in my hands, I sense a strange mix of emotions swirling inside me, and I can't quite grasp what I'm feeling. Is it shock? Is it anger? Maybe too much time has passed, or perhaps I'm just so numb from everything that I can't even process this revelation. It's almost like my brain is trying to protect me from the magnitude of it all.

The last thing I take is the vase I got for my mother. With the final boxes loaded up into my car, I stand at the threshold of her apartment and take one last look around. At the now-empty rooms that were once filled with memories and my mother's presence. But it's time to move on. Maybe one final memory. Hold your breath. Freeze Frame. Click. With a heavy heart, I close the door behind me, the sound echoing through the empty hallway. I take a deep breath and start to make my way down the stairs.

I can't really tell you why I kept my apartment here, or my old shitty car for that matter. Maybe, deep down, it's the thought that if everything falls apart in LA, I can always retreat back to my old life. The thought of failure lingers in my mind like a shadow, but It's like a safety net that I know is there, even if I hope I never have to use it.

As I carry the boxes up to my floor, the weight of everything hits me all at once. I'm exhausted, both physically and mentally. Pushing open the door, I step into my apartment, greeted by the familiar, stale air. I drop the boxes on the floor with a thud and take a seat on the couch. For a moment, I simply sit there. Scrolling through my phone, I come across the photo of my mother and me at LAX. It's a bittersweet memory, but I feel compelled to share it with the world, so I post it on Instagram before reaching for the remote control. Turning on the TV, I look for something to fill the void. After all, it's Christmas Eve, so I should probably watch *Home Alone.* As the screen comes to life, I notice that the white spot on it has grown again, and it's even more noticeable now. It's like a cancer, slowly consuming the panel. The more I stare at it, the more it feels like it's staring back at me, taunting me with its existence.

I start the movie, and the theme music fills the room. The nostalgic melody transports me back to my childhood, and for the first time in days, I don't have to think about the fact that my mother died. I can actually breathe without feeling like the air is made of concrete.

But then the TV starts to flicker, the screen pulsating on and off like a frenzied strobe light. The flickers intensify, growing more frequent and violent, accompanied by a buzzing sound, until the image goes completely black. Leaving me in the dark, both literally and figuratively. It's like the universe is playing a sick joke on me, trying to tell me that I should leave this fucking place behind. Or maybe it's just a malfunctioning device, and I'm reading too much into it.

I jump off the couch, snatch the faulty television and lower it to the floor. I then reach over and grab one of my mother's boxes, feeling its weight in my hands– the one containing the projector. I unpack it, pulling out the pieces and arranging them on the coffee table. I pick a random reel with no label, no indication of what's on it. And without thinking, I feed the filmstrip into the machine.

The projector starts, and the reel begins to turn, casting a glimmering light against the wall. The footage is in black and white, with no sound. I see a six-year-old version of myself, running through the house, toys in hand, giggling and carefree. The image is haunting, almost ghostly, and it's as if I'm watching a stranger's memories rather than my own. Fuck, I want to be six years old again. I miss the simplicity, when my biggest problem was how to convince my mother to buy me those damn Ninja Turtles action figures. When all I had to worry about were Saturday morning cartoons and which cereal to eat for breakfast. I feel envy for my younger self, with his innocence and carefree attitude. He doesn't know what's coming, what to expect, and that is exactly why he can feel that way.

And suddenly, there she is, projected onto my wall: my mother. Young, beautiful, and brimming with happiness. It feels like she's here with me, and I sense tears welling up in my eyes. She was always so strong, even when life was tough. But now, with the knowledge about my father's death and the way she had to deal with it all on her own, I see her as even stronger. My heart aches with love and loss, and I wish I could go back and tell her how much she meant to me. But it's too late now. All that remains are these flickering images on my wall and the memories that they bring.

My thoughts are abruptly interrupted by the buzzing of my phone on the table. I grab it and see a text from Maria. "Richard, I just saw your post; I am so sorry. I am here for you if you want to talk."

I think for a split second, but I give in to my impulse and type out a quick reply. "Thank you, I appreciate it,"

Yes, I am well aware what it means to give in to a narcissist, giving them the very thing they crave - attention. To feed the monster. But right now, at this moment, sitting alone in my apartment on Christmas Eve, I just don't give a fuck. Maybe she's changed; she may not be the same person she was before. Or maybe I'm just desperate for any kind of familiar connection in this world that feels so painfully isolated.

The constant clatter of the projector became my background noise. As I watch reel after reel, lost in a world of black-and-white memories. But eventually, the images become unbearable, and I have to turn it off. Collapsing onto my bed, tired from the turmoil of the day. I reach for my phone and start watching *Home Alone* on it. Tossing and turning, trapped in this endless loop of thoughts and emotions until finally, exhaustion overtakes me, and I drift off into an uneasy sleep.

Fade out.

31

asting my life seems to be taking forever. It's Christmas day, and the tradition persists. The destination remains the same, but it sure as hell doesn't feel the same. And this time, I'm alone. The air is frigid, and my breath creates a cloud of fog in front of me as I walk through the cemetery gates. It's been a year since my last visit, but now I'm faced with two graves, instead of one. And to make matters worse, the disillusionment about my father's death has become an unwelcome guest in my already burdened heart. Standing here feels like a bad dream, making me realize the gravity of what I've lost.

Why is it that whenever someone dies, our minds automatically go to the last time we saw them? What did they say? What did we say? It's like we're just playing a fucked up game of memory, trying to piece together some sort of narrative to make sense of it all. But does any of it really matter in the end? Does it change the fact that they're gone? No, it fucking doesn't. Suddenly, all those little things we used to worry about or made us angry seem so insignificant. It's all just noise. And we're left here, standing in a cemetery, wondering what it all meant, if it meant anything at all.

Since replying to Maria's message last night, she and I have kept up with our casual texting, but let's be real - there's nothing casual about it. There's a weight, a heaviness to each message. And somehow, the simple act of communicating with her in the midst of all this chaos makes it all a little more tolerable. It's like I'm reaching for something familiar, something that I know, even if it's not the best thing for me.

But despite our complicated past, the thought of meeting her for coffee when I'm back in LA is strangely comforting.
It seems we share an unspoken understanding that we're both damaged goods, and that makes it easier to connect.

As I stand here, staring at the two graves, I feel like I've fulfilled my obligation to the tradition. I take a deep breath, then finally turn to leave the cemetery. The sound of my footsteps reverberates in the stillness like a solitary heartbeat. While walking through the rows of headstones, I realize that I'm the only one here. Everyone else is out there with their families, enjoying the holiday festivities.

I hear a plane pass above me and wish I was on it. But where do you go if you don't want to be anywhere?
Back at my place, I'm listening to old Christmas Music on my phone. Trying to force myself into the holiday spirit, but it's not really working. It's like trying to perform a lobotomy on myself. I still feel like shit. Reaching for my bottle of Phenibut, the little capsules that make everything feel a little less heavy, only to find that it's empty. Fuck. Despite being an unregulated supplement,

it's not something I can simply purchase at a pharmacy–I have to order it online. But then, a glimmer of hope, I remember the small gift Emily gave me "for emergencies ."A couple of 2 mg bars of Xanax. And if this isn't an emergency, what is? Right now, my brain could really use a warm hug. I hesitate for a moment, weighing the consequences, but then I break off a quarter and pop it into my mouth without another thought.

Merry fucking Christmas.

32

I spent most of the holidays alone, my only companion being my mother's laptop. I watched a marathon of Christmas movies on it and devoted the remainder of my time to writing. The days flew by one after the other, and before I knew it, the holidays were over. But when I write, something strange happens. It's like I'm bending time to my will, manipulating it to fit my needs. Hours can fly by in what feels like seconds, while days can stretch on endlessly. That's my superpower. I wrote over 80 pages that I'm fairly happy with, or maybe they are complete bullshit. Who knows? But it might be said that the most profound and beautiful creations often emerge from the abyss of agony, so here I am.

After my Instagram post the other day, my inbox was flooded with DMs yet again. Among the messages were local women from Seattle; some of them claimed I was their "favorite writer," ready to meet up. I couldn't resist the temptation to have a little fun and use it as a distraction from my self-pity. So, I decided to invite some of them over in between my writing sessions. And I don't see anything wrong with it. They must have felt the same kind of loneliness that I felt during the holidays. So we distracted each other. It's an honest transaction, nothing more, nothing less. They got to have sex with their "favorite writer," and in return, I enjoyed a bit of company.

Feeling numb from the benzo, I'm walking through the chilly Seattle streets. It's freezing out here, but I like it. As I stroll past the *Secret Garden* bookstore, I notice my self-published novel displayed in the window. Below it, a sign reads, "Soon to be a major motion picture - We're proud of our local writers," and that makes me happy. No matter how chaotic things become, I never want to forget where I come from. Then, I spot something even better. Right next to my book is another one, titled *Art in Your Heart* by Laura Barlowe–the woman who shared her work the last time I was here. The very same Laura whose words stirred something within me that I couldn't quite describe, and seemingly, my words had a similar impact on her. Finally, true Art found its way to the public, and her work gets the recognition it deserves. Seeing her book next to mine fills me with so much joy.

I step inside the store, determined to buy a copy of Laura's book. And the first thing that hits me is the sudden rush of people and voices. It's Friday, I realize. Even right after the holidays, the place is teeming with writers eager to showcase their latest work.

Approaching the "Local authors" table, I see Laura's *Art in your heart* proudly positioned in the center of it. As I reach for it, a young woman's voice interrupts me.

"Excuse me, are you Richard Bryght?" she asks, with a hint of nervousness in her voice.

I turn to her and nod, offering a smile, "Yes, that's me."

She introduces herself as Amber, her face lighting up as she pulls out a copy of my book from her bag and timidly asks if I could sign it for her. Of course, I oblige. As I'm signing the book and realize once again how terrible my handwriting is, she asks me a question that catches me off guard. "Why is your book called *Serendipity*?"

I pause for a second, thinking about my answer. It's simple enough, but no one has ever asked me that before. I quickly compose myself and tell her, "It's my favorite word in the English language. And that's what the novel is all about - life's unexpected twists, turns, and serendipitous moments that make it all worthwhile."

I'm handing the signed book back to her, and she thanks me for both the autograph and the answer to her question. I notice a glimmer in her eyes as if she's star-struck by my presence. It's crazy to me; I'm just little ol' Richard. In a way, I'm still the same guy I was when I was 12, nothing special. But it's endearing, and I guess that's the power of Art—you never know the impact your work might have on others. I watch as Amber walks away, her steps light and her smile wide, but she still appears somewhat nervous.

Then I navigate to the row of chairs in front of the podium, settling into a seat for the evening's readings. Glancing around, I notice that some of the other writers seem to recognize me— which is still new and a strange experience. The anxiety keeps gnawing at me, clawing at my insides like a rabid animal.

Instinctively, my hand reaches for the Xanax bottle, quickly breaking off half a bar and swallowing it down, hoping it will calm me. Suddenly, people start clapping, and I raise my eyes to see Amber at the podium, a piece of paper in her trembling hands. Then I realize that her earlier nervousness wasn't due to me but because of the fact that she was about to read in front of an audience.

After introducing herself, she starts reading–her voice quivers at first but soon steadies as she continues. It's evident that what she's written is personal, raw, and filled with emotion. As she reads, I find myself hanging on to every syllable, my own pain and sorrow mingling with hers. Time seems to pause, and it's just her words and the collective silence of the audience. I can feel the tears prickling at the corners of my eyes, realizing that I'm not the only one. Seeing others wiping away theirs, sniffling, and trying to keep their composure. And then, as she finishes, the room erupts into applause. Not just for the bravery it takes to stand up and read something so personal but also for the connection we all felt through her pain. It's as if we've all lost something, and for a moment, we bear this burden together. As Amber steps down from the podium, our eyes meet–I can see the glistening moisture in hers, and I reciprocate her emotion with a thumbs-up and a nod. In that exchange, I sense a mutual understanding and connection between us. It's like we're both a little less alone in our grief. Her words ignited something inside me, like a fire in my belly, and I know what I have to do. I have to reveal something personal as well.

The cemetery is cloaked in darkness, and I can hardly make out the words on the tombstone. Yet, I'm back in front of my parents' grave, driven by the urge to be raw. I reach for my phone, and the artificial light casts an eerie glow on the burial sites around me, cutting through the darkness like a blade. My fingers tap on the screen, scrolling through my notes until I find the words that have been brewing inside me. With shaking hands in the cold air, each visible breath a testament to the frigid temperature, I clear my throat and start reading. The words pour out of me like a river of emotion.

"Dear Mom, the other day, I visited the cemetery alone, trying to keep our tradition alive. I can't believe you're gone. It still feels like a sick joke, as if you're hiding somewhere, waiting to pop out and surprise me. But that's not the case, is it? It's reality, and you're not coming back. Leaving you in Seattle to pursue my writing dreams in LA was a necessary evil, but it's hard not to feel guilty about it. I suppose I succeeded, but at what cost? Was it worth it? Your memory was erasing itself daily while I was typing away in the sun.

You were always my biggest supporter, my number one fan. In a way, everything I wrote was for you—it just took me this long to actually acknowledge that. Here's something I didn't tell you, I wanted to buy you a house to repay you for all the love and support you gave me over the years. But fate has a way of laughing at our plans.

Regarding Dad's suicide... I'm aware of it now, and I understand why you kept it from me. You were shielding me. I wish I could have been there for you more, Mom. But know this, you were the most important person in my life–and I love you. I really hope you did find the light.
Richard"

By the time I finish, I'm gasping for breath, tears streaming down my face. The words, heavy with the weight of all the things I never got to say, linger in the air. But somehow, reading them out loud in the darkness of the cemetery makes it feel like she can hear me. Like maybe, just maybe, she's still there with me, listening to every word. I pause, staring at the graves as if I'm waiting to get some kind of a sign that my message has been received.

Follow your heart, and you will die every day.

DANIEL RUCZKO

PART III

33

Returning to LA feels like coming home to a dysfunctional family: they drive you crazy, but deep down, you know you can't live without them. As soon as I step out of LAX and inhale the air, heavy with smog and aspirations, I feel as if I'm back where I belong.

Back in the land of broken promises and shattered dreams, where everyone is just one audition, one script, one deal away from making it big. Sure, it may be colder than usual for Los Angeles in January, but it's still a vast improvement from the gray, rainy Seattle skies I left behind.

The Uber pulls up to the curb. I step out, feeling the familiar warmth of California greeting me once again. The sun shines, the palm trees sway in the breeze—it's good to be back. As I approach the house, I notice how quiet it is. Danny must still be sleeping, so I try not to wake him. He went back to Los Angeles after our little "bar incident." And despite it being Christmas, I wanted some alone time to sort through my mother's things as well as my own emotions.

I head to my room, drop my bags and collapse onto the bed. My phone vibrates in my pocket, and I see a text from Maria, checking if I made it back to LA okay. I quickly reply, confirming that I did. I decide to take my last Xanax bar, fishing it out of my carry-on. As the pill dissolves on my tongue, I close my eyes, letting the drug do its work. It's been a long trip; I'm exhausted and instantly drift off to sleep.

I wake up to the sound of my phone ringing; reaching for it, I see that I've slept for five hours straight. Emily's name flashes on the screen. Still groggy, I answer, "Hey,"

"Hi!" Emily says, "Are you back in LA?"

"Yeah, I'm back."

"That's great! Listen, my friend, and I are going to this rave in downtown tonight. We thought you might want to come with us. It'll be fun—a little reunion!"

I hesitate. The last thing I want to do is go to a crowded club. "I don't know, Em. I'm not really feeling it after the shitty holidays in Seattle."

"Come on, we'll take care of you and cheer you up, I promise!" Emily insists.

I sigh, giving in. "Alright, fuck it. Let's do it."

As I hang up, I decide to ask Danny if he wants to come with us. I knock on his door, but there's no answer. Perhaps he's asleep, or maybe he's gone out. I try knocking again, but still nothing. Looks like it's just going to be me and the girls tonight. It could be worse. My spirits remain low, but the show must go on. I shrug it off and prepare for the night.

Upon arriving at the club, called 1720, I see the line outside is already insane. The heavy beats from inside are reverberating through the walls and into the night air. As I approach the line, I spot Emily and her friend waving at me. They both look breathtaking, with their hair perfectly styled and their outfits accentuating all the right curves. Nothing about their looks is a coincidence. Emily instantly wraps her arms around me. "I'm sorry about your mom, babe," she whispers into my ear before giving me a soft kiss on my lips. It's a small gesture, but it means the world to me. Emily quickly introduces me to her friend April who, without hesitation, smiles and gives me a hug. We hit it off immediately.

With a sly grin, Emily declares, "We're your dates for the night," as April enthusiastically nods in confirmation. They each take one of my arms, and we head towards the entrance with confidence. I feel lucky to be in the company of these two beautiful women—maybe this is exactly what I needed.

As we approach the bouncers, Emily secretly slides a pill into my palm, barely acknowledging the action as she continues to walk. She flashes me a swift look. I know what it is; I don't even have to ask. Without a second thought, I pop the pill into my mouth, feeling like a total junkie.

Thanks to Emily, our names are on the guest list, so we're able to bypass the line and walk right in. The club is like a dark warehouse, with exposed pipes, flashing strobe lights, and a sound system that could awaken the dead. It looks like a scene straight out of a dystopian movie. The beats are pounding so hard I can feel them deep in my chest. It's a physical force that's taken over me. The DJs are playing Half Time Drum & Bass and dubstep throughout the night. The heavily distorted low frequencies intertwine with the thumping drums, creating a crazy sonic experience.

One guy recognizes Emily and April as adult film stars and asks for a photo. He's obviously nervous, fumbling with his phone. The two are total pros, posing for the shot with their arms around each other. But as soon as the photo is taken, their attention turns back to me. It's like they're both hyper-focused on making sure I'm having a good time.

All around us, people are dancing and sweating, the air thick with the smell of alcohol and body odor. I glance over to Emily and April, who are passionately making out with each other. The strobe lights flicker and blaze, illuminating their faces and bodies as the bass sounds vibrate through the club. It's a captivating scene.

Emily catches me watching them and shoots me a quick glance before she pulls me in with a smile. Without hesitation, she presses her lips against mine, and I feel her tongue sliding into my mouth. Soon, another pair of lips join in–it's April. Her mouth is hungry and aggressive, and I can feel her hands going down my body. Our lips meet in a continuous cycle—mine, then Emily's, then mine again. I can feel the eyes of strangers on us, but I'm too caught up in the moment to give a shit. I'm in the middle of some kind of fantasy come to life. I notice some people taking pictures or videos to post online, but none of us care. The music mixed with the Xanax hugging my brain and the sensation of kissing two gorgeous women simultaneously, everything becomes a blur.

I can feel Emily's breath on my ear as she whispers, "Let's get out of here." Before I can even respond, she and April are pulling me toward the exit. We maneuver through the crowd, bodies pressing against us, finally making it out to the cool night air. We jump into an Uber; our make-out session continues almost immediately. Suddenly, Emily pulls out more pills from her purse and puts one into my mouth. I don't even bother to ask what it is— I simply swallow it down, feeling the rush of chemicals hitting my bloodstream. Both girls take one as well.

Before I know it, we've arrived at Emily's place in Santa Monica. I stumble out of the car and into her apartment, the girls leading me along like a lost puppy on Molly. Fuck, why did I just think, Molly? This doesn't feel like Xanax. I turn to Emily and ask her what she gave us, but I already know the answer before she could even open her mouth. It was fucking Molly. But whatever.

We make our way to the bedroom. Emily and April take turns kissing me and each other, their hands exploring every inch of my body. As the Molly hits us, time seems to lose all meaning. The next few hours are like an x-rated hazy dream, a blur of sex and drugs, body parts, and oral pleasures. This isn't my first threesome, but it's my first one with two porn stars, and on Molly, no less.

One thing is for sure, Emily kept her promise to take care of me.

But is this really the level of intense stimulation required to blank out my mother's death for a few hours?

If so, then I'm in trouble.

As the night wears on, the drugs start to wear off, and the sun begins to rise. I peel my eyes open, the stale taste of guilt and the lingering ghosts of last night's escapade mingling in my throat. My head is pounding, a relentless jackhammer threatening to split my skull in two. I gently move the two naked bodies next to me aside and reach for my phone. The alerts are blowing up, demanding my attention. Instagram, the cesspool of our generation's narcissism. I scroll through the endless stream of notifications. Another video, another photo - Emily, April, and I, making out at the club like there's no tomorrow. It's all over social media. But I don't care. Not really.

Then I see a message from Maria, pulling me back to reality: "It looks like you had a good night :) When do you want to grab coffee?"

I remind myself that I shouldn't give a shit about what she thinks. After all, she could be happily married with three kids and a dog named Charlie by now. We haven't been in each other's lives in years. I don't regret last night at all. I'm a little fucked up right now and simply wanted some distraction. So I shouldn't fucking care.

But somehow, I do.

When the music changes, so does the dance

34

Over two years have passed since I've last seen Maria. Two years of silence and distance that I never thought we'd break. And now, here I am, about to meet her for the first time in what feels like forever. I have no idea what to expect. Is she still the same person I knew? Fuck, I hope not. I know I'm not the same. Our initial plan was a casual coffee meet-up, but then Maria suddenly switched the location to a bar, asking if that was okay. Yep, that is what narcissists do, as she wants to be the one in control.

I step out of the Uber and take a deep breath, trying to savor the cool breeze of the evening air. The bar Maria picked is right on Sunset Boulevard, with neon lights illuminating the front entrance. The atmosphere feels nice, but my anxiety keeps creeping up on me, always lurking in the back of my mind like a shadow. The allure of taking a Xanax is tempting, but I'm out of pills, and I know I shouldn't rely on them too much.

I walk into the bar, trying to locate her, but it seems like she hasn't arrived yet. The place is packed, every seat taken, people spilling out onto the sidewalk. It's a cool-looking bar, mostly made of wood - dark oak, I think. A nice contrast to the metal accents and glass panels scattered throughout the space. Despite the chaos, I manage to find an empty booth near the back. I navigate through the crowd, heading straight for it. I sit down and reach for my phone.

I'm never nervous about meeting a woman, but there's something about her that still has power over me. Even though I didn't want to admit it. I look around the bar and then, as if on cue, the door swings open, and Maria walks in. Fuck. She's stunning, maybe even more so than I remember. Sure, I encounter gorgeous women in LA every day, so much that I almost get numb to it, but Maria stands out. There's just something about the way she carries herself with such confidence and charm. She's my kryptonite, and I'm fully aware.

As soon as she spots me, her smile is like a burst of sunshine that floods the entire room, and she begins to walk over. I feel a surge of excitement and anticipation mixed with a hint of nervousness. Maria used to be a model, and given her physique, it's evident why. But she is more than just a pretty face; she blends intelligence, humor, and ambition seamlessly. Yet she decided to trade in the runway for the courtroom, and from what I hear, she's been kicking ass ever since. In a city where people cling to the fantasy of becoming a model or actor to escape the monotony of their day job, she went against the grain - turned her back on the limelight. Her choice wasn't due to a lack of success but rather a calculated move.

"Richard!" she calls out to me, rushing in for a hug, and it feels like deja vu, yet so different. It's almost as if we've stepped into a parallel universe where everything seems possible. As she pulls away and takes a step back, her eyes scan my body. "Wow, you look fucking hot!" she exclaims. I return the compliment and take a moment to soak it all in. We chat like old times as if all the heartache and the last two years of silence never happened. She's effortlessly charming; it's like she never left. She congratulates me on my success and tells me how proud she is. It feels genuine. I didn't really think about reconnecting with her in that way.

Yet, my eyes briefly dart to her hands, searching for any sign of a ring. But damn, she's got so many on, it's hard to tell which, if any, could be a wedding ring. Is she married? Divorced? Single? Who knows. It's like trying to decipher a secret code, and I'm not sure if I want to know the answer.

Deciding to let it go, I focus on the present moment, enjoying the company of this woman who I never thought I'd see again.

I sit here, listening to her talk, occasionally feeling her hand brush against mine. The magnetic pull she has on me is undeniable, but I'm trying to keep my cool. We talk about everything and anything, exchanging questions and stories with natural ease. The wine flows, and so does the conversation. Amidst the small talk and catching up, she suddenly pauses and gives me a look of sympathy. "I'm so sorry about your mother," she says softly. I simply nod, murmuring a quiet "thank you."

I have a philosophy when it comes to asking too many questions, a kind of "less is more" approach. If someone wants me to know something, they'll tell me, and if they don't, well then, it's probably none of my damn business. But then, Maria challenges that very philosophy with a pointed question: "So, are you dating one of the two porn stars?" I chuckle and try to play it off, telling her that the two are simply friends, nothing more. She lets out a laugh and says, "You've got some nice friends."

My anxiety intensifies. And she shifts her attention to me, sensing that something is off. We always had this mutual ability to read each other's thoughts and feelings like a book. Straight away, she asks me, "What's up?". Reluctantly, I admit that I've been struggling with anxiety lately. She's quick to pull out her Xanax bottle, which seems to be a common accessory in this city. "Do you want one?" she asks, offering me a small white bar. I stare at it, turning it over in my hand.

She looks at me, her expression filled with understanding. "It's okay. Keep it and take it when you need it," She says" And you know what, just keep the entire bottle. I have more at home," And hands it over to me.

I take the bottle, feeling a mix of gratitude and unease. But in the blink of an eye, the weirdness dissipates. We carry on talking and laughing, losing track of time, until we eventually realize that the night has reached its end. As we step outside to wait for an Uber, Maria thanks me for the evening. Then, she takes my hand and looks at me with those piercing eyes. "Can we do this again soon?" she asks, her voice soft and sincere.

I want to say yes immediately, but I'm a cautious person. I need to know her situation first. So, I hesitate for a moment, but then I finally say: "Yeah, sounds good."

In the next instant, something shifts in the air. Maria's expression changes, her voice quivers as she hesitates, attempting to gather her thoughts before finally speaking. "There's something else I need to tell you," she says, and the tone of her voice alone makes my heart drop. I can see that something is weighing heavily on her, and it's not just the influence of the alcohol. This is not going to be an easy confession for her. Tears fill her eyes, and it's eating away at her. She hesitates once more before starting. "You were always so good to me; you deserve to know," she says, her voice breaking.

Reaching out, I wrap my arm around her, trying to offer some comfort. "What is it?" I ask softly, hoping to ease the tension.

And then, finally, she blurts it out between sobs. "I'm so sorry. When we were dating, you were right. I cheated on you. Please don't hate me, but I HAD to tell you."

My mind is racing, struggling to process what I just heard. Back then, she called me crazy, paranoid, and jealous. Anger and betrayal mix within me, yet there's also a sense of relief that the truth is finally out in the open, confirming what I always suspected. But it may be too late for that to matter. Why would she confess that now? Was this the whole reason she wanted to meet? Countless questions swirl in my mind, but I can't bring myself to ask any of them.

Maria sobs uncontrollably, apologizing profusely for the bombshell she just dropped on me. My heart feels heavy as I try to digest the news, but at the same time, I appreciate that she had the courage to come clean. All I can manage to say is, "It's okay."

As the Uber pulls up, Maria hesitates. She looks at me with pleading eyes, hoping for some kind of forgiveness.

"You should hop inside," I say calmly, "We'll talk." Nodding through her tears, she climbs into the car and drives away with a final sob. I stare blankly at the empty street, my mind overwhelmed by a whirlwind of thoughts. I reach for the bottle of Xanax in my pocket, unscrew the cap, and shake out a single pill before quickly popping it into my mouth.

Your favorite person has the potential to become your least favorite person.

35

You can dance with drugs all you want but don't forget they lead the waltz. I know that my Xanax consumption has been a little extreme lately, and the fact that Maria casually gave me an entire bottle, doesn't really help the situation. A lot of times, It's easier to say yes, than no. I've also noticed that Xanax stifles my creativity. Whenever I try to write while under its influence, it feels as if my brain has been put in a straight jacket. So to move away from benzodiazepines, I've ordered Phenibut online.

I'm on my way to meet Alessa to discuss the book release. Danny was supposed to roll with me, but at the last minute, he texted me, saying he'll meet me there. Since I returned to LA, our communication has been reduced to a mere stream of texts. Nothing happened; he just spends a lot of time in his room, sleeping. It's like we're two strangers living in different time zones, even though we're in the same damn house.

Entering Alessa's office lobby, I'm greeted by the sight of Tara's beaming smile. These past few months have been a cluster-fuck of emotions, but finally, something positive is starting to come together.

Inside her office, Alessa is pacing around, her eyes bright with excitement. "Richard! So good to see you," she says, giving me a quick hug before gesturing to the leather chair in front of her desk. As we sit down, Alessa launches into the good news. "So, the publisher is fast-tracking the re-release of your book; they want it to be out before the movie," she says, leaning back in her chair. "We're looking at a release date in three months."

Three months? That's insane. But even as we make progress, I can't shake the feeling that something is missing. Danny was supposed to be here, but he's nowhere to be found. He's my manager, after all, and this is a pretty big deal.

"Wow, that's amazing," I reply, struggling to contain my excitement. "I can't thank you enough for making this happen." Alessa smiles and waves a dismissive hand. "It's what I do," she says, as if it's no big deal.

We dive into the nitty-gritty details of the book release: the cover art, the marketing strategy, and interviews. Alessa has thought of everything, and I feel like I'm in capable hands.

She smiles, and I can see that she's genuinely happy for me. "We're going to make this book a bestseller, Richard. You just wait and see."

My head is spinning with all the details she just laid out for me, but I'm blown away by Alessa's organizational skills and her ability to make everything look effortless. Then comes the dreaded question, "What's next?" She wants to know what I have planned for my next project, even before the first one is released.

I sheepishly admit to having jotted down some ideas over the holidays, but don't have a solid concept yet. She says, "I'm sure it'll come to you organically soon."

Since my mother's passing, I've been on autopilot, but I know I need to snap out of it. I don't take my current life for granted. Not for a second. I've worked my ass off to get where I am today, and the last thing I want to do is fuck it all up. The one thing I have control over is my work, and I'll try to focus on that. Each constructed paragraph becomes a stepping stone, a breadcrumb trail leading me back to the land of the living.

I won't fuck it up.

I won't fuck it up.

I won't fuck it up.

As I rise to leave, Alessa interrupts me with a final piece of news. "Oh, and Richard," she says, a mischievous grin spreading across her face. "We're in talks to get a segment of your book published in Playboy magazine."

Playboy magazine? The very same publication that adorned teenage dreams, a forbidden fruit shared in secret by adolescent hands. Despite the fact that I've had sexual encounters with a woman gracing its cover, I never thought I'd see my own work within those iconic pages, never imagined my words would mingle with the scent of cologne samples and the seductive gazes of centerfolds. The connection between my teenage self and the man I am today collides with a perverse synchronicity.

I try to maintain my composure, to play it cool, but I can feel a grin threatening to split my face in two. "That's... that's incredible, Alessa. Thank you." I say, with excitement evident in my demeanor. "I'll keep you updated on that front," she says before waving me off. She does not fuck around.

Stepping out of Alessa's office, I'm still riding the high of the surreal news she just shared. As I stroll to my car, my pocket buzzes with an almost rhythmic alert. It's Maria. Her name illuminates the screen, accompanied by the words "How are you?" staring back at me. Simple but loaded with layers of unspoken meaning.

I can't lie—meeting with her left me confused. Her daily text messages are starting to wear on me. I can sense the guilt that seeps through each pixelated word like a thick, viscous layer that clings to my consciousness. But what am I supposed to do with that? It's not that simple. Sliding into the driver's seat, the urge for a Xanax gnaws at me, insistent and unrelenting, like an itch that demands to be scratched. The thought of that tiny pill, solace offering temporary relief, lures me with a seductive whisper.

But I'm smarter than that; I need to preserve my creativity, no numbing allowed.

Arriving at home, Danny is nowhere to be found.

Undeterred, I head straight to the game room and fire up the PlayStation 2. The familiar hum and glow of the screen serves as a reminder that sometimes, the best way to escape is by immersing yourself in another world, far from the grasp of chemical crutches. After all, this is what we set this room up for. The room with no tomorrow, my escape from the outside world, where you leave your problems by the door.

How many days have we already wasted freaking out over things that "could" happen? But most likely, never will. All those horror scenarios our brains come up with, as if we're torturing ourselves for no reason. We must shift our focus to the present and let go of all that unnecessary worry. It's like that old saying goes - "don't worry about the future; it hasn't happened yet." So fuck that.

I choose to embrace the present moment, on the simple pleasure of playing *Silent Hill 2*. Simply because I fucking can, my career is going great, and we all have to hit "pause" on life from time to time to let our mind rest for a few hours. This isn't avoidance; it's essential for our survival.

I remember playing this game right after its release. Being a devoted fan of the original, I couldn't wait for the sequel.

This wasn't just a game - it was a full-blown experience. The story, the music, the sound design - everything was exceptional. It was just so different and unique.

And now, here I am 22 years later, and I'm just as excited as I was the first time around. The intro still gives me goosebumps - "In my restless dreams, I see that town, Silent Hill." It's as if the game is reaching out to me, calling me back to that nightmarish, haunted place.

But isn't it just the perfect twisted coincidence? In the realm of this game, where nothing is quite as it seems, one of the main characters just happens to share the name of the very person who's been haunting my thoughts lately–Maria, who isn't quite as she seems. I had completely forgotten about that. Back then, I could lose myself in a video game for hours on end, ignoring everything else around me. But now, even when I have the time, my mind refuses to let me sink into that world as it once did.

Perhaps it's the weight of responsibility that comes with age, the knowledge that there are always other obligations to fulfill. Or maybe it's just a sign that my brain has become too cluttered, too consumed by the demands of modern life, to fully surrender to the fantasy of a video game. But I miss that. While everyone keeps talking about mindfulness, I'm craving mindlessness.

The door creaks open, and Danny walks in like a zombie, "There he is," I say, "my manager... DJ Fluxx,". I'm relieved to see him alive, although he looks like he's been through a meat grinder. His face is a roadmap of stress and exhaustion; the bags under his eyes look like they could hold all his worldly possessions. So, I quip, "You look like shit, man."

But he ignores it all, pretending like nothing happened and as if he didn't forget about our meeting this morning. "I fucking love that game," he says, referring to *Silent Hill 2* on the screen in front of us. And for a moment, we just sit there in silence. It's strange– I've known Danny for years, and yet, lately, it feels as if we're worlds apart. He has become distant and absent.

"You missed the meeting," I say; my words come out like a punch, but I can't help it.

Danny looks like he's been caught with his hand in the cookie jar. "Fuck man, I'm sorry," he responds, and I can hear the genuine regret in his voice. Yet, it doesn't change the fact that he's been dropping the ball a lot lately.

"Are you okay? What's wrong?" I ask. It's a loaded question, I know.

Danny shrugs and gives a half-hearted chuckle before replying, "Nothing a lobotomy couldn't fix."

I look at him, really look at him for the first time, and I can see the darkness in his eyes. How could I have been so oblivious to his suffering? The signs were there, but I was too absorbed in my own shit to notice. The weight of my guilt settles in my stomach like a lead balloon. I feel like a piece of fuck.

Danny turns to me, guilt on his face. "I know I've fucked up," he admits. I want to reassure him that it's okay, but before I can say anything, he asks, "How did the meeting go?" I start my recap of everything that happened–Previously on Richard's life: the book release, the potential Playboy magazine feature–and I see His eyes light up with excitement.

"Fucking Playboy?" he says, his voice rising with enthusiasm. "That's insane!" Suddenly I can see that spark returning to his eyes.

He looks at me and says, "In a time where we are constantly bombarded with mass-produced content, designed to be consumed and forgotten right after, like shitty fast food for your mind. Yet you decide to go with the gourmet dinner and write books. The right people will appreciate that." And again, he just randomly drops a bomb like that.

His statement hits me like a wave, an unexpected surge of validation that I didn't even know I needed.

I hand him the controller, and for a while, we forget about the world outside; we hit start on the game and simultaneously "pause" on life.

Click.

36

Creativity is the fuel that keeps my engine running. It's what makes me jump out of bed before the alarm gets off and what makes me forget that 5 am is a little past my bedtime. The feeling of creating something from nothing is unmatched by anything I've experienced so far.

But now I'm sitting here, staring at a blank screen in front of me, unable to conjure anything. I never believed in writer's block; I thought it was just an excuse for lazy or wannabe writers. But now I find myself a victim of it. This feeling is new to me, and it's unsettling. The words that used to flow effortlessly from my mind to the page now feel like they're trapped inside, locked away by some unseen force. It's as if I'm suffering from creative impotence —I have the desire, the drive, but I just can't seem to get it up to produce something that feels worthwhile. Maybe it's just a phase, a temporary blip in the grand scheme of things. And perhaps it's the pressure that's weighing me down. Nonetheless, I'm desperate for a solution.

I arrive at the *Chateau Marmont*, the epitome of old Hollywood glamour, a place that has seen more stars than the night sky. Walking through the vintage and opulent lobby, adorned with plush furniture and exquisite chandeliers hanging from the ceiling, I notice the portraits of famous guests lining the walls. James Dean, Marilyn Monroe, Jim Morrison–they've all graced this place with their presence. It's like a tribute to Hollywood history.

Making my way to the back patio, I see Lana sitting at a table, exuding the charm of a Hollywood starlet with her effortless beauty and sophistication. If anyone belongs here, it's her. She looks up as I approach and flashes me a smile that could light up the whole city. We hug and catch up on our lives, discussing work and relationships, but as usual, our conversations have a tendency to steer towards the unconventional.

Lana tells me about her latest fiasco. Apparently, she had crashed into a car the other day, adding another dent to her already sky-high insurance. She explains how the guy got out of the car, and they exchanged phone numbers, a standard move in the aftermath of a fender-bender. However, the story takes an unexpected turn when she gets home, and the guy sends her a text saying, "I think I know you." Lana found herself in a unique position and ended up trading sex for lower insurance rates.

She insists it was an honest transaction and actually preferred this unorthodox solution to the alternative. The guy was able to fulfill one of his fantasies while she got away with a bargain, at least in her mind.

The benefits of being an A-list adult film star, I suppose. I laugh about her story and her unique business instinct, using sex as a form of currency.

As we sip on our drinks, I bring up my recent struggles with creativity. I explain how I've been feeling blocked and unproductive, and Lana nods in understanding. She then tells me about micro-dosing–a practice she's been experimenting with that involves taking small amounts of psychedelics to enhance creativity and focus. For a moment, I think that we probably shouldn't talk about stuff like that in public, but this is the Chateau; everyone here is probably on something.

Suddenly, she asks me, completely serious, "Do you want some Penis Envy?"

"What do you mean?" I ask, wondering if I heard her correctly.

She explains that it's a specific strain of mushroom, highly potent, but that she has microdose capsules of it.

I hesitate at first, telling her I have a photo shoot for my book in just two hours, and the last thing I want is to be tripping out during it.

But Lana assures me that micro-dosing is subtle and that I won't feel anything. It's just enough to give my mind a gentle push in the right direction. It's the kind of thing the Silicon Valley types have been doing for a while, she says, micro-dosing all kinds of psychedelics like LSD, Psilocybin, and Mescaline.

Lana hands me the green and yellow capsule, and I swallow it down with a sip of water. I wait, expecting some kind of immediate, mind-bending effect. Will the world around me suddenly be coated in vibrant, neon hues?

But even after an hour...nothing changes. The world around me remains as mundane as ever, and I feel no different than before. And that's probably the whole point.

I check my watch, realizing that my photo shoot is fast approaching. Maybe it's for the best that I'm not tripping out right now and fuck up my first real photo shoot.

I say my goodbyes to Lana, thanking her for yet another interesting encounter. Before leaving, she looks at me and says, "Let me know how you like it." I nod, then head out.

The valet brings me my car, and I hit the road, the regular scenery passing me by. Who knows, maybe one day I'll be one of the Silicon Valley types, micro-dosing my way to success. But for now, it's just another peculiar experience in the weird and wonderful world that I live in.

Arriving at the photographer's studio, which Alessa hooked me up with, I'm feeling a mix of excitement and nerves. I've never been a fan of being in front of a camera and having my photo taken, but I understand the necessity of it for promotion. Stepping out of my car, I look up at the building in front of me. The outside appears unassuming, just another old warehouse; like any other nondescript building, you'd find in this part of town. But once I step inside, it's a whole different world. The space has been transformed into a photographer's paradise. Different backdrops and scene setups are scattered throughout the modern, sleek interior, and there's a plethora of equipment -

lights, cameras, lenses, props - all meticulously organized and ready to be used.

As I enter the studio, the staff greet me like an old friend, anticipating my arrival.

And I'm acutely aware of the fact that this photographer, Charlie Shaw, has snapped pictures of every big celebrity that walks on this earth. Now, it's my turn. Charlie is a pro, no doubt about it, and he seems nice enough, but there's a certain arrogance about him that rubs me the wrong way. But I don't have to be friends with the guy, so it's not a big deal.

A staff member guides me to a changing room. Stepping inside, I spot a vibrant red couch and notice something strange. The colors appear more saturated than they should be, and now that I think about it, I'm starting to feel a little funny. Oh shit, are the mushrooms kicking in?

The thought alone sends a ripple of laughter through me, and I feel a warm, tingling sensation spread throughout my body. It's becoming increasingly difficult to suppress the idiotic grin threatening to take over my face.

My thoughts feel the same, but It's as if every color is brighter, every sound sharper, and every touch electrifying. My body feels like it's humming with energy, like a coiled spring ready to burst forth. It's really more a body high. Well, and things just seem funny.

A knock on the door interrupts my thoughts: "Richard, we're ready for you." I emerge from the room and into the bright lights of the photo studio, fighting the urge to grin like a dumbass. Charlie's assistant, a petite blonde girl with a clipboard, greets me, and I follow her like a lost puppy on Penis Envy. With every step I take, these sensations intensify. Fuck. And yes, I do see the pattern here—either unknowingly taking drugs or taking too many.

Charlie and his team are prepared, and I take my place in front of the camera, attempting to act as normal as possible. But the very act of *trying* to be normal is a surefire way to fuck up. My body is betraying me, my face is betraying me, and I know I'm on a collision course with the absurd. Charlie barks instructions at me, and the more he wants me to be serious, the harder it is for me to keep a straight face. I keep apologizing, but the laughter and grinning just won't stop. It's like trying to keep a balloon from flying away in a hurricane. Every time the shutter clicks, I feel like a ticking time bomb. Charlie is yelling at me, but I can't hear him over the sound of my own laughter.
I know I'm fucking up, but there's nothing I can do about it.

He is getting frustrated, and the crew is getting antsy, but I'm not in control here. Not anymore. And in that moment, I realize that maybe, just maybe, the real me is the one who can't stop laughing, the one who can't take anything too seriously. Okay, no, it's probably just the drugs. Either this wasn't a microdose, or I'm just way too sensitive to substances like this.

But as the photographer's lens keeps capturing my altered state, I can't help but find the entire situation hilarious. I let go of my inhibitions and let the laughter take over; just embrace that shit; it's authentic. And suddenly, Charlie's scowl slowly turns into a grin, and even the staff members can't help but chuckle along with me.

With the ice broken, I don't want Charlie and the team to think I'm an asshole or that I don't appreciate their work. So, I decide to come clean. "I apologize," I say, trying to sound earnest. "I took some mushrooms - I was trying to microdose, you know, to be less nervous. Sorry, guys. It's the Penis Envy."

The room explodes with laughter, the rest of the tension dissolving as if it had never been there. Everyone seems completely understanding, and we carry on with the photo shoot. In retrospect, I probably should've told them about the mushrooms from the get-go. But now that the truth is out, the atmosphere is lighter, and we're all having a good time.

Finally, after what feels like an eternity, the photo session is over. I'm exhausted, and my face hurts from the excessive smiling. I stumble back to the changing room, feeling as if I've just run a marathon. When I catch my reflection in the mirror, I realize that I look like a cross between a clown and a maniac.

Before leaving, Charlie calls me over to his computer, showing me a few of the unedited photos. To my surprise, we actually managed to capture some shots among the chaos that are not bad at all. In fact, they're pretty damn good. For a moment, my smile fades, replaced by a look of disbelief. Charlie notices my reaction and chuckles. "Yeah, man, we got some good stuff. You look great," he says.

I've always hated taking photos, but here I am, high on mushrooms, and somehow managed to pull off a decent shoot. I suppose that's why Charlie is the professional earning $25.000 per client. Everyone in the studio appears satisfied with the outcome, their smiles genuine and wide. I express my gratitude to each person for their hard work and understanding and walk out of the studio with a peace sign.

The door closes behind me, and I step into the bright sunlight, the day's events playing out in my mind like a chaotic, surreal movie. But you know what they say, sometimes, the unplanned is what turns out best. Serendipity. Some things are just too big of coincidences to be labeled coincidences. Maybe it was serendipity that led Alessa to get me this photographer, that led me to take mushrooms, and that allowed me to be my true self in those photos. Maybe it was serendipity that led Lana to trade sex for insurance rates.

Or perhaps it was just a series of bad decisions, yet everything somehow fell into place, by serendipity.

37

f you had told me at the age of eleven that I would one day write a book that would be adapted into a movie, I would have said you were full of shit and doubled over in laughter. I wouldn't believe it. Fuck, I still can't believe it. But here I am, years later, with the remnants of that laughter still ringing in my ears. Principal photography for *Serendipity* - the movie is officially done, and tonight is the wrap party. Allen's invitation was a no-brainer - I had to attend. I wanted to bring Danny, but he didn't feel like it, so Emily becomes my plus-one for the evening. I don't know if they'll keep the name of my book for the film, but who cares, these things can change last minute.

It's been a solid two months since I've been able to write something, and the micro-dosing has certainly played its part in getting me back on track; I've perfected the dosage now, so I don't feel any weird effects - just the way it's meant to be. As an added bonus, it really seems to lift my mood, but something is still missing. Maybe I have some living to do before I can write another book. Who knows. Tonight might be a good night for that.

Emily looks stunning, as always, effortlessly sexy, with a black dress framing her slender figure perfectly. But it's her smile that truly takes my breath away.

The doors of the elevator slide open, revealing a rooftop venue, the night sky above us, the city sprawled out below. The view is both exhilarating and unnerving, and Emily and I exchange uneasy glances. We both silently hope the evening won't end with someone jumping off the edge tonight. Both, Literally and figuratively. As we walk through the door, I notice a few familiar faces from the set, and we exchange greetings. The space is open and filled with all kinds of people from the industry, the chatter and music filling the air. The lights are low, giving everything an intimate feel. And then I see Allen - he's talking to someone, but when he sees me and Emily, he excuses himself and makes his way over to us.

He greets me warmly, but his eyes quickly shift to Emily. He looks at her like he's trying to place her, "Do I know you from somewhere?" he asks.

Emily shakes her head, her lips curving up into a smile. "I don't think so," she replies, her voice smooth as silk.

"I feel like I've seen you somewhere before," he says, but Emily just shrugs it off, and I immediately know what's up. He probably knows her "work" from lonely late-night browsing sessions on the web. I think it's funny, and I know Emily doesn't care, either. She wears her profession with pride and doesn't give a fuck about the opinions of those who'd judge her. And besides - times have changed, with every other girl now having an OnlyFans account, especially in this town.

I tell Allen that we're just gonna roam around and get the vibe of this rooftop bash. Emily and I are checking out the crowd and exploring the venue. The movie is wrapped, and everyone is in a good mood. Emily had a few drinks, and I can tell from the way she giggles and flirts with me that she's feeling good. In between sips, she pulls me close and plants a kiss on my lips. This girl is something else.

I opt to stick with water since I'm driving us back later. No Benzos, no mind-altering drugs, no nothing, just plain old me. Watching Emily get a little tipsy is already very entertaining to me. She dances, she's like an Energizer Bunny, and then she comes back to me, that sly grin on her lips. "I can't wait to seduce my designated driver later," she whispers in my ear.
I just nod my head with a grin. "Thank you for bringing me here," she says, "this is so much fun."

As the night unfolds, I strike up conversations with some of the crew and various people I've met before, while Emily continues dancing, moving her body to the beat with fluid grace. Suddenly, my phone buzzes in my pocket. It's a text from Maria, and I can feel the weight of the message before I even read it. "Hey, what are you doing? Are you free to help me with something?"

I type out a fast reply, my thumbs moving quickly across the screen: "Just at a wrap party for the movie; what's up?" I hit send and turn my attention back to Emily, who's still dancing and enjoying herself. But in the back of my mind, I know that Maria's text is like a ticking time bomb, waiting to go off and disrupt this perfect evening. Maria responds right away, "Oh shit, I'm sorry; I don't want to interrupt. Have fun." She knows exactly what she's doing, and of course, I'll bite. I turn to Emily, who's now taking a break from dancing and sipping on a drink. "Hey, I gotta take care of something real quick," I tell her, holding up my phone. "I'll be right back." She nods and gives me a smile, but I can't help feeling a twinge of guilt as I walk away. I dial Maria's number, and as she answers, her voice is trembling, and her sobs are audible through the phone. "Hey, what's going on?" I ask with concern.

She replies," I really don't want to ruin your night," which is already in full motion.

But I insist on hearing her out. Finally, she tells me that she got into a massive fight with her husband and wants to leave, but he's taken the car. Well, now I can stop wondering what her situation is; this new information hits me hard. I hesitate for a moment as she apologizes for contacting me. I know she is manipulating me, but I still allow it. She says that I'm the only person she wants to see. I look over to Emily, who is dancing like a free bird again. I have to make a decision, tipsy porn star or narcissistic ex? I'm such a fucking idiot.

I think for a second before quickly saying, "Text me the address, and I'll come get you." As soon as I say the words, I feel a pang of regret. Maria has always had a way of pulling me back in.

I hang up the phone; Emily looks up at me with a curious look on her face. "Is everything okay?" she asks.

As I break the news to Emily, her expression softens. "A friend is in trouble and needs my help," I explain, trying to keep things as vague as possible.

Emily smiles at me, "You're such a good guy," she says, clearly impressed by my willingness to drop everything and go help a "friend." I can feel a knot forming in my stomach. "I'm such a dumb guy," I think to myself. I offer to call her an Uber, but she shakes her head and says she wants to stay at the party a bit longer. She flashes me a smile and assures me that she'll find her own way back. I tell her, "Just make sure no one jumps, okay?" Maybe that one was too soon, but she laughs; I give her a quick hug and tell her to text me later. I still feel guilty as I head out to help my troubled ex-girlfriend and leave Emily behind. Wondering if I'm doing the right thing.

I arrive at Maria's house, and she's already waiting for me outside. It's dark, and the street lamps cast a yellowish glow on her face. Her makeup is smeared from crying. She gets into the car and gives me a tight hug, which lingers a little longer than it should. She apologizes for calling me, but I tell her it's okay. I ask her how she's doing, but it's a stupid question.

I can feel her anxiety radiating off of her as she tells me about the fight she had with her husband. It's strange hearing all this from her, especially since we used to be together. And up until an hour ago, I wasn't even sure if she was married. I try to be supportive and tell her that everything will be alright, but I'm not sure I believe it myself. I don't know anything about them, and the truth is that relationships are complicated. They can be beautiful and fulfilling, but they can also be messy and painful. And sometimes, no matter how hard you try, things just don't work out.

Then she tells me that he's filed for divorce. Out of nowhere, she leans in for another hug, and I welcome it. But then, she kisses me. Her lips press against mine, and for a split second, I'm transported back to a time when things were simpler between us. But just as quickly, I snap back to reality. I pull away gently but firmly. She's not even divorced yet, and I'm her ex. The last thing I want is to add another layer of problems to the ones she's already facing. She apologizes again, and I can hear the regret in her voice. It's not like I don't want her too, but there are some things that are better left in the past. She's impulsive, maybe just looking for something familiar. I take a deep breath, trying to steady myself before I speak. And assure her that it's okay.

As I look at Maria, I can see that she's a wreck. It's obvious that she doesn't want to be at her own house right now. Maybe being alone in a place that reminds her of her crumbling marriage is too much to bear. So, without really thinking about it, I blurt out, "Do you want to stay at my place? We have a guest room. You can have some space and time to clear your head."

She looks up at me, her eyes red and puffy. "Are you sure?"

I nod. "Of course."

Her eyes widen in surprise. "Yeah, that would be nice. Thank you," she says softly. I fire up the engine and pull out of the driveway. The drive to my place isn't long, but it feels like an eternity with the silence hanging in the air. As we pull up to the house, she looks up and gasps in awe at the sheer size of the place. "Wow," she mutters under her breath; it's not a mansion, but still pretty impressive. I unlock the front door and lead her inside. The house is quiet and still, with only the distant hum of the AC filling the silence, no sign of Danny. I show her to the guest room, and she looks around, taking in the sights and sounds of the place.

"This is really nice," she says.

I nod, unsure of what to say.

"If you need anything, just let me know."
Her eyes meeting mine for a brief moment before she looks away. "Thank you," her voice barely audible.

Is it really a good idea to have her stay here? What if she gets the wrong idea? Fuck, what if I get the wrong idea? I leave Maria in the guest room to get some rest. It's strange to have her here, in my house, after all this time. I head to the living room, take a seat on the couch next to Salem, who is sleeping, and turn on the TV, but I'm not really paying attention to it. It's all background noise to me, something to keep me company while I process what's happening.

Moments later, Maria emerges from the guest room and walks into the living room. She stops for a second, her eyes wandering to the view outside the big window, the sprawling city of Los Angeles at night, twinkling with lights like a million fireflies. Without a word, she walks over to me and asks if I mind if she sits down. I say no, and she settles in next to me. We watch TV for a while. At some point, she leans in and rests her head on my shoulder. I could feel the weight of her head pressing against me, and for a moment, the room seems quieter.

I feel a vibration on my wrist; glancing at my watch, I see a new text from Emily. "I made it home; I hope your friend is doing better." Before I can even process the words on the screen, I feel Maria's hand slowly inching toward mine. And though I know I should, I don't fight it. I let her hold my hand, silently acknowledging that this is a mistake, but unable to resist the pull of her touch.

Reuniting with an ex is like sticking your hand in a garbage disposal and expecting a different outcome the second time around.

38

Cranking up the volume of "New York State of Mind" by Nas as I hit the streets of West Hollywood. The warm evening sun shines on my face, and I feel alive. There's something about cruising through LA with the windows down, music blasting, that never gets old. This city never sleeps, and neither do I; I just dream. I'm on my way to *Book Soup*, my favorite bookstore on Sunset Boulevard, where I have a reading scheduled for tonight. Alessa and Allen think it's a smart move to generate some hype for the upcoming movie and re-release of the book, and I'm all for it. I've chosen my favorite chapter, and I'm eager to share it with anyone who shows up.

Stepping into the bookstore, I take a moment to survey the scene. I notice a small crowd already gathered. Glancing around the room, scanning the attendees for Danny, who was supposed to be here to handle some of the logistics, but he is nowhere to be found. Once again, he has left me hanging. However, to my surprise, I catch sight of Alessa, standing at the back of the room. A small smile creeps onto my face as I make my way toward her, grateful to see someone familiar in the sea of strangers.

"You made it," I say, relieved to see her.

"Wouldn't miss it for the world," she replies with a big smile. She always knows how to get things done. With her by my side, I can finally focus on my reading. This is my first one in LA, and it feels different than the last one I did in Seattle.

Alessa leans over and asks me if I'm nervous. I reply, "A little bit." But it's the good kind of nervous–the kind that keeps you on your toes and makes sure you don't fuck up.
I look out to the gathering, and my heart skips a beat. There are more people here than I had ever anticipated.

"You would think no one gives a shit about book readings anymore," I say to Alessa, "but these people prove the opposite."

She nods and gives me an encouraging pat on the back. "You'll kill it; I know it." And damn, that makes me feel better. I mean, this is a book reading, not a UFC fight, but still, it's nice to have some moral support. Finally, an employee of the bookstore walks up and announces my name. The audience breaks into clapping, and I take a deep breath before striding up to the podium. I see a blown-up cover of my book proudly hanging next to me, daring me to fuck up. But I don't have time for doubt or hesitation. I introduce myself with a confident tone and begin to read.

My words spill out, and it's strange. I wrote them so long ago when I was a different person, and they had a different meaning. As I come to the end of the chapter, I pause, soaking in the silence. I can feel the crowd's attention fixated on me. Then I deliver my favorite line, "How are we supposed to meet and fall in 'love' if I am so fucking busy and you don't exist?"

And then the applause comes, crashing through my thoughts like a wave. I see Alessa clapping with a look of pride on her face. Gazing at the multitude of faces, I notice that some of them have brought copies of my book, hoping for an autograph. It's humbling to think that something I wrote has become important enough to these people to show up, wanting my signature. Alessa walks up to me with that smile on her face that says everything she doesn't need to say. She congratulates me and gives me a hug that feels like a cozy blanket on a cold day. Then she pulls away and says, "I have to go, but this was amazing!" as she turns to leave, I catch her last words: "Take care of your fans," accompanied by a sly wink. I give a quick wave to Alessa and watch her walk away before turning back to the crowd.

After signing the last book and exchanging pleasantries with the final fan, the bookstore empties out, leaving me to wander aimlessly amongst the shelves myself. I fucking love bookstores.

Then I hear someone saying, "You must be a big deal," I turn my head to the direction of the voice and see a brown-haired beauty staring at me, book in hand. She's gorgeous.

I reply with a chuckle, "I'm no Hemingway, just a guy who scribbles down some words, hoping they'll resonate with someone out there."

She smiles at me and continues, "Well, all these people lining up to meet you says you're not doing a shitty job."

I walk towards her and introduce myself. She tells me her name is Emilia. There's something about her scent that is intoxicating.

We start discussing books, and I can tell she's intelligent and witty. I'm intrigued by her, and the conversation flows effortlessly. She says, "I really liked the last line you read." She's got a kind of quiet confidence about her that's hard to ignore.

"Thanks," I reply," Can't take credit for it, though; I stole it from a fortune cookie."

We share a laugh, trying to keep things going; I ask her, "So, what's your story? What do you do when you're not reading in bookstores?"

She leans back, running her fingers through her hair, and tells me, "I'm a registered nurse," It's refreshing to meet a woman who doesn't fit the mold of a typical LA beauty. I was hooked the moment she said, "I'm neither a Model nor an actress," which is a rare thing to hear in this town, even though she could very well be either. Not a porn star, not a manipulative ex-girlfriend–just a normal woman from the real world, with schedules and an alarm clock that needs to be set. She's not trying too hard to impress anyone. She's just herself, and that's what makes her so intriguing to me. I don't want to beat around the bush, so I cut right to the chase and ask her what her plans are after the bookstore. She raises an eyebrow and gives me a curious look. "I don't really have any plans," she says, shrugging her shoulders. "Why do you ask?"

Trying to appear casual, I say, "Just thought maybe we could grab a drink or something. Talk more about fortune cookies."

She laughs, and damn, it's a good sound. "Sure, I could go for a drink," she pauses, "but not too long; I have to pick up my boyfriend from the airport in the morning." And just like that, the fantasy crumbles.

I ask, "LAX?" and she nods.

"You know it's serious if she picks him up from LAX," I say with a hint of sarcasm, trying to play it cool.

She chuckles, knowing exactly what I mean. "Yeah, I guess it is," she replies.

The bar is situated right by the street across from *Book Soup*. We sit at a table, the neon lights reflecting off the shiny countertop, and the smell of cigars is in the air. Emilia and I share one drink. I have no ulterior motives, no moves to make. I respect the fact that she has a boyfriend. I just enjoy her company, and I can tell she feels the same way. After a while, I sense the conversation winding down, and I know it's time for Emilia to go. I offer to call her an Uber, knowing that I don't want to be the reason she stays out too late. After all, I made her drink; the least I can do is make sure she gets home safely. She looks at me and nods her head, the slightest hint of a smile on her lips.

We step outside, the sound of car engines and laughter fills the air, a soundtrack to the city that never sleeps. As we wait, we make small talk, and I can't help but admire how down-to-earth and genuine she is. Then, I see the Uber pull up. I open the door for her and watch as she gets in and flashes me a smile, "Thank you, this was nice." Her words echo in my mind like a bittersweet symphony.

As the Uber drives off, her scent still lingers in the air. I take a moment to soak in the cool night atmosphere. I don't know how it happened, but after meeting with Maria, my words started flowing again. Maybe it's the memories of our tumultuous past that's fueling my creative juices, or maybe it's the new emotions she's stirred up inside me. But there's no denying it—something has shifted in me since we reconnected. She's like a fucked up muse, inspiring me in ways I can't quite understand. Mirror, mirror on the wall, who's the most fucked up of them all?

Turning around to face the bar, I can see a group of gorgeous women giggling and flirting with the guys around them.
I know I have a choice to make: girls or writing? Lust or creativity? Each path calling me with its own seductive voice. The attractive women at the bar are tempting, but so is the call of the blank page. Fuck it, I turn around and head to my car. The night swallows me, windows down. Neon flashes punctuate the urban orchestra of wandering souls and racing cars, beating the rhythm of the sleepless city. Parking my car, I step out onto the pavement with a sense of relief. It feels good to be home. I make my way toward the house, fumbling with my keys for a moment. It's dark and quiet when I walk in, except for the muffled sounds emanating from the game room. Danny couldn't be bothered to come to my reading, but he's got all the time in the world for

video games. I shake my head in disbelief, but I don't want to deal with this tonight. Walking to my room, the only source of light is my laptop as I boot it up. For a moment, I just stare at the blank screen. However, the words begin to flow as if they were always there, waiting to be written. The tapping of keys becomes my sole sound as I lose myself in my writing.

For me, writing is like sex; if you don't enjoy it, you're doing it wrong.

39

unyon Canyon, the hub of Instagram dreams and selfie sticks. I've only been here a handful of times, and it's like a runway for the attractive people of Los Angeles; it's almost like a social experiment, in a way, to determine who's the hottest of them all. They come here to hike and show off their toned bodies, designer sunglasses, and expensive workout gear. Today, Maria wanted to meet me, so I suggested to join me here. I try not to be alone with her too much, and a public place like this is ideal for avoiding any awkward situations. I can sense an uneasy feeling rising in my chest as I see her walking towards me in her tight yoga pants and baseball cap. She looks incredible, but I try not to show any interest.

The sun beats down on us as we begin our hike. Maria and I skillfully manage to keep the conversation light, steering clear of the landmines that are our shared history, as well as the current situation she's facing. We're both experts at this dance by now, and the small talk flows smoothly. In spite of everything, I still find a strange comfort in talking to her, as if she understands me on a level no one else does. However, I can't let myself be deceived; it's all a facade, expertly crafted to draw me in.

Suddenly, my phone rings, and Alessa is on the other end. I answer, "Hey, Alessa, what's up?".

"Hey," she says, a hint of frustration in her voice. "Do you know where Danny is? I've been trying to reach him."

I glance at Maria, who casually sips her drink, her eyes glued to me.

"No clue. Why?" I admit.

Alessa sighs heavily. "He's rescheduled our meeting twice already, and now he's not showing up.

I'm surprised and say, "I didn't even know you guys had a meeting.".

"I know you are friends, but he's really unreliable lately. I didn't want to mention it before, but it's becoming an issue." As she speaks, I can't help but think about how Danny's been holed up in his room lately, likely in the throes of a depressive episode. Offering help to a person drowning in depression is like trying to grasp smoke; they slip through your fingers, a dark cloud that resists taming. He's my best friend, and I feel fucking helpless.

"I'll talk to him when I get home," I assure her, the weight of the situation settling upon me.

"Thanks," she says, and we end the call. I slide the phone back into my pocket and turn my attention back to Maria, who studies me with a mix of concern and curiosity.

"Everything okay?" she asks, raising a perfectly arched eyebrow.

"Yeah," I say, forcing a smile. Maria and I keep talking, but my mind is miles away, fixated on the inevitable confrontation with Danny. I'm overthinking it, once again, letting it fuck up the here and now.

As we navigate the rugged terrain, we adeptly maneuver around the subject of her impending divorce and our tumultuous past, narrowing the scope of conversation to the point where it feels suffocating.

"How have you been?" I ask, trying to find a safe topic to discuss.

"I've been... managing," she says. "But work is good."

I nod and say, "I'm glad."

We walk in silence for a moment, the tension in the air thick enough to slice through. Maria stops abruptly, drawing in a deep breath as if she's preparing to dive into uncharted waters. I turn to face her, bracing myself for what's to come.

"Can I be honest?" she asks.

"Of course."

She exhales, her shoulders sagging as if she's releasing a burden she's been carrying for miles. "I have no idea what the fuck I'm gonna do," She says, her voice cracking, "and I can't really talk to anyone about it."

For a moment, I don't know what to say. And I realize that beneath her polished and confident exterior, Maria is just as lost and confused as the rest of us. "Hey," I say softly, trying to catch her gaze. "None of us really know what the fuck we're doing."

Maria chuckles. "Yeah, I guess you're right."

"You know, Danny is all about manifesting," I begin, a wry smile tugging at the corner of my mouth. "He keeps saying everything will be great as long as you believe it, and so far, he's been right. It's just hard to see when it's hailing shit sometimes." I say, laughing.

"You're such a great person," she says, her eyes cast down. "And I fucked it all up."

Her words strike a sharp pain in my chest, but I don't say anything. Part of me wants to reassure her, to tell her that it's all water under the bridge, but that would be bullshit. If that were the case, then it wouldn't feel the way it feels. Heads, I love you, tails, I don't even like you.

Just then, Maria's phone interrupts the uncomfortable silence, and I thank fuck for it. She answers the call and begins talking, but I purposefully tune her out, deciding that ignorance is bliss in this situation. I simply don't want to know more than I'm told.

After a few moments, she hangs up and apologizes, "I'm sorry, but I have to take care of something. It's a work thing."

I wave off her apology and say, "Don't worry about it."

We turn around and start making our way back, and all I can think about is how I'm just trading one uncomfortable situation for another. The tension with Maria will be replaced by the conversation I need to have with Danny once I get home. It begs the question: where do you go when you don't want to be anywhere? My Apple watch vibrates, informing me that I've reached my exercise goal, but it may very well just be my anxiety that accelerated my heart rate.

As I maneuver my way through the winding roads of Mulholland, my mind drifts off, thinking of the first weeks in LA with Danny. Everything was so new and exciting, but things have changed. He used to be my co-pilot, but now I'm mostly flying solo. And I want to change that; maybe I can help him somehow.

I pull up in front of the house, the tires of my car crunch against the gravel as I park.

Stepping inside the house, I call out, "Danny!" but receive no answer. Maybe he's out, and we can postpone this. I head towards my room, seeking refuge from the world outside. And there, on the nightstand, the small amber bottle of Xanax that Maria had given me not too long ago. I almost forgot about it. It seems to stare back at me, whispering promises of temporary relief from the mounting anxiety.

I hesitate for a moment, my hand hovering above the bottle. Then, with a quiet sigh, I pick it up, clumsily fumbling with the cap. The pill tumbles into my palm, its chalky texture contrasting against my skin. I swallow it dry, the bitter taste lingering on my tongue, preparing myself for the confrontation to come once Danny finally drags himself home. As the Xanax starts to work its subtle magic, my body relaxes, sinking into the plush comfort of my bed. Now all I can do is wait for Danny to return, mentally preparing myself for whatever storm is brewing between us. I want to support him as a friend, but his dual role as my manager complicates matters, and his fuck-ups are accumulating, making it difficult to separate the two. A door slams like a shotgun blast, yanking me off the bed and into the hallway. There he stands, my best friend, my manager—a human wreck, appearing as if he's been chewed up and spat out by life itself.

"Yo." I exclaim, and he flinches, resembling a deer caught in headlights. He acknowledges me with a trembling nod. My voice, stern but concerned, cuts through the tension, "We need to talk." We stumble toward the living room, with Danny leading the way. The stench of alcohol clings to him like a ghost of bad decisions trailing behind. The fading sunlight casts long shadows, creating an eerie stage for the inevitable showdown between friends. We sink into separate couches, facing each other, the burden of unspoken thoughts and unasked questions weighing us down. I steady myself, inhaling deeply and attempting to exude an air of calm.

"How you doing, man?" I ask gently.

He glances up, his face contorted with disbelief as if my sincere question is nothing more than a twisted joke. But there's no laughter here.

"Talk to me, man," I plead, my tone steady yet laced with the concern of a friend trying to understand. However, he remains silent, hollow-eyed, his lips pressed into a thin line. Each moment ticking by in agony as the silence stretches, making an already difficult situation even more unbearable.

"I want to help you; I want to understand," I offer, my words drifting through the tense air between us, searching for the key to restore the connection we once shared.

The room grows heavy as he opens his mouth and quietly utters those words. His voice is barely audible, and it's as if he's afraid that someone else might hear him. But I hear him loud and clear." You really wanna know how I feel?" he asks, my eyes lock onto his, and I give a slight nod. He inhales deeply, then continues, each word pouring out like a secret confession: "It's like being trapped in a never-ending nightmare," he admits, his voice trembling slightly. "The world around me loses all its color, and everything seems gray and hopeless." I witness the pain etched onto his face, and the words form a bleak, monochromatic painting of his reality. He continues, "Each dawn I die. My mind is telling me to get up, to be productive, to do something meaningful, but my body is weighed down by the crushing weight of sadness and hopelessness."

I'm left speechless. His words cut into me like a surgeon's scalpel. And in that moment, I know that I'm witnessing something raw and genuine. Something that has been festering inside him for a long time, threatening to kill him from the inside out. The words tumble out of my mouth, urgent and determined: "We need to get you some help." Our gaze remains locked, the connection between us now unbreakable, as I continue, invoking his own teachings: "You always told me everything will work out, that everything will be okay."

He replies in a defeated whisper, "No one can help me. And nothing will be okay, at least not for me."

My heart seizes up, frustration and fear clawing at my insides. I shoot back, incredulous, "So what now? You're just gonna wither away while I stand by and watch?" The words tearing into both of us. A torrent of emotions flood through me—anger, desperation, helplessness. His eyes meet mine, and for a moment, it's as if he can see the battle raging within me. And as we sit there, locked in this silent struggle, I realize that it's not just about saving him. It's about saving us both. I thought I had hit rock bottom when my mother passed away, but he appears to be in an even deeper pit. No matter how bad things are, there's always someone more fucked up than you. Which is extra painful to witness when it's your best friend.

So I take a deep breath, steel myself, and reach out to him once more, my voice steady, my determination unwavering: "We'll find a way through this. Together." I tell him, "Listen, man, you need to take a step back. You can't keep putting all your energy into managing me when you're struggling yourself."

He looks at me with eyes that betray his rage. "What the fuck are you talking about? You're gonna replace me now just because I missed a few fucking meetings? After all I've done for you?" His words, like hot acid, burn through the air.

I try to reason with him, but he is too far gone, consumed by his emotions" No, you're my brother. It's not about replacing you. It's about you taking a step back and prioritizing your own well-being. I want to help," I say calmly. But he's not even trying to hear it.

"How do you want to help me? You're the one popping Benzos and fuck pornstars to distract yourself from the ex you're not over," he retorts. Although his words cut deep, I am aware that he's projecting his pain onto me. I try my best not to take it personally." You wouldn't even be in fucking LA without me," he adds, his voice shaking. "Who was there for you when your mother died? Who's been by your side this whole fucking time?"

And, of course, he's right. Everybody wants to be around for the party, but only real friends stick around when you're a pain in the ass. He's been there for me through some of the toughest times in my life. But that's exactly what I'm trying to do for him. "That's my point," I say, "I appreciate everything you've done for me, and now it's my turn." I try to talk sense into him, but it's like talking to a wall. He's too consumed by his anger and refuses to listen to reason. "Come on, man, don't be like that; I'm trying to help you," I plead.

Abruptly, he jumps up and turns towards me, his face twisted with rage. "Fuck you! Help yourself. You're so fucking self-absorbed. Go take another Benzo." he says, throwing his hands up in the air. "I don't need this shit. I don't fucking need you." With that, he storms out of the room, slamming the door behind him.

And I'm left alone, with nothing but the echoes of his rage bouncing off the walls.

Depression is a twisted dance partner, leading its victim in circles; the more you try to pull them apart, the tighter its grip becomes.

Following Danny's advice, I go to my room and pop another Xanax.

40

A shitty day in Los Angeles is still better than a shitty day in most other places. We may have our issues, but at least we got sunshine. And even when things are bad, they still look pretty damn good. Today, Emily's got a shoot and invited me to tag along. And come on, I'm a writer, a man of curiosity. My inner researcher can't pass up the chance to visit and explore a porn set. It also serves as a good distraction from the fight with Danny. I'll give him some space, but it doesn't lessen the ache I feel in my chest.

I drive up to the villa in the hills of Laurel Canyon. It's an architectural masterpiece, with a stark white exterior contrasting with the lush greenery that surrounds it. It's the type of place you usually only see in movies or on the pages of glossy magazines—or, well, while driving through LA. Exiting my car, I take a moment to appreciate the panoramic view of the city below. With my sunglasses shielding my eyes, I walk through the open doors, greeted by the sound of laughter and music. The interior of the villa is a testament to excess, with marble floors, gilded furniture, and floor-to-ceiling windows that flood the space with golden sunlight. The room is alive with activity, a chaotic ballet of individuals running around, setting up cameras and lights. My presence seems to draw attention, an unfamiliar element in this well-oiled machine. A guy with a clipboard approaches me, his face expressing concern. "Are you the new PA?" he asks, eyeing me up and down as if trying to assess my usefulness.

I shake my head, offering a wry smile. "Nah, just here to see Emily."

He relaxes slightly, apologizing for the mix-up before leading me through the organized chaos toward the makeup area. We weave our way between half-naked performers and harried technicians. Upon entering the room, I see Emily positioned gracefully in a chair, bookended by two women working on her hair and makeup. When she catches sight of my reflection in the mirror, her eyes light up, and a genuine warmth spreads across her face. The two women working on her step aside as she rises and walks toward me.

"Hey, you made it!" she says, giving me a hug.

"Of course," I tell her. "You look gorgeous!"

Her laughter is light and sincere as she replies, "Thanks. Inner beauty hasn't done much for me."

I let out a chuckle at her clever remark and notice her T-shirt that reads, "Former baby, future ghost." I point at it. "Nice shirt."

She responds with a playful smile. "I'm almost done," she says, gesturing to the activity around her. "Make yourself at home. April should be here somewhere too. And I'll come find you in a bit." she adds before turning back to the two women working on her. I nod and begin to wander around the set, taking in the details of the luxurious villa. I walk toward the pool area, surrounded by palm trees and the hot sun. The crew members are all courteous to me, nodding and giving me welcoming grins. In one corner, a guy casually flips through a magazine, his erection a bizarrely normal part of the environment. On the terrace overlooking the canyon, something catches my eye–a large bed with a camera rig that looks, unlike anything I've seen before, featuring two cameras mounted side by side.

Suddenly, I hear footsteps approaching behind me, and I turn around to see April, dressed only in underwear, showing off her perfect body. She greets me with a warm hug and a kiss on the cheek. After we exchange pleasantries, I gesture toward the camera rig and ask her what it's for. She smiles and tells me it's for a VR scene. My eyes are wide open with curiosity.

"Porn in VR?" I exclaim. "Holy shit, no nerd is ever going to leave their basement again."

April chuckles and responds," Well, they are kind of annoying to shoot. But it's definitely the next big thing in the industry." She continues, "Although you're not exactly our target audience."

My mind races with possibilities as I try to wrap my head around the technology of VR Porn. The implications are mind-boggling.

Just then, another girl enters, wearing a sweat suit, sunglasses and carrying a smoothie from *Erewhon*.

"Oh, there's the other one," April says, motioning towards the newcomer.

"How many scenes are you shooting?" I ask her, trying to focus on the matter at hand.

"Just one," she replies, "but with three girls."

I raise an eyebrow and say, "Lucky guy." Even though that sounds exhausting as fuck. While it may sound awesome in the fantasy of someone who has never had one, even a threesome can already be overwhelming, sensory-wise.

April points to a large African American man seated by the pool. He's wearing a black T-shirt, tattoos covering his arms, and a stern expression on his face. She says, "Yep, that's him." This dude could snap me like a twig if he wanted to.

She continues, "He's a total sweetheart. You should see him with the girls. He's like a teddy bear."

I laugh and say, "Seems like it."

Staring at April with a mix of disbelief and fascination.

"I'm the one doing Anal with him in the scene," she says casually. My mind tries to comprehend how that would even fit. Before I can process it, she adds, "It became my specialty, almost like a party trick. Like, 'Hey, look what I can do.'" She smirks, a mischievous glint in her eye. "And it pays more."

"Wow," I say, "you're quite the Harry Houdini of giant dicks"

April laughs at my silly joke. Suddenly, our attention is drawn to some commotion involving the third actress. And we overhear the conversation between her and the assistant. She refuses to sign the release form, and the assistant demands to know why. "It's mercury retrograde," she explains as if that should be common knowledge. "I can't sign anything until May 15. You have to understand."

I burst out laughing at the absurdity of the situation. This is some next-level LA shit.

Out of nowhere, Emily comes rushing towards us. Her makeup is flawless, and her eyes gleaming with excitement, holding something in her hand. She wraps her arms around me in a tight embrace, the scent of her perfume entering my nose. "Oh, congratulations! Why didn't you tell me?" her voice tinged with both delight and a hint of playful accusation.

Caught off guard, my eyebrows knitting together as I try to decipher her words. "Tell you what?" I ask, genuinely puzzled.

"Playboy magazine?" It takes a moment for her words to register. The issue with my chapter in it came out. As Emily holds up the magazine, my heart races with excitement. I quickly flip through the glossy pages, my eyes scanning the articles until I finally see it. There it is, my chapter. My name stares back at me in bold letters. It feels surreal, as if I'm living in a dream. " H o l y fuck!" I say.

Emily and April grin at me, their eyes sparkling with pride. "I'm so proud of you," Emily says, embracing me tightly.

Her excitement is contagious, and April pulls out her phone to capture a picture. "Let's take a photo together with the magazine!"

she exclaims. Within seconds, we snap the picture, immortalizing the moment on Instagram.

However, the excitement is short-lived, as my immediate instinct would be to call Danny the person I truly wanted to share this moment with. I make a mental note to show him when I get home. Then, I observe as the producer gathers the girls, motioning for them to come over. Mercury Retrograde joins them, and the girls prepare themselves for the stills shoot. I take a seat and watch the scene unfold before me. I didn't know this, but apparently, stills take longer than the actual scene itself. Yet, the girls seem unfazed. They are true professionals, preparing themselves like soldiers gearing up for battle. I flip through the pages of the magazine again, making sure my chapter is indeed there and not just a figment of my imagination. But there it is, in print, for the whole world to see.

Hold your breath.

Freeze Frame.

Click.

I spot a crew member with a VR headset on and driven by my curiosity, I walk over to him. He removes it and senses my interest. "Have you ever tried it?" he asks, offering me a chance to experience it for myself. I shake my head, and he carefully places it over my eyes.

Suddenly, I'm transported to a different reality. I know that's the point, but it's still crazy. I see a body that's supposed to be mine, and then Emily enters the scene. It's a surreal feeling, almost like a lucid dream. I can look around in 360 degrees and feel as if I'm truly there, while Emily starts climbing on top of me. I can understand why the nerds would be obsessed with this technology. But for me, it's just strange. I actually had sex with this very woman in real life, multiple times. So I guess April is right—I'm not the target audience for this. Nevertheless, it's pretty fucking impressive.

The day on set stretches on, a relentless parade of flesh and moans, until it finally comes to an end. Emily slides up beside me and asks if I want to come back to her place. It's hard to believe that after an entire day of exposed bodies and simulated ecstasy, she still craves more. Fuck, I'm not even sure I'm in the mood for it. I've seen some shit, literally. Although April's party tricks were pretty impressive. But I tell her I should probably head home. There's the whole situation with Danny I need to confront, an attempt to stitch together the torn fabric of our connection. She nods and presses her lips to mine in a tender kiss. I exchange goodbyes with the cast and crew, the chorus of farewells a testament to the day's strange allure. Then, with a final glance, I set off, leaving the scene behind me.

The sun dips low in the sky, casting a warm, golden glow upon the sprawling city of Lost Angels, as I navigate the labyrinth of streets. The car hums beneath me, the familiar purr of the engine providing a backdrop to my thoughts. I can't deny it—today was a uniquely intriguing experience. The kaleidoscope of encounters dances through my mind, a Technicolor mosaic of the unusual and unexpected. The day's peculiarities blend together like the vibrant hues of the setting sun, painting the sky with a fiery intensity that matches the memories seared into my consciousness.

I pull up to the house, and I notice Danny's car parked outside. However, as I enter, the silence envelops me.

It's quiet, too quiet. The only sound is the gentle purring of my cat Salem, who pads over to me to offer a welcome-home nuzzle. But something is off. His car is here, but the house is empty. I call out Danny's name, but there's no response. With rising anxiety, I move through the silent house. It feels like I'm walking through a movie set after the director has called "cut." I check every room, but Danny is nowhere to be found. Defeated, I slump onto the couch in the living room. That's when I see the note on the coffee table. My heart sinks as I read Danny's words. He's gone back to Seattle and doesn't want me to contact him.

I can't believe it. This is not how I wanted things to end between us. But it's clear that Danny needs some space, and I have to respect his wishes. I sit there for a while, staring at the note, attempting to process everything. It feels like the world is crashing down on me, though I know I have to keep moving forward. With a heavy heart, I get up and walk over to Salem, who rubs against my leg. The sun has fully set now, and the room is bathed in darkness. It's a fitting metaphor for how I feel - alone, in the dark, and lost.

But you're not lost if no one is looking for you.

41

No one will ever tell you, "These are the times; enjoy them while you can." It's been two weeks since Danny left, and I'm still trying to wrap my head around it. I did what every best friend should do: ignore what he said; and I tried calling, texting, emailing, but no answer. I can't help but try. The house, once alive with Danny's presence, is now an empty shell, haunted by the ghost of our friendship. His room, a shrine to the cherished memories we shared, remains frozen in time, the bed unused, and his belongings lie untouched, gathering dust like unclaimed treasures.

As I pace the hallway with the phone glued to my ear like a lifeline, I wonder if I'm chasing a ghost. I feel like the Protagonist in the third act of Fight Club, trying to chase Tyler Durden. Calling every last dialed number, flying to each airport last traveled. Maybe I should just go to Seattle and talk to him face-to-face. But then again, would that be too much? Would he even want to see me? I sit down in the game room and try to clear my mind. But I can't think of anything else; I feel cognitively depleted while trying to untangle the chaos. Maybe he knows he overreacted, but the weight of his decision has left him paralyzed, incapable of reaching out and admitting he was wrong. But I won't give up. I'll persistently call, text, and break down the walls he's built until I reach him. Nevertheless, I also can't lose myself in the process. Especially now.

Sipping on my cold coffee, the bitter taste of caffeine and regret coating my tongue, as I stare at the calendar with wild eyes. The days seem to fly by faster as the re-release of my book approaches, and I am already feeling overwhelmed. Without a manager to handle the mess that is my life, I'm left to manage myself. Just me and my chaotic tendencies. Now that Danny isn't here, I realize how much shit he handled for me. Everything is important, and nothing can wait. I am Sisyphus, rolling the boulder up the hill, only for it to roll back down again. I've got a TV interview coming up this month a local morning show that wants to pick my brain. Plus a handful of podcasts. I've never done anything like this before, but I guess I'll figure it out along the way. I'm pretty good at confidently pretending like I know what I'm talking about even though I'm completely clueless; I can bullshit with the best of them.

Standing in the middle of the game room, surrounded by every console and video game I would've wanted in the 90s, I feel like an intruder. Being in here by myself is weird, reminding me that playing video games is an activity I only enjoy with my friend. The feeling of being completely fucking alone in a city of millions. It's the kind of feeling you get in the aftermath of a painful breakup, except it's even worse. Even Emily, my go-to distraction, is out of town. And Maria, well, she's not an option, not now, considering her ongoing divorce. I tried writing, but the words just won't flow. In a city this big, with endless possibilities, one would think I'd have something better to do besides sit around and feel sorry for myself. But we're all special cases.

I pull out my phone and start scrolling through social media. The flood of notifications is overwhelming, and I can barely keep up with them. Everything I wanted is happening, but it's like I'm watching it happen from the outside; it feels hollow without Danny next to me. A message pops up from Maria, asking if I want to hang out tonight. But I can't bring myself to respond. When something terrible happens, we sometimes believe that time would stop. But why? Because of us? Why are we so arrogant? Time doesn't give a shit about us. It moves on either way. The real question is, are you gonna use it? And right now, I'm not. I'm just wasting it. But fuck that. I grab my keys and jump into my car, turning up the volume on the radio, blasting Marilyn Manson's *The Mephistopheles of Los Angeles*. My head nods along with its very fitting lyrics as I cruise down the highway toward Santa Monica. The sun beats down, making the leather seats sticky and uncomfortable. But I don't care–I just need to get away.

As I pull into the parking lot at Santa Monica Pier, the salty sea air fills my lungs, and I can already see the chaos. Tourists swarm everywhere, snapping photos and chowing down on overpriced fast food from the stands. I make my way to the edge of the pier and stare out at the vast expanse of blue. Ocean waves crash against the rocks below, and I can feel the mist on my face. For a moment, everything else fades away as I get lost in nature's beauty and power. I'm grateful that all this is only a 30 to 90-minute drive away, depending on the time of day. This is exactly what I needed. These moments remind me why I fell in love with this city in the first place.

After soaking in the sights and sounds of the crashing waves, I turn away from the water and head towards the Venice Beach Boardwalk. I observe the vibrant characters lining the path, embracing the freedom to be themselves.

Eventually, I turn to the *Sidewalk Cafe* and navigate toward the adjacent bookstore, *Small World Books*, discreetly nestled beside it. A sanctuary masquerading in the shadows of the surrounding mayhem. The scent of old books fills my nostrils as I enter the dimly lit store, lined with shelves upon shelves of paperbacks and hardcovers. The hip-looking guy at the register acknowledges me with a nod as I walk past him. The space itself is quiet, except for the gentle rustling of pages being turned by a few scattered customers. Approaching a shelf, I start browsing through the titles, looking for something to catch my eye. Then I spot it—my book, *Serendipity*. The self-published edition that I put together myself. I pick up one of the copies, running my fingers over the cover, remembering how I hired a guy from Fiverr to design it for me. I had no clue how to do it myself. It's not perfect, but it's mine.

Flipping through the pages, I remember the late nights I spent writing, editing, and formatting. And then I see the portrait of me in the back, staring at me. It's strange to see myself frozen in time like that, unchanged while everything around me has shifted and evolved. I feel like an asshole standing in the middle of the bookstore, looking at my own literary creations. But it's more like revisiting a time capsule for me, a snapshot of who I was when I wrote it. I never had any desire for children, yet each piece I've written feels like an offspring, a fragment of my soul manifested on paper.

As I stand there holding my child, a sweet voice drifts to my ears. "Richard?" I turn, and there stands Emilia. She's just as captivating as ever with that intoxicating perfume.

I greet her, and she looks at the book in my hands with a smile and asks, "How do you like it?"

I laugh and tell her, "Well, I heard the author is a bit of a self-absorbed jerk, but It's perfect for propping up that wobbly table in my kitchen."

Emilia's laugh is like music to my ears. "Wanna get a drink?" she asks, tilting her head slightly.

"No stranded boyfriends at LAX today? Or are you on break?" I ask.

Her smile widens, revealing her perfect teeth. "Ex-boyfriend!" she corrects me. I feign surprise, putting a hand to my chest. "I'm sorry?" I say, my voice rising in pitch as if asking a question. Emilia just laughs.

"So, drinks? I'm buying." She says.

"Actually, I have a better idea," I tell her, and we leave the bookstore together.

By the time we reach the Mulholland Overlook, the sun sinks low in the sky, offering its usual breathtaking view. I pull out the bottle of wine we grabbed from Whole Foods on our way here, along with two cheap plastic cups. We lay down on the hood of my car, feeling the warmth of the metal against our backs while watching the colors of the sky change. Another perfectly manufactured moment in paradise city. Emilia and I share thoughts and stories, from deep and meaningful to light and funny. Then she tells me that her ex confessed to cheating on her after she picked him up from the airport. Surprisingly, she seems unfazed by it all, which works just fine for me. I make it my mission to keep her amused by cracking some jokes.

We continue talking and laughing until the wine runs dry and the temperature drops a notch. Reason tells me I shouldn't drive, but my house is only three minutes away, and the temptation to continue the evening is too strong. So, I ask if she'd like to accompany me to my place. With a nod and a smile, she agrees, and we make our way to my house.

The Hollywood sign may gleam by day, but the real stories begin when the stars come out to play.

I love the nights. Some of my best days were nights.

42

The sound of leaf blowers and chirping birds outside my window wakes me up, and I'm greeted by a bright blue sky, without a single cloud in sight. As I get out of bed, I notice the sheets are slightly rumpled, reminding me of Emilia, who stayed over last night. She's a creature of the world outside these walls, with a real job bound by responsibilities and obligations, her life a stark contrast to the chaotic nature of my own. But somehow, it seems to be working, at least for now. We've been hanging out a few times over the past two weeks, and I genuinely like her. However, there's a mutual understanding between us, an unspoken agreement that we're not looking for anything too committed, that puppy thing again. There's just no emotional bandwidth for another person. Fuck, I'm not even emotionally available for myself. So we just go with the flow.

I leave my bedroom, still feeling tired from the night, and for a second, I forget what day it is. But as I check my phone, I remember—today's the day. The day of my book's re-release, a work that has been out in the world for some time, almost invisible. Now it's like a phoenix rising from the ashes, with a new cover, new promotion, a fresh coat of paint. And professionally published. It's as if I was underground before, waiting for this moment, and now I finally get to see the light. Like transitioning from overlooked to recognized.

The gears of Alessa's plan are in motion—a three-stage operation: first, the re-release of my debut novel, followed by the film adaptation hitting theaters, and finally, six short months later, my brand new book *Hard to Find, Easy to Lose* will be unleashed upon the world. Money is no longer a worry. My phone is vibrating non-stop, exploding with social media posts and tags about my book, while my messages overflow with congratulatory notes, including one from Maria—and excluding one from Danny. It leaves a bitter taste in my mouth, one that even the money can't seem to wash away.

It's weird how such a small detail can fuck up the entire experience. But I have to force myself to enjoy it, the here and now. I owe it to Eckhart Tolle.

I'm getting ready to do my first interview to promote the release on a podcast. It seems that everyone and their mother started a podcast during the pandemic. It's as if the entire world clamored to be heard, desperate to fill the void left by human connection with the sound of their own voices, verbalizing their thoughts and emotions. But today, I'm talking to someone who's been in the game for years, long before it was even a thing. And not just anyone, mind you. This guy has millions of listeners. I took a Modafinil to boost cognitive performance, a Phenibut to relax, and an Alpha GPC for focus and memory.

The studio is located in West Hollywood, inside a generic building that could be anything from a dentist's office to a Scientology recruitment center. Inside, the walls are plastered with stickers and scribbles, the battle scars of countless guests who have left their mark in a world that's constantly changing. The staff warmly welcomes me, escorting me to the recording room where I meet Larry, the host, for the first time. He's a tall, buff guy with long hair and an infectious charisma. I can see why people like to listen to him speak.

As I settle into my seat, Larry–a man with a voice like whiskey and gravel–leans back in his own chair, his fingers drumming an impatient beat on the table.

"Alright, let's do this," he grunts, and I brace myself for the onslaught of questions. Wondering how interesting anything I'd have to say is, but maybe that's just my imposter syndrome kicking in.

I ask Larry, "Can I cuss on here?"

He pauses for a moment as if considering the question and then bursts out laughing. "Fuck yeah!" he exclaims, grinning from ear to ear. I feel relieved and grin back, knowing I can be my raw, unfiltered self. With a light chuckle, he continues, "You know, we actually have a 'fuck' counter here," he says. "We count every f-bomb our guests drop. So far, the guest holding the record made it to 88 in one interview. It was a rapper."

Smirking, I eagerly welcome the challenge to surpass that record without sounding forced. The glow of a crimson sign illuminates the room, signaling that our broadcast is live, streaming into the ears of listeners all over. After Larry's introduction, it's my turn to thank him for the invite. As I hear my own voice through the headphones, it sounds like a stranger, completely unfamiliar to me. I can already tell this is going to take some getting used to.

I'm an interview virgin, but Larry is very gentle with me. Within a minute, I'm in the zone, as if I've never done anything else. We cover all the basics–where I was born when I started writing–, and he delves into my childhood and beyond. It's like being in a confessional booth, and I'm spilling my guts for all the world to hear.

Larry listens intently, nodding along as I speak. Our conversation flows as if we're just two friends talking, and I completely forget about the millions of listeners tuning in to our every word.

But then, out of nowhere, Larry asks me directly: "So, who is your book about?"

The question takes me off guard, although I should've expected it. Of course, the book is about Maria. Every word on every page has her name written all over it without me ever mentioning it explicitly. However, I can't tell him that. And I refuse to feed the narcissist, to give her the satisfaction of knowing that she's the star of the show. Her ego is already inflated enough. My words stumble, trip, and fall from my lips like a drunken tap dancer.

"It's just a character I made up," I lie, trying to sound casual. "It's all fiction, you know."

Larry raises an eyebrow, clearly not convinced. But he lets it go, and we smoothly transition to the next topic. And before I know it, the time has flown by. The interview is over, and I'm left feeling exhilarated as if I've just climbed a mountain. Suddenly, Larry screams out, "Oh wow, you did it, you broke the record. 95!" and I can't lie—I am weirdly proud of my accomplishment.

Driving down Sunset Boulevard, music blasting, I'm feeling fucking invincible again. And then, out of the corner of my eye, a billboard captures my attention. But it's not just any ordinary advertisement; it's for my book. The sight startles me, nearly causing me to swerve and hit the curb. Everywhere you look, there are signs and displays screaming for attention, promoting new crappy superhero movies, local dispensaries, and TV shows. Yet, in the midst of it all, there it is—a billboard for a book. MY fucking book. I'm sure they pushed it even more to generate some hype for the upcoming film. I'm not mad about it. And who knows? Maybe someone driving by right now will notice it and decide to give my book a chance.

I pull over to the side of the road, just staring at it for a few minutes, absorbing the surreal experience. It feels like a dream come true, a moment I'll never forget. I take out my phone and snap a picture for Instagram. Click. I post it just with the caption "Bruh!" Clearly directed to Danny.

A text notification abruptly jolts me back from my post-billboard daydream. It's a message from Emilia; she's done with work and wants to know when I'll pick her up. Alessa invited me to a small social event to celebrate my book release tonight, and I invited Emilia to be my plus one.

We arrive at the restaurant in the heart of Hollywood. The place looks fancy, with soft lighting and tasteful decor.
Alessa welcomes us at the door, a huge smile on her face as she congratulates me. The patio area is reserved exclusively for our group. It's an intimate but meaningful event, with only about twenty attendees, all genuinely happy for me. Although the sales of my book have yet to be determined, but in this moment, it doesn't even matter.

Emilia, elegantly attired in her black dress, is taking everything in with wide-eyed wonder. This is her first taste of the Hollywood scene, and it's all new to her, but she seems to enjoy it.
I order a drink from the bartender and lean against the bar, taking it all in. The sounds of laughter and chatter filling my ears, and everyone seems to be enjoying themselves. Alessa gracefully approaches me, wearing a confident expression.

"I know this will be big, Richard," she says.

I raise an eyebrow, waiting for her to elaborate. "How are you so sure?"

"You know why?" she asks, leaning in close. "Because a) you are an amazing writer, and b) everyone has or had a 'Maria' in their life. Your book resonates with people on a visceral level. And that's what makes it special."

Hearing that from her with such confidence makes me feel good. I smile and thank her for her kind words.

"Is that your girlfriend?" she asks, pointing to Emilia.

I shrug, "Meh."

Alessa lets out a laugh and shakes her head in amusement. "She's pretty, though," she says, glancing over at Emilia. I nod in agreement, my gaze fixed on her as well. And yet, my mind involuntarily drifts back to Maria. I know it's unfair to compare the two, especially because it's not even the real Maria, but some bullshit idealized version of her that my mind created and put on a pedestal–the way I want her to be. Why can't I let go of the past and embrace the present? It's my constant struggle. I feel like I need a fucking lobotomy to erase her from my mind.

Alessa redirects the topic and asks, "Have you heard from Danny?".

The mention of him cuts through me like a knife. He's the one person who knows me better than anyone else in this damn city. He should be right next to me, celebrating this moment. I shake my head. "No," I say, my throat dry and raw.

Alessa places a comforting hand on my shoulder. "I'm sorry," she says. I manage a weak smile, grateful for her kindness, but inside, I'm still hurting. Emilia approaches me, leaning in to plant a soft kiss on my lips, in full view of everyone at the event. And to my surprise, I let it happen without hesitation. Fuck the chaos in my head, I think to myself; it's just noise. I'm here to embrace the now, to celebrate the release of my book with an amazing woman next to me. As the night wears on, I successfully push those thoughts aside, and it feels like a small victory in a sea of uncertainty.

Emilia and I take an Uber back to my place, and she falls asleep with her head resting on my shoulder. The sound of the engine humming in the background like a monotone lullaby. Then I feel a buzz in my pocket, and I pull out my phone to see Maria's name flashing on the screen. Those fucking Synchronicities. Glancing down at Emilia, her face peaceful in sleep, I ultimately choose to ignore the call and let it go to voicemail. But it's easy to pretend like you're over someone when you're with somebody new.

At some point, we were both strangers, but she was stranger than me, which was unusual.

43

The sun is shining, casting a warm glow on my face as I walk toward the office building. I'm usually not the biggest fan of Monday mornings, especially when my alarm clock rings at such an early hour, but the weather today lifts my mood. And I'm excited for the day ahead. I ride the elevator up to the office with a sense of purpose and make my way inside. Looking around, I notice that there aren't many people here yet. Damn, am I early? I check my watch and see that, in fact, I am. The few people that are here seem to be busy, heads down, focused on their tasks. In their own little worlds, completely unaware of anyone else around them. I scan the office, taking in the monotonous hum of keyboards clacking and printers whirring.

Then, I notice a guy standing by himself in the break room, lost in thought while staring down the food. I walk over, knowing that he's the only one here who's not too busy to chat. I have to admit, he's a good-looking black dude, but it's his presence that makes him stand out. It's the kind of charisma that draws you in without even trying. And I can already tell he's not like the rest of these corporate drones here. As I approach him, he turns around and greets me with a smile, revealing pearly white teeth that could blind a man. "What's up, man?" he says.

I greet him with a nod, then he points at the food with a look of disgust on his face.

"Look at this shit. It's all vegan. I need meat!" he exclaims. I can't help but laugh at his strong reaction. "So, would you say you have beef with vegans?" I ask, feeling pretty damn pleased with myself.

The man erupts into laughter as if I've just delivered the punchline of the century. "That's a good one, man. You got jokes!" He says, grinning.

He extends his hand and introduces himself, "I'm Daniel, but most people call me Danny." Shaking his hand, I tell him my name is Richard, and his eyebrows shoot up in recognition. "Ah, you're the new guy, the hacker," he says, his voice dripping with a mix of amusement and condescension. "Good to meet you, dude."

We continue talking, exchanging jokes and stories back and forth as if we've known each other for years. Our twisted senses of humor and shared interests in music and movies create an instant bond. Danny's the kind of guy who could make even the most mundane task seem like an adventure. Put him in the DMV, and he'll have fun. And just like that, a connection is forged–a connection that seems destined to evolve into something more than just a chance encounter between strangers in an office, a connection larger than life.

Now, a decade later, we're best friends, going through all the ups and downs together. And here I am, chasing after him into a different city like a crazy ex-girlfriend. It's already getting dark, and I know this may seem extreme, but I've tried everything with no response, and I'm desperate. He did the same for me at my mother's funeral, and this is the least I can do. The memory of his comforting presence, unwavering support, and loyalty flood my mind, pushing me to try harder. Stepping out of the black Uber, the cold droplets of Seattle rain assault my senses like tiny daggers. And it's fucking July.

The gray sky above seems to mirror the gloom I feel as I look around at the dreary cityscape. I have a feeling that something is wrong, that he needs me like I needed him.

I reach the entrance and ring the buzzer, hoping beyond hope that he'll answer. But there's no response, only the sound of the rain pounding against the pavement. Then, like a sign from the universe, another resident of the building exits, allowing me to slip inside unnoticed. I make my way to the elevator, anxious to get to his apartment.

Finally arriving at his door, I ring again, but there's still no answer. My heart sinks, the weight of dread and worry bearing down on me. I raise my fist to knock but hesitantly pause, trying to recall our last conversation.

"Danny, it's me, Richard," I say as I knock, my voice hoarse with emotion. No response.

I knock harder this time, hoping he'll hear me. But again, nothing. Realizing I have no other choice, I pull out the spare key I keep on my keyring and insert it into the lock. As I turn it, my heart rate increases, and my palms start to sweat. "I'm coming in," I announce, just in case he's in there, my voice quivering slightly. Then, with a deep breath, I slowly push the door open. The apartment is dark and silent, the only sound coming from the rain outside. Cautiously, I step inside, calling out his name. But there's no answer, only the faint hum of the appliances and the steady ticking of the clock on the wall. My footsteps echo through the empty space as I make my way through the apartment, my heart pounding in my chest as I search for any sign of my friend. A sense of unease fills me, but I suppress it and keep moving forward.

The living room is empty, the kitchen pristine, and the bathroom unoccupied. However, one door remains closed–the one leading to his bedroom. My hand trembles as I knock on the door, my stomach churning as I wait for a response. But there's only silence. I try the doorknob, finding it locked. Dread coils in my gut, and panic sets in; something is terribly wrong.

I know I shouldn't, but without a second thought, I take a step back and kick open the door. The wood splinters and cracks under my foot, causing me to stumble into the room. As I regain my balance, I'm hit with a sight that makes my blood run cold– here he is, suspended from the ceiling, his lifeless body swinging gently like a gruesome pendulum, his head lolling to one side.

And that's when the smell hits me. It's a putrid stench of decay and death, overwhelming my senses, and I can feel bile rising in my throat. It's clear that he's been here for days, his skin discolored and bloated flies buzzing around his body like a grotesque halo, and there's a dark stain underneath his dangling feet.

The sight of him sends a shiver down my spine, like a cold hand gripping my heart. I cover my nose and mouth with my hand and try to breathe through my mouth, but It's futile. The stench clings to me. I force myself to take a step forward, to get closer to him, but every inch feels like I'm trudging through quicksand. The flies are everywhere, landing on my face and arms, making my skin crawl. I can't take it anymore. I stumble back, desperately fighting the urge to vomit. The scene before me is like something out of a horror movie, but this is all too fucking real. I realize that I need to call the police, but my hands are shaking so badly that I can't even hold onto my phone.

Everything around me fades away as I stand there, frozen in shock and disbelief. The only thing I can hear is the sound of my own heartbeat, pounding in my ears like a mournful drum. The image of him hanging there, lifeless and alone in his own sanctuary, a twisted testament to the darkness that had consumed him.

I finally step out of the apartment and into the hallway. Fumbling with my phone, trying to dial 911. The operator answers, and I struggle to find the words to explain what I've just discovered. My voice quivers, and I can barely get the words out. The operator assures me that help is on the way, and I hang up, feeling numb and helpless. He was right; no one can help him, not anymore.

I sit on the curb outside the building and wait. The rain intensifies, soaking through my clothes. Sirens echo from far away, growing louder and closer. But it all feels like a nightmare. As the paramedics and police arrive, I watch from a distance, feeling like an outsider in my own body. They rush into the building, and I'm left sitting there, alone with my thoughts and my guilt. Our last conversation drove him out of town. Was this his plan all along?

As the first responders carry his lifeless body out of the apartment, the reality hits me–I am alone. I know that life will be forever altered. My best friend is gone, and I'll never be able to make sense of it. All I can do now is seek closure and strive to understand the world without him.

It seems that sometimes the pain of living outweighs the fear of dying.

Hold your...

Fuck it.

293

PIECES OF A BROKEN MIND

PART IV

44

Dear Norma,

I don't know how to begin this letter because the weight of my decision to leave this world is overwhelming. I know it will bring you more pain than I could ever imagine. I'm sorry for everything. For not being the husband you deserved, for not being the father Richard needed, and for not being the man I wanted to be. You've always been stronger than me, and I know you'll take great care of our son better than I ever could. I couldn't bear the thought of him growing up with a father like me, someone who is broken and lost.

How did I ever expect to help others when I can't even help myself? My demons have been chasing me for far too long, and I can't keep running away from them. Is this a graceful exit? No, it's a cowardly one. But please don't blame yourself for anything that has happened. This was my decision and mine alone. I'm sorry for the questions that will never be answered and for the years that we'll never have together. But I hope that in time, you'll find happiness again.

I love you more than words can say, even in death.

Stephen."

My father, at least, had the decency to leave a letter for my mother—a final goodbye that brought some semblance of closure. But Danny left nothing behind, no note, no email, no explanation. Just his lifeless body hanging from the ceiling like a macabre ornament.

Going through his things is a painful reminder of his absence. Each item is a piece of the puzzle that will never be complete. I search desperately for something, anything that might give me a clue, a hint, an explanation for what happened.
But there's nothing. It's as if he vanished into thin air, leaving me with a tangled web of riddles. It's frustrating, infuriating, and, above all, heart-wrenching. Missing someone is like living with a phantom limb—the pain never quite goes away.

I stare out the window, my eyes fixated on the somber reflection of the overcast skies. Seattle, this fucking city, now carries a bitter aftertaste. It has become synonymous with the worst kind of pain and despair I've ever experienced, and I will forever associate it with terrible reasons to be here. It has taken everything from me, leaving behind an empty void that can never be filled—a void that now defines me. It all appears hazy as if I'm viewing the world through a foggy lens. But the pain is crystal clear, sharp, and unrelenting. I reach for the Xanax in my bag, hoping it will numb my pain. But there's not enough Xanax on this planet to alleviate the agony that claws at my insides. Danny is gone, and nothing feels real.

As I continue to search, I come across his will. It's a brief and simple document; his final wishes are clear—no funeral, no memorial, just a direct cremation. Was this his way of sparing us the pain of a public goodbye? Or was it a final act of rebellion against a society that never fully accepted him? This is fucking breaking me.

I find myself staring at the cover of *The Secret*, the book that sold millions of copies and which Danny treated like it was his personal bible. It lies on the coffee table. He would always say that the law of attraction would bring him everything he ever wanted, that he had the power to manifest anything. But now, what good are all those fucking affirmations? The book feels like a cruel joke, a sick reminder of all the things Danny wanted but could never have, all his dreams shattered.

He didn't have much of a family, and I am left to deal with this whole situation by myself. After some effort, I manage to track down a distant aunt named Laura, who hasn't heard from Danny in over a decade. As we talk, I learn that he had cut off contact with most of his relatives, leaving only a few scattered breadcrumbs to track him down. Laura sobs as she recounts the tragic fate of Danny's father, a man who also suffered from depression and ultimately ended his life. And now he was following in his footsteps. It's as if Danny and I had a bond we didn't even know about, a shared pain that brought us closer, even in death.

Laura asks me about him, seeking insight into his character and how his life was. Memories flood my mind as I speak, telling her about our move to LA, how Danny became my manager, and how he helped me navigate the entertainment industry. But it all feels so superficial, like I'm painting a picture with a few broad brushstrokes and missing all the intricate details that made Danny who he was. It's strange; I was actually closer to him than her. We can be blood-related to people yet still know absolutely nothing about them or who they really are. The world is full of these hidden connections, bonds that we never knew existed until it's too late.

Eventually, there's nothing left to say, and we hang up, both of us grappling with the same anguish. The guilt inside me consumes my soul like a virus, knowing that our last conversation ended in a huge fight. Maybe he was right; I was too self-centered to lend a helping hand. But now, it's too late to fix that.

There's not much left here–Danny's possessions here are sparse and scattered, most of his things are in LA. Looking around, I reach for *The Secret* and stuff it into my bag. It meant so much to him; it only seems right to take it with me. And now it's time to leave this place behind to let Danny rest in peace. Farewell, my brother.

As I exit the unit, I take one final glance at the empty space, a solemn reminder of how fragile life can be.

I'm back in my car, driving towards my own shitty apartment, when my phone vibrates on the passenger seat. I pick it up and see an email notification from the publisher. The subject line reads: "First Sales Numbers." Who gives a fuck? The numbers are sky-high, they've surpassed even their wildest expectations, but it's all fucking meaningless. A deep sigh escapes me as I toss my phone back onto the seat, the sound of the muted thud against the leather resonating through the car. It's not that I'm ungrateful or anything. It's just that success doesn't solve everything.

I unlock the apartment door and step inside the place that once felt like home but now resembles an empty shell. The artificial Christmas tree is still in the corner, a reminder of the holiday I spent alone after my mother died. The loneliness and emptiness I experienced then is the same feeling I have now. Slowly, I make my way to the couch and sink down onto it, the cushions feeling too soft beneath me. This is where it all began. This is where I wrote that book, where Danny and I spent endless nights watching movies and laughing at dumb jokes. Suddenly, the couch feels too big, like it's swallowing me whole. The night feels endless, as if time has ceased to move forward. Leaning back, I stare at the ceiling. I've come to realize that this place no longer fits my soul. It's like an old pair of shoes that used to feel comfortable but now just hurts my feet. I no longer belong here; I've outgrown this place and everything that came with it. Once I handle it all and tie up loose ends, I'll sell this apartment and never look back. I don't need a safety net anymore.

And with that decision made, I reach for my MacBook and open a blank document. It's time to start something new, a fresh chapter in the book of my existence. The past two years are a blur of memories, experiences, and emotions, and I need to put them down on paper before they fade away completely. It's also a way to immortalize Danny and our friendship. I type out the opening sentence, the words flowing out of me like water from a broken dam. The cursor moves across the page, forming sentences and paragraphs that capture the essence of my life. I don't hold back and pour my soul onto the digital pages. The love, the loss, the drugs, the sex, the fights, all of it. Uncensored.

Follow your heart, and you will die every day.

301

DANIEL RUCZKO

45

ome is where the heartbreak is. Before preparing to leave Seattle, I had hired people to pack up everything in my apartment–an impersonal, mechanical process, but one that had to be done. The furniture, the trinkets, the memories–all left behind, I have no use for it. The belongings that I wanted to keep were shipped off to LA. Now, my apartment is up for sale, a final tie cut from a city I once believed I loved. The hardest part was the final goodbye to my best friend, Danny. After his cremation, I knew I had to find a way to honor him. In a way, I wanted to unite the two people who meant the most to me in this world. Taking the vase, I once bought for my mother and have Danny's ashes filled inside. It feels right–a last act of love and tribute to those who have departed this world. I make a quick detour to the cemetery, the final resting place of my parents. Since I don't know when or if I'll ever return, so I need to pay my respects, saying goodbye for now.

As I board the plane to Los Angeles, the vase remains by my side, an odd yet comforting presence on the seat adjacent to mine, almost as if Danny is with me on this journey. I even bought an additional ticket for it.

Grief is like a dark cloud that follows you wherever you go, even when you return to the sun-kissed chaos of Los Angeles. But I genuinely love LA because this city is just as fucked up as me.

I walk through the front door of my house, releasing a deep breath. Salem meows, brushing against my legs. I pick him up and hold him close, feeling his warmth against my chest. Emilia has been checking on him daily, but I'm relieved to find that she's not here right now. I need to be alone with my thoughts to process everything that's happened. I set Salem down again, and he runs off, chasing a stray sunbeam across the room.

The house feels different, and not just because I've been away. It's weird coming back to LA now that Danny's gone. The safety net of being able to return to Seattle whenever I wanted is gone too. With a thud, I set down my backpack and take a seat on the couch. Reaching for the vase, my fingers glide over its smooth surface. It's bittersweet to have Danny's ashes with me, intensifying the reality of the loss. I hold the vase for a moment, lost in thought, before setting it down on the table in front of me.

I swipe through the notifications on my phone. My book is creating quite a stir, and I appreciate the support. But despite everyone seeming to understand my situation, I know there's a lot that needs to be done. I should call Alessa to check-in. Allen wants to discuss something with me "Whenever I'm ready." But not right now; I'm not fucking ready. I also need to reach out to Emilia; I don't want her to think I'm just using her as a cat-sitter. Emily offers to be my sexual distraction, and it's tempting, just like a Xanax would be so fucking tempting in this vulnerable state. But I believe I need to fully experience this, with no distractions and no escapes. I need to let it consume me, let it break me down until there's nothing left but the raw, unfiltered truth. So I politely decline her offer. And Maria's message, I didn't even fucking read. Right now, the only thing I want to do is write. So with Salem settled beside me, I unzip my backpack and pull out my laptop. I start typing, letting the sound of the keyboard mingle with the soothing purr of my cat. As I pour my heart and soul onto the page, I begin to feel a sense of catharsis, a release of all the pent-up emotions that have been building inside of me. It's not a cure, but it's a start. I didn't choose writing; it chose me.

The hours pass by in a blur as I continue typing, the setting sun casting long shadows across the living room, leaving the space only illuminated by the bright glow of my computer screen. Suddenly, I hear the front door opening and the sound of footsteps echoing through the house. I look up to see Emilia walking in.

"Hey, you're back!" She exclaims a hint of surprise in her voice. Shit, I didn't even tell her I was coming back. I'm such an asshole.

"Yeah," I reply, feeling guilty. "I'm sorry I didn't let you know."

"It's fine," she says, smiling. As she walks over to me, she gives me a kiss on the lips, and it feels intimate and relationship-y. I wonder if she's just being nice or if she wants more from me. Breaking the kiss, I look at her, studying her face. "Thanks for taking care of Salem," I say, attempting to change the subject.

"Of course, no problem," she replies while sitting down on the couch next to me. "Are you okay?"

"Yeah, but It was rough."

"I'm so sorry," she says, placing a hand on my shoulder. "Is there anything I can do?"

I shake my head. "No, I just need some time to process everything."

She stands up and heads to the kitchen. "Do you want anything to eat or drink?"

"No, I'm good," and I continue typing. I can feel her eyes on me as she rummages through the fridge. She clearly doesn't know what to do in this situation, which is understandable. It's unnerving, but I don't say anything. Finally, she returns with a bottle of water and sits back down on the couch, her fingers gently stroking my back. Then she says "I missed you." And I can feel my skin crawling from discomfort. While I do like her and appreciate Emilia's efforts to be supportive, her presence is starting to annoy me.

"Yeah," I reply curtly, "I missed you too." But did I really? Or was it just the convenience of having someone to take care of Salem, and I'm trying to be polite? I had too much other shit on my mind to miss her. Taking a deep breath, I try to shake off the uneasy feeling that's settled over me.

"Can we talk?" she asks. I know what's coming next.

"What is it?" I say, trying to keep my voice even.

"I know we didn't really talk about what this is, but I can't control how I feel about you," she confesses. Here it is, the moment of truth. Houston, we have so many fucking problems. I knew this was coming, but I didn't expect it to be so soon.

"Emilia," I begin, but she cuts me off.

"Please, just hear me out," she pleads. "You're going through a tough time right now, but I want to be here for you. I care about you, more than just a fuck buddy."

I told her early on that I don't want a relationship, at least I think I did; with everything else going on, it's hard to be sure. The last thing I need right now is the added pressure of a commitment. I understand that she's trying to show how much she cares, but I just need space. As I open my mouth to respond, she cuts me off again with a quick apology.

"I'm sorry, forget what I said. I know this isn't the right time; I was being impulsive."

Man, even in this moment, she is being cool. And the last thing I want is to fuck with her feelings.

"Let me know if you want to be alone," she says softly. "I didn't want to ambush you like that. I'm sorry." She's too damn cool for her own good, and it's throwing me off.

I hesitate, unsure of what I want. But then again, maybe I should stop being so fucking selfish. "No, stay," I finally say, closing my laptop. And so we sit, two lost souls in a world that doesn't seem to care. I tell her about Danny—how we met, all the crazy adventures we've been on, the moments that defined us.

Emilia listens intently, nodding along like she can understand the pain I've been carrying around. It actually feels good to talk about him, to share these memories with someone who cares.

As the night wears on and the conversation turns to lighter topics, I realize that Emilia is still here, still listening, still being cool.
And perhaps, I'm not as alone as I thought I was. Maybe there's hope for me after all.

Hours later, I randomly wake up with Salem sleeping by my feet. I can feel the warmth of Emilia's body next to mine, her breathing steady and even as she sleeps soundly beside me. Then my phone lights up on the nightstand, casting a blue glow across the room. I reach for the device and see that I have five missed calls and three messages, all from Maria, at 3 AM. Shit, this can't be good.

My heart starts racing as I read her desperate plea for help. Without waking Emilia, I slip out of bed and silently tiptoe towards the door, phone in hand. I feel like an intruder in my own home, sneaking around in the dead of night. With a mixture of fear and adrenaline, my trembling fingers dial Maria's number. She answers on the third ring, her voice strained and frantic on the other end. "Thank god you're awake; I'm so sorry to call you," she says, and I can tell she's not in a good place. She tells me that her ex-husband-to-be hit her, and for a moment, I'm stunned. Something feels off, but I can't be an asshole and question her right now.

"I called the cops," she sobs, "but he's already taken off." I don't care who you are or what your reasoning may be; no one should ever raise a hand to a woman, no exceptions! But she has a history of exaggerating things. Is she crying wolf? And the fact that I'm even thinking that is a red flag alone. Fuck it.

"Okay, I'm coming over," I say firmly before ending the call. I look to Emilia, who's still fast asleep, and for a moment, I debate waking her up. But this isn't her problem. It's mine. I quickly get dressed, grab my keys, and head out into the night.

The city is alive, even at this ungodly hour, and I can feel the adrenaline pumping through my veins. I'm merely running on autopilot at this point.

I pull up to Maria's house, the engine idling as I wait for her to emerge from the shadows. When she steps out, I notice she's carrying a small bag with her. She climbs into the car, her body trembling against mine as she hugs me tightly. I remain silent, simply turning the key in the ignition and easing out onto the road. She tells me the whole story as we drive, her voice shaking with emotion. Maria mentions that the police wrote everything down, I glance over at her, and I see a black eye forming. She doesn't know about Danny yet, and this is not the time to burden her with my grief.

I assure her that she can stay with me, that she'll be safe with me. And I mean it.

Upon arriving at my place, I notice the lights are off, indicating that Emilia is still asleep. Inside, I lead Maria to the guest room, making sure she has everything she needs. She thanks me softly, and I tell her to get some rest, that I'll be just down the hall if she needs anything. She hugs me tenderly to say good night. Her embrace lingers a little too long, and I can feel myself getting uncomfortable. Glancing at the door leading to the bedroom, where Emilia is peacefully sleeping, unaware of the situation outside, I gently pull away from the hug and watch as Maria walks through the door.

I let out a deep sigh and make my way down the hallway, dreading what's to come. I can already picture the awkwardness in the morning. Me caught in the middle of two women, dating neither of them, yet still involved with both of them. It's a tangled mess, and I know that I need to figure out my priorities before this all blows up in my face.

There's no way I'm going to sleep tonight, so I walk toward the living room.

For a fleeting moment, it feels like I'm not alone. I swear I see Danny sitting on the couch, a ghostly apparition haunting me in the middle of the night. But just as quickly as the image appears, it fades away into nothingness. It's just my mind playing tricks on me. I settle onto the couch and grab my laptop, feeling the smooth surface cool against my fingers as I open it up.

I try to focus on my writing, but my mind keeps drifting to the two women in my house. One in my bedroom, the other in the guest room. And I can't help but feel like I'm being torn in two different directions. But for now, all I can do is write and try to forget about the chaos surrounding me.

We fight demons from our past only to face new monsters.

DANIEL RUCZKO

46

Did you know that most life insurance policies include a suicide clause? It denies the payout if the insured takes their own life within a set period after the policy's start - typically two years. My father didn't know that. Just a year before he chose to end his life, he had changed his life insurance policy, sealing his fate and unknowingly subjecting my mother to a long battle she never asked for. Evidently, his suicide wasn't a calculated move but rather the desperate flailing of a man drowning in his own misery, leaving behind a tangled mess of bureaucracy.

My mother left to pick up the pieces, fought the previous insurance company tooth and nail, struggling to secure the money she believed was rightfully hers. It became a grief-fueled war that lasted for years, pitting her against a corporate behemoth that couldn't care less about the shattered lives left in my father's wake.

It's a perverse dance, this battle with a company that sees us as nothing more than numbers on a balance sheet. A grotesque reminder that even when your world crumbles, the gears of life grind mercilessly on, indifferent to the dust and debris left behind. Time doesn't give a shit about us.

Back then, I was too young to grasp the weight of my father's death, too innocent to understand the tangled web of grief and greed that my mother was trapped in. I had no idea how my father died, and my mother rarely spoke about it. I saw the struggle through the eyes of a clueless child, and I couldn't comprehend its significance and complexity. But it's all so clear to me now, the puzzle pieces fitting together perfectly.

Today, I get a call from Danny's life insurance company. Apparently, he took out the policy just before we decided to move to LA together. This leaves me wondering: why did he do that? Who was it for? Certainly not his family. The insurance agent then tells me that Danny named me as his sole beneficiary. However, since it's been less than two years, there won't be any payout for a self-inflicted injury. Obviously, it's not about the money anyway; it's the thought behind it that cuts deep, leaving a bitter sting of love and friendship. I knew Danny struggled with depression, but I never imagined it would come to this.

The day drags me along, my body obediently following, but my mind is elsewhere. I'm on my way to meet Allen, although I don't particularly feel like it. But work is the best distraction. We're meeting at Laurel Tavern, as I suggested it. I like the place - it has this unpretentious vibe that suits me.

I push open the door, the familiar scent of worn-in leather and lingering whiskey hitting me. It's comforting. Anton is working again today. I really like him - he's the kind of guy who knows when to chat and when to let a man drink in peace.

Sliding onto a barstool, I greet him with a simple "Hey, Anton,"

"What's up, man?" he replies, flashing a toothy grin. "Long time no see."

I order an old-fashioned, which Anton skillfully prepares with practiced ease. We chat, the conversation remaining light and simple, a welcome respite from the heaviness of recent days. He mentions he's read my book - says he loved it. A smile tugs at the corner of my lips, a rare sight these days. I express my gratitude, remembering his help with my first screenplay. The guy has a knack for storytelling.

After taking a sip of my drink, I notice Allen walking in. He's dressed in his usual crisp suit and tie, perfectly embodying the image of a thriving Hollywood producer. He approaches me, and before I know it, he does something rather uncharacteristic for LA standards - he apologizes for being late. A simple gesture, really, but in a city filled with a thousand excuses - where traffic serves as the perfect scapegoat for tardiness - his apology is as refreshing as a cool breeze on a hot day.

He pulls me in for a hug that feels genuine and honest. It's a long hug, the kind that only comes from someone who knows what you've been through. He had actually called me right after he heard about Danny, and we talked for a while.

He slides onto the stool beside me and says, "I hope the city of angels is treating you like a son." His voice, a soothing blend of sincerity and showbiz charm, makes the phrase sound like a strange kind of poetry, but I like it.

He asks how I'm doing, dipping his tone the way you do when you ask a question you know will come with heavy answers. After we bounce some small talk back and forth, Allen hits me with the real reason for this meeting.

"What are you working on these days?".

I tell him that I'm lost in the maze of my next novel, trying to piece together fragments of a story I've yet to fully understand. The words tumble out, a confession of sorts, a writer's lament for the tale that hasn't quite found its path yet.

He nods and asks, "Would you write the script for our next movie?"

There it is, a proposition disguised as a question. He wants to take advantage of the hype surrounding my book and keep the momentum going. Hollywood doesn't sleep; it merely waits for the next big thing. Sell the dream. And I can't lie; it feels nice to possibly be considered that next big thing. Allen then adds, "There will obviously be more money for that one." But I don't give a fuck about money. And I know that's easy to say when you have it. I'm not rich by any means, but I'm comfortable. And money is not what drives me. It's never been about that.

I take a sip of my drink, trying to buy myself some time to consider. The ice cubes clink against the glass, a sound that seems to echo in the otherwise silent moment.

Allen must sense my hesitation because he leans in and speaks in a lower tone. "Look, I know it's been tough for you. But writing is your gift. It's what you were born to do. I think this project could be the perfect outlet for you, and we're willing to give you creative control."

Fuck, this guy sure knows how to sell and how to pull the strings. But I find myself teetering on the precipice of a decision, a coin flip suspended in mid-air. The timing is strategic and calculated. On one hand, he's asking me for another script before the first movie even hits the screens, before the reviews and box office numbers are in. Which could be a blessing or a curse.

 If the movie turns out to be a massive hit, then this offer will look like pocket change. On the contrary, if it flops and it face-plants into the unforgiving concrete of Hollywood Boulevard, I might not even get an offer like this again. Money talks, but so does pride.

So, here I am, weighing my options like a goddamn fool. Should I take the chance and write another script? Or play it safe and wait to see how the first one does? It's a gamble, a game of Russian roulette, and I can almost hear the spinning of the barrel, the click of the hammer. I nod slowly, still unsure. But then I contemplate the alternative. Sitting alone in my house, drowning in my grief and self-pity. At least with this project, I'll have something to focus on, something to keep me going. There's no rush for the next book.

"Fuck it," I say, my voice steady, my heart pounding the beat of a rebel drum. "Let's do it."

Allen's face breaks into a grin, a Cheshire Cat smirk. "Great," he purrs with satisfaction. "Expect an offer tomorrow."

And just like that, amidst the half-hearted small talk and the stale smell of spilled beer, our fates are sealed. We're all in, placing our bets on a dream that's yet to prove itself. And I know that my attorney, Ava, will negotiate the shit out of their offer. She's more shark than woman, circling the waters of this Hollywood sea, teeth bared at the scent of a fresh contract.

Back at the house, with a potential new deal under my belt, I unlock the door and step inside. The only sound is the gentle hum of the air conditioning unit. Passing through the living room, I drop my keys onto the table by the door and notice Salem curled up on the couch, his eyes half-closed as he basks in the warmth of the room. He meows softly as he sees me but doesn't move.

That one night, I've offered Maria a place to stay whenever she needs it, and she's been occupying the guest room ever since. But it seems that she's not here right now. It's nice to have some solitude, and I make my way to the game room. I sit down in front of the PlayStation 2 and boot up Burnout 3, the game that had kept Danny and me up until the early hours of the morning.

If he were still here, he'd be sitting right next to me, eagerly waiting to hear all about my meeting as we crash virtual cars. This game still holds up, even now. "Just one more race," I think to myself multiple times. The hours seem to melt away like wax on a hot stove, but I'm not complaining.

Suddenly, the door creaks open, breaking the spell. It's Maria, standing there with a smile on her face. The sounds coming from the TV must have alerted her to my late-night gaming session. "You're up late," she says, a hint of amusement in her voice. I ask her for the time, trying to sound casual, but the truth is that I've totally lost track of it. She informs me that it's 2 AM. Shitness. Part of me wants to ask her where she's been, but I remind myself that it's none of my fucking business.

Knowing she's not really into video games, I hit pause and ask her, "Want to watch a movie instead?".

She nods, and I can tell she's had a rough day. "Sure, and some wine, if you have any,"

I grab two wine glasses and a bottle of red from the kitchen, uncorking it with a satisfying pop. Pouring us both generous glasses and hand one to Maria.

We settle onto the couch, scrolling through countless horror films on Netflix, a genre that intrigues us both. Eventually, we choose a random one and press play. The wine flows freely, and I find myself pouring a second bottle before I even realize it. It's as if my "just one more" game mentality has carried over, and I can feel the room spinning slightly as I take another sip of wine. The movie is playing, but I'm not really paying attention anymore. All I can think about is how close Maria is getting. She claims the movie is too scary and inching closer with every jump scare. A charged silence lingers between us.

And then, without warning, she suddenly turns around and kisses me. Fuck. I can feel the effects of the alcohol, making this seem even more surreal. Despite knowing that this is all kinds of fucked up, I can't bring myself to stop. Our past sexual chemistry is taking over; it's like we never missed a beat. It's an escape from reality, a chance to forget about all the bullshit in our lives and just exist in the present moment. Fuck it.

I am Icarus, flying too close to the sun, watching the wax of my wings melt away.

47

itting inside a small coffee shop in Glendale, the first thing that comes to mind is that it looks like it's straight out of *Twin Peaks*. The walls are lined with vintage black-and-white photos of old Hollywood stars, and the rich aroma of freshly brewed coffee fills the air. I love it. However, the motives for my presence here aren't quite as positive.

Emilia lives in this part of town, and I suggested we meet at a coffee shop as a neutral place for emotional armor. Maria and I had just hooked up, and now I'm meeting with another girl who I know has feelings for me. It's like I'm playing a fucked up game of emotional hot potato. And even though I'm not technically with either of them, I still feel shame that's crawling all over me like a million tiny spiders. So I think it's only fair that I have a conversation with Emilia. I can't bear the thought of leading her on, making her believe there's a chance for us when there isn't. I mean, who am I to go around toying with people's emotions like they're my own personal playthings?

I'm a fucking idiot. Emilia is a real person with hopes and dreams and a future that very well could have included me. Yet here I am, cutting her off like a limb on a diabetic. I could try to play the incident with Maria off as a drunken mistake, an evening of blurred lines and fuzzy decisions with my ex. But who am I kidding? It's only a matter of time before she sucks me back into her world of chaos and destruction. Fuck, I'm already in it.

We've all been through the ex-lovers dance, a performance choreographed by nostalgia and blind hope. We swear it's going to be different this time. Convincing ourselves that we can turn the tides, that the ending can be rewritten. But we're just setting up the stage for an even greater fall. Fuck. The past is a boomerang, always returning with a vengeance, and this time, it's not just my heart that's in the line of fire. It's Emilia's as well.

I glance at my phone, checking the time. Then, Emilia steps through the coffee shop door, disrupting the mundane hum of the place. My gaze lifts from the worn tabletop, meeting her eyes. It's like I'm seeing her for the first time. The scent of her perfume trickles into my nostrils before she's even close, a gentle tide preceding the storm. She folds into the chair across from me, her eyes soft and inquiring. It's all so nauseatingly cliché, like a scene straight from a mediocre rom-com. But the thing is, we're not dating. So technically, there's no relationship to end. Nevertheless, here we are, each of us anchored to the moment by the weight of what's to come.

"How are you?" she asks, a small smile tugging at her lips with that look like she knows a storm is coming but can't quite make out the dark clouds on the horizon.

"Can't complain," I reply, the words a familiar tune on my tongue. We engage in a strained exchange of pleasantries, each sentence carefully chosen, like stepping stones across a river of awkwardness. But the inevitable can't be held at bay for too long. Taking a deep breath, I spill out the truth.

I tell her about Maria, about how we hooked up, and the overwhelming guilt I feel. Emilia's smile freezes, the light in her eyes dimming ever so slightly. She doesn't say anything, just blinking at me, processing the words. In a rush, I blurt out my well-rehearsed line, "I told you from the beginning, Emilia, I wasn't looking for a relationship." It's a shitty thing to say, I know. And I've said it so many times before, to so many women. It's like I've sucker punched her with a truth she already knew but didn't want to hear.

But she's quiet, disturbingly so. Is she overthinking what I'm overthinking? She looks at me, her eyes wide, and for a moment, I swear I can see a flicker of something vulnerable and wounded. But in an instant, it vanishes, replaced by something else.

Then, she breaks the silence, her voice as steady as a surgeon's hand. "It's unfair what you do," she says, locking her eyes onto mine, a spark of defiance lingering in their depths. "Someone like you–intelligent, charming, creative–you let an ordinary person in, and it's... it's just fucking unfair."

Ordinary? Nothing about her is ordinary. Hearing that stings like a slap, a raw honesty I wasn't prepared for.

"We don't stand a chance but to fall for you, no matter how much you insist you don't want a relationship," she continues, the words spilling out in a torrent of frustration and hurt.

"You show us something we can't keep, and that's fucked up, man." She leans back in her chair, running a hand through her hair. "You can't just let someone into your world, cause chaos. And then, tell them to fuck off. I think you're just scared of anything real." It's a punchline, delivered with the timing of a seasoned comedian; only this joke isn't funny. It's as raw and bitter as the coffee cooling between us. But she's right. It's like I've been walking through a minefield blindfolded, and the explosions are starting to catch up with me. The shrapnel of my own stupidity and selfishness raining down on my head.

But I can't help it. I never promised her anything more than a casual fling. And yet, here she is, pouring out her heart to me in the middle of a fucking coffee shop.

"I know it's unfair," I say, attempting to sound sympathetic. "And I never meant to hurt you." It's all up to her now.

"Intentions don't mean shit, Richard," she retorts. "Actions speak louder than words." I'm the villain of this piece, the architect of this mayhem, and there's no way to argue with the truth. The moment stretches out, tense as a tightrope, before I watch her rising from her seat. The chair scrapes against the floor, a harsh, grating sound that carves its way through the ambient hum of the space.

"Goodbye, Richard," she says with an unwavering voice, matter-of-fact, as if she's talking about the traffic, not the end of... whatever this was. Then she turns and adds," Good luck with your fucking book." her tone is cold and final, a little too sharp. It's a parting shot, a jab that hits its mark like a sniper. And I can't blame her.

She doesn't look back as she pushes the door open and steps out into the world, leaving me in the quiet aftermath of our collision. The bell above the door chimes, a cheerful note that feels jarringly out of place. Right now, even my regrets seem pointless. It's like swallowing shards of glass—it's vile, it's bitter—but somewhere in the pit of my gut, I know it was the only move to make.

The coffee mug meets my lips. It's a bitter kiss goodbye, the final act in this tragic play. I push the empty cup away, staring at the ring-shaped stain it leaves. Rising to my feet, I drop a couple of crumpled bills on the table, the currency of guilt.

As I step out of the establishment, the world outside remains apathetic. The sun blaring down with unyielding brightness, the birds chirping their merry tunes. They didn't get the memo - their world should have stopped turning.

These are the times when I'd typically reach for my phone, dialing Danny's number, ready to spill my guts. I can almost hear his voice in my head, cracking a joke or a clever metaphor to make me feel better. But that's a phone call that ends in a dial tone now. Yeah, I could really use a Danny-ism right now.

Memories of him, as vivid as the city's neon lights, flash through my mind. His laughter, loud and uninhibited, echoing off the walls of my head. "Fuck," I breathe out, my voice lost in the city's symphony, "You'd know what to say."
It's like I'm alone in a crowded room. And I wonder if this is what Danny felt like before he died.

I'm behind the wheel of my car, navigating through the traffic of the city of angels. My phone vibrates in my pocket, and I pull it out to see an email from Ava. It contains Allen's offer for the new script, a financial declaration of belief in my talent: $500,000 spelled out in cold, emotionless numbers. The sum feels surreal, like a fictional currency in a video game. Plus, a bigger percentage than last time to be confirmed. And that's before Ava has even started twisting arms and breaking kneecaps. The deadline, six months, sits like an open invitation, generous and inviting.

Los Angeles always seems to find unique ways to show you why you belong here. It's a city that knows how to play the game, how to bluff, how to make you go all in, even when the odds are stacked against you. It's a constant, relentless reminder that this is the city where dreams really can come true.

But there's a nagging sensation, a prickly unease that's been gradually creeping up on me, slithering in like an insidious intruder. Anxiety, my unwelcome passenger, has strapped itself in for the ride. It lurks in the shadows, conjuring fake scenarios, a shapeless monster that feeds on doubt and uncertainty, growing stronger with each passing day. I hate this shit. But it's the strange bipolarity of life—the exhilarating highs and the crushing lows. On one hand, my career, it's like a rocket aiming for the stars. And the flip side, my personal life, it's a goddamn minefield. Dead friends, anxiety, toxic Ex-girlfriends, potential girlfriends—they all lay in wait, all rigged and ready to explode at the slightest misstep. Their detonations echoing through the caverns of my mind.

The adrenaline of success mingles with the dread of emotional upheaval, creating a strange cocktail that leaves me reeling. It's a paradox, an internal conflict, a battle between the professional and the personal, between the excitement of the future and the ghosts of the past. And yet, I laugh. I laugh in the face of the absurdity, the sheer insanity of it all.

And as the sun sets on another day of triumphs and tribulations, I tip my hat to the havoc prepared to navigate the labyrinth that is my existence.

So here's to the mess- Bring it on. I'm fucking ready.

At least, I think I am...

DANIEL RUCZKO

328

48

The city outside pulses a low electric symphony that never ends. Yet within these walls, there's just Salem and me, my black-as-the-night cat, the only creature in LA that doesn't demand anything from me. My head is resting on his side, his fur a prickly warmth against my cheek. His body rises and falls in this slow rhythm, a living metronome that doesn't keep time but anchors me to the present moment. I close my eyes and focus on the sound, the gentle purr resonating from his throat. This is my own version of white noise, my furry Zen master teaching me about the power of simplicity. Sometimes, when the night is too quiet, and the thoughts in my head are too loud, insomnia becomes an unwanted guest, and I find comfort in this ritual. I'm tired of being tired and not being able to sleep. Like I forgot how to sleep.

Earlier today, the final keystrokes of the script echoed in the emptiness of my house. I hit send, and it's like watching a digital bird take flight. A pixelated phoenix emerging from the ashes of my late nights and countless cups of coffee. And with that, the first draft was sent off to Allen and his people. Six months later and a cool half a million dollars etched into a narrative arc. 125

pages, each worth $4,000 if you do the math. It's been a hell of a half-year - an eternity or a blink–depending on who you ask.

Anxiety, the bastard child of fear and uncertainty, has made a comeback, not just that, a grand, theatrical return. It's like a star that's been absent from the limelight too long, now back on stage savoring every minute of it. It's no longer a whisper in the back of my head; it's a deafening siren blaring out of control, drowning out any remnants of peace. Thus, I'm back on Xanax, my chemical pacifier. My tolerance is high–two, maybe three pills a day, just to function and to numb the pain. It's pretty damn bad, and I'm not proud of it. But when your own mind is your worst enemy, you grasp whatever reinforcements you can get.

And then there's Maria, another thing I'm not particularly proud of. With her freshly inked divorce papers and her seductive smile, we are involved in a chaotic dance that some might call dating. What a beautiful disaster. It's like we're playing with fire - except that I'm a moth, being drawn to her flame. I'm all too aware of the burning, of the inevitable pain, but damn it, the light is too irresistible. Right now, we're still in the beginning–the "love bombing" or "idealization" phase, as the therapists call it. It's the part of the narcissist's performance where they make you feel like you're the center of the universe, their sun, moon, and stars. It's a beautiful lie, and we're both eager to believe it. The sex is mind-blowing and soul-shaking. The kind of sex that burns itself into your memory. She's constantly whispering sweet nothings about soul mates and destiny, but they're just echoes, hollow and meaningless. Her voice, like honey, poured over broken glass.

But it feels nice. The sweet poison that you knowingly drink because, for a moment, it makes everything a little less painful. For now, it's our reality, our beautifully constructed lie. And in the grand scheme of things, it's not such a bad lie to live. But I know what's coming. I've seen this movie before, and I know how it ends. We clearly have an expiration date.

On top of all that, I wake up every day with the same thought. Danny is gone. Months have passed, but it still feels like yesterday. And it doesn't fit my soul. Every little thing reminds me of him. The idea that time heals all wounds is a fairy tale we tell ourselves to make it through the day. In reality, some wounds never heal; they just become a part of who we are. Perhaps it's this calendar page flipping over to November and the realization sinking in that my first holiday season in California is approaching. I'm used to snow and shitty weather. Here, it's sunny and warm, and the only cheer seems to come from people spending money they don't have. Or maybe it's because this is my first holiday season without Danny—my first Thanksgiving, birthday, Christmas, and New Year's Eve, without my best friend. I'm not looking forward to this. I guess everything comes with a price.

The glow of my phone's screen pierces the darkness of my room, an interruption to my sleepless stare at the ceiling. Emily's message, like a virtual post-it note stuck on the screen: "Are you still coming?" I forgot. It's her birthday. Emily knows about Maria , that I've been dancing on the knife edge of her world. And she understands the labyrinth we're trapped in. But she wants me there, not as a lover, but as a friend. It's 1 AM, and despite Salem's hypnotic purring, sleep remains an elusive phantom.

Fuck it, I think, as I open the Uber app. A little white pill, my Xanax-shaped parachute, finds its way down my throat as I hit "confirm ride." Then it's out the door and into the night that's as restless as my mind.

Arriving in Santa Monica, the sound of the party reverberates through the streets. Emily's face lights up when she sees me, her excitement almost infectious, grinning from ear to ear as she welcomes me in with open arms. The place is packed, wall-to-wall, with people. The crowd forms a vibrant mosaic–a blend of influencers, DJs, NFT Artists, YouTubers, and girls aspiring to make it in the adult film industry, all in their early twenties. The scent of weed and alcohol wafts through the air. In the sea of her guests, I feel like an old man, a vintage vinyl in a world of Spotify playlists. Maybe it's because I am, in fact, old, or maybe it's the Benzo making me feel even more disconnected from the room's energy.

Emily drags me through the throngs of people, introducing me to her friends. They all seem nice enough, but I can't shake the feeling that I don't belong here. She introduces me as a writer, and I can't help but wonder if these kids even read anything besides texts, tweets, or Instagram captions. And just as that thought slips from my mind, I'm struck by a sudden realization that this is the epitome of "Old-man" thoughts.

I accidentally bump into a character named Ryan, only he insists on being called "Lyrical Mirage." The irony of the name isn't lost on me–a walking, talking contradiction in the flesh. He's one of those Soundcloud rappers, a skinny white dude with a wildly mismatched thrift store outfit. And has got this cocky grin plastered on his face, the kind that shows he's in the habit of believing his own hype.

"I'm going to be the next Eminem," he declares, chest puffing out with a bravado that's almost endearing in its naïveté. It's a bold statement, and I can't help but smile, amused by his audacity. Can't fault the kid for dreaming big, though, can you? We are all just playing our parts.

I mean, what the fuck do I know, anyway? Maybe he's got bars that could outshine the sun. Or maybe he's another wannabe, lost in the sea of internet fame chasers. Either way, it's not my circus, not my monkeys.

The party swirls around us, a sea of young, hopeful faces, and there I am, standing in the epicenter with a Soundcloud rapper who dreams of fame and respect. Welcome to California. It's a glorious, fucked-up mess, and I'm just along for the ride. Then Ryan, I mean, "Lyrical Mirage," moves closer and starts rapping directly into my ear as if he was auditioning for me. My body involuntarily cringes, but I put on a fake smile and try to be polite, nod along to his inane lyrics. I know rap, and I love rap.

But he sounds like he'd be right at home spitting over that 808 autotune garbage that passes for music these days. I know, yet another old man's statement.

Suddenly, like a guardian angel, Emily comes to my rescue. She pulls me away from the wannabe rapper and hands me a drink. "Drink with me," she says; I don't even ask what it is and obey without question. I don't care if it's spiked with arsenic as long as it keeps me away from that autotune nightmare. Emily introduces me to more and more people, and I can feel myself starting to relax. My memory is terrible, and their names and faces are blending into a smeary watercolor of youthful exuberance and ambition. The drinks keep flowing, and I'm actually glad that I came out. I let the alcohol flood my senses, and the world slows down. One of them wants to be a comedian, he cracks a joke, and laughter bubbles up from somewhere deep inside me, surprising in its authenticity. It's loud and contagious, and soon, others join in. We're all laughing together, these strangers and I. Are we laughing about the joke itself or the absurdity of this city that brings us together?

Each person celebrates in their own way, and drugs are the confetti. Molly, coke, X, and every other substance under the sun is being snorted, popped, and gulped down. Someone is even smoking DMT somewhere. I notice Pupils dilated like black holes, consuming the scant light. I watch them, their minds adrift on the tides of dopamine and serotonin. However, I stick to the booze, a lot of it. Enough to make the world spin around me like a demented carnival ride. My speech slurs, and I'm two drinks away from an Ouija board.

Suddenly, as I navigate through the crowd, my legs feel weak, and I'm not sure I can take another step. I need to sit down before I fall. I suppose I'm getting too old to party with the kids. Emily quickly notices the change in my demeanor; she rushes over. "Are you okay?" she asks, but her voice sounds distant, warped like she's speaking from the bottom of a well. I open my mouth to respond, but nothing comes out. She doesn't wait for an answer, wrapping her arm around mine and guiding me through the crowd. My vision blurs, and I can barely keep my eyes open. We reach her bedroom, where I catch a glimpse of a couple mid-coitus. Emily doesn't even flinch as she interrupts them and commanding them to leave. "He needs to lay down," she says, her tone brooking no argument.

Emily lowers me onto her bed as the room tilts and swirls. Her voice fades in and out as if controlled by a shitty DJ, and I try to focus on it, try to anchor myself to something solid. And then the nausea hits a tidal wave of sickness and the taste of bile burning the back of my throat.

My limbs feel heavy, unresponsive like I've been encased in lead. I can feel myself sinking, descending deeper and deeper into the dark abyss. I struggle to claw my way back, to fight against the drowning tide, but it's like trying to swim through tar. I feel like I'm about to die. Just waiting for that bright light to appear, the one that signals the end of the tunnel.

And then, everything goes black.

Fade out.

49

Symphony of sensory stimuli buzzes around me before I dare to open my eyes. The shrill beep of machines, and I am a passive listener, an audience of one, as I teeter on the edge of consciousness. The rhythm of my own heart beats in my ears, a reminder of the life that still insists on coursing through my body.

Closer to me, there's the soft drip-drip-drip of the IV forming a metronomic rhythm.

I can smell it before I see it. The hospital room, I mean. It carries an antiseptic sting of sanitized air, a clean, cold aroma. A scent that conjures images of white walls and fluorescent lights, of hushed voices and echoed footsteps. My head is pounding like crazy, a desperate SOS from the neurotransmitters pleading for that precious Choline.

My tongue feels swollen and dry against the roof of my mouth. The aftertaste of pills and alcohol lingers, bitter and chalky, a grim reminder of the path that led me here. Slowly, as if surfacing from the depths of the deepest ocean, I strain against the weight of my lids, and crack my eyes open, one at a time. The world comes into focus, an amalgamation of white and grey gradually forming into the sterile hospital room I had imagined. And there, in the harsh reality of fluorescent lights, sits Maria.

When my eyes finally meet hers, there's a silence that's louder than any words we could exchange. She's usually the one who fucks up, so this feels unfamiliar. She's about to tell me what happened, but I don't need her to. I am very aware what this was. Overdoses are the footnotes in the book of life, where the protagonist decides to skip a few chapters, maybe even the whole damn story.

It's just another cliché fulfilled–I've got a tiny bit of success in Hollywood and already my first overdose under my belt. It's almost laughable, in a tragic, twisted sort of way. It's a hollow, bitter sound, the laugh of a man who's danced with the devil and lived to tell the tale. Another day, another disaster. Such is life in the fast lane.

Maria's face is a mixture of relief and concern as I struggle to sit upright. Giving her a weak smile, a feeble attempt to reassure her that I'm okay, although we both know it's a lie. You don't end up here if you're fine. Uttering a mumbled apology for worrying her, I notice tears welling up in her eyes. I know they must have given me Naloxone, depending on how bad my overdose was. I also need to apologize to Emily for ruining her birthday with my questionable choices.

I ask Maria when I can leave, trying to sound indifferent despite the fact that my insides are churning with anxiety. She confirms what I already know–that since it wasn't a suicide attempt, I can leave whenever I feel like it. And it's fucked up; I've just woken up from an overdose, mixing Benzo's with alcohol, my body still protesting the abuse it's taken, and yet, all I can think about is taking another Xanax.

Feeling like I forgot something, I ask Maria what date it is. When she answers, my mind races to remember why the 28th was important, and then it hits me. Fuck, tonight is the premiere of *Serendipity*, the movie. Yeah, they kept the title. They kept my words.

"I can't miss this premiere," I say, as much to myself as to Maria. The words sound surreal, a bad punchline to an even worse joke. Fresh from an overdose, and here I am talking about a fucking movie premiere. Maria looks at me, her eyes widened and concern etched onto her face. But she doesn't argue, doesn't tell me I'm crazy. I wouldn't listen either way, and she knows that. She just nods - a slow, resigned movement.

Several hours later, the Uber pulls up to the Chinese Theater, a relic of Hollywood's Golden Age, with its stone dragons coiling around pillars standing sentinel at the entrance.

I get out of the car, and the first thing that hits me is the paparazzi's flashing cameras. I'm momentarily blinded by the bright lights as we step on the Walk of Fame. Maria is next to me; she's dressed to kill, and with her past modeling experience, she knows exactly what she's doing.

Alessa, already waiting for us, guides us among the throng of fans and photographers like a ninja cutting through the madness. This whole thing feels like a tightly choreographed ballet. She pushes me forward, leading me to a face that's as surprising as it is familiar–Cora, My publicist. She greets me and flashes a smile that's more like a warning. "Don't worry about the video," she reassures me. "I'll do some damage control."

I try to keep my cool as I ask her, "What video?" But my voice cracks, betraying my fear.

She hesitates for a beat before answering, her words carefully chosen.

"The one from last night," she finally says.

Apparently, some kid at Emily's birthday decided to turn my overdose into a short film and share it with the world. The thought of someone filming me while I was at my worst is fucking nauseating. Just what I needed on the night of my movie premiere. "Focus on the press," Cora advises, her tone an odd mix of maternal care and mechanical. Maria's hand remains warm in mine as we walk down the red carpet, attempting to project the illusion of the successful writer whose book has been adapted into a film. Yet, I can't help but feel like a fraud, standing here pretending like everything is alright, like I didn't wake up in a hospital because of a fucking overdose this morning. Maria, on the other hand, seems to be thriving in the attention, basking in the flashes like she was born to be here. Every time the camera clicks, Cora raises that sign with my name on it. A reminder. A brand.

An overdose in the morning, red carpet in the evening. Only in Hollywood.

After what feels like a million photos later, we finally make it to the end of the red carpet and spot Allen. I extend my hand, congratulating him on the movie, and he returns the gesture to me.

Feeling the moment is right, I drop the question, a seemingly innocent inquiry, "Did you get a chance to read the script yet?" The discomfort in his eyes is as clear as the Hollywood sign.

"Yeah," he mumbles, his gaze darting off as he rubs the back of his neck–a nervous tick betraying his unease. "Let's... Let's talk about that on Monday, alright?"

His words echo in my head, a hollow promise or a grim prophecy; only time will tell. Fuck, I could really use a Xanax right about now.

Undeterred, he quickly recovers, slinging an arm around my shoulder, his grin reappearing on his face. "Enjoy the night," he commands, his gaze darting away from mine. "This is going to be big for you!" Then he disappears into the sea of Hollywood elite. Meanwhile, Maria lingers by my side; she leans in, catching me off guard with a kiss that's as intoxicating as the second Benzo. It's familiar yet foreign, a dangerous cocktail of past mistakes and future regrets. Breaking away from it, we stand there, two misfits playing dress-up in the land of make-believe. And I can see it in her eyes, the same destructive potential that mirrors my own. We're a ticking bomb; it's only a matter of time until we fuck this up. The question is, who will it be? Because the way things are going, all bets are off.

Will it be my ex with her Ph.D. in narcissism? The woman who, with one flip of her hair, can make me forget the countless nights of arguing and the bitter taste of betrayal? Or will it be yours truly, with my new best friend Xanax and self-destructive tendencies?

There's a grim poetry to our predicament, two broken pieces of a jigsaw puzzle that never quite fit together. The question isn't if, but when - and who's going to crumble first? Place your bets, ladies and gentlemen.

And the situation is just like this goddamn movie. It could be amazing and a big win, or a total flop and ruin us all.

As we inch our way into the grand theater, the air is filled with a mix of popcorn, expensive perfume, and anticipation. I try to push aside these thoughts and focus on the moment at hand. We slide into our plush seats, right in the middle of the theater, the perfect vantage point.

I'm just a writer, but this is surreal—a trip down the rabbit hole to a world where my first book is now a Hollywood movie. Maria leans in, her voice a hushed whisper against the din of the crowd, "I'm so proud of you." Her words hit me like a shot of straight vodka, and it's then that I realize the enormity of what's about to unfold.

She's about to see a movie, a goddamn movie based on a book that's all about her, about us. Our raw, messy love story playing out on the big screen in front of a room full of strangers. Such a full-circle moment. I never thought I'd talk to her ever again when I wrote that book; now, here she is at the premiere with me. The lights dim, the crowd falls silent, and I take one last look at Maria.

Fuck. I wish Danny were here.

50

remiere Nightmare: Writer Richard Bryght Overdoses at Porno Starlet's Birthday Bash, Just One Day Before Movie Launch! That's what the headlines read. Fucking TMZ, always at the forefront of exploiting other people's pain for profit. They were the first to thrust the video into the public eye, it spread like wildfire, and now the whole world seems to know. But what can I expect from a culture that feeds off of the misery and misfortune of others? I don't really care.

Since then, Paparazzi camp out in front of my house, with those unblinking, glassy eyes of their lenses waiting for me to fuck up again. But in a strange way, this whole thing might have helped the film. It was like free promotion - the kind of PR money can't buy. People wanted to see what kind of story came from a mind spiraling out of control.

The movie had a budget of 15 million dollars, and we just made double that on the opening weekend alone. It's not a blockbuster hit yet, but it's a promising start. The rule of thumb is that a movie has to make 2.5 times its budget to start making money, and we're well on our way. And after watching it, I have to admit, I actually really liked it. They did a great job, but it's still hard to believe that my words have come to life on the big screen. It's like a dream, a surreal fever dream on celluloid.

And then there's Maria. You'd think she would be pissed, but she loves it. She knows it's about her. She knows she's the muse, the inspiration, the spark that ignited the story. Her ego, it's like a scalpel, carving away the negative, the ugly, the inconvenient. The criticism, the pain, the parts of the story that cut too close to the bone? She probably thinks those are just the fiction, the parts I fabricated. And she's like a black hole, sucking in all the attention. So we're kind of good.

My brain chemistry is all kinds of fucked from taking so much Xanax. I'm not as resilient as I used to be, unable to deal with even the slightest problem without popping a pill. The more I take, the less I can handle. And the less I can handle, the more I take. It's a never-ending cycle. I try to mix things up, toss a little Phenibut in between the Xanax binges, but it never hits the same. Sure, it's less addictive, but it feels like a different beast altogether. It's like trading one demon for another, still trying to outrun the darkness that follows me everywhere.

And now here I am, stranded in this Kafkaesque purgatory of the unknown, waiting for a call from Allen. With his thoughts, his verdict on the new script.

LA, the city where everyone's constantly waiting for their phone to ring, and I'm part of it. And I fucking hate waiting.

Then it happens, the phone finally sings its song of relief. Allen's voice same as ever, smooth as a radio DJ with a hint of a smile always clinging to his words. He asks about the weekend, like a concerned parent, tiptoeing around the TMZ headline, telling me not to sweat it. "It's all part of the game", he says. And then he transitions to the movie; he's happy with how it's doing, with the numbers, the reviews. But he's not getting to the point; it's all white noise, empty calories. He's warming me up, softening me for something.

While Allen's voice keeps flowing through the line, my hand casually reaches for that little bottle of tranquility. It's a motion so natural, so rehearsed, you'd think I'm reaching for a bag of chips while watching a game. I snap a bar in half with the ease of practice and toss it back, swallowing it dry. The half dissolves in my mouth, and the bitter taste lingers. Then, there's a subtle shift in the tone of his voice, and I can feel it coming, like a storm brewing on the horizon. We are approaching the elephant stomping around in the room, the script. His voice, light as a feather on the breeze, attempting to soften the blow. But I cut him off mid-sentence,

"Allen, give it to me straight. None of that sugar coating. I can handle it."

There's a long moment of silence on the other end, just the gentle rustling of paper in the background, and I can almost hear him gathering his thoughts, perhaps even his courage. Then, he lets out a sigh, deep and heavy, the kind you'd expect before a confession.

"We...we don't like it, Richard. At all."

His words detonate in my ears, the echo reverberating like the aftermath of a grenade blast. Well, I thought I could handle it." What are your notes? You want to email them?" I ask, trying to keep the desperation from seeping into my voice. The contract clearly includes three rewrites, three attempts to make it right, everything after that costs extra. I can make changes, adjust, adapt.

But Allen, he's the grim reaper of creativity, mowing down my expectations. "Richard," he says, a hint of pity in his voice. "It's just... it's too much. Too many notes. The entire approach... it's not what we envisioned."

That's the thing about creative freedom; it's a double-edged sword - It's all on me, my vision, my fuck-up. Do I have to start from scratch now? Fuck.

But then, Allen delivers the real plot twist and says, "We need to move quickly. And we're bringing in another writer for this one." His voice is light as if he's just talking about the weather. "And you can focus on your next novel," he adds as if that's meant to be a salve to the sting.

My head drifts back to recent headlines I found myself in. Maybe that's the real reason they're dropping me. Is this the silent judgment of Hollywood, a silent punishment for a scandal too public, too raw? Am I being fucking canceled? One minute they're toasting to your success; the next, they're watching you crash and burn. The love is rented, but the hate is real.

But wait, did I really just get half a million dollars for a script that's going to end up in a trashcan? The irony is not lost on me. A hefty paycheck for a project that's going to be butchered by someone else.

"We'll be in touch," Allen says, and I can almost hear the condescension in his voice. As if he's doing me a favor by keeping me on a leash, dangling the vague promise of future work in front of me. The call ends, the line goes dead, and I'm left here with the deafening silence of my own thoughts, my own doubts. And yet, I am still breathing, still fighting, still dreaming. Because that's what we do, us storytellers. We dream, we hope, we bleed our hearts onto the page. And even when the world turns its back on us, we keep going.

Because the story isn't over.

At least, not yet.

51

After Allen essentially told me to fuck off, the only thing that's hurt is my ego, but I'll get over it. Now I have time to continue working on my book; however, the words just won't flow. I've had a good start after Danny's death, but since then, I've been too occupied with the script Allen ended up hating anyway.

Maybe it's the lack of deadlines or pressure now that the film project is no longer on my plate. Or maybe it's because I don't have to worry about money anymore. My book is on the cusp of being a bestseller; the cash for the script is digital confetti in my account. And with the movie doing well and my contractual percentage attached to it, I know there's more to come. However, money has a point of saturation where the amount you possess becomes irrelevant. Once you hit that threshold, everything beyond that is just empty numbers on a screen, at least for me. And I know people that would disagree, the pursuit of wealth becomes a never-ending hamster wheel to them. But to me, it's just noise. A pleasant hum in the background, but noise all the same.

My mind is as empty as the page in front of me. And besides the cash, the only thing that's flowing is my frustration. Normal people in my place, they would probably be booking first-class tickets, packing their bags, and setting off on a year-long journey around the globe. They'd fill their Instagram feeds with sunsets in Santorini and selfies in front of the Taj Mahal, drinking Mai Tais on Caribbean beaches and dancing the night away in Ibiza.

But I'm unapologetically abnormal when it comes to that; I don't dance to the same rhythm. Money may be able to purchase a round-the-world ticket, but it sure as shit can't buy passion. The joy of creation, the thrill of birthing a story from the womb of my imagination—that's my true wealth. Creativity is the only currency that truly matters. So if I'm not inspired, then it might as well be fucking monopoly money. And right now, there's nothing. I'm creatively broke. Perhaps it's time to flirt with the psychedelic mistress of micro-dosing again. But I'm not exactly the guy with a "guy." I'm the guy with a "girl," and her name is Lana.

I reach for my phone, scrolling through my contacts until I find her. She's my connection. Her voice, sunny and full of artificial sweetener, vibrates through the speaker; it's the kind of happiness that only LA can produce.

"Hey, stranger," she says as if I'm some long-lost lover instead of an uninspired author looking for a psychedelic pick-me-up. Part of me cringes. I feel like a typical LA douchebag now, the guy who only calls when he needs something. But Lana, she gets it. After all, she's the one who introduced me to psychedelics in the first place. She just laughs and says, "Of course, anything for you."

After a brief moment of silence, she invites me to a party at her place tonight. My mind instantly flashes back to the last adult film star soiree I attended. *Do I really want to do this?* I ask myself, looking at the empty page before me.

"Sure," I say before I even have a chance to think it over, a slave to my own self-destructive tendencies, "I'll be there."

"Great, I'll have the capsules ready for you then." she trills through the phone.

I don't even ask what she's celebrating, but in this city, we don't need an occasion to party.

And I'm getting excited. Yeah, I know it's fucked up to get psyched over drugs, but creativity requires its fuel. Here I am, the man who writes for a living, now depending on a fungus-induced inspiration. But hey, it's all for the art, right?

That's what I keep telling myself anyway, the words becoming a mantra, a pathetic justification. Which, of course, reminds me of Danny. As if repeating it enough times will make it true. It somehow makes it acceptable that I'm about to attend an A-list adult film stars party just to pick up mind-altering substances like they're vitamins, all in the name of art. I end the call and look around the house.

I don't remember the exact moment when Maria moved in; we never had "the talk," no agreement. It simply happened. And I don't really care. Her clothes now hang next to mine, her perfume mingling with the stale air of my closet, and her toothbrush resting beside mine. I just allowed it to happen. I'm standing on the sidelines, observing the gradual takeover.

Danny's room transformed into a mausoleum of memories. Everything in its place, untouched since he left. It's like time froze in there as if I could step in, and he'd be back, laughing, living. But he's not. The emptiness screams at me, echoing through the silent space. Sometimes, when the void gets too loud, I sit in that room, just sit, surrounded by his stuff, immersed in his memory. Maybe I'll write in there.

The garage became a storage unit. My old Seattle apartment is squeezed into boxes inside its walls, mixed with Danny's belongings. Like a museum of bad decisions, a monument to our past lives. This house is supposed to be a symbol of my success, but all it does is remind me of what I've lost along the way. I'm trapped in this luxurious hell, suffocating under the weight of my own ambition.

Another fucking cliché.

I'm sitting in the living room, with Salem by my side, staring at the vase of Danny's ashes that's resting over the fireplace.

Suddenly, the front door opens, and Maria enters. She's had a long day, but damn, she still looks incredible. A simple 'Hi' slips from her lips. She walks over to me and gives me a kiss, dragging me out of my melancholy haze.

"How was your day?" I ask. I want to know about the world outside that she's just returned from. It's a simple question, but for us, it's a bridge that connects our separate lives, our distinct realities. She begins unraveling the story of her day, how she's been busy with clients and meetings. Her narrative, a vibrant tapestry of structure and logic, starkly contrasts with the chaotic canvas of my life. It's a dance of opposites.

Our relationship, if you can call it that, is built on foundations of sand. I can't deny that she believes in what we have, that her feelings are genuine in her own twisted way. A narcissist resides in a reality of their own creation, and in her world, she's the protagonist of a grand romance.

But facts are stubborn things. They have an inconvenient way of demanding attention. Like the fact that she found a sanctuary in my home and my life, after her own world crumbled. Post-divorce, a fresh start with an ex-lover who had conveniently evolved into a successful writer is more than just a coincidence. It's a survival tactic. Narcissists usually bounce around between two people.

"I'm going to take a shower," she says, her voice pulling me from my internal monologue. She adds, "Want to watch a movie after?" It's an invitation to further immerse into our shared illusion, to drape ourselves in this carefully constructed normalcy. It's like a sitcom, and I swear I can almost hear the laugh track.

As Maria begins to peel off her work persona along with her clothes, I say, "Actually, I'm going out tonight,"

Her hands halting their task midway through the act of releasing her bra.

"Out?" she echoes, a hint of surprise in her voice. "Where to?"

"Lana's throwing a party," I tell her, dropping the name like a lit match onto a gasoline-soaked floor.

"Lana?" The name falls from her lips, sharp and laced with acid. She knows exactly who Lana is. The porn star. The one who can make a Tuesday feel like a Saturday night. The woman who is not her.

I did end up in the hospital last time, sure. My veins were a cocktail of good intentions and bad decisions. But tonight, I'll be careful. Jealousy flares in her eyes as if I'm the one who cheated, the one who betrayed and shattered the trust. Not her. Never her.

But I refuse to play this fucking game. I've done nothing wrong. My cards have always been face up on the table. "You're welcome to join," I toss out a half-hearted invitation, knowing full well she'll decline.

And, true to form, she does. She shakes her head. "No, I don't feel like it," She wants a reason to be angry. She's building an ammunition depot out of thin air, preparing for a war I have no intention of fighting.

"Just make sure you stay out of the headlines this time," she spits out. A punchline. I'm the joke, and she's the audience, laughing at her own comedy.

"I'll try my best," I answer because what else is there to say? The door shuts behind me with a finality that echoes through the quiet house, a clear punctuation to our latest chapter of drama. And there it is, another perfect night in our sitcom of a relationship. Cue the laugh track.

There's a certain satisfaction I get as I step out of the Uber. The undercurrent of Xanax and Phenibut in my system amplifies this feeling. It's not euphoria, more like a pleasant sense of detachment, a warm hug from a chemical friend. There's no need for alcohol, not tonight. I'm here to experience everything while feeling nothing at all. I approach Lana's hillside villa, and the thumping of generic house music bleeding into the night air. The driveway is jam-packed with High-end cars, polished to perfection.

The front door swings open before I can even knock, and there she is, Lana herself, as polished as the cars lining her driveway. Dressed in something that clings to her like a second skin, she's a living, breathing piece of art. "Lana," I manage to utter, my voice more stable than I feel. Her hug is warm and enveloping, a welcome reprieve from the emotional warfare I left behind.

I cross the threshold into the pulsating heart of the party. It's in full swing, people, beautiful people, laughing and talking over the music, creating a symphony of human connection. And amidst them all, like a black swan in a sea of white, I spot Emily. Wearing a little black dress, she exudes an aura of elegance and confidence.

Feeling a bit self-conscious because of her birthday fiasco, I contemplate my next move but decide to face it head-on. I approach her, my eyes meeting hers, and her lips curve into a soft smile.

"I'm sorry about your birthday," I say.

She waves it off dismissively, her smile indicating that it's water under the bridge. "No worries," she replies, her voice barely audible over the music. "I'm just glad you're okay. I should be the one apologizing. I didn't think anyone would be low enough to film you and post it online. What a dick move."

I laugh and say, "I swear it was fucking 'Lyrical mirage'!" Emily chuckles, and Lana appears, holding a glass of something sparkling in her hand. She offers it to me, but I decline, raising my hands in defense. Tonight isn't about drowning sorrows; it's about floating on them.

"But we're celebrating," she exclaims, a twinkle in her eye.

Intrigued, I ask, "Oh, what are we celebrating?"

She grins, a triumphant look on her face. "I'm retiring from porn."

I stand there, absorbing the revelation, the party around me blurring into background noise. The insanity of it all hits me, and I can't help but laugh. For most people, this would be like a break from reality, but this IS my reality. And I am well aware that the life I lead is far from ordinary, but damn, it makes for a fucking good story.

"Congratulations," I say. The word is sincere, despite the oddity of congratulating someone for retiring from the adult entertainment industry. Yet, it feels entirely fitting.

"Thanks. Yeah, I've had enough of faking orgasms and getting cumshots in my eyes for money," she jokes, her laughter ringing out in the room. She's moving on to the fashion world with plans to start her own clothing brand. It's no surprise, really, with the kind of wealth she's accumulated over the years, she can live life on her own terms. Lana and Emily clink their glasses together, the crystal sound echoing through the space, a celebration of Lana's achievement.

Then Lana asks her, "And you? Ever think about retiring?" Emily laughs, her dark eyes sparkling with amusement. "Fuck no," she replies. "I still love it too much. I was born for porn."

And there she is, a young woman who's found joy in an industry that the world looks down upon. I have to admit, I'm pretty damn impressed by both of them. One, courageously stepping away from the familiarity of an industry that has been her world, and the other, fully embracing it with open arms. The whole idea of 'right' or 'wrong' dissipates into oblivion. We all must make our own choices based on what we believe is best for ourselves.

Lana's voice cuts through the ambient chatter, suggesting we take a photo together - a slice of time immortalized in pixels. Her, Emily, and me. A strange echo of the day when Emily and I first crossed paths. We assemble ourselves, Lana in the middle, while

Emily and I orbit her on either side. Click. Three lives intersecting in this one moment now etched in binary code.

Lana turns to me, her voice velvety smooth. "Oh, before I forget," she says, delving into the labyrinth of her purse. Her fingers emerge with a small bag filled with yellow and green capsules, which she holds out to me. "Your penis envy," she says with a smirk. The mere mention of its name makes me laugh, reminding me that I am still 12 years old inside.

I take the bag from her hand, feeling its weight and the promise it holds. A grin creeps across my face, "Thanks," I say, tucking it carefully into my pocket. My watch buzzes on my wrist; I glance down at it, the bright screen illuminating my face. I read Maria's message: "Hope you're having fun with your porn star friends. I'm going to bed now. I love you..."

I let out a sigh, wondering why she has to bring that up again and strategically combine it with "I love you. Dot dot dot". Another punchline. She wants a reaction, but I choose to ignore it.

Hours have passed, but I've been a good boy, resisting the temptation of alcohol and sticking to sugar-free Red Bull. The conversations were interesting, the laughs were plenty, but I'm ready to call it a night. I'm getting *Stand by Me* vibes again. I say my goodbyes to Lana, casting a final glance at her–silent tribute to our shared moment in time, a quiet understanding. Then I seek out Emily to do the same. When our paths cross, she pulls me into a lingering embrace–a hug that feels like a final farewell, as if acknowledging the transient nature of our connection.

Then with a few touches on my phone screen, I call an Uber, witnessing a symphony of endings and beginnings unfold in the cold light of the screen. A nod here, a hug there, and I make my way to the front door. The party fades away behind me as I step outside.

The Uber arrives, and I slide into the back seat, greeted by the sanctuary of faux leather and air freshener. The driver, a middle-aged man with a receding hairline, seems to have found in me an unwilling participant to his one-sided discourse. I nod, offering non-committal hums in response. Lost in my thoughts, I stare out the window. The city passes me by in a blur of neon lights and shadowy alleys as we navigate the streets of West Hollywood.

My phone vibrates in my pocket—it's an Instagram notification: "One year ago today." showing a picture of Danny and me, smiling. Memories of him flood my brain, bringing back the good times, the bad times, and the times I've tried to forget.

However, everything changes in an instant as we cross an intersection.

The screech of tires, LED headlights blinding, the impact that shakes my entire body. A black Tesla hammers into the driver's side of the Uber. Time seems to warp and contort. Each moment stretches out, agonizingly slow yet horrifyingly fast. The sound of metal twisting and bending fills my ears as the world spins around me. I watch in horror as we flip over and over, like a tumbleweed caught in a storm. The driver screams, but it's like listening to someone underwater. His body - this man I know only by his first name, a detail shared by an app - crumples like a rag doll in a macabre ballet of broken physics, a grotesque dance in the strobing light. A warm spray of his blood hits me, a Rorschach test of life's fragility painted onto the fabric of my shirt. I attempt to scream, but no sound comes out. My mind struggles to process what's happening, but before I know it, the world goes black.

52

The world blurs in and out, and I can't tell if I'm dreaming or if this is my new reality. I'm paralyzed, and my brain feels like it's been scrambled, thoughts slipping through my fingers like water. Everything is dark. My mind feels untethered, unmoored from my physical form. I seem to float above my own body, the world around me taking on a surreal, otherworldly quality. Caught in a limbo between consciousness and unconsciousness, reality and fantasy.

Memories come in flashes, a flickering slideshow of chaos and disaster. There was the party, the Uber, an impersonal ride in a stranger's car—And then the crash, a violent dissonance of screeching tires, shattering glass, and the sickening crunch of metal on metal. The driver's blood and the mangled Tesla, twisted like a croissant.

Fuck, am I dead? This question echoes in the empty cavity of my brain. Will I be the writer to pen down the sensation of dying? The first to paint a vivid picture of this unknown realm between life and death?

Machines beep, and voices murmur. It's a strange sensation, being here but not quite here, an odd state of semi-presence. The more I struggle, the further away from my body I seem to drift, until I'm nothing more than a spectator to the scene below.

As I look down at my anatomy, lying there motionless, I feel a sense of detachment, as if I'm watching a movie of my own life. Is this really me? Time feels like it's moving in slow motion, every second dragging into eternity. But if this is really it, that would be fucking disappointing–a story without an ending. A writer left on a precipice of a cliffhanger. Below, my body lies dormant, an empty husk. A body with a story still left to tell. One more book, one final wordplay, one more plot twist, that's what I want. A writer deserves a grand finale, a climax. Not this shit, not hovering in this purgatorial slowness, a fucked up astral projection experience peering down at the mess I've become.

But then it hits me–perhaps I'm not dying. Maybe I'm just high as fuck, my senses blurred and distorted by the drugs. I'm in a hospital, filled with sterile smells and bright lights. They've pumped me full of painkillers, my veins humming with chemical relief.

An extra life. That's what it feels like. Like I've stumbled upon a hidden cheat code in the video game of life. I may be down, but not out. I can hit 'continue' and keep playing. Maybe I've had some dying to do before I can write another book.

And I will. I've got a story to tell.

Then, Fade in: My consciousness re-entering my body like a character respawning in some glitchy video game. And here I am. The moment my eyes blink open in the clean wash of hospital lights, it's a stark contrast to the chaotic haze of my memories. It feels like hitting the reset button. I'm back, baby.

A nurse is hovering in the periphery of my blurred vision. She's a vague shape of blues and whites, a smudge against the harshly lit backdrop of the room. Her eyes shift to me, widening slightly when she notices my consciousness creeping back. Her lips move, forming words that my brain fails to process, as my system is still booting up. Then she disappears out the door, her footsteps echoing in the sterile hallway beyond. A few long, drawn-out moments later, the doctor walks in and gives me a recap of what happened in the previous episode of my life, the one I fell asleep during.

They've got me on a cocktail of drugs that would make a pharmacy blush. Loaded me up with Oxy and muscle relaxers, inducing sweet synthetic oblivion into my veins. This is pharmaceutical nirvana. I've never had Oxy's before, but damn, It's like sinking into a soft pillow, making the world become a blurred watercolor painting, all gentle edges, and mellow hues. And the muscle relaxers, they're the cherry on top, smoothing out any roughness, making every movement feel like I'm made of rubber. In a good way.

It's a level of relaxation I never knew existed– like floating in a warm pool, the world drifting by in slow motion.
Every breath brings a fresh wave of euphoria; every exhale is a sigh of relief. The pain, the fear, the confusion, all of it fades into the background, replaced by a profound sense of calm and peace.

It's the ultimate power-up, the perfect extra life. The kind of high that would have made Hunter S. Thompson jealous.

But waking up here feels like déjà vu, like the worst kind of Groundhog Day. I've been in this scene before, only a few days ago, but this time it's got a twist. I didn't OD, didn't dance too close to the edge of my own volition. This time it's not my fault. I also didn't ask for the Uber to be T-boned by a speeding Tesla. And the truth is, It's a miracle that I'm still alive–I survived a fatal car crash. The Uber driver's life was extinguished in the blink of an eye, caught in the deformed wreckage of the car with me. Reduced to a tragic footnote in the events of the night. The Tesla driver's life abruptly snuffed out upon impact. Just a sudden, violent goodbye.

And me? I'm only left with a brain that feels like it's been put through a blender, a neck that screams bloody murder with every move, and a few hours of time sucked into a black hole of nothingness, as if edited out. Yet, considering the alternative, I'll take it. There are still stories to tell. So I'll embrace the concussion, the sore neck, and the lost moments in time. Ironically, I can already see the next headlines: "From OD to ICU: Richard Bryght Cheats Death Twice in Triple-Thrill Week!" I swear, this movie is getting more free press by the day. At this rate, I should have Ava re-negotiating my cut.

A knock interrupts my thoughts, and Maria enters the room like she's walking onto a movie set, a leading lady entering the scene. But before she can get a word out, I shoot her a peace sign

—a silent declaration of my survival. I'm still here, still breathing, still capable of making light of a situation that's anything but. Despite the groovy vibes of the Oxy and muscle relaxers coursing through my veins, I'm lucid enough to read the relief washing over her face.

She crosses the room in a couple of quick strides, and her arms are around me before I can react. Her kiss is soft and warm, like a grounding presence, and when she finally pulls away, her face is a mix of relief and that all-too-familiar "I told you so" expression. The latter doesn't surprise me. And maybe it's the influence of the drugs talking or my attempt to lighten the mood, but I say, "You know, the same thing could've happened on the way to *Whole Foods*."

Her eyes roll, but I can see the corners of her mouth twitch, fighting a smile. "Let's get you home," she says firmly but gently.

I nod at her. "But I think we need more Oxy," I say, my voice slurring slightly. In my current state of blissful oblivion, fueled by a newfound ambition and the reality of two lost lives that could have included my own. I know it's all plastic, an emotional dead end. But I don't give a shit. As fucked up as it may be, our "relationship" is exactly what I need right now. It's just real enough to make me feel something. And I have a vision, to find meaning in the madness. Because that's what I do. I take the absurd, the tragic, the beautiful mess of life and turn it into words.

Life's funny in its cruel kind of way; it serves you tragedy on a silver platter, then slips you a second chance under the table, like a secret handshake between you and fate.

53

Writing is the enduring love that never abandons me, the one constant in a world of fleeting emotions. Even after periods of separation, its appeal never dissipates. This creative process, I love it more than I could ever love another person. The ability to build entire worlds with nothing but my thoughts and a few well-chosen words. Writing has a certain power; for example, by reading this very line, you allowed me to control your mind for a moment.

I may not believe in a god, but if creating something from nothing isn't godlike, then what is? We're all divine architects in our own right, master builders of creation.

It's been two weeks since I left the hospital, or 75 pages of my book ago. Depending on how you measure it and writing is all I've been doing.

Maria is physically present but not really here. The tide of her narcissism has turned, and we're now in the devaluation stage, the inevitable next phase of her cycle. And I'm drowning in the icy depths of her indifference, a far cry from how affectionate she was just two weeks ago. I can see it in the way she looks at me, the way her eyes flicker with annoyance and impatience. It's like she's bored with me, like I'm a toy she's tired of playing with. I'm not the great writer she once swooned over anymore; I'm the flawed, ordinary human being that doesn't quite measure up. A narcissist's love is a switchblade kiss, sweet and sharp. One moment they are the sun, radiating warmth and light in abundance; the next, they transform into a bitter winter, leaving you yearning for the summer that once was.

I don't know if she knows that I know. Maybe she doesn't even realize that she's following a script, but I do. And that gives me an edge, a small sense of control in an otherwise chaotic situation.

But the irony is, knowing about these cycles and understanding the nuances of her narcissism doesn't make it any less painful. The knowledge of her patterns is not a shield; it's a magnifying glass, making every slight, every indifference, more pronounced. It's like anticipating a punch - you still feel the impact.

Yet, there's something about her twisted manipulation that ignites my inspiration; it fuels me, a dark and dangerous muse that sparks something in me. It gives me a depth of emotion that I wouldn't have otherwise. I'm not just writing; I'm bleeding onto the page, pouring out my soul one word at a time. It's a fucked-up kind of inspiration, but it's inspiration nonetheless. Maybe we can turn this pain into prose, this chaos into a masterpiece. She was my inspiration for my first book, and now, even in the midst of her emotional abuse, she's inspiring me once again. Fuck micro-dosing; I'm on a full-blown Maria trip. She's not a drug; she's the entire damn pharmacy. And what's wrong with that? Well, what the fuck is right with that shit? I don't know.

And then there are the new companions, the chemical comrades who've stormed the fortress of my psyche. Oxy's, muscle relaxers–the whole pharmaceutical circus has come to town. They're all invited–Xanax, Phenibut–each providing a different brand of forgetfulness, each adding their own flavors to this twisted recipe. Sure, I'm feeling fucking miserable, but at the same time, I'm feeling fucking amazing. Oscillating between states of agony and ecstasy. It's like the drugs and the creative process are taking me to places I've never been before. That's a high you can't bottle, a trip you cannot prescribe.

However, being able to say that "I'm an artist" is like a get-out-of-jail-free card, an excuse for any self-destructive behavior I choose to indulge in. But it's all for the sake of my art, or so I tell myself. The more I bleed, the more authentic my work. The more I suffer, the more profound my voice is. The more I lose myself, the more I find my art. And the idea of sacrificing my sanity for my work feels almost noble. I am a walking contradiction of self-destruction and artistic passion - it's all worth it if it means creating something truly great. We are all special cases.

I hear the door swing open and shut. It's Maria, returning from work. There's no kiss, no hug–just a quick and cold "Hi" before she walks right past me. It's as if she's allergic to me, annoyed by my very presence. And yet, this is my house, the one I paid for, the one she's living in for free. She plays the charade well, a puppeteer pulling the strings of our routine, the 'nothing-is-wrong' dance in full swing.

I attempt to break the tension. "Wanna watch a movie?" I ask, but she immediately declines, disappearing into the other room without a word. We haven't had sex in a while, and that's usually a good indicator of a bigger issue. Maybe it's me, maybe it's her, maybe it's both of us.

Fuck this; I need a change of scenery. And so, I grab my MacBook and summon an Uber, directing it towards Laurel Tavern. Feeling strange now as I climb into the backseat, with the memory of my last ride still fresh in my mind. But the drive is uneventful, no crashes, no dead people. The driver remains silent except for the occasional grunt in response to my small talk.

I push open the door to the bar. The place is noisy and crowded, but it's a welcomed change from the silence of my house. I survey the room, searching for an empty table, a sanctuary where I can disappear into my own world. Finally, I spot a table in the far corner, away from the chaos of the bar. I navigate through the crowd, avoiding spilled drinks and stumbling patrons. I notice some of them giving me that look, like they know who I am. They probably recognize me from recent TMZ headlines. Or maybe I'm just being paranoid.

I sit down, open up my MacBook and start typing. Time becomes fluid, and the hours seem to melt away as I type, lost in the world I'm creating. Occasionally, I notice someone staring at me, but I ignore them, determined to finish my work. Here, in the dim light of the bar, I'm no celebrity, no headline. I'm just a writer, fully absorbed in my craft.

Suddenly, I'm approached by a guy demanding my attention. "Are you Richard Bryght?" he asks, and I nod without looking up from my screen. Anticipating the inevitable conversation about my latest scandal, I'm already pre-annoyed. However, instead of launching into a predictable barrage of questions, he throws me a curveball. "I'm Tom, Maria's ex-husband," he says.

My mind stumbles for a second, trying to reconcile this figure with the monster she painted. I offer him my silent condolences, my mental fingers crossing for his sanity. But then something in me snaps, and I find myself blurting out a question that's been burning in my mind for months. "Oh, you're the guy that hits women?" The words spill out before I can even think, propelled by a cocktail of drugs and anger.

But his reaction is immediate, his face twisting into a picture of hurt and indignation; he looks me straight in the eye and denies it vehemently. "I never laid a hand on her," he protests. "She probably punched herself and then called the cops."
And somehow, I find myself believing this stranger.

Maria's stories had portrayed a vivid and brutal picture of the man in front of me. Yet, from up close, he's just a man. A man worn down by the same relentless tide that's eroding me. Under normal circumstances, I would have questioned his story, but this is Maria we're talking about. The woman who twists reality to suit her own needs, who plays the victim even as she inflicts the most cruel emotional abuse on those around her. The rabbit hole of her deceit runs deep, and I'm just starting to comprehend its extent.

As he talks, I remember that night I picked her up, the night she'd spun that horrifying tale of abuse. I'd opened my home to her, offering her safety and solace. Had it all been a plan, a carefully orchestrated play in the twisted theater of Maria's mind? Narcissists usually bounce around between two people, and I think in Maria's case, right now, they are looking at each other. We're just two puppets in her game.

I gesture for Tom to take a seat. Over the clinking of glasses and low murmur of the bar, we swap war stories from the front lines of Maria's fabricated world. He recounts her infidelity, the countless times she'd been unfaithful, and her baffling rage when he'd caught her red-handed, as if he was the one in the wrong. It's a mirror of my own experiences–a pattern of manipulation that's hard to break free from. And right now, she's in my house, in my bed, and in my heart.

As Tom continues to speak, I'm wondering why he even bothered to approach me. He's off the hook now, free from Maria's grasp, so what does he want from me? Is he trying to bond with someone who's experienced the same thing he has? Or maybe he saw my TMZ headlines and thinks that my current situation is a direct result of Maria's behavior. If it's a warning, telling me to be careful, then his words are falling on deaf ears. Because the truth is, I don't care. I don't want to be saved. I know the risks, I know the danger, but I'm in too deep now. I use her just as much as she uses me– it's a sick and distorted kind of codependency. I know it's fucked up, to use her to fuel my creativity, to keep myself miserable and inspired. And it's also fucked up that she uses me for a place to stay, for the validation and desire that I can offer her. It's the worst of both worlds.

Last time, I was clueless, ignorant to her manipulations and her true nature. But now, it's different–I know what's happening, and I am aware that I'm allowing myself to be used and abused. I see the storm; I know it's coming, but I'm strapping myself to the mast all the same. This isn't ignorance; it's a deliberate dance with disaster.

Or maybe it's just the fact that I'm too broken to want anything else, anything real.

Emilia might've been right.

54

There's a dull throb in the back of my skull, an unrelenting tension that's been there ever since I spoke to Tom. It has become a chronic condition, a tumor made of truth. Maria's truth. Or lies. Can't say which, at this point, it's all the same. She has twisted my brain into knots, my thoughts tangled in a web of deceit and manipulation. But today is Thanksgiving, and Maria has left the premises. She's boarded a plane to visit her family in Oklahoma. And, damn, it feels good. As if the sun has broken through the clouds after a week-long rain. This time apart gives me the space I need to write. No more switchblade kisses, no more emotional exploitation.

The sound of the Macy's Thanksgiving Day Parade fills the room, and it's just me, my cat, and my MacBook–a blank canvas for my words to flow. But that's as far as I indulge in the festivities; I'm on a water fast right now. Zero calories. I am aware that it's an unusual choice for a holiday centered around food, but I have my reasons. The lack of nourishment is supposed to clear my mind and make me more productive. And it does; it's like a mental reset, a way to clear out the cobwebs and make room for new ideas.

However, I have to be extra careful with my drug consumption while fasting. My body, starved and raw, absorbs everything like a vortex, pulling it in, crushing it down, amplifying the effect until it's a symphony playing at full volume inside a closet. Half a Xanax will feel like two, and I can't afford to lose control. While the rest of the world is feasting, I'm weaving a delicate web of deprivation and intoxication.

It may seem like a strange way to celebrate, but in this moment, in this silence, it's perfect. But the silence is abruptly broken by a text from Maria, wishing me a "Happy Thanksgiving." There are no sweet nothings, no whispered 'I love you's—nothing but a cold, calculated text. Maria deliberately starves me, savoring my thirst for her affection, on purpose. She's playing hard to understand. The DSM that my father handed me is sitting right in front of me on the table, and I can't help but crack a grin. I don't need to flip through its pages to find the section on "narcissistic personality disorder" - I know that thing cover to cover.

I could directly confront Maria, expose her lies, and rip off the mask she's been wearing. Shove Tom's tales right in her face, and ask her if the domestic violence was just a plot device. But when it comes to narcissists, you have to be careful, strategic. The timing has to be right, like a sniper. The moment you call them out, they'll flip, turn the tables, transforming themselves into the victim. How dare you see them for who they truly are? It is like poking a stick into a hornet's nest; you better be ready for the swarm. And then, they will discard you, like a rusted car, too damaged and broken to be worth fixing.

And so, I smile, a mask of my own. Silently holding the truth like a venomous snake, waiting for the right moment to unleash it. While observing her from a distance, like a scientist studying a dangerous, unpredictable creature.

On the other hand, I keep checking IMDb for box office numbers. Although math was never my strong suit, this is the sexy kind of math. *Serendipity*, the movie so far, pulled in over 60 million dollars. Subtracting the 15 million they spent to make it, that's a profit of 45 million. Thanks to Ava, I'm entitled to 7% of that, a sweet 3,150,000 Dollars. Alessa gets her well-earned 10%, and Ava gets her 5% share. If Danny were still around, he would have gotten his 15% manager cut, which I would have gladly given to him. So after the dust settles, and if the movie wouldn't make another dime, I'm still left with a sweet 2,677,500 dollars. Minus taxes, of course. Writing is something I'd do for free and have for years, but this is still pretty nice. You can either sell your soul for a dollar or sell your art for a fortune.

I get up to feed Salem; after all, she's not fasting, and it's Thanksgiving, so I splurged on the fanciest cat food I could find. He circles my legs, his green eyes tracking my every move, a purring engine of anticipation. I open it with a hiss, revealing the pungent aroma of salmon and chicken, and the cat dinner is served.

Returning to the keyboard, my fingers dance across the keys, the words cascading from my mind like a waterfall of twisted thoughts. There's something strangely liberating about fasting, about not being a slave to my body's demands. It gives me space, freedom to dive into the realms of my mind. Hours pass in a blur, with only a few sips of water providing respite.

I carefully break off a quarter of a pill. My need for Xanax is growing with each day, ever since Maria's sudden change in behavior. At this point, I think it's pretty safe to say that I'm addicted to it. I can't remember the last day I went without it; I didn't even try.

I reach for my phone - a tap, and a swipe, immersing myself in the social media rabbit hole. Maria's story with some faceless smiling Joe pops up, leaving a bitter taste in my mouth. I Don't know the dude, but that's probably the point. It's a performance, yet another staged scene in the Maria show. I keep scrolling, and Emilia pops up—on a hike, Fryman Canyon, by the looks of it. It's a breath of fresh air. A selfie with the canyon sprawling behind her, no makeup on, and looking breathtaking—a sunrise in a world of neon lights. The caption reads, "I am grateful for this! Happy Thanksgiving". She's alone, much like myself. And it seems like she's enjoying it, just as I am.

A warmth spreads through me, a fuzzy feeling that's far from the cold prick of Maria's post. Emilia's presence, even though it's just a digital imprint, feels genuine.

Perhaps there's a plot twist here— she is actually the one that got away, and I was too fucking stupid to see it. Maybe I should also write about that, write about my mistakes, my fuck ups.

If you want to make an impact, write about the things that everyone is afraid to talk about.

55

t's a sunny Christmas day in Los Angeles, a far cry from the chilly and snowy holidays of my youth. It's my first time celebrating it in California, and the sunshine feels wrong, like a misprint in the calendar. Additionally, It's also the first festive season without Danny, and the reality of his absence hits me hard. The cemetery in Seattle, where my parents are buried, also goes unvisited. The traditions are slipping away, leaving me feeling out of place, like I'm the one ornament that doesn't belong on the tree.

Despite the high temperatures, there's still an intangible chill in the air, and it's not just the air conditioning. Maria, the emotional Grinch, has returned from her trip to Oklahoma, attempting to pretend like everything is okay. I didn't expect her to come back so soon, and I can feel the tension brewing.

I observe her trying to act normal, trying to project like everything is fine, the way every family does on Christmas. She's constructing a Hallmark holiday moment, but the colors are too bright, the smiles too wide, the laughter a fraction too forced. I can see right through her. But I don't care. I won't let her ruin this day for me. I've bought a big tree and have been blasting

Christmas music for days. I'm force-feeding the holiday spirit. And I'm ready to play the game. To act, to pretend, to fuck under the mistletoe.

I've got *Home Alone* cued up, it's my personal tradition, and she knows it. The glowing TV screen promises a safe haven of nostalgic holiday comfort. She reaches for my hand, her touch gentle and warm. But the warmth is a lie, an illusion. It's a mechanical act devoid of feeling and of connection. I reciprocate, playing along with the facade. There's a paradox here, I hate that I love her, despite everything, or am I confusing the emotion with something else? I can't fucking tell anymore.

I press play, and the theme song fills the room. The opening credits roll as we sink into the couch cushions. Maria turns to me; her eyes, those deceivingly beautiful traps, meet mine, and she says, "I love you." Her voice is a lullaby, and I don't know if it's true, but I don't care, because I don't feel the difference. Maybe I'm too numb, the counterfeit sentiment still lingering in the air with the same intoxicating fragrance. She then kisses me before resting her head on my shoulder. And we watch the movie together. It's a picture-perfect scene, on the surface, made in Hollywood. The lights from the tree twinkle, casting a warm glow throughout the room. And for a fleeting moment, it feels like we're just two people in love, spending the holiday together like any other happy couple.

And amidst this, the real Christmas miracle is unfolding. My new book is nearing its completion; at this pace, I should be done sometime after New Year's Eve. I can smell the ending; it's close, the final piece of a jigsaw puzzle. It's the unwrapped present under the tree, the promise of completion, of accomplishment. It appears that creativity thrives in the darkness of the mind. Every single miserable moment over the past months, has helped me with my writing - it's all just fuel for the fire. And the flames burn brighter than ever before.

I reach for the bottle of pills resting on the table and fish a muscle relaxer out from within. The persistent pain in my neck is both a constant reminder of the accident and a good excuse to consume more drugs, to push myself further.

Then Maria starts kissing me, her lips urgent, insistent. She's the one who initiates, not me, her hands and mouth moving with a certainty, and I just give in. It's like she's attempting to prove something, to me, to herself, or perhaps it's a diversion. She tastes like peppermint and red wine, an odd combination that somehow works.

Before I know it, we're naked, illuminated by the soft glow of Christmas lights. It's an interesting experience, sex on muscle relaxers and Xanax. Like I'm feeling everything through a thick layer of cotton, or engaging in intercourse underwater— everything becomes slow and distorted. It's not unpleasant. In fact, there's something almost surreal about it. It feels appropriate. And then it's over, like a hiccup in time. But as we lay there, I'm left feeling hollow and disconnected. Maybe this is my life now, a series of bizarre meaningless moments all strung together.

I finish dressing myself as Maria steps away from me, walking naked over to the kitchen counter, reaching for the wine bottle like a drunken ballerina. My phone vibrates on the counter next to her, and I ask her if she could bring it. Her gaze instinctively shifts to the screen as she picks it up and says, "It's from Emily," the words dripping with suspicion and jealousy. She tosses it over to me like a grenade with the pin pulled out.

The message is innocent, just a simple "Merry Christmas." Yet, it's enough to ignite the flames of Maria's paranoia. Then comes the loaded question, one she has asked before, "Did you fuck her that night?"

The hypocrisy is overwhelming, coming from the one who previously admitted to cheating on me during our relationship. It is her way of projecting her own issues and insecurities onto me, transforming our relationship into a theater for her inner demons.

I roll my eyes and sigh." No, I didn't fuck her that night."

The look on her face reveals that she doesn't believe me, but I don't care. I've never given her reason to doubt me, yet here we are, a tableau of suspicion and mistrust set against the backdrop of tinsel and twinkling Christmas lights.

Then she asks," Why would I believe you?"

She stole my line, and of course, the question is rhetorical, a declaration of her disbelief. I shake my head as I take a seat on the couch.

"I can't trust you with all your fans and porn star friends," she says, bitterness lacing her words.

I know that it's pointless; my response to her accusation is nothing–a void, an abyss of indifference. In that moment, I realize that I no longer care. I'm numb to her words, her accusations, her anger. And it feels liberating.

"Say something!" she demands, but I find nothing to say. Our fraudulent Christmas has come to an end, the illusion shattered. Instead, I reach for the remote and search for Home Alone 2 on TV. This apathy fuels her anger. It's a mirror reflecting her own behavior back to her. The bitter taste of her own medicine, like a Xanax without water, and it's not going down well. She looks so vulnerable–this woman who struggles to control her own emotions–standing there naked, both mentally and physically exposed. And I feel a strange sense of detachment.

She breaks the silence. "You're fucking pathetic!" she spits at me.

Without looking away from the television, I respond with a simple truth and a shrug: "No, I'm apathetic." I correct her, "There's a big difference."

She doesn't know how to react. I've been tiptoeing around her constantly, suppressing my voice time and time again, all in an effort to prevent her from getting angry. And I think to myself, this is the beginning of the end; I'm fucking ready. Letting her know that I'm on to her, Initiating discard.

"Oh, and Tom says Hello," I say casually, watching as she covers herself up.

Confused, she asks, "What?"

I've got that 'I'm-about-to-kick-your-puppy' tone in my voice when I reply, "Yeah, I ran into him at Laurel Tavern, and he told me a few things. Nice dude, though."

My words sound casual, the implication anything but. It hangs between us—a silent accusation, a shared secret brought into the light. She's caught off guard, her vulnerabilities laid bare, her sins exposed under the harsh spotlight of reality. It's a small victory, a turning point, a shift in the dynamic. She explodes with anger and storms off to the bathroom, slamming the door behind her—a tactical retreat to contemplate her next move. I know it's fucked up, but it was long overdue. And it was worth it for how long it lasted; every damn minute of it was worth the trouble, in so many ways.

I finish the movie, feeling the urge to use the bathroom, but Maria has been holed up in there since her exit. I can use one of the other ones, but I decide to check on her anyways.

I knock once, twice, but there's no answer. "Maria?" I call out, my voice bouncing off the silence. Nothing. An uneasy feeling stirs in my stomach as I reach for the door handle. It turns easily— the door is unlocked. I push it open, and my world tilts on its axis. Maria, naked and pale, is slumped against the white tiled wall, blood seeping out of her wrist. Empty pill bottles scatter the floor around her. It's an instant flashback to the moment I found Danny.

I rush to her side. She's still conscious, her eyes glassy and unfocused. It's clear she didn't cut deep enough to kill herself, just enough to bleed, to create a scene, a diversion from the real issues at hand. She will go to any extreme to be the victim and to get the attention she craves. As she looks up at me, she whispers, "I'm sorry. I love you." But she really turned the shit dial-up. I'm sorry, but I'm in love with someone else—anyone else. A reaffirmation of everything I have come to understand about her, but understanding doesn't mitigate the fear, the urgency.

I dial 911, my hands trembling, my voice steady as I relay my address. I feel numb as I wait for them to arrive. Sirens blare in the distance, growing louder until they stop outside the house. Paramedics storm in, their trained eyes taking in the scene, their hands moving with practiced efficiency, bundling Maria onto a stretcher.

All I wanted to do was watch holiday movies and continue writing. This was supposed to be a silent night with the soft hum of a keyboard—not a soundtrack of sirens and muted screams.

Merry fucking Christmas.

56

These are the hazy in-between days, the limbo when the holidays have dissolved and the dawn of the New Year is just around the corner. Following Maria's 72-hour 5150 hold, she returned briefly to gather most of her belongings. There was no need for me to confront her; I never had to reveal all the secrets I'd learned or the truth Tom had shared with me. She knew I had seen through her carefully crafted facade and that I was aware of her deception. But she couldn't admit fault; instead, she played the victim one last time, blaming me for her desperate act and insinuating that I was responsible for her attempted suicide.

Fortunately, the paparazzi camping out in front of my house took the holidays off when Maria was taken away in the ambulance– one less headline to worry about. She instantly blocked me on all platforms, and within a day, we went from "I love you" to "user not found." I can't believe how much power she had over my emotions, and now, in the aftermath of her exit, I find happiness. The air is lighter, and the atmosphere is cleansed of her toxic presence. The world is now still and quiet, the perfect backdrop for my creativity to flourish. However, it's a strange paradox: I'm torn between the desire to finish my book and not wanting it to end. After this chapter, I only have two more to go, and I want to savor that. So it's time for a break.

I gather Maria's remaining belongings from around the house and take them to the garage–a silent funeral procession for a long-dead relationship. The garage carries the distinct aroma of a space neglected, a mixture of musty cardboard, stale air, and lingering hints of motor oil. Surrounded by boxes filled with memories from my old Seattle home, I realize it's time to let go of the past entirely. Not only the ghost of Maria but also the echoes of my former life. I stand there, contemplating. Why keep the relics of my Seattle existence? These boxes, a cardboard labyrinth, with their dust-covered memories and stale air, serve no purpose.

I must move on, but I'll go through these boxes one last time. It's more than just a physical clearing out; it's a mental decluttering, too. I crack open a box, and the first thing I see is the gold trophy I won for that short story I wrote. Underneath it are notebooks filled with the raw, unformed thoughts that would eventually become *Serendipity*. As I flip through the pages, I find myself lost in memories of late-night writing sessions and moments of pure inspiration.

Lifting one of the notebooks, a scrap of paper flutters to the ground like a dying butterfly. Twelve words stare back at me: raccoon, evolve, motor, employ, apple, dilemma, color, hockey, capital, laundry, quiz, problem. It's the seed phrase for my long-lost Bitcoin wallet. Fuckness.

With a newfound sense of excitement, I eagerly delve into the remaining boxes, and there it is—my mother's old laptop. I carry it to the living room and set it down on the table as if it were some ancient artifact, waiting for it to boot up. Finally, I'm in; the desktop materializes, and I open the Bitcoin wallet, entering the twelve words.

And then I see it - a digital treasure of 49.90403071 BTC, now roughly worth 1.4 million dollars.

It's funny; the closure of the missing Bitcoin wallet case fills me with more joy than the money itself.

Two years ago, this sum would've completely changed my life, but now it's a quirky footnote, a serendipitous bonus. It's not like I need it to keep the lights on, not anymore - my writing has taken me to places I never thought possible. I have earned my way here, grinding through the trenches, sculpting worlds with words. This unexpected treasure doesn't really alter the course of my life too much. But hey, maybe I'll buy a new coffee maker, a fancy one with automatic brewing options and Wi-fi connectivity. Because, after all, I fucking love coffee.

My phone buzzes, dancing over the tabletop next to me; it's Alessa calling me via FaceTime.

"Hey, Richard, how were your holidays?" she asks, her voice bright and effervescent.

I force a laugh, bitter and hollow, "Eventful, to say the least," I respond, leaving out the details on purpose.

Alessa gets straight to the point. "What are your plans for New Year's Eve?"

I shrug, "No plans, really."

"Well, there's an industry New Year's Eve party at the *Chateau Marmont*. I'd love for you to come. It starts at 9 PM," she suggests eagerly.

Without a second thought, I say, "I'll be there."

"Great, bring a date," she replies, "I'll see you there, Richard."

We end the call, and I wish I had a date. Of course, I know who I'd want to take. The pill bottle rattles in my hand, and I pop a Xanax. Unlocking my phone, I open Instagram, my fingers swiping through an endless parade of images. My follower count has skyrocketed to over 2 million– it's surreal. I find myself on Emilia's profile, scrolling like a voyeur, a desperate fan. There's an undeniable allure to her. "Fuck it," I mutter under my breath, the Xanax lending me courage. I decide to text her, gambling on a second chance. My fingers tap out the message: "Hey Emilia, I hope you had a fantastic holiday season. If you're not busy tomorrow, there's a party at the Chateau."

As soon as the message goes through, instant regret sinks into me. What a fucking simp move.

In the tense minutes that follow, I find myself fixated on the screen, waiting for a response that might never come. The screen stares back, a blank face hiding a thousand potential responses.

Fuck it; it was worth a shot. Sometimes you have to try a few times to know it's wrong, and that's okay.

I realize that no matter what happens - whether it's heartbreak, rejection, or the cruel hand of fate - the one thing that will always remain is my ability to create. To mold the chaos of existence into something tangible, something that transcends the boundaries of my own reality.

I toss my cell phone aside and reach for the laptop in front of me. Opening it, my fingers fly over the keys with practiced ease. Hours pass, and I barely notice. The sun sinks below the horizon, the sky turning a deep shade of blue-black.

And I gladly sacrifice sleep for my writing, as well as other things.

57

've always had this idea, this stupid, ridiculous notion, that I could do anything I wanted to. Well, maybe not anything, but at least in the realm of creativity. It's a stubborn, relentless belief that's been pushing me forward, and so far, the universe hasn't intervened to prove me wrong. I always called it creative confidence. Sure, I've made mistakes along the way. I've failed, stumbled, fallen flat on my face. But each time, I've dusted myself off, learned from my missteps, and tried again. And my instincts, when it came to my art, were never wrong. I knew that I was destined to be a writer.

And now, here I stand on the sidewalk of Sunset Boulevard, gazing through the window of *Book Soup*, seeing my work displayed in the storefront. Not only that, this one's a successful movie now; it's like seeing my thoughts vomited up in Technicolor, my words dragged kicking and screaming into existence. All those dreams I had in Seattle, they actually came true. They have been manifested. The last two and a half years feel like a fever dream, a relentless rollercoaster of events, all happening so goddamn fast, and I didn't even have time to stop and absorb it all. It's as if someone pressed the fast-forward button, and suddenly, everything was happening at once.

I think, in a way, that first book was more luck than anything else. I didn't know what the fuck I was doing; I just followed impulses, driven by emotions. But this new one is different. It's the product of those two years of living, of feeling, of suffering, and grasping it all in my desperate, ink-stained hands. I had to go through it all–every high and low, every twisted turn of fate–to be able to write it, to infuse my very essence onto the page, and create something that's truly mine. I owe it to everyone I lost along the way, the people that helped me get here, to make it the best thing it can be. But I know that there's still more work to be done, more dreams to pursue.

And now, on this final day of the year, a taste of accomplishment lingers on my tongue. There's just one last chapter to write, just beyond the horizon of today. But I choose to savor it a little longer, like the last note of a beautiful melody. Because, eventually, all good things must come to an end.

Out of nowhere, my wrist vibrates, jolting me back to reality. It's a text from Emilia, consisting of just two words: "What time?" My heart leaps, hammering against my ribcage like a trapped bird desperate for freedom. She's considering it, actually thinking about coming. It's a simple gesture, but the impact is monumental. And so, with a touch of newfound confidence, I send her a reply: "9PM !" It's the way a simple text message can turn the tide of an entire evening.

As the sun begins to set on this year, I'm in the back of an Uber, navigating its way toward the *Chateau*. My hand slips into my pocket to fish out the familiar cylinder. This time, it's not the anxiety but the genuine, unadulterated nervousness brought on by Emilia. I'm excited to see her, but I'm not even sure how to approach her. I pop a whole bar between my lips, swallowing it down like a sacrament. I can't remember the last time I felt nervous because of a woman. Okay, that's not entirely true. I can. It was when I first met Maria again. But this, this is different. There is potential for something real with Emilia. The thought of opening myself up to someone and making myself vulnerable is terrifying, but it could be worth it.

Entering the hallowed grounds of the Chateau - the heady aroma of cigar smoke and the sound of music flowing through the air. The attendees are dressed up in their finest attire to farewell the old year while warmly embracing the arrival of the new one.

As I venture out to the back patio, my eyes scan the crowd, settling on the familiar face of Alessa, standing among a group of industry insiders. I approach her, and she greets me with an enthusiastic hug and starts introducing me to the crowd. "This is Richard Bryght," she proudly proclaims, her arm around my shoulder, "the genius behind *Serendipity*, both the book and the movie." I try to hide the fact that I hate being called that behind a polite smile. I shake hands, engage in small talk, playing my part. Knowing I am far from a genius, I'm just a writer tethered to prescription drugs. But Hollywood only cares about the numbers, indifferent to the personal toll taken to produce them. Yet, I don't let that stop me from mingling with the vultures. They're still good people, just doing their jobs.

I notice Allen nearby, his wife by his side. Excusing myself, I head their way and offer my hand. "Hey, Allen. Good to see you." He responds with enthusiasm, reaching out to shake my hand. "Richard!" he exclaims. "I'm glad you could make it. How's the new book coming along?"

"The first draft will be done tomorrow," I say with a smile. "Wow, congratulations!" He says before introducing me to his wife, a tall blonde, easily 15 years younger than him, with a sharp wit and a quick tongue.

We chat for a few minutes, exchanging pleasantries and making small talk. But my mind is elsewhere, scanning the guests for any sign of Emilia. The gathering's growing increasingly lively and raucous, with clinking glasses and laughter filling the air. Then, out of the corner of my eye, I see her by the entrance, surveying the room. Dressed in a stunning black dress, her hair styled in loose curls, she captivates my attention. My heart starts racing as she begins to approach me. I don't know how to react, but I force myself to walk towards her.

She looks me straight in the eyes and says, "I have no idea why the fuck I came."

Without thinking, I wrap my arms around her in a tight hug. "Me neither, but I'm so fucking glad you did," The words raw and genuine. Stepping back, she tries to hide a smile creeping up on her. "Look," I tell her, "I'm really sorry for everything."

She gestures toward the bar. "Come on, buy me a drink."

"Yes, ma'am!" I say without a second thought, and we start walking over, elbows brushing against each other in a delicate dance of reconnection.

With each drink we share, the tension between us gradually dissipates. We talk, we laugh, and I crack jokes as midnight creeps ever closer. This goddamn year - a year where I lost my best friend, nearly lost my mind, and almost lost my life - is on the verge of being history. Emilia and I join Alessa and the other guests, anticipation crackling in the air like static.

The countdown begins, echoing through the room: "Ten, nine, eight, seven, six, five, four, three, two, one... Happy New Year!" We all shout in unison, and I turn to Emilia, hugging her tightly. "Happy new year!" I say, and as we pull away from the embrace, I can feel my heart beating faster. A symphony of cheers and clinking glasses fills the air. And then, without thinking, I lean in and kiss her. Everything else fades away; this feels so fucking right. Fireworks burst in the night sky, illuminating the scene as if applauding our reunion.

We pull away, and she grins. "Happy New Year!" she exclaims, and then she kisses me again, her lips warm and soft against mine. I grab my phone, pulling her close, our bodies pressed together. Emilia flashes a beautiful smile as I snap the picture and post it on Instagram.

Before I know it, we're back at my place, the night's revelry nothing more than a blur. The new year stretches out before us, full of unknowns, but for now, we're just here, together. And that, in itself, is more than I could have ever asked for. I've spent way too much time looking for the right things in all the wrong places. But lying here with Emilia, I feel something I haven't felt in a long time: hope. Emilia, a beacon of grace and forgiveness, and I, a flawed soul seeking redemption. It's impossible to predict what this new year has in store for us, but I am grateful for our reunion and my relentless desire to dive headfirst into the unknown; to give our connection the honest, raw chance it deserves. Here's to new beginnings.

Happy new year.

58

'm still struggling to wrap my head around it, but this - this right here - is the final chapter of my new book, *Pieces of a Broken Mind*. Typing these words is surreal; I never thought I'd get to this point, yet here I am, staring at the blinking cursor on the screen. This is almost ceremonial. And I feel a strange sense of loss, like I'm saying goodbye to a part of myself.

But with that loss also comes a sense of achievement, of having conquered the demons that drove me to write this in the first place. It's like standing in a dimmed theater, the final scene fading to black, and the end credits start rolling on this twisted, gut-wrenching drama of a book.

Taking a moment to pay tribute to the cast of characters who've populated these pages - the heroes and villains, the broken souls seeking redemption, the lost ones aching for solace. Their faces materialize in my mind, each one a reflection of some fragmented part of myself, a mirror held up to the darkest recesses of my being. And as I mentally type their names, one by one, I bid them farewell, grateful for the lessons they've taught me, the pain they've shared, the hope they've inspired. I am determined to immortalize them.

In the background, a haunting melody plays, a requiem for the lost, a hymn of hope for the found. The steady thrum of the printer fills the room, working in unison to bring my creation to life. Ink and paper fuse together, page by page, a blood-soaked marriage of my mind's debris. The first printed copy of a new manuscript always holds a special significance– it's when you can hold your thoughts in your hands. As the stack of papers grows, I am filled with a sense of pride, knowing that these words will live on beyond me, that I will not be forgotten.

These two and a half years have been the most intense, the most emotional, and the most eventful of my life. I've experienced the highest of highs and the lowest of lows, and somehow managed to survive them all. I may be too old to die young, but I'm not too old to be remembered. These words, these pages, they are my legacy, my gift to the world. To all those who have loved or hated me, who have understood or misunderstood me, who knew me or are just now learning about me. An echo that remains long after I'm gone. And if your life isn't a piece of art, you're living it wrong.

However, the end credits also signal the beginning of a new chapter, a fresh start, a blank page waiting to be filled. As the music fades and the last words of *Pieces of a Broken Mind* dissolve into the void, I know that this isn't truly the end. While I hold the finished manuscript in my hands, I know that I'll never forget these years, no matter how much time passes. They will always be a part of me.

My gaze drifts to the vase perched on the fireplace mantel, containing Danny's ashes. A constant reminder of his presence and the impact he had on me. I know how much I owe him, the fact that I wouldn't be here if it weren't for him. The last time we talked in this very room was a heated fight that left a bitter taste and made me question everything. Yet, I refuse to let that single, dark event overshadow all the good times we had–the laughs, the gaming sessions, the unconditional love. Those are the things I hold onto and the things that keep me going. And I swear, in this moment, he is looking at me, and he is fucking proud of me, like he always was. The same goes for my mother, who has been my biggest fan. Every word, every sentence, every page, is for her. God, I miss both of them so much.

I reach for my pill bottle, unscrewing the cap, and taking out an Oxy. I swallow it, feeling its bitterness and acrid taste slide down my throat.

I grab my phone and flip through the flood of messages I've received. A couple of them stand out - Emily and Lana among them. These women have given me a glimpse into a world that most people can't fathom, and for that, I'm grateful. I have stories to tell, ventures that have shaped me.

This introspection brings forth a wave of emotion, and it's not just a momentary burst of emotion; it's something that has been building for a long time, something that has been simmering beneath the surface. And now, as I contemplate the words that have just come out of my mouth, I know that they are true.

As I sit here, surrounded by the artifacts of my life, I realize that I have been chasing goals for far too long. And there is a difference between a goal and a purpose. I have been so focused on achieving success, on making a name for myself, that I have lost sight of my purpose. But now I feel a sense of clarity that I haven't felt in years.

My purpose is to create, to tell stories that move people, to make them feel something deep inside. It's not about accolades or recognition; it's about connecting with others on a fundamental level. And it's important to let others in, to take a chance, even if it means being vulnerable. Genuine connections are so fucking rare and precious, and we can not allow them to slip through our fingers. Because, in the end, they're what makes life worth living. And I am genuinely excited to welcome Emilia into mine, to reveal my true self, and give us a real chance, a shot at something meaningful. Let's see where this road takes us.

The doorbell rings - it's her. I had plans to take her out to a fancy restaurant to celebrate the completion of my book, but she had other intentions in mind. She simply wanted to stay in and drink wine. And who am I to say no to that? It sounds fucking perfect.

I fumble for the Xanax bottle, shaking out another pill and tossing it back, hoping it'll relax me. As I open the door, there she is, standing on my doorstep like a vision. She's dressed in a simple outfit that looks both elegant and comfortable at the same time. Holding a bottle of wine in her hand, and her eyes shine with excitement. She greets me with a kiss, and I feel my heart skip a beat.

"Congratulations on finishing the book," she says, with a smile to die for, "this is incredible." I invite her in, and we make our way to the living room. Taking our places on the couch, I pour us each a glass of wine. With a gentle clink, our glasses meet, and we drink, savoring the smooth, rich taste.

Time slips away unnoticed, the hours marked by empty wine bottles, yet I'm not concerned about the time. For once, I am free from thoughts of deadlines, books, or anything else that might pull me away from the present moment. I am right here, and it's just me and Emilia.

As the last bottle of wine is emptied, I realize that I've never felt this content in my entire life. All of the stress, all of the anxiety, and all of the doubts that have plagued me for so long seem to have faded away. I'm left with only this moment, this perfect evening with the woman who gave me hope, celebrating the birth of a new project.

Intoxication courses through me, my head swimming in a delightful haze. Drawn together like magnetic forces, Emilia and I stumble toward the bedroom, beginning a wild dance of passion and desire that seems to stretch on for hours. It's raw, it's real, and it might just be the best sex of my life.

Eventually, she drifts off to sleep, her breathing steady and peaceful. But the bigger the high, the worse the low. I carefully untangle myself from Emilia's soft embrace and stumble out of bed to try and tiptoe toward the bathroom. The new manuscript sits proudly on a small table, its pages bathed in a rogue beam of city light that sneaks past the curtains, casting an ethereal glow onto it. As I pass it, the world around me tilts and sways like a ship on a stormy sea. My feet stumble, threatening to send me crashing to the floor, but I catch myself, regaining my balance just in time, and reach the haven of the bathroom.

Flipping the switch, the sudden brightness nearly blinds me. The alcohol and the sex are taking their toll on me, leaving my mind in a blur. I reach out to the bathroom counter to steady myself, looking at my reflection in the mirror, the light above it flickering for a second. Suddenly I feel the past clawing its way back, each memory a vivid Polaroid dangling before my eyes, every single "click" clear as day. As I stand in this luxurious bathroom, I'm compelled to confront some tough questions that I was too afraid to ask before: the lessons learned and the prices paid. In the end, was it all worth it? Should I have just remained in Seattle, taking care of my mother and being there for my best friend? Instead of being so selfish. Both would probably still be alive, even if I might be dead inside. These fucking "what if's" are driving me insane. I can't escape them, no matter how hard I try. I feel like Schindler. A man questioning if he could've, should've, done more for those he left behind. Sometimes it's best to leave your dreams untouched; they're fragile like butterfly wings.

I open the drawer, my eyes are blurry, and my vision is hazy, but I can still make out the shapes of the pill bottles. My hands tremble as I reach for them and twist off the caps, revealing the pills inside. I can't fully read the labels, but it doesn't matter. Taking one of each, just to be sure. I just want to sleep through the night and wake up fresh to start my new life. Though deep down, I know that I can't keep going like this. Something has to change. Starting tomorrow, I'll do everything I can to get off the pills. I'll gradually decrease the dosage, weaning myself off them.

But there's one last thing I have to do; I have to be honest with myself, for once. The man in the mirror, Richard Bryght, is suffering from a Bipolar disorder–Bipolar 2, to be exact, with a sprinkle of a general anxiety disorder on top. Cognitive dissonance. It's a cocktail of mental struggles that I've been too afraid to face, too preoccupied with analyzing people around me to distract from my own problems. The mirror bears witness to my internal battle, the silent struggle of a man seeking redemption for the life he's lived.

Follow your heart, and you will die every day.
The sterile glare of the fluorescent light makes the reflection of my face look pale, and I am surprised when I see a tear rolling down my cheek. I haven't cried in months, maybe even longer. But it feels good, cathartic.

No one can ever prepare you for the life you imagine for yourself, especially when it unfolds exactly as planned. Trapped within a self-fulfilling prophecy.

But what would it take to get there? What if you're on top of the world and you feel absolutely nothing? I stare into my eyes in the mirror until they seem foreign. Taking a deep breath, I splash water on my face and leave the room.

The bedroom is shrouded in dim light, illuminated only by the rays of the LA skyline slicing through the gray curtains. A police helicopter circles a small area in the distance somewhere in Laurel Canyon, but nothing happening outside is important right now; only what's inside matters. Two stained glasses and an empty bottle of wine sit on the nightstand on my side.

Seeing her silhouette lying in my bed still feels surreal, as if turning on the light would make her disappear, and the bed would be empty again. The simple act of talking to her was absolutely unthinkable less than a week ago. I lie down next to her, kiss her neck, and wrap my arm around her body. She reaches for my hand, holding it tightly.

There were moments in the last couple of weeks where I would've killed just to smell her one more time. And now, here she is, giving me another chance, and I just want to fall asleep next to her. I didn't know it before, but this moment right here is what it's all about; it completes me.

I will be remembered.

I will be remembered.

I will be remembered.

I inhale deeply before closing my eyes.

Hold your breath.

Freeze Frame.

Click.

LOS ANGELES POLICE DEPARTMENT
OFFICIAL POLICE REPORT

Case Number: 2024-0102-03782

Date/Time of Incident: January 2, 2024, between 0300 hours and 0700 hours

Reporting Officer: Officer Marisol Garcia, Badge Number 8256, and Officer Vincent Reed, Badge Number 5026

Involved Parties:
1. Deceased: Richard Bryght, Age 41, Male, Occupation: Author
2. Reporting Party: Emilia Sinclair, Age 34, Female, Relationship to Deceased: Unspecified

Location of Incident:
Mulholland Drive, Los Angeles, CA

Summary of Incident:
Upon arriving at the scene, we were met by Ms. Emilia Sinclair, who was visibly shaken and distressed. She reported that she woke up at approximately 700 hours and found Mr. Bryght lying next to her in bed, unresponsive.

Ms. Sinclair disclosed that they had been involved in consensual sexual activity the previous night.

The scene was a second-floor bedroom in a well-maintained, modern home overlooking the city. The room was neat, save for a few items on the nightstand beside the bed where Mr. Bryght was found.

On the nightstand, we observed one empty wine bottles of a 2018 Pinot Noir from Sonoma County, two half-filled wine glasses, a manuscript titled "Pieces of a Broken Mind" bearing Mr. Bryght's name as the author, credited to Mr. Bryght, located on a little table in the bedroom, and a couple of prescription pill bottles. Upon closer inspection, the pill bottles were identified as Xanax and OxyContin, both prescribed to Mr. Bryght.

More empty bottles of wine were found in the living room.

Ms. Sinclair informed us that Mr. Bryght had a history of substance abuse, including a previous overdose a few months back. She stated that her and Mr Bryght had been drinking wine the previous night and he had also taken his prescribed medications, though she could not specify the amount.

The body of Mr. Bryght showed no outward signs of trauma or struggle. He was found lying on his back, one arm draped across his chest and the other resting by his side.

Preliminary Findings:
Los Angeles County Medical Examiner was called to the scene and took possession of the body for further examination. Initial assessment suggests that Mr. Bryght's death might be a result of an overdose, potentially a fatal interaction between his prescription medications and alcohol. However, the final determination will be made after a full autopsy.

Next Steps:
The investigation is ongoing. We are currently awaiting the medical examiner's report. In addition, Ms. Sinclair will be interviewed in a more formal setting, and we will reach out to Mr. Bryght's prescribing physician for additional context about his medication usage. The manuscript and notebook found at the scene will be analyzed to gain potential insight into Mr. Bryght's state of mind prior to his death.

Investigating Officer: Detective Elijah Bennett

Attachments:
1. Crime Scene Photographs
2. Preliminary Interview - Emilia Sinclair
3. Prescription Pill Bottles
4. Manuscript - "Pieces of a Broken Mind"

This report is confidential and is intended solely for the use of the individual or entity to whom they are addressed. If you have received this report in error, please notify the system manager.

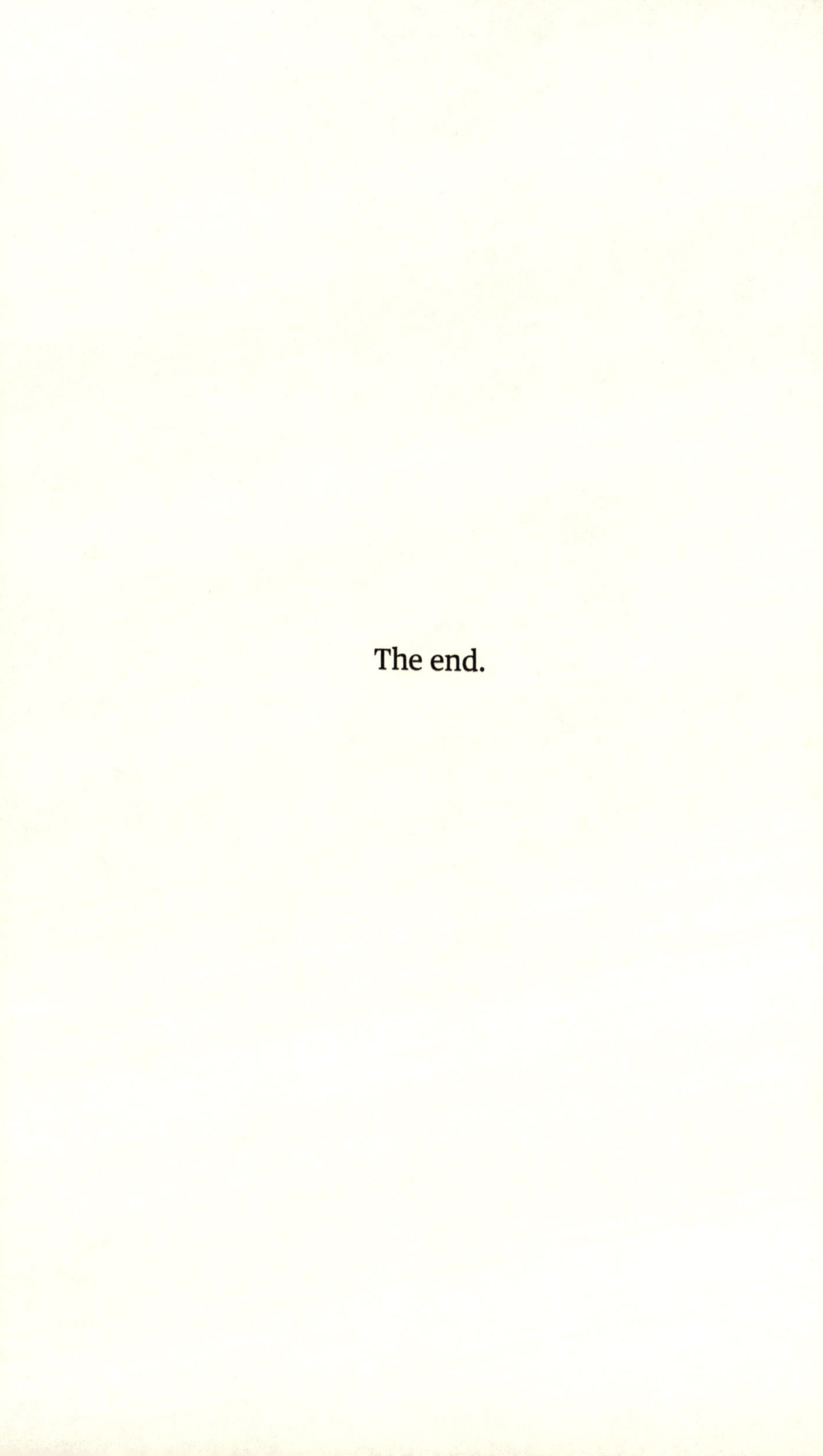

The end.

Richard's LA Playlist

ABOUT THE AUTHOR

Daniel Ruczko is an award-winning autodidact artist from Bremen, Germany. He has achieved recognition across multiple creative domains, including directing, writing, composing, music production, and visual art. His debut work, *Pieces of a Broken Mind*, extends his storytelling abilities beyond screenplays to a full-length novel. Currently residing in Los Angeles, California, Daniel remains actively engaged in the various realms of his creative work.

Author photograph by Liz Napino